CHANNELING
BO

G. L. Keady

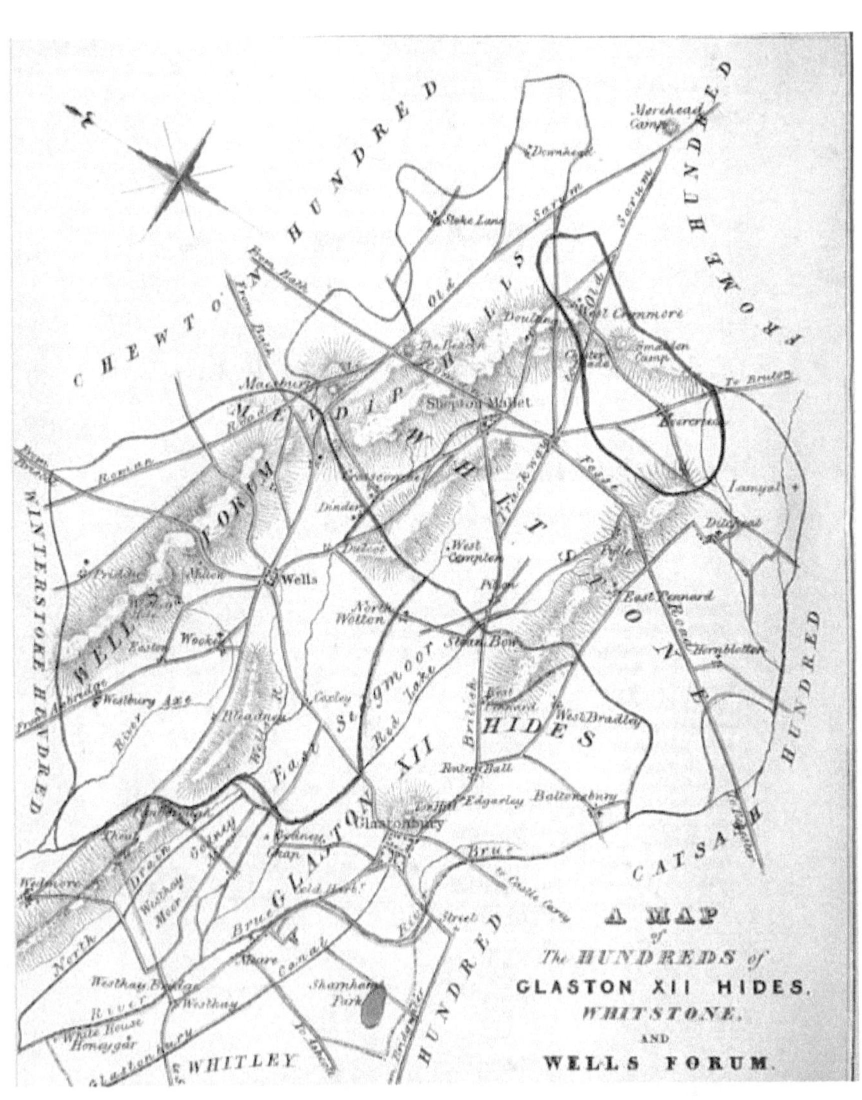

The Twelve Hides of Glastonbury.

TABLE OF CONTENTS

CHAPTER
I

And did those feet in ancient time
Walk upon England's mountains green?
And was the holy Lamb of God
On England's pleasant pastures seen?
And did the countenance divine
Shine forth upon our clouded hills?
And was Jerusalem builded here
Among those dark satanic mills?
Bring me my bow of burning gold!
Bring me my arrows of desire!
Bring me my spear! O clouds, unfold!
Bring me my chariot of fire!
I will not cease from metal fight,
Nor shall my sword sleep in my hand,
Till we have built Jerusalem
In England's green and pleasant land.

William Blake

It feels like years ago that I last sat on this lovely porch to reflect on my life. Though the view of the lake hasn't changed in the slightest, my life certainly has. As a matter of fact, it is barely recognisable. If you knew me then, I doubt you'd even think I was the same person now. Such has been the impact of the events of the last ten months. You might ask if I've been affected in a bad way. Well, you be the judge. Am I a better person because of it? Who knows! However, this much I can say: my husband and I have survived an ordeal few could hope to imagine. Have I changed the world? Yes, absolutely. The influence of what we achieved is ubiquitous. You might ask if, at sixty-three, I am content with my life. My answer is simple: no bloody way... to quote one of my favourite authors: "The best I will ever write, I will write tomorrow." Do I have regrets? Fuck yes. Do they bother me? Fuck no. It isn't over yet. So, if you're interested to know what I have done that could well affect you... read it and weep.

Ten months ago...

Sometimes, I like to just kick back on the porch with the sun on my face and conjure up dreams. Years seem to have flitted by of late, giving me the feeling at times that I'm running out of life. With retirement age only two years away, it surprises me to think I have lived this long. When I was young, I could never have imagined being sixty-three. But with that said, retirement isn't something hubby and I intend dealing with by having a blanket over our knees.

Though we live relatively stress-free, far from the maddening crowd on the South Coast of New South Wales in Australia, it has always been our intention to extend our lives here—not terminate them. So it came as a shock when we moved here from Sydney four years ago, bought a house, and then learned that due to the huge number of resident retirees, the younger residents nicknamed Tuross Head 'God's waiting room.' But we don't care. One warble from a magpie or the fragrant scent of the Frangipani blossoming immediately below the balcony quickly dispels any such notion. My loving husband is content with writing his memoirs, while I'm delighted with my part-time job as a social worker in the nearby town of Moruya. Only three days a week... and on days off, I get to laze on the balcony, feasting on the bucolic charm of Coila Lake that today is gleaming in the late morning Spring sunshine like the mirrored facets of a D-colour flawless diamond—and to top it off, I'm expecting a visit from my young niece, Cleo. She lives in Sydney with my sister, and I haven't seen her since we moved down here. She phoned from Canberra yesterday to say she'd drop by today for a cuppa and a chinwag.

Searching the azure sky for remote memories, I suddenly became aware of prying eyes. You know the feeling... I guess derived from experience of days now more numerous in arrears than ahead of me, but it turned out the eyes belonged to Cleo. She was standing on the balcony, angelically backlit by the sun, looking at me. Is it her aura I can see, or her corona? I questioned myself.

"I didn't hear you come in, love."

"Hi Aunt Bo," she said, intoned of tender years. "Reminiscing?"

She smiled before shyly giving me a tender peck on the cheek.

"You can drop the aunt bit, Darl. Bo will do just fine. Aunt has a past-your-use-by-date vibe."

"You were staring at something in the sky. What was it?" she said, looking up at the heavens for a sign of something.

"My life, love."

"Oh," she said with a quizzical look on her pretty face.

"Sit down, and I'll write you into my introversion. Did you see Jackson on your way in?"

"No," she said cutely, her slender body sinking into the director's chair beside me. "I snuck up the stairs just to catch you unawares." As she smiled cheekily, the sun caught her sparkling eyes, filled as they were with youthful enthusiasm and intellectual vitality.

I leaned close and delicately brushed a long strand of red hair out of her eyes.

"You remind me of myself, Cleo."

Her smile was warm. "No offence, Bo, but it's not easy to picture you at twenty-four."

"Hey, time may have robbed me of my youthful appearance, love, but it has left my memories intact, for the time being, at any rate."

"Which brings me to why I'm here."

"Ah, so there is more to your visit than meets the eye?"

"Yes, afraid so. I'm doing a degree in writing at Uni and have an assignment to complete that I thought you might be able to help me with."

"Why me? What about your mum?"

"Um, well, I asked her, but she said you've got a better story."

"A better story! Hmm, now you've got me intrigued. So what's the topic?"

"I'm to write a biographical essay about an older relative when she was my age."

I knew why my younger sister Maureen, or Mo as I called her, had concluded that my story from forty years ago would surpass hers.

"So, Mo thought I'm more intriguing than her, huh? Well, that's quite remarkable."

"Mo and Bo, similar in name but entirely different in nature... Yes, she was quite emphatic about it. Mind if I record our conversation?" Cleo asked.

"Hold your horses, girl. I haven't given my consent yet. What exactly did Mo say about me back then?" I asked, raising an inquisitive eyebrow.

"She said you were the black sheep of the family, a free spirit, an advocate for feminism, an anti-war protester, a poet, um, and an eccentric individual with remarkably vivid visions."

"Hey, I take exception to that! It was women's liberation back then, not just feminism, if you don't mind," I joked.

It wasn't difficult to realise that it would be far better to share my peculiar story with Cleo than to let it fade away solely within the failing memories of those involved.

"So, is that okay?" Cleo asked, preparing her iPad to record our conversation.

"I suppose so, but it must be an honest account, flaws and all. And I want final approval on the finished draft—the writer's cut, so to speak."

"Agreed!" she exclaimed with a mischievous grin.

"Just remember, there are three sides to every story: yours, mine, and the truth."

"Alright, even with the imperfections. Let's delve into the truth then. So, what was the most significant life-changing event for you when you were twenty-four years old, Aunt Bo?"

"Event, hmm, well, perhaps that won't be as challenging to answer as you might think because I can recall 1974 as vividly as if it were yesterday. It was the year Richard Nixon resigned the US presidency, the year Cyclone Tracy devastated Darwin, Gough Whitlam was re-elected as Prime Minister of Australia, and the year I met a man who would forever alter the course of my life and whom I would eventually marry."

"That's a good starting point. So, how did you come across Dr Jackson Bolt?" she prodded me.

I delved into my memory, seeking a trigger—a scent, a sensation, a song—and one promptly emerged.

Songs from the previous year were still playing on the radio, and Helen Reddy's anthem 'I Am Woman' sprang to mind first, followed by Carly Simon's 'You're So Vain,' and then Roberta Flack's 'Killing Me Softly With His Song.' Each of them fuelled the momentum of the women's liberation movement. It's worth noting that 1974 was a year of protest—peaceful and, at times, less peaceful demonstrations against the Vietnam War and civil rights were in vogue. We, the young generation, rallied as an army for our rights... not solely to be heard, mind you, because our voices were already channelled through our music... no, we yearned for more. We yearned to be listened to and, above all, taken seriously.

A chant came to mind, "One, two, three, four, we don't want nuclear war, five, six, seven, eight, we don't want to radiate!" I chanted those words in the scorching September afternoon heat during a massive anti-war peace rally that wound through the streets of Sydney like a colossal serpent, culminating in Domain Park. I was attired for the occasion, wearing a suede Apache Indian vest adorned with swaying tassels over a loose-fitting, revealing purple tank top that accentuated my figure. On the lower half, I had on high-waisted, snug blue bell-bottom jeans embellished with embroidered flowers encircling the flares. And of course, there was the obligatory rainbow headband that kept my unruly, curly red hair at bay. Oh, and let's not forget my beloved funky white platform sandals that elevated me from a meagre five foot seven inches to an impressive five foot ten. After the gruelling march, I slung them over my shoulder to provide my blistered feet with much-needed respite on the cool, lush green grass of the Domain.

The Domain was the chosen venue for free speech—Dad cynically referred to it as soapbox city. A gathering of hippies congregated there, creating a symphony of poetry, radical speeches, and folk songs that captivated our consciousness. It was a happening place to spend a couple of hours after a rally, not just to socialise but to connect with like-minded individuals.

I had connected with a strikingly attractive man who invited me to his apartment in nearby Woolloomooloo for some intimate moments.

Things got steamy on the couch in his cramped terraced flat... until he offered me a tab of acid. Foolishly disregarding the consequences, I mindlessly consumed the tab, and we engaged in passionate activity. However, when the hallucinogenic effects kicked in, my mind was blown—I was losing control in a major way. I remember gazing down between my spread knees at the stranger's animalistic eyes as he forcefully thrust himself, and it completely unnerved me. For him, it was mere carnal pleasure, but for me, I was being ravaged by a demon—it was an intensely horrifying trip. I was overcome with unease, paranoia, anxiety—every negative sensation imaginable washed over me.

I abruptly leaped up and hastily departed his apartment, still in the process of dressing. I recall sprinting barefoot down Forbes Street at dusk, overwhelmed and desperately pulling up my jeans while carrying my platforms in hand, observed by a group of homeless winos. All I desired was to reach home and have the dreadful trip come to an end. I longed to curl up in the safety and comfort of my own bed.

Eventually, I managed to convince a cabbie to take me to Coogee, and once there, I stealthily slipped into the house, careful not to disturb Mom and Dad. At the time, I was unemployed and temporarily staying with them. Mo was up in Noosa Heads, Queensland, with her friends, so I had the privilege of occupying her bedroom. While your mother embodied the surfer type with her obligatory bleached blonde hair and fondness for the Beach Boys, I represented the complete opposite, immersing myself in bands like Osibisa, the Moody Blues, and King Crimson. In those days, one's taste in music, style of dress, and hairstyle essentially categorised them as a hippie, a surfer, or a straight.

I crawled into bed and lay there, curled up in a foetal position, willing myself down.

The next morning, at the breakfast table, my parents were furious with me. Apparently, I had awakened them in the middle of the night, screaming incoherently. They accused me of being hysterical, even insane, claiming they had a difficult time calming me down. I couldn't recall any of it and assumed it was just the aftereffects of the acid. I assured them it wouldn't happen again, but my father wasn't satisfied. He believed my behaviour confirmed his suspicions that I was a drug addict. I tried to brush it off with a laugh, but that didn't work. Both my parents came from conservative backgrounds and had never embraced the flower power counterculture of the sixties and early seventies—free love, unconventional behaviour, eccentric clothing, and wild hairstyles. They saw it all as an act of rebellion against tradition, and in hindsight, they were somewhat correct. Regardless, my father was livid and arranged an appointment with a doctor through a golfing acquaintance who happened to be a psychiatrist.

"I'm not going to see some shrink!" I protested. "I'm over twenty-one, you can't tell me what to do."

But my father, a tough, imposing figure standing at six feet two inches with a decorated military background and a penchant for control, wasn't someone to be reckoned with. When he raised his voice, you listened, or else.

"You listen to me, young lady," he bellowed. "You're my daughter, and as long as you're living under my roof, you will do as I command. This is not up for negotiation, Bonnie. Either do as I say or find yourself somewhere else to live!"

He knew full well that I didn't have the means to leave, so I found myself trapped between a rock and a hard place. As he stormed out of the kitchen, I shot my mother a pleading, teary-eyed look, hoping for some sympathy. But she simply lowered her eyes in guilt—a verdict had been reached, leaving me feeling isolated, cold, and alone.

A couple of days later, I reluctantly arrived at a private psychiatric practice for my appointment—an experience that would forever remain etched in my memory.

Macquarie Street in Sydney was the prestigious domain of high-priced psychiatrists and medical specialists, and it still holds that status. The entrance door to the office had the name "Dr Winston Gibson-Smith MB, D.P.M (Eng), F.R.C.P., F.R.C. Psych" stencilled on it. Inside, the decor belonged to a fading era: dark timber-panelled walls and a stale, musty atmosphere that evoked images of a Dickensian television adaptation. I half expected to find a clerk seated at a desk, writing with a quill pen. Instead, I noticed a print on the wall depicting a 19th-century fox hunt, with aristocratic English riders on horseback galloping through the idyllic countryside. Against the wall stood an olive Chesterfield lounge with spider-web cracks, exuding a distinct odour, eagerly awaiting an occupant. The room had a perpetual library-like scent, intermingled with another aroma—pipe tobacco.

Behind an Edwardian desk sat not a quill-pushing clerk, but an immaculately dressed middle-aged woman wearing an expression as if she had just bitten into a lemon. We exchanged pleasantries, but when I apologised for being late, she peered disapprovingly at me over her horn-rimmed glasses and sharply reprimanded me for my lack of punctuality, explaining that my tardiness resulted in missing my appointment with Dr Gibson-Smith. Consequently, he had taken on another patient. A wry smile crept onto my face, but just as I was about to make my exit, she informed me that I would now be seen by his intern, Dr Bolt, and that Dr Gibson-Smith would join us later.

She led me down a dim, narrow corridor adorned with wood paneling, devoid of any signage. Knocking once on a door, she gestured for me to enter. I glanced back along the corridor, taking in the sight of the coarse, olive green carpet that resembled poorly knitted horsehair. Drab. From inside, I heard the muffled word "enter." She ushered me in and closed the door behind me. I was relieved to bid her farewell.

The room was relatively small, but its decor remained consistent with the rest of the establishment, except for one striking detail—an incredibly attractive guy of my age sitting behind a desk. The atmosphere instantly brightened as he rose from his seat, towering over six feet in height. With utmost courtesy, he stepped out from behind the mahogany desk and extended his hand in greeting. He gestured for me to take a seat on a brown leather two-seater couch, a less luxurious relative of the old Chesterfield in the reception area, while he settled into one of the two matching single armchairs across from me. I thought to myself, here we go—the classic psychiatrist's couch treatment.

He exuded an air that suggested I was his first-ever patient, a notion he confirmed when I mentioned it.

"Don't let that concern you, Miss Leigh," he replied calmly. "I completed my degree in parapsychology at Sydney University with honors. Do you mind if I call you Bonnie?"

"No," I replied, feigning disinterest as I glanced at the leather-covered door and the matching leather-topped desk.

"I know what you're thinking. The room could do with a spruce-up. It's pretty old hat."

"If that's what parapsychology entails—mind-reading—then I don't have to tell you anything. You should already know what I'm thinking," I remarked.

He beamed at me, his smile nearly melting me on the spot.

"Parapsychology is a separate field from psychiatry."

"So, does that make you or Gibson what's-his-face the quack?" I added, giggling and not expecting a serious answer.

I had never been fond of suits, but his well-tailored pin-striped number, along with his white shirt and thin, hip blue and white paisley tie, elevated him in my estimation above the other suits I had encountered in this part of town. Macquarie Street was the Sydney equivalent of Harley Street, populated by esteemed medical chambers and practices.

"I'm not a psychic, Bonnie," he responded calmly.

"Must be a breeze raking in loads of cash just by lending an ear to people and letting them spill their hang-ups?" I asked, imagining the hefty fees psychiatrists must charge.

"Well, there's a bit more to parapsychology than that. Shall we get started?" he said, signalling the end of the pleasantries. He crossed his legs and opened a manila folder on his lap.

Leaning back in my chair, I mirrored his relaxed posture. The little white cotton frock I was wearing had ridden up when I sat down, revealing my legs. I wanted to see if he was attracted to them, but he paid no attention. So, I began rocking my leg back and forth, still no response. As a last resort, I let my sling-back shoe dangle from my heel while seductively flicking a strand of hair away from my face. I figured that would be enough to convey my interest, but despite all my best moves, he remained unresponsive. Frustrated, I decided to shift my focus to studying him and pondering why he was so unresponsive. He had attractive black hair, cut to medium length, with a part on the left side. Occasionally, he would flick a stray lock away from his right eye with a quick toss of his head. It wasn't a nervous gesture; it was actually quite endearing. His skin was pale, his lips full, and he had noticeably long, thin, artistic fingers. In short, he was quite the catch... and still is.

"I need to ask you a few questions," he said, his voice carrying an air of authority.

"Why?" I retorted.

"Because I'm conducting a preliminary assessment, which means I'll be doing most of the talking."

Cutting him off, I joked, "So, because I was late, Doctor What's-his-face dismissed me, and you got the gig?"

"Did you purposely arrive late?" he inquired.

"Let's just say I wasn't in a hurry."

"Fair enough," he smiled knowingly as he reached for a gold fountain pen from the top pocket of his suit coat, removing the cap to jot down notes. "Do you use drugs?" he asked sternly, giving me a piercing stare.

"No more than anyone else," I shot back.

"Hmm, it says here that you suffer from violent nightmares."

"Shouldn't I be lying down on a couch for this?"

"No, Bonnie, this is not a therapy session. I'm simply going through the questions provided by Dr Gibson-Smith. You're..."

"Twenty-four, a Cancer, ruled by the moon, born here, currently unemployed and down on my luck, but not out of it," I interjected, trying to maintain a nonchalant attitude. I detested following protocols.

"Why do you think you're here, Bonnie?" he asked, shifting gears.

"To appease my old man. He thinks I'm a drug addict. And for the record, he thinks anyone under thirty is a drug addict."

"And does that make you angry? Do you resent him?"

"No, why should I? I'm not the one with the complex."

I wasn't enjoying the line of questioning. Despite my initial attraction to him, he was starting to get on my nerves.

"Tell me about your nightmares," he probed.

"I never remember them. I only find out later that I've been screaming, going insane in the middle of the night, speaking some kind of gobbledygook."

"Gobbledygook?" he inquired.

"Yeah, some strange language. Look, if the people who complained actually understood what I was babbling about, maybe they wouldn't have a problem with it."

"How long have you been experiencing these nightmares?"

"Oh, the past two months, since my birthday in July, I suppose."

"And how often do they occur?"

"I don't know, a couple to three times a week."

Something I said seemed to change his demeanour. He became noticeably more excited, perhaps because of the mention of a foreign language.

"Have you ever been hypnotised, Bonnie?"

"Not that I know of. But then again, would I remember if I had?"

"I like your sense of humour. Look, I'd like to try a process called hypnotherapy with you."

"You want to hypnotise me?"

"Yes."

That piqued my interest. The idea conjured up images of people acting like chickens or zombies.

"Cool," I agreed.

"Okay, just recline on the couch and relax. I'm going to turn on a reel-to-reel tape recorder, which is right over here. Now, close your eyes and focus on my voice..."

He modulated his tone, and it was indeed hypnotic. The next thing I knew, I was abruptly awakened, not by Dr Hypno-Voice Bolt, but by the opening door, the smell of pipe tobacco, and a gruff voice.

"What in God's name are you playing at here, Bolt? Huh? I asked you to take preliminary notes, not to embark on some experiment better suited for parlour games. This girl has a drug problem, as reported by her father. Drug dependency requires specialised psychiatric treatment, and as an intern, you are certainly not qualified."

"But, sir," Jackson stammered, rattled by the old man's tirade, "she suffers from recurring dreams, multiple instances even, and—"

The grumpy old man glanced around the room, as if assessing it for an auction bid. Removing the smouldering pipe from his mouth, he pointed it threateningly at Bolt and growled, "I have no interest in your parapsychology prognosis, young man. Now, please excuse us."

With his tail firmly between his legs, my handsome intern made a swift exit, and Doctor What's-his-face continued to interrogate me about my hypothetical drug addiction. When my time with him was finally up, I was overjoyed to get the heck out of there.

CHAPTER
II

A couple of days later, a report from Doctor What's-his-face arrived at the house. I thought about lifting it from the letterbox and ditching it, but I figured my old man would only hear it firsthand from his golfing buddy anyway. So the folks went into a private huddle to discuss it. I was eventually summoned to the old man's study, given a dressing down on the importance of punctuality, and then ordered to attend weekly therapy sessions with Doctor Plum-in-the-gob, and no buts. I realised right there and then, it was time to move out—but where on Earth to?

The answer arrived divinely, courtesy of a call to arms from my girlfriend, Flea. She was a member of the Women's Liberation Action Front and she called to invite me to join the front in a protest at Glebe that coming Friday night. I knew Flea, whose real name was Susan, was gay, and that I was her crush since we were in high school together, but it never got in the way of our friendship. I also knew her dad had bought her a two-bedroom flat in Kings Cross, and I figured if I helped her out with the protest, there was a chance she'd offer me the spare room.

I turned up at the trendy Black Widow Café in Glebe where I found Flea waiting at a table. It was all a bit strange, but I went along with it, my mind set on securing a place to stay. The reason it felt weird was that there were eight seriously butch-looking women with Flea, all of them in their thirties, and all of them seriously fired up about something that I couldn't, for the life of me, work out. Then, just as Flea was about to fill me in, another woman poked her head in through the café front door and screeched out, "He's here! He's here!"

With that, they all sprang to their feet and hoofed it out of the café as if it were on fire. I followed them, totally bewildered. Outside,

I watched them race across the road to a guy getting out of a parked car. He looked up sharply at the marauding herd of screaming Banshees coming at him and freaked out. As he tried desperately to get back into his car, the women descended upon him. He was quickly overpowered. Then, to my shock and horror, they began kicking and punching the living crap out of him. As they hammered him to the ground, he threw a desperate punch that connected with my chin, and I hit the deck, out like a light.

When I opened my eyes, I was on my hands and knees, staring at the ground. Droplets of blood were falling in slow motion and exploding in splashes on the gravel. It was my blood. I looked up through a dizzy haze and recognised the leafless branches of a tree spread overhead like withered claws. The sound of voices shouting in the heat of a fight flooded my senses. As I rocked back on my haunches, I noticed my hands were different—filthy—grubby fingernails, cut short, ragged, and ugly. My forearms were muscular and scarred. These weren't my hands or my arms; I felt giddy. An instinct was driving me to reach out for something I needed. I picked it up from the ground beside me and studied it in my hand. It was a sword. I rose slowly to my feet, holding it, drawing in deep breaths, struggling to regain my equilibrium. Then, suddenly, a hand grasped my arm and scared the living shit out of me. A voice spoke with urgency, but I couldn't recognise it or the language, though somehow, I kind of understood the meaning.

"You've killed him," the voice growled. "You killed the rapist!"

It was all too much information for me, and I passed out. When I awoke, I was on the back seat of a moving car. Startled, I struggled to sit up and immediately recognised from the haloed streetlights and neon signs flicking by that we were driving through Newtown. It was a relief to see Flea sitting beside me. I looked at my hands—they were mine—more relief.

"Guys," Flea squealed excitedly, "Bo's back in the land of the living! Are you alright, love? Thought we'd lost you after that bastard king-hit you." She added with that distinctive little girl smile of hers.

"What on Earth was all that about?" I mumbled, feeling my sore chin and checking my fingertips for blood.

"He was the Glebe rapist, and didn't we give the bastard one hell of a hiding!" she crowed proudly.

The car was full of smoke from the driver and the girl next to her puffing cigarettes like steam trains.

They burst into a triumphant chant, "Terrorise men as men have terrorised women for centuries! Rape will be revenged!"

Flea explained that we had attacked the alleged rapist outside his Glebe home. The guy was all over the news at the time, along with American President Tricky Dicky Nixon's Watergate denials. The Women's Liberation Action Front had taken the law into their own hands and given the alleged rapist a beating he would never forget, intended to set an example for other potential rapists. Now we were on our way, armed with paint, to plaster Sydney with the slogan: "Rape will be revenged!" I sat back on the bench seat of the Holden Monaro thinking that though he might have been the Glebe rapist, I had been in a different fight. After getting whacked on the head, I had been in a sword fight in which I apparently killed someone. How weird.

I moved in with Flea and got on the dole to tide me over while hunting for a gig. A few days later, I was walking down Victoria Avenue at Kings Cross when I heard my name called. A cab pulled up, and out jumped Doctor Bolt. My first reaction was to turn and run, but he quickly caught up with me at the El Alamein fountain.

"Wait, Bonnie, I need to talk to you," he pleaded warmly.

I stopped, sat on the edge of the fountain, folded my arms, and grumbled petulantly, "Go on, but I'm not going to any appointments with Doctor What's-his-face if that's what you're after."

He sat down beside me. The sun overhead was scorching, but the fine spray from the fountain cooled me down.

"Remember I recorded you under hypnosis?"

"Yeah, old chimney pipe wasn't too impressed, was he?" I giggled.

"Don't worry about him, Bonnie. I didn't get to tell you what happened under hypnosis. You spoke in a foreign language."

"Yeah, like far-out, tell me something I don't know... gobbledygook."

"Yes... no... look, I took the tape-recording to a friend at Sydney University, and he wrote the words down, then researched the language."

"Funky, what did he find out?"

"He rang me yesterday, excited," Jackson said, drawing a notepad from his pocket. "Iad a mharú... do you recognise that?"

"Nup, sounds like mumbo jumbo to me."

"It means 'killed them!'" he said as though he'd just discovered the Ark of the Covenant. "And what makes that more profound is that it's a dead language. You were speaking Manx, Bonnie, a dialect of Brittonic, which is a derivative of Celt."

"More mumbo jumbo," I scoffed.

"Listen ...it was the language of the ancient Britons, Bonnie, don't you see? It isn't spoken anymore; it's a dead language. So how could you know it?"

"So what's that supposed to mean? Maybe I read it or saw it on TV or something."

"No, no, no, this was from your subconscious mind while you were under hypnosis." He was excited. "Bonnie, I believe you were channelling a person from ancient times, maybe from the Iron Age, possibly a kindred spirit. Carl Jung, the renowned psychologist, believed it possible. I need to put you under again to find out."

"No friggin' way, man!" I jumped up, adamant.

"To make contact with this person, Bonnie ...this is the opportunity of a lifetime."

"Maybe for you, but not for me. No, mate, I'm too busy." I reiterated stubbornly and then strode off, hoping he would follow. Don't ask me why I was so pertinacious back then, but I guess it was the courting ritual. Though I must admit pretty much all the women's liberation philosophy then was coming from lesbians who'd labelled just about all Aussie men that weren't gay male chauvinist pigs. It was almost an automated response not to agree with a guy—otherwise, you might be letting him think he was superior. Seems stupid looking back on it now. Anyhow, I slowed down for him to catch me up, and he took hold of my arm.

"Look, I'm sorry for being so forceful, Bonnie. I'm just keen to stick it up old pipe-smoking What's-his-face, that's all."

He seemed so sanguine about it. I fired him my best lost-puppy-dog look that had failed to work with my mum. "But why?" I pleaded, and boy, that was chucking the Female Eunuch axiom right out the window. I had him hooked.

"I didn't like the way he treated you, Bonnie. You and I both know you're not a drug addict. He's just a supercilious old fart wearing his self-importance like a crown—he can't dig that young people might know something he doesn't."

Well, that had me hooked. This was a guy after my own heart. He understood me, and that was pretty much the first time I could say that about any guy.

"Okay, doc."

He took my hand. His were soft and sexy.

"Call me Jackson."

"When do you want to do it? I mean, put me under, you know," I corrected myself, not wanting him to think I wanted a bonk, even though the desire was ubiquitous.

"How about tonight? I have to get back to the practice now. Um, we could have dinner first."

"Are you asking me on a date?" I blushed.

He blushed. "Um, yes, let's call it that. Um, a date,"

We arranged to meet at the Cauldron Restaurant in Darlinghurst at 7 p.m.

When I got home and told Flea, she was seriously impressed. The Cauldron was the hippest bar in town at the time, and that presented me with a dress dilemma—what the hell was I going to wear? I'd bailed so surreptitiously from home that I'd brought bugger-all with me.

But good old Flea came to the rescue. She opened up her wardrobe and with a courtly wave of her arm, proudly proclaimed, "Take your pick, kiddo." And boy, did she have some groovy threads to choose from!

The Cauldron is on Darlinghurst Road, close to where it meets William Street in Kings Cross. Looking back now, it seems funny, but at the time, it was embarrassing. When the cab pulled up out front of The Cauldron, I struggled out and immediately went over on my platforms in full view of a long line of punters waiting to get past the doorman into the club. My legs went everywhere when I hit the deck... it must have been a sight for sore eyes. Undaunted, I jumped up, assessed the damage—none done—brushed myself down, and then swallowing my pride, strode past the line up to the doorman, like nothing had happened, and dropped the name Dr Jackson Bolt. Well, if looks could kill, the entire line of at least thirty punters fired daggers at me when I was ushered inside ahead of them.

A single-story sandstone house built by convicts in the nineteenth century, The Cauldron was unique and the in-place to be seen in Sydney. Just inside the front door, I waited for the maître d' to take me to a reserved table. He led me past a packed bar from which I felt every pair of male eyes undressing me. That wasn't a problem; I was garbed for exactly that reaction and lapped it up big time.

The dining room was small, cosy, with a fireplace. Each of the twenty or so tables was occupied. With my heart pounding at ten to the dozen, I felt a rush of calm when I spied Jackson sitting alone at a table, studying the menu. He looked stunning, dressed in blue flared jeans and a matching denim jacket over a beige and maroon satin cowboy shirt. I hadn't expected him to be so hip, and by the admiring glances I was getting from the other diners, I must have looked a dish myself in my white lace, see-through mini and platforms that made my ever-so-shapely legs seriously desirable. My mum always envied what she termed my dancer's pins.

Always the gentleman, Jackson rose to greet me and then waited for me to sit before pushing my chair in and then taking his seat.

We chatted about the ramifications of Nixon's resignation the month before and which team might win the rugby league grand final in a couple of weeks. And then when the waitress arrived, we ordered an aperitif. Sydney rock oysters au naturel—still our favourite till now. Jackson ordered a bottle of red wine—I hadn't tried Australian wine— it wasn't so common in those days. I can remember it was a 1970 Killawarra Cabernet Sauvignon, and it was so good that after we polished it off, he ordered another bottle. No blow-in-the-bag booze buses lurking the roads back then.

After dinner, we had a drink at the bar where Jackson introduced me to the barman, John, or Flaps, as he was known to his friends. It seemed Jackson was a bit of a regular at the Cauldron, and maybe a little more of a groover than I had credited him. I was thrilled when he asked me back to his flat for coffee, knowing full well what that implied.

CHAPTER
III

By the time we arrived at the door of Jackson's upscale Darlinghurst apartment, just walking distance from The Cauldron, I was feeling tipsy. Thinking that once inside the flat, he would whisk me off to the bedroom for a romp, I was seriously disappointed when that didn't occur, and he began to talk about his work.

"Sit down, I'll get the tape recorder ready, and then we'll start," he said.

Bemused, I sat on the three-seater purple vinyl couch and took in the living room. We were on the 17th floor with an unobstructed view through large plate glass sliding balcony doors of the city of Sydney, the Harbour Bridge, and the Opera House, which had only opened a year ago—it was simply breathtaking.

Jackson switched on a reel-to-reel tape recorder he had set up next to his stereo unit, a turntable, amplifier, and two large speakers, then returned to place a small microphone on the coffee table in front of me. I would have preferred him to put Barry White's 'Can't Get Enough of Your Love Babe' on the stereo, but I went along with it, hoping for a novel approach. He leaned forward, not to kiss me, but to speak into the microphone.

"Test, one two," he said, checking the levels. "Right, rolling. Um, Tuesday, September 17, 1974—the day the Southern Cross was beaten by USA Courageous in the 23rd America's Cup—it is twenty-two hundred hours, and with her permission, I am placing Miss Bonnie Leigh under hypnosis."

I closed my eyes... my head was swimming from the wine, and it wasn't difficult to let the dulcet tones of Jackson's voice envelop me. Then, like someone had changed the TV channel, I was overcome by a vision so clear that I can still see it now.

I found myself inside a large round wooden room with big timber crossbeams holding up a thatched roof. A smouldering fire in a hearth in the centre of the room caused skeins of smoke to hang in the air like a gossamer veil. Fine rays of moonlight descended through tiny gaps in the thatch around the chimney, adding an otherworldly ambiance to the room. The bed was covered with thick animal pelts, and leaning against the bed were a round wooden shield and a long sword with a rusty blade. They seemed familiar. The carved face of the shield caught my attention—it was embossed with three hares and a raven, the artistry was stunning. I walked over to a large bronze standing mirror and peered at myself in the polished surface. My heart skipped a beat—though the image was blurry, I could discern that the nude female body I was staring at was definitely not mine. She was a larger woman than me, robust, with a mass of long curly red hair— that much we had in common. But she had big full drooping breasts, a muscular body, and powerful hips and thighs. I turned to gaze at my rear and was shocked to see deep weeping welts on my back. I turned back and moved closer to the mirror. Within the huge bush of red pubic hair, there were angry festering sores. I realised I must have been whipped and raped. Though the painful wounds seemed to be healing, the mental anguish and hunger for retribution were all-powerful and omnipresent in my mind. A knock at the door had me quickly covering up. When I spoke, like before, I couldn't recognise the language, but I fully understood what I was saying.

"Wait, I'm getting dressed. Who is there?" I asked.

"Domnall, my Queen," a grave voice replied. "There has been a reaction from procurator Decianus Catus to your slaying of the rapist Lovernius."

"Huh! That was to be expected—wait, Domnall."

A queen, no doubt! Well, I hadn't expected that! But even so, I couldn't get over how weird it was seeing through the eyes of someone else but being unable to do anything other than tag along for the ride. All my senses were functioning, but I couldn't speak and couldn't connect with her mentally. It was like I was a visitor or a ghostly guest. I quickly plaited my hair, tied it back with a leather thong, got dressed, placed a golden Torc of eminence around my neck, collected my sword and shield, and then pulled open the door. Waiting for me in the moonlight was a frightening ogre of a man, his face tattooed with blue Celtic motifs, a full ginger beard, long thick hair glistening with red ochre, and bare muscly shoulders. At six feet tall and just as wide, he towered over me, even after lowering his head to me in reverence. He looked back up, then shot me a huge broken-toothed grin.

"Queen Boudicca," he said.

I thought, Boudicca: Bo, hey, we have something in common.

"Call the Ricons to assemble. It is time they learned firsthand about the rape and the beating of my daughters and myself at the hands of the Romans."

My voice had a take-no-prisoners edge: this Boudicca bird was obviously one tough mother.

I felt robbed when Jackson's voice suddenly invaded Boudicca's world and dragged me back to reality. In a flash, the Queen's world evaporated, replaced by the lights of Sydney flickering in the yawning night outside the balcony windows. The mystical haze cleared, leaving Jackson looming over his stereo. It was surreal—there was no way I wanted to be back there. I wanted to be the Queen.

"Wow, that was mind-blowing!" I said, sitting up and knuckling my eyes.

Jackson sat down opposite me.

"You're not wrong. You were rambling on like there was no tomorrow."

"Yeah, do tell. What was I saying?"

"I've got no idea. You were speaking in... what did you call it?"

"Gobbledygook," I chuckled.

"Yes, that. I'll need to get the tape to Professor Harris to interpret."

"Can I have a glass of water, please?"

"Sure, sorry."

He got up, went through to the kitchen, continuing the conversation on the go. "What can you remember?"

I took the glass of water from him and had a sip. "Plenty this time."

"Really! Can I tape you?"

"Sure." I was keen to talk about it. He stopped the tape recorder, then sat opposite me, legs crossed, just like at the office.

"Okay, what do you remember from your vision?"

"Well, most importantly, I learned her name. The woman I was seeing through is a Queen. Her name is Boudicca, and she was talking to a guy called Domnall."

Jackson's mouth dropped open with astonishment. It was the first time I'd seen him lost for words.

"Are you saying you see through her eyes?"

"Yeah, it's like her point of view. I can hear, smell, think, taste, feel... everything she does. But I can't speak and can't connect with her, or at least I don't think I can. But I know what she looks like because I saw her in a mirror, and I know what had happened to her. What a trip! She killed the guy who had raped her."

"Are you serious? This Boudicca, a Queen, had been raped? But how could you tell?" Jackson asked, still in disbelief.

"Believe me, a woman knows these things. She had also been whipped—her back was cut to ribbons."

"So you could understand the language then?"

"That was the really mind-boggling part. I couldn't recognise any of the words she spoke, but I understood exactly what she meant."

Jackson leaned forward, turned off the microphone, and then slumped back in his chair, gripping his chin, lost in thought. I searched his face, and he appeared lost, like the lights were on but there was nobody home.

"Hello... Jackson? ... knock, knock!" I said, trying to bring him back to the present.

Finally, he snapped out of his daze.

"Oh! Sorry... Um, I do that... you know, disappear into my thoughts every so often."

"It's okay, I just thought you'd wigged-out or something."

"No, it's your ability to understand and speak a language you have no knowledge of that's left me astounded."

"What do you mean, speak it?"

"You were speaking the language during the session, that's what I recorded. Hey, I've read plenty about past life regression and multiple personality syndrome, but this is something completely different."

"That sounds like a scene from a Monty Python sketch," I joked, but he seemed lost in his own thoughts and didn't hear me.

Then, he had an epiphany. "The library! I need to go to the library to research this Queen Boudicca."

I checked my wristwatch. "Well, it's nearly midnight. I think the library might be closed."

He sat up, startled, as if someone had taken his lunch money. "Midnight! Oh, Christ, I'm so sorry. I need to get you home."

"It's alright, Jackson. Take it easy. I'm not going to turn into a pumpkin. Here, come here."

Thinking he might be shy, I patted the cushion beside me. He hesitantly rose and obediently sat next to me.

CHAPTER
IV

"Did you two do it on your first date?" Cleo asked, eager to know.

"No, even though there was plenty of free love back then, a girl didn't want to be seen as an easy target by someone with prospects," I replied.

"Ladies!" a voice interrupted us.

"Speak of the devil," I said. Cleo and I looked up sharply as Jackson appeared on the balcony, carefully balancing three mugs of piping hot coffee on a tray.

"I thought you might like a brew," he said with a warm smile.

"Wow, how well-trained are you uncle Jack?" Cleo smirked cynically.

"Actually, he's not trained at all. He's just an incredibly considerate guy," I countered.

"That's my girl," Jackson beamed.

I looked up at him, admiring his grey hair that he still flicked away whenever it drooped over one eye. His fingers, once slender, now marked with age spots, but underneath the signs of time, he remained my debonair knight in shining armour, my hunk of a doctor. I loved him as much now as I did back then.

"I was just telling Cleo the story of how we met. She's taping it for her master's in writing," I explained.

"Recording, love? They don't use tape anymore. I hope she doesn't let the truth get in the way of a good story," he said smugly.

Cleo looked embarrassed. "Don't worry, she demanded it to be warts and all."

He sipped his coffee and smirked with his green eyes shining. "My little socialist feminist wouldn't have it any other way."

"Alright, run along, you. I'm busy talking about you behind your back!" I playfully scolded him.

"As you please, but Cleo, if you need factual confirmation direct from the horse's mouth, he'll be in his stall," he quipped. "And remember, Cleo, story is the hub of the moral compass."

"Thanks, Uncle Jack," Cleo replied.

Jackson walked back inside, and I turned to Cleo. "For a while, I used to call him 'Aunty Jack' whenever I got angry at him."

"Why 'aunty'?" Cleo asked.

"Oh, you missed the joke. There was a show on ABC TV in the early seventies called 'The Aunty Jack Show.' It was a bit like an Aussie version of Monty Python—seriously off the wall. Grahame Bond played Aunty Jack, a motorcycling transvestite boxer. He even had a hit song in '74, 'Farewell Aunty Jack.' She'll rip your bloody arms off."

"Ugh?" Cleo seemed perplexed.

"That was one of the lines from the show. Aunty Jack would say that if you didn't watch it, she'd find you and rip your bloody arms off. By the way, are you still recording?"

"No, I turned it off for coffee. Do you want to continue now? I have some questions," Cleo replied.

"Yes, let's bat on, love, but save the questions for later. Now, where was I?" I asked.

"You were on Jackson's lounge in his flat," Cleo said, hitting the record button again.

"Right. He put me in a cab—"

"Wait, did you kiss? Was there any romance?" Cleo interjected.

"If there was, I would have mentioned it. But no, nothing like that. Anyhow, we agreed to meet on Saturday at a café in the city."

When I returned to Flea's place that night, things took a weird turn. She was eager to hear all the details about my night at The Cauldron. I went into her bedroom to return her clothes.

"So, what was The Cauldron like, Miss Funky Bum?" Flea asked, flopping onto her waterbed, causing it to slosh loudly. Dressed in a flimsy satin nightdress, she sat up and folded her shapely legs up to her chest, wrapping her arms around them.

"It was groovy. Your mini attracted a lot of prying eyes," I replied.

"Was it sexy enough for you to get laid?"

I took off my top but kept my bra on. "No, none of that happened."

"Bo! What the..?" Flea gasped, her hand over her mouth in shock, as if she had seen a ghost. "Your back!"

She grabbed my shoulders and turned me to face the full-length standing mirror. There, on my back, were whip marks— the same pattern I had seen on Queen Boudicca's back. I quickly pulled down the front of my panties and checked my shaved pubic area. Similar marks were there, but they were faded, not weeping or sore—only a faint resemblance. They weren't real.

"Okay, Bo, time to fess-up," Flea said, studying the marks with astonishment. "Is this guy into S&M?"

"No!" I rebuked her. "It's nothing like that. He's as gentle as a lamb. It's something else."

"Wait." Flea rushed over to the vanity table, pulled open the top drawer, and took out her brand-new Minolta XE SLR camera and flashgun.

"Lucky the flash is charged. Take off your bra, I'll take some shots," she suggested.

"No!" I objected, covering my breasts, not wanting to pose topless for her. But the flash fired, and by then, it was too late to stop her. So, I reluctantly showed my breasts.

When she finished, she smiled suggestively. "Are you sure I can't turn you? You've got a scandalous-looking pussy."

"No, Flea. But if I ever decide to change, I promise you'll be the first to know," I said, making a quick escape to my bedroom.

Strangely enough, Flea didn't ask me any further questions about the strange marks. After a few days, the marks faded completely, and I forgot about them.

The rendezvous with Jackson was at the City Café on Elizabeth Street, just opposite Hyde Park. It was a blustery day with a storm expected in the late afternoon. In those days, the city would be crowded with shoppers on Saturdays, but once the shops closed at noon, it became virtually deserted until the evening. Only a few people lived in the city back then. I remember worrying that I was going to be stood up as I sat there for over an hour. I had already finished two coffees and a round of raisin toast smothered with butter. The caffeine had my heart racing, and I was getting jumpy. Just after 2 p.m., as I was about to leave, I saw him enter the café, looking roughed up like a tumbleweed blown in from the street. He was apologetic. I pretended to be cross with him, but once he sat down and beamed that magical brown-eyed smile, the beast within me calmed down, and my claws retracted.

The café was closing, so we decided to go across to Hyde Park to continue our conversation. He explained that he was late because he had been at the Mitchell Library, researching Boudicca. I remember it well because as we left the café, he took my hand and rushed me across Elizabeth Street, between two green and yellow double-decker buses. I refused to let go of his hand once we were on the other side. With a hot westerly breeze at our backs, we strolled through the park like lovers, heading towards the Archibald Fountain.

"What I discovered today at the library is going to blow your mind, Bonnie," Jackson said, excitement evident in his voice.

Just the way he said it already had my mind half-blown. "What did you find out?"

"Boudicca existed! She was indeed the Queen of the Britons, and get this... in 60 AD!"

"Far out!" was the only suitable exclamation I could come up with.

"She was the ruler of the Iceni tribe, which inhabited an area of Britain corresponding roughly to modern-day Norfolk. And she spoke Brythonic, or ancient Celt. So Professor Harris was right when he said you were speaking ancient Celt."

We sat on the edge of the fountain, allowing the fine spray to cool us from the suffocating heat of the day. I glanced up at the statue of Diana on the fountain, the goddess of purity and peaceful nights, a symbol of charity. She seemed to watch over my morals. Then my thoughts turned to Theseus and the Minotaur, and the image of Domnall sprang to mind. The fountain felt connected to my visions somehow, with Apollo at its apex, holding his right arm out as a sign of protection. Memories of mythology from my school days flooded back. At the touch of Apollo's rays, men woke, trees and fields turned green, animals went out into the fields, and men went to work at dawn. Boudicca had awakened within me, and now she had awakened within Jackson. I already knew Boudicca was real, and now Jackson knew it too.

"I'm glad you were able to verify her existence. So, what now?" I asked.

"I want to hypnotise you again," he replied.

"Why?"

"So we can gather more confirmation on tape. Once we have enough evidence, I'll be able to convince Professor Harris to take a serious academic look at it."

"That's all well and good for you, but what's in it for me?" I questioned.

He stared at me, his brow furrowing, and then it seemed to suddenly dawn on him what I was getting at. A wicked smile broke across his handsome face. "I'll write a book about it, and you can share the income. How does that sound?" he said excitedly.

"Hmm, only if you pay me a weekly retainer while we work on it, so I don't have to find another gig," I suggested.

He thought it over for a moment, then his smile widened.

"Done," he agreed happily.

Jackson called me the next day at Flea's apartment to discuss our schedule. It was exciting to have a job and be able to afford to pay rent to Flea. Finally, I could revel in the freedom of my independence—or so I thought. But my plans were abruptly overshadowed when I received another call from Jackson a couple of hours later. His voice sounded grave, and something was clearly wrong. He didn't want to discuss it over the phone and asked to meet me at the City café at six o'clock.

It was a wicked day, raining cats and dogs and blowing like the devil. I caught a bus down William Street and jumped off at the corner of Park and Elizabeth Streets. As soon as the bus moved away, a gust of wind caught me and turned my umbrella inside out. Trying to fix it felt like wrestling an octopus, and I ended up getting drenched. Frustrated, I abandoned the broken umbrella in a bin and hurried through the pouring rain across Elizabeth Street, seeking refuge in the City Café.

Jackson was already waiting at a table, and I'll never forget the look on his face when he saw me—I must have looked like a drowned rat. He stood up, a perfect gentleman, and greeted me with a sympathetic smile.

"I'm sorry to put you through this, Bonnie. I wasn't expecting such terrible weather," he said.

I sat down, water dripping from my hair, and watched him take his seat. "You don't control the weather, mate. It's not your fault."

I picked up a napkin and began to towel my face dry, giving up on the hopeless task of fixing my hair. "Sydney weather is full of surprises. Sometimes we experience four seasons in a day... and Mondays... oh, I hate Mondays. So, why the distress call and all the gloom and doom?"

The sparkle of sympathy in his eyes suddenly faded, and I knew that whatever he was about to say wouldn't be pleasant.

"Your father—" he started.

"Oh, right," I cut him off. "He's freaked out about me missing appointments with Doctor What's-his-face and has blown up, right?"

"Close, but there's more to it than that. When Doctor Gibson-Smith found out that I've been seeing you privately and that we planned to continue the regression hypnotherapy... well, he—"

Realisation suddenly hit me like a punch to the gut.

"He sacked you!" I exclaimed.

"Yes, but there's more," Jackson continued.

"You've got to be fucking kidding me. My fucking father..." I was seething with anger.

"Shush! Shush, settle down, Bonnie!" Jackson urged, looking around the café with a conscious awareness of the raised eyebrows from other patrons.

I lowered my voice to a harsh, angry whisper, still using some expletives. "That bastard! What else did he do?"

"Doctor Gibson-Smith is going to discredit me professionally, so I won't be able to practice psychiatry anymore," Jackson revealed.

"Aw bullo! How can he do that? Doesn't that restrict your right to work or something?" I asked, stunned.

"I'm afraid he can, Bonnie. He has influence, and I stepped out of line. I'll just have to accept it and face the consequences," Jackson explained sadly.

"After three years of uni..." I muttered.

"And more," Jackson added.

"No way! You have to fight him!" I snapped.

"He doesn't like me, especially after he found out that I got out of national service by taking the government to court. He's ex-British military, you know?" Jackson said.

"Ahh, so that's the connection with my dad. He's an ex-major," I realised.

"My breach of ethical protocol goes against everything people like him stand for," Jackson said.

"Yeah, just like how all rock band members are drug addicts and how everyone except females should do a stint in the army to toughen them up for the real world. Fuck! Where do these old farts get off? My dad even told me that there's no place for women outside the kitchen. They're the male chauvinist pigs, not young guys like you," I ranted.

"They suffer from the hangover of a bygone era, where women were regarded as less than equal," Jackson explained, his face drawn with worry, lost in his thoughts. He didn't seem to hear my words.

"Hey, do you think Bugs Bunny had Daffy Duck for dinner?" I quipped, trying to lighten the mood.

"Hmm?" he groaned, his stare distant.

Taking his hand, I looked into his sad eyes. "We can beat this, Jackson. Doesn't it mean anything that I asked for your help because

I felt uncomfortable with Doctor What's-his-face?"

Suddenly, his eyes began to shine again. "That's brilliant! Theoretically you're right."

"It's just the truth, well, sort of," I said.

"Okay, Miss Bonnie Leigh, I think we have a defence. If you're with me, we'll take them on," he declared.

Still holding his hand, I gripped it a little tighter. "Call me Bo."

CHAPTER
V

It was the night to end all nights. I, I mean we... or her—well, Boudicca—was standing on a dais up front of a score of Ricons, which is what they call the chiefs of the provinces, and they were very angry. Behind them, sparks rose like a hoard of swirling fireflies from a massive bonfire that cast an eerie orange flickering glow over everything and everyone. Above me, the leafless branches of an ancient oak spread like claws into the abyss of the night sky. The sea of fierce, bearded warrior faces stared up at me, their giant bodies casting shadows from the bonfire much larger than they were in reality. Their gravelly voices rumbled, competing with the crackling of the bonfire; they were talking amongst themselves. They had gathered to listen to the speech I had just delivered, and I was awaiting their response. If they refused to follow me into battle, then I had threatened to go it alone with my own army... that's what I had told them, well, she did, Boudicca. They didn't like ultimatums, but with a tight grip on their balls by Rome, they knew it was a case of fight or capitulate. I had warned them the time was nigh to strike while Governor Gaius Suetonius Paulinus was campaigning in Wales and had left the Roman garrison in Colchester vulnerable. I had forewarned them that procrastination was not an option: a united decision to follow me was what was needed tonight.

I had learned much about this mighty woman warrior from her speech and the respect garnered as a leader, a queen, and a warrior. I had also learned from the cat-calls of some of the Ricons that the Romans had mocked her threats, which was understandable, considering the Roman propensity to treat women inferior to men.

Recently widowed by the death of her husband Prasutagus, Boudicca had inherited sovereignty over the Iceni Kingdom, as was the tradition. But Rome had other ideas and claimed Prasutagus had, prior to his death, bequeathed half of the Iceni Kingdom to Emperor Nero. When Boudicca had publicly refuted the claim, she and her two daughters were arrested, publicly flogged, and then raped. Believing the humiliation would put an end to her rebellious impertinence, the brutal act had had the reverse effect.

Suddenly, someone appeared right out of the bonfire like an apparition. Unscathed, garbed in a pure white caftan, he glided towards me as though on a cloud. Who was this spectre to not only perform a miracle before my eyes but also look like a god? I turned sharply and looked down at the bulk of Domnall.

"It is Arch Druid Bran, my queen," he croaked.

Right, so this guy was like Merlin, a sorcerer: a pagan priest. Was this really a time of magic and sorcery as depicted in Arthurian legend? The Ricon ranks parted to allow Bran passage to reach me, their piety for him obvious. I could feel the radiance of his power: the raging bonfire at his back created an aura around him. He stopped a few paces from me, his face in darkness, shrouded by a hood, and when he lowered it... it was Jackson!

He turned to face the Ricons and spoke with an air of dignity and righteousness. It struck at the very hearts of all within earshot.

"Boudicca speaks wisely. As I speak, Gaius Suetonius Paulinus marches his legion on the defenceless Druid stronghold at Mona. Heed the words of Boudicca, unite under her as one for your will against Rome to be done."

His poetic words resonated with the Ricons.

Bran pulled the hood back over his head of long hair and walked back towards the bonfire. As the Ricon ranks closed around him, he disappeared.

"Bo, the phone! There's a call for you!" a voice resounded.

I sat bolt upright in bed with my heart beating at ten to the dozen.

Flea's voice boomed again from the hallway outside my bedroom door. "Wake up, Bo... the phone!"

That was the first time I had channelled Boudicca since Jackson had last hypnotised me, and the first time I remembered so much detail. This dream had been the most vivid so far, more realistic than before. I felt angry at being brought back prematurely. I slipped a robe over my nakedness and went to the phone.

"I've got it, thanks Flea. Hello. Jackson, oh hi."

He had news and wanted to meet up to tell me. I was desperate to visit the Mitchell Library to read up on Boudicca, Bran, and Gaius

Suetonius Paulinus, so we agreed to meet there in an hour.

The rendezvous was at the top of the exterior stone stairs to The Mitchell Library or State Library of New South Wales as it's now called—the oldest library in Australia, I might add. As was becoming the norm with us, I was first to arrive. Five minutes later, Jackson came charging up the stairs like Rocky Balboa.

"Who?" Cleo asked.

"Rocky, the scene from the mid-seventies movie Rocky, when... oh, it doesn't matter, you can research it later... "

Anyway, Jackson was eager to tell me his news, so we hurried inside to the foyer and sat down by the wonderful Able Tasman map on the marble floor. We had to whisper because our voices resounded loudly off the marble walls and floor surrounding us.

"I've got good and bad news. Which would you like first?"

I pondered it and decided, "The good news."

"Okay, Professor Harris has agreed to collaborate on a research study into your experiences from a historical perspective."

"That's a good thing, I expect..." I said a little unsure. Academic stuff was streets beyond me at that time.

"It means the study will be published by the University of Sydney Department of Ancient History, and in the academic world... that is indeed credible," he said, with an excited gleam in his eyes.

"I still don't get it."

"Hmm, let me put it this way: it will fall into a grant from the University, so I will be able to keep paying you, and I'll have a job to boot."

Now that made perfect sense.

"Great! So when do we start?" I said excitedly.

"Pretty well immediately, but then there's the bad news."

"Don't tell me you're going to be an Indian giver."

"Not exactly. There is to be a hearing at the University of Sydney Psychiatry Department to determine whether Dr Gibson-Smith's claim that my hypnotherapy results on you, which he believes to be a case of psychic determinism, and my neglect of his direct order to stop hypnotising you, amounts to a violation of professional ethics and warrants the stripping of my academic credentials. If he's successful, we will lose the grant and the opportunity with Professor Harris."

"What the hell is psychic determinism?"

"A Freudian theory that professes all mental processes are not spontaneous but are determined by unconscious or pre-existing mental complexes. In other words, all that you are experiencing derives from your childhood."

"But that's ridiculous."

"In short, it's a rejection of regression hypnotherapy, the very basis of parapsychology. It has been a contentious debate between Jung and Freud theorists since forever."

"Schizophrenia amongst the academic psycho ranks, huh? So, when's the hearing?" I queried.

"Hmm, I've never thought of it like that. But yes, you're right... Oh, the hearing? Next week."

"Can they do that? Isn't that restricting your right to do your work?"

I could tell by the grave look on his handsome face that he didn't hold out much hope of success.

"Yes, they can revoke my degree and end my career in psychiatry. Those are the rules."

Rules were my pet hate, and I barked, "Stuff the rules! Why not use the findings of Professor Harris to support your case, along with a statement from me, of course?"

"No, I can't implicate him; it would mean putting his reputation at risk. He has already taken a big chance to convince the faculty to sanction a collaborative research study with me. No, I need solid evidence, something beyond the doubt connected with hypnotherapy."

"Well, we've got a week to come up with something."

"I love your optimism, Bonnie," he said with a look that almost melted me.

We ventured inside the library and spent hours scouring the catalogue and then reading up on Roman Britain, Gaius Suetonius Paulinus, the Druids, and the histories of the Roman senator Cornelius Tacitus, upon whose book Agricola much of the history of Roman Britain is based today. What we found on Boudicca was intriguing, to say the least. Roman Procreator Decanious Catus had ordered Boudicca and her daughters punished for resisting the seizure of their property, deemed following the death of Boudicca's husband Prasutagus to be the property of the then Emperor Nero. Now Queen of the Iceni, Boudicca wouldn't accept the Roman law of possession after death, which Catus claimed her husband had agreed to. So, Catus ordered Boudicca and her two daughters whipped and raped, publicly humiliated, and her possessions seized. This confirmed what I had already learned from my vision.

The library boasted the latest fandangle gadget: a Xerox RiCopy DT 1200 photocopier. It wasn't due for retail release until 1975, and

Jackson immediately fell in love with it. For 10¢ a page, he copied pertinent sections from various history books for us to study later.

We left the library mid-afternoon and walked to Jackson's apartment, which wasn't so far away. We stopped along the way at a café on William Street to buy donuts and coffees—it was a hot day, and luckily I was dressed for it whereas Jackson wasn't. Wearing a suit, by the time we had taken the tiny, stuffy elevator to the 17th floor of his apartment block, he was sweating up a soup.

Handing over his photocopies, he gestured for me to sit and make myself comfortable while he went to freshen up and change. He had been specifically researching Gaius Suetonius Paulinus, the Roman governor of Britain at the time of Boudicca, while I was chasing up Decanious Catus, Boudicca, Druidism, and Tacitus. It was interesting to read from the photocopies that in 61 AD, Paulinus had indeed led an assault on the island of Mona or Anglesey, which is known today as the refuge and stronghold of the Druids. The tribes of the southeast took advantage of his absence from his barracks and staged a revolt led by Queen Boudicca of the Iceni. I remembered what Bran had told the Ricons.

"Boudicca speaks wisely. As I speak, Gaius Suetonius Paulinus marches his legion on the defenceless Druid stronghold at Mona. Heed the words of Boudicca, unite under her as one for your will against Rome to be done."

When Jackson returned from his bedroom dressed in a loose singlet, AFL shorts, and bare feet, I was immediately distracted from reading. He sat on the lounge beside me and took the pages from me.

"Anything interesting?"

He didn't notice my amorous glance at the lump in his shorts and me licking my lips.

"More than you can imagine."

"It's hard to say who was the biggest threat to Boudicca, Paulinus, or Catus?"

"I just read about Paulinus taking his legions to rout the Druids at Mona and remembered Arch Druid Bran, who incidentally looked for all the world like you, telling the Ricons at the gathering that Paulinus was on his way there."

"That's fascinating! You realise that your vicarious visions will allow you to verify historical accounts, which at the best of times, have, to date, been biased."

"Yeah, why's that?"

"Because history has always been written by the winners."

"Oh, I see. I get the feeling Bo seeks revenge on Catus because he ordered her and her daughters whipped and raped."

"You're probably right, though Catus would have taken his orders from the governor Paulinus, so maybe she wants to settle a score with both of them."

I slipped off my sandals and manoeuvred a bare foot on top of his, hoping a little body contact might arouse him. It worked.

CHAPTER
VI

It was midnight when I entered Flea's apartment. I found her naked on the lounge with a skinny little blonde thing. She stopped and checked me out over her bare shoulder.

"Oh, hi Bo, this is Vanessa," she purred puffing out of breath.

"Hi Vanessa," I said, nonchalantly.

"Hi Bo," a small voice squeaked. I couldn't see her face for the mop of unruly hair.

"I'll just leave you guys to it. Goodnight."

I retired to my bedroom and closed the door to keep out the groaning. I relaxed on my bed and eventually drifted off to sleep.

I felt a hand on my shoulder shaking me awake. My eyes opened to see Domnall staring down at me. I was back with Boudicca!

"My Queen, my Queen, the Ricon's have voted you Arviragus! You will lead them into war!" He said excitedly.

"By the eyes of Andrasta, I knew it Domnall! The prophesy of high druid Bran was true."

Dawn was breaking. I was sitting with my back against the massive trunk of an ancient oak tree. Domnall offered me a hand up.

"You must convene a war council."

"No Domnall, first I'm must pay homage to Andrasta. Bring me oil."

He nodded obediently and left in a hurry returning few minutes later with an amphora. By then I was standing naked.

"Anoint my body."

He handed me the amphora and from it I poured olive oil into his cupped hands. This he spread over my skin. His calloused hands were made soft to the touch by the precious oil. When he finished my body glistened in the first rays of dawn. I had him pour oil in my hands and then drenched my hair with it. Domnall had also brought blue dye extracted from the woad plant. This he streaked on my face and forehead and then finger-painted spirals on my chest. I took a generous handful of it and rubbed it through my hair. I was ready.

"Do I look worthy Domnall?"

Domnall took two steps back and looked me over, head to foot, front and rear. Then with a broken tooth smile announced, "Yes my Queen, you are ready."

I immediately took flight and ran like the wind into the forest. It was a mystical experience running like a wild animal through the rays of light that cut like a blade through the canopy of high trees down onto the forest floor. I felt the sting of plant fronds whipping my naked body and the sensation stimulated me even more. I was connecting more with Boudicca—sensually and physically—it didn't matter that I had no idea where I was running to or why—when suddenly, I slowed as I entered a misty valley. Water, I could hear running water. A veil of mist hung in a gorge that contained a lake, I could just make it out through the thicket. I made my way tentatively through the thickening fog to the waters edge. Skeins of the mist floated on the surface of the lake. Peering through it my reflection looked back at me from the mirrored surface. Suddenly, a ray of light sliced through the trees and mist veiling me in a pool of heavenly radiance. I turned slowly and found majestic Arch Druid Bran standing right behind me.

"You have come to pay homage to Andrasta and she accepts your will," his warm, deep, voice resonated all the way down to my lady garden. "I have come to tell you of your destiny," he continued.

He let his grey hooded caftan drop to the ground, which left him naked. Anointed with oil, his beautifully proportioned body glistened in the light. His arms spread inviting me into his embrace and without hesitation I fell into them. The fragrant scent of oil on his skin made my senses swim ...we kissed ...and in our rapture, he lowered me down to the soft grass, gently laying me on my back and then he entered me.

It was the first time she had been entered since she had been raped and it hurt at first. But quickly her passion overcame the pain. When it was over my mind was left afloat in a sea of ecstasy.

He leaned forward, cupped my face in his hands locked his eyes on mine in a mystical stare and said, "Take stare into my eyes Boudicca for through them you will see as the raven, and sight your destiny."

I did as he asked and saw flames within his pupils ..then the vision slowly cleared and I was looking down at the land from a great height as from a bird in flight. Below I could see Roman legionnaires slaughtering people with sword and spear: men women and children being cut down while running to escape. It dawned on me I was watching the fall of Mona, the slaughter of the unarmed innocent, and it was terrifying. I saw Bran, his body cut, torn and bleeding ... legionnaires, in their bloodlust, as savage as a pack of wolves crucifying him on an oak tree. Then my tearful vision clouded over. When it cleared again, I saw a town below and recognised it as Camulodunum. Within the high ramparts smoke billowed from buildings set ablaze. My army were setting the fires, slaughtering and routing the legion of Petillium Cerialis.

I suddenly snapped out of the vision and to my horror, found a raven perched on my chest, staring at me. It squawked, and then flew away. I sat up sharply looking for Bran. Had he really been with me? Did I really see him killed at Mona? Was it a premonition or remote viewing? Then I realised what it was ...I had communed with the goddess Andrasta—her will be done.

I knelt at the bank of the lake, splashed water on my face and then peered at my image in the water. She wasn't Boudicca! I was annoyed at being back in the 20th century ..I felt robbed, cheated. That terrible sense of loss was staying with me longer now that the dreams were becoming more realistic, more graphic. My nerve-ends still tingled with the warm afterglow of lovemaking. Though it felt wonderful, it was at the same time disturbing. It made me question my sanity: how could this be happening? Why was I having a physical reaction to a phantom event? I needed to talk to someone about it. Jackson, yes, he would understand.

A loud thump, like a sack of potatoes hitting the floor, jolted me back to reality. Cleo and I exchanged quizzical looks.

"What was that?" she said, closing her iPad.

I stood and called out, "Jackson, was that you?"

I checked the time and was surprised to see it was 3 p.m. I had been talking for hours. When Jackson failed to answer, I ventured into his office and found him unconscious on the floor, a pool of blood surrounding the back of his head. The shock hit me like a ton of bricks. I stood there frozen for a moment, staring at him, and then screamed out, "Cleo! Quick, call an ambulance!"

Cleo and I waited anxiously in Moruya Hospital's emergency department for what felt like an eternity. Though the wall clock indicated it was only 9 p.m., I had lost track of the day. Worry tends to do that to you. Cleo was comforting, holding my hand as we sat there, both anxious for a doctor to appear and provide a diagnosis. Eventually, a nice young man, originally from Sri Lanka, arrived to deliver the news.

"Mrs Bolt?" he started, with an exotic accent.

"Yes, Doctor," I peered at his nametag, "Issuru."

He took my hand and looked deeply into my eyes.

"Now, I don't want to alarm you, but your husband lost consciousness."

"Yes."

"He fell and bumped his head."

"Oh!" I exclaimed, tears welling up in my eyes. "Will he—?"

"He is currently out of danger, but I will need to keep him here for a day or two under observation."

"Can we see him?" Cleo asked politely.

"It would be best for him to rest for now, so I think you should go home and then phone in the morning for an update on his condition. Okay, Mrs Bolt?"

"He's not going to die, is he?" I blurted out, tears streaming down my face.

"I do not expect so, Mrs Bolt. He appears to be a strong man, and he has a lovely wife and daughter to live for."

I wasn't about to correct him that Cleo wasn't our daughter. It didn't seem necessary.

We drove home, and Cleo stayed the night in the spare room. We agreed to pause the interview for the time being. Boudicca would have to wait; the health of my love was all that mattered.

The next morning, at breakfast, kind-hearted Cleo offered to stay until Jackson returned home. I graciously accepted; I didn't feel like being alone.

Later that day, Cleo drove me to the hospital, and I went in to see Jackson alone. He was sitting up in bed, his head bandaged, looking, for the first time since I had known him, like a sick man. Pale, drawn, and teary-eyed. I could see in his eyes that he needed me there. I held him, offering my comfort for what felt like an eternity. It's an awful feeling when the fragility of life becomes apparent, and the light of youthful exuberance that had flourished in his eyes until a day ago is dimmed by a silly accident. It wasn't long before Doctor Issuru arrived. Always pleasant, he checked Jackson's vitals and assured us that he was on the mend but would need another day in the hospital until the remaining test results came in. The prognosis brightened Jackson's spirits somewhat.

On the way home, Cleo mentioned that she was eager to continue the interview, but I was still a little shell-shocked. It was a murky, cold day, and rain fell steadily. I stoked up the fire, and we took an armchair each in front of it, sipping piping hot chocolate. Cleo had her ever-present iPad and was checking her email.

"I suppose you'd like to pick up where we left off, huh?" I suggested with a knowing glance.

Cleo snapped to attention. "Are you sure? That would be great."

"Okay, now where were we?"

"You were going to speak with Jackson about the erotic dream you had."

"Ah yes, Boudicca's world through the mystical eyes of the raven... and poor dear Bran..."

CHAPTER
VII

ackson wanted to meet up at Broadway Café, just a short walk from the University of Sydney, which was a regular spot for caffeine-loving students.

"I can relate to that," Cleo chuckled.

I arrived at the café after the lunchtime rush and spotted Jackson sitting at an outside table, engrossed in the newspaper. The headline caught my attention: "France to continue nuclear testing in South Pacific." I decided to sneak up behind him.

"Boo!"

"Argh!" he shrieked, nearly jumping out of his dapper suit. "You startled me."

"It's all that caffeine you've been consuming. It makes you jittery," I teased.

I gave him a hug and took a seat across from him.

"I've only had two," he defended himself.

"Yeah, two short blacks, I bet."

"It's no good polluting good coffee with milk."

"Polluting what's already poison. It'll get you one day, mark my words."

Little did I realise at the time how much truth there was in that statement, as years later, he suffered a dizzy spell, fell, hit his head, and ended up in the hospital after indulging in one too many coffees.

He smiled. "Surely you didn't come here just to scold me for drinking coffee. So, what does this stunning lass want from him?" he asked cheekily, referring to himself in the third person.

"Ah, he might well ask. But first, I'll take all the flattery I can get."

"That's it, huh?" he replied, folding his arms comically.

"Hmm, okay, short but sweet. Order me a cappuccino, oh sophisticated man, and then I shall grace you with my confession," I purred.

He got up, went inside, and returned moments later with my coffee.

"Two sugars and gently stirred, madam."

"Oh, how urbane of you, Doctor."

I watched him as he sat back down, took a sip of my coffee to gather courage, and then proceeded to tell him about my dream. Throughout the story, he stared at me wide-eyed. It felt as though I was narrating a cheesy sword-and-sandal porn flick. When I finished, he got up, went back inside the café, and returned with a fresh short black coffee.

"Did I freak you out that much?"

"Well, I went from casually reading about Frank Sinatra's feud with the Australian media, describing 'the broads who work in the press' as 'the hookers of the press' and saying 'I might offer them a buck and a half,' to visualising you in 60 AD having sex with an Arch Druid who looks exactly like me. So yes, you definitely freaked me out. I needed a top-up, and to make matters worse, David Bowie's 'Sorrow' was playing on the radio inside, which made me feel like slashing my wrists!"

I reached across the table and gently took his hand.

"Oh, don't feel that way, Jackson. It was just a dream. Besides, Bowie is singing about a girl with long blonde hair and blue eyes. That's not me, is it?"

He smiled warmly. "No, you're my 'Ruby Red Dress' by Helen Reddy, aren't you?"

"Exactly," I agreed.

"Look," he scowled at me, "on a serious note, I think it's time you had a word with Professor Harris."

"But I couldn't tell him about..." I protested bashfully.

We crossed Parramatta Road and entered the campus of Sydney University. After a brief walk, we arrived at an inconspicuous door on the top floor of the stately Brennan MacCallum Building. Jackson knocked once, opened the door, and ushered me inside.

On the other side, there was a small wood-panelled room with an antique desk. Behind it sat an elderly man who resembled Albert Einstein. He rose gracefully and gestured for us to take a leather chair each opposite his desk. In his sixties, with owl-like eyes, a prominent Hungarian nose, and a tendency to gesticulate broadly with the flat palms of his hands, he wore a crisp white shirt and a dark blazer that had replaced tweed as the uniform of the academic class. His white, curly hair looked as though it had been tousled by the Sydney wind.

"I presume, Doctor Jackson, my presence is being graced by the infamous Bonnie Leigh?" he said in a warm voice that emanated from a face that had witnessed and remembered many summers.

"Indeed you are, Professor," Jackson beamed.

"My dear, you are a source of copious fascination..."

"Thanks, Professor Harris. I appreciate all you've done to help us," I acknowledged. "But I'm not quite sure how to put this..."

Jackson interjected, "The dreams are becoming more vivid, Professor, and she is left with more than just a memory. She also experiences physical sensations."

"Such as?" the professor inquired.

I felt embarrassed, but I took solace in knowing that the wise professor was on my side.

"I made love with a man in my dream, and when I woke up, I could still feel—"

"I see," he said, pushing back in his chair and staring up at the ceiling. His hair and bushy eyebrows made him the perfect embodiment of a professor. A deathly silence enveloped us as he carefully considered my admission.

"Are you sure you hadn't...?" he trailed off, leaving the question unspoken. I knew he was wondering if I had masturbated in my sleep.

"No, I know the difference. You know, in the feeling," I blushed once again.

"The other thing is, Bo is becoming increasingly depressed each time she returns to the 20th century," Jackson added.

"Do you prefer staying in your dream time?" the professor asked.

"It's just so different there. I feel more connected than I do here, if that makes sense."

"Tell me the dream in as much detail as you can, and please don't feel embarrassed," he smiled.

I understood the importance of being definitive, especially when dealing with academics. So, I made sure not to leave out any detail as I recounted my dream. This time, during the course of my story, I had two men ogling me. When I finished, the professor, without uttering a word, slipped on a pair of round reading glasses and hurriedly went to the wall of books behind his desk. He began scouring through them, and to my surprise, Jackson seemed untroubled by this behaviour.

Eventually, the professor returned to his desk, clutching a big old leather-bound book that he had marked. He explained, "Here... Bran, Arch Druid of Britain in the days of the Roman invasion, seems to have been conjured up by the Welsh antiquarian Iolo Morganwg."

"Are you saying he never existed?" I asked, intrigued.

"Oh, no, no, no... What that means is that, like much of British history corrupted by Christianity, especially Druidism, it was the main opponent to Christianity. Even before Christianity reached Britain, during the Iron Age, Druidism was demonised by the Romans." He glanced at me over his glasses. "You see, history is mostly written by the winners, and the Druids never really had a voice. Furthermore, they had no written records of their own. All we know about them is derived from the surviving poetry, myth, and songs in folklore... and even those have been corrupted by the Church."

It was a revelation to realise how much of the history I had learned in school was distorted or outright false. It angered me to think that Boudicca and Bran were likely written out of history because they were the enemies of the conquering Romans.

The professor flipped through the pages of the book until he found another reference and added, "Here... Bran was thought to be the father of Caradoc, better known in history as Caractacus, the Chieftain of the Catuvellauni tribe. He led the resistance against the Roman conquest." He looked up, peering over his glasses at us again. "Now, this Caradoc is an interesting character because the Romans captured him and took him to Rome. According to the account, in Rome, he impressed the Senate, and they granted him his freedom on the condition that he stayed in the city for seven years. Nothing more is mentioned of Bran, but if you're saying he died in the massacre on Mona... well, that does make a lot of sense."

"Maybe if I could identify things in my dreams, archaeologists could go there to excavate, and we could rewrite history... properly," I suggested, hopeful.

The professor chuckled. "What a wonderful concept... I only wish it were that simple, my dear."

"Perhaps not, Professor Harris," Jackson interjected. "But it certainly would be worth a try, wouldn't it?"

Harris put the book down and looked at me thoughtfully over his glasses. "You know, you might just have a point there, Jackson. I have a friend in the UK who might be interested in Bonnie's recollections. I suggest that whenever you wake up from a dream, you make a detailed record of it. This could greatly contribute to our research, Bonnie."

"I can do that," I said happily.

"Mind you, like all things academic, we'll need evidence to support the theory," he added.

"Evidence?" I queried.

"It could be argued that you're simply dreaming about things you've seen in movies or read in books. But Jackson and I don't believe that to be the case. Some of the linguistic evidence that Jackson has provided from your sessions will go a long way toward supporting the regression theory. However, those feelings you've been experiencing can only remain conjecture for now, I'm afraid."

After the meeting with the professor, we went to Jackson's apartment. As we entered the foyer, he checked his letterbox and found a letter from the Australian Institute of Psychiatry. Instantly, his mood shifted from affable to foreboding. He remained silent about it until we were inside the apartment. With tentative hands, he opened the letter and read its contents, his face turning ashen grey.

"What is it?" I asked, concerned.

"I've been struck off as a practicing psychiatrist, and I'm required to appear before a hearing next Wednesday," he revealed, his voice filled with despair.

"What? Oh, how terrible. That only gives you five days to prepare," I said, shocked.

He slumped into an armchair, dejected. "I don't really have anything to prepare, Bo."

I sat in his lap, wrapping my arms around his neck, trying to console him. "You have me to help you prepare. We can beat this, babe. We just need to stay positive. You'll see, something unexpected will come our way. It always does when you're in the right."

"Bo, the letter states that your parents will be present, supporting Doctor Gibson-Smith. That's going to make it tough," he lamented.

Anger surged through me, and I jumped off his lap, pacing about. "What can they say? I'm over twenty-one. They have no right to dictate my life."

"Legally, you're correct. But ethically, they can claim that my actions could have caused damage to your mental health, and that's akin to professional negligence. No, we need solid evidence to prove your case and justify my decisions. Right now, we have nothing."

"Something will turn up, just wait and see. It's karma. You've done nothing wrong, babe," I insisted.

We shared a passionate kiss, and it led to an afternoon of incredible intimacy, providing a momentary respite from the weight of our worries.

Over that weekend I thought a lot about what Professor Harris had suggested and from then on kept a notepad beside my bed to jot down notes after a dream. But that Sunday the thought was nagging me that it would be better if I were taped as well. I knew it would be too difficult to set up a tape recorder to leave running all night in the hope that I might have a dream, but me speaking in a foreign language, especially one that I have no comprehension of, would surely be great evidence for Jackson's hearing. I rang Jackson and he agreed. We decided to try some more regression therapy and tape it, so I went to his apartment that afternoon for a session.

It was all set up for me when I arrived. A small table beside the three-seater lounge for the tape recorder and a comfy pillow for me to rest my head. It wasn't long before I was laid back on the lounge comfortably drifting off, mesmerized by Jackson's hypnotic voice.

The view of the burning town and warriors executing the remainder the Roman garrison was gratifying. Domnall was beside me, his forearms bloodied, his long hair matted with Roman blood.

"While Suetonius marches his legion back from Mona, we must continue crushing their diminished forces," I said urgently.

"Are you sure the tribes will continue to support us?"

"What makes you doubt them Domnall?"

"When they are done looting Camulodunum, they will have quenched their thirst for blood and bounty. It is then they will want to take their prizes home... you must remember Cadeyrn, only few are soldiers most are farmers. See, as we speak the chiefs are coming our way."

"Then I will need to make my plans convincing to them."

"More than that, you will need for them to know there will be Roman riches to fill their greedy pockets... none of them fight for the cause we do," he grinned.

Seven chieftains', in bloodied battle dress, were tiredly making their way up the hill towards us. I raised my sword in the air and shouted. "Today Ricons, today has been a historic victory!" They stopped a short distance from us. "Your names will long be sung in praise to this conquest. We have garnered revenge on Suetonius and Rome, for the murder of our brothers, sisters and the Druids on Mona by destroying the legion of Petillius Cerialis. We have burned the Colonia and Procurator Catus Decianus is running with tail between his legs to Londinium!"

The Ricons raised their swords in the air as one and then slapped their shields with them, a rowdy triumphant salute. I lifted a hand to quieten them.

"But the deed is not yet complete. There are greater spoils to be had in Londinium and Verulamium."

"One win over depleted forces and you act as if you are Vercingetorix, Boudicca!" A big ugly Chieftain roared.

"I haven't used that title. Vercingetorix was a hero of the people murdered by Rome. I am Boudicca, and I say to you... the depleted Roman legions offer us a chance to strike a killing blow! We need to move now to keep surprise our weapon. They will not be expecting us to continue but to withdraw with our plunder."

"What will Suetonius do in revenge if we kill more Romans?" Another Ricon bellowed. The rest of them grumbled in agreement.

"No more than for what we have already done!" I growled back like a savage beast. "Look behind you, see, Camulodunum ablaze... it's people and army slaughtered. We have no choice now but to continue on to Londinium!"

They squabbled amongst themselves until finally they reached a consensus and Addedo, chief of the Trinovantes, stepped forward. I liked him, he was a true believer and a great warrior—a proud, tall, powerfully built man with a shock of long auburn hair and a voice that reverberated right down to your very boots.

"Cadeyrn!" he called to me. "Two Ricons will take leave of us with their warriors... they wish to fight no further. We bid them thanks for their fight today. You have the support of the Trinovantes, Dobunni, Belgae, Coritani and the Artebates. With your Iceni warriors, we are force strong enough! This day we praise you Boudicca. Your name means victory, and it is the sweet taste of victory we have on our breath! We first drink in triumph, and then we march on Londinium!"

Suddenly, I wasn't looking at Addedo but at Jackson. I was back and I didn't like it at all.

"No Jackson, send me back, there's more I need to know!"

CHAPTER
VIII

Jackson was taken aback by the sheer intensity of my demand. "Fine, fine, I'll send you back, but only after an hour or two. It's not good for you to be hypnotised for too long," he said, sounding like a true doctor.

My mind was in a haze. I could see that it was already dark outside. "How long have I been under?" I asked groggily.

Jackson looked at me with concern. "Nearly three hours," he replied.

"Wow, it felt like no time at all. Did you get much on tape?"

"I certainly did. You were jabbering away like you were giving a speech or something. I have no idea what you were saying, of course. We'll have to leave that for Professor Harris to determine."

My mind drifted, and I babbled, "Greater spoils to be had in Londinium and Verulamium I, I—"

Jackson stood up, worriedly saying, "Bonnie, you're talking in another language... you're back... You're back." He took my hand and peered into my eyes. "Are you with me?"

"Yes, yes, I'm fine... um, I was making a speech to the chiefs of my army," I said vaguely.

"You need to clear your mind. Sit back, take a deep breath, and focus on the here and now. I should record you recounting this, as the Professor suggested."

Squinting, I stammered, "Fine, fine... But you know what?"

"Hmm?"

"It's in order—"

He turned from setting up the recorder. "Order? Oh, I see what you're saying... your dreams are in chronological order, sequential."

Holding my brow, I was able to focus again; the fuzziness was wearing off. "Yes, yes, if I went—"

"Wait, let me get this on tape—" he said quickly, activating the tape machine.

"Before you do, I'm sorry for snapping at you. It's just... I don't know... it's difficult when I'm drawn back from so much going on."

"That's okay. I'm beginning to understand... Okay, speak up; it's recording."

"Oh, right... the dreams are in sequence. Like, if I was brought back from a vision and then hypnotised again, say ten minutes later, I'd go back to the vision, and the same ten minutes would have elapsed."

"That's interesting. It's as though you're living a parallel timeline to Boudicca."

"Seems so, but how come?"

"Describe your vision, Bonnie."

Jackson took notes as I prattled on about my vision, and then we discussed the notes later over dinner. An interesting thing came up: the time difference between Sydney and London was being accommodated for in the vision. For example, if it was 7 a.m. on Tuesday, when I was standing on a hill in Britain in 61 AD, then it would be 4 p.m. the same day in Sydney, when Jackson hypnotised me in 1974. Pretty weird.

A few hours later, I was back on the couch, ready to be hypnotised again.

"I'll allow you a short session only, Bonnie. We need to be careful, okay?"

"Okay," I said, settling back in expectation of his soothing voice.

I looked down... my feet and legs were bare. Then, a strange sensation came over me. My nerves tingled as they came to life. I became aware of the cold, but it didn't bother me. I was naked and anointed with oil. I could smell it—pungent but fresh, herbal. I was in a forest, where obviously, I was again seeking the goddess Andrasta. She was the medium through which I had contacted the spirit of Bran the last time. I needed to find running water. I felt instinctively that it was an integral link to the spirit connection. The forest was dark and silent, with only the sound of sticks breaking under my step and a distant whirring sound creating a magical ambiance. Ahead, through the bushes in the radiant glow of the full moon, I heard a babbling brook. I stopped at its bank, knelt down, and scooped up some water into my cupped hands and drank... it was cool, clean, and invigorating. I heard a rustle on the opposite bank and caught sight of a hare darting into a thicket. Where it disappeared, a shaft of moonlight had cut through the tree canopy, and I could see a dark figure standing in the light. She was naked, full-breasted, with long red hair like my own, falling all the way to her knees. She was the crone of the dark of the moon, the cutter of threads—the one to whom all return—the lunar goddess of war, the mother, and the most venerated maiden—she was Andrasta. With her arm raised, a finger beckoned me to enter the water and approach her. I waded through the fast-running, knee-deep water, and as I stepped up onto the bank, I found no-one there. Had she really been there, or was it just in spirit? The temperature suddenly changed, the air became much cooler, and goose bumps rose on my skin. Then, I felt light fingers stroking my back and buttocks. I turned sharply and found no-one. I felt dizzy, like I was going to faint. My heart was pounding like a war drum.

I looked down from a great height and realised that I was seeing the world again through the eyes of a raven in flight. Below me was the isle of Mona—the Roman legion, XIV Gemina, moving out across the flat of land that at low tide linked Mona to the mainland. It was a long line that scarred the snaking road with torches and crimson uniforms, like a river of blood. No living creature had been spared on Mona—it had been Pax Romana: annihilation. I landed on a branch of the giant oak tree upon which Bran was crucified. Barely alive, his face battered almost beyond recognition, and his body torn, he was hashed naked to the trunk of the oak—the most sacred icon of Druidism. His body had been brutalised by countless spear thrusts. From his wounds, his lifeblood drained, running as a rivulet down the great girth of the ancient tree to enter its roots. Bran opened his parched lips and spoke to me with a serene and warm voice.

"I am close to my physical passing, Boudicca... In life, there are duties that in death are no longer relevant. You will defeat the Romans at Londinium and Verulamium, and then, before you become one with Andrasta, you must prevent the life's work of the dying sage from falling into Roman hands. Boudicca, I entrust to you this most sacred duty: bury the sage and his gospel in safe but separate unmarked graves. Boudicca, my life has been sacrificed to this sacred cause. Now, as distinct from my youth when years seemed endless, I come down to seconds, and the very last second is as significant as the first, the most significant."

The light suddenly left his wondrous eyes. A final tear rolled down his beaten and bloody cheek, dripping as a glistening red diamond that exploded into a universe of particles on the soil, then entering the roots of the tree. Bran would become one with the ancient, sacred magnificent oak.

The cold immediately left me, replaced by warmth. I sat up abruptly from my bed of dewy grass, conscious of the enormity of the secret Bran had bestowed upon me—a sacred undertaking far beyond my own mortal capacity. I pledged then that I would fulfil my vow to Bran.

"Can you hear me, Bonnie?"

My eyes finally focused on Jackson's face as I took a deep breath. I sat up and drank some water. I was back.

"That was incredible! Finally, it's becoming clear, Jackson," I said excitedly. "Bran is dead."

"Wait, let me turn on the recorder. Okay, what do you mean when you say it's finally becoming clear?"

"There is a reason for the connection... you were right, Boudicca and I are locked in some sort of parallel world. We're both exactly the same age, with similar looks... maybe even genetically linked or kindred spirits. But more importantly, she has a quest for me."

"A quest?"

"A secret that could be important to the world now."

"Unbelievable!"

"Turn off the tape recorder, Jackson. This secret is so valuable we can't risk it falling into the wrong hands."

I arrived home still buzzing from the vision and still feeling the pain of Bran's loss. I found Flea on the couch, watching TV. I flopped down beside her.

"Hey, Flea."

"Where have you been, girl... with Dr Wonderful?"

"Sure have," I said coyly.

"Lucky girl, all that sex."

"Not tonight, Josephine. Anyhow, you've got nothing to be envious about. You're not into pinkies," I emphasised by wiggling my little finger.

"Don't you worry, I've had my fair share of stiffies."

"Ah, so you admit to being a switch-hitter!"

"It depends if I want to whet my appetite on fish fingers or bangers and mash!"

"You're crazy!" I giggled.

"Like it or hump it is my philosophy, honey. For me, it's all about orgasms... the more, the merrier, I reckon. And how they're delivered doesn't really bother me. Hey, speaking of orgasms, how's the dream therapy going? I heard you rabbiting on in some weirdo language again the other night. It sounded like you were getting bonked."

"I'll be honest, Flea, it's getting pretty far-out. You're right, I did have sex in my vision the other night, and I could still feel the sensation after I woke up, like it really happened."

"Hmm, lucky you. So, do they fuck the same way back then, or is it only doggy style?"

I playfully slapped her on the arm. "You! I think that's one thing that hasn't changed since we were cavemen."

"You mean cave girls, honey," she scoffed.

"Goodnight, Flea."

I gave her a hug and then wandered off to bed.

Wednesday arrived quickly, and even though I wasn't attending, my thoughts were with Jackson at the hearing. I was in the kitchen at Flea's, making a cup of coffee, when the phone rang. It was Flea, on a break from a television commercial shoot, and she wanted to meet me at the East Sydney Pub in Woolloomooloo. I told her I wanted to stay near a phone in case Jackson called, but she insisted it was important. Since it was just a walk down the hill and it was a nice sunny day, I trotted off to meet her.

I found her at the packed public bar with a group of arty film types. The slightly battered old pub, with its wooden floors, was known as the last country pub in Sydney.

"Hey, Flea, what's the news?" I greeted her.

"Hey, guys, meet my spunky flatmate Bo. She's straight," she announced with a cheesy grin. The alluring ogling from her six friends—two females and four others—indicated their sexual preferences.

"Do you want a drink, love?" Flea asked.

"No thanks. Look, I really need to be at home—"

"Shush!" she hushed me. "Come over here."

She physically dragged me away from her friends, and we found a spot near a side door.

"You've gotta see these," she said furtively. "Lucky I had a friend of mine develop them in his darkroom. We'd never have gotten them back from Kodak, too racy."

It felt so clandestine, as if we were doing a drug deal. She handed me a packet of photographs and then looked around to make sure nobody was watching us. I opened the packet and thumbed through the pictures. Immediately, I understood their significance. They were the photographs Flea had taken of my naked back and other parts on the night I came home from my first date with Jackson. We had been to The Cauldron, then to his apartment, and then he had regressed me. The photographs clearly showed the grisly whip marks on my back and the terrible scores around my genital area from Boudicca's rape. They were graphic, embarrassing even, but I knew that this was exactly the evidence Jackson desperately needed for his defence. I needed to get them to the hearing in Pitt Street before it finished.

"Thanks, Flea. You're a diamond!" I yelled, racing for the front door.

I made it to the Angel Place Law Courts in the city in record time, only to be confronted by a huge board in the lobby that listed an awful lot of courts and hearing rooms. Which one? I yelled inwardly. I was just about to give up when I spotted Professor Harris.

"Professor!" I cried out in desperation.

"Bonnie! Are you all right? You look frazzled, dear."

"Look at these," I said excitedly, handing him the photographs. He flipped through them one at a time. I bit my lip when he came to the shots of the welts around my shaved pussy.

"These were taken an hour or so after the first time Jackson used hypnotic regression on me. See, they're date-stamped on the back. Those marks on my back mirror Boudicca's wounds after she had been whipped. All of the marks had completely disappeared a couple of hours later."

"Were they painful?"

"No, I didn't even know they were there until my flatmate saw them when I was taking off the clothes she had loaned me that night. She immediately grabbed her camera and took the pictures. We had forgotten all about them until she picked them up from her photographer friend this morning and then called me. Do you think they will help Jackson?"

A huge smile broke on his wise old face. "Indubitably, my dear, indubitably."

"Are you going there now?"

He checked his watch. "Yes, I'm due to make a statement in five minutes," he said diligently.

"I thought you couldn't help him?" I queried.

"That's what Jackson thought as well, but I have other ideas," he smiled warmly.

"Thank you, Professor Harris. I'll leave the photos with you then."

He pulled a pen from his top pocket and handed it to me. "Here, sign the back of each photograph with today's date... that way, I can witness your signature, and they will be admissible as evidence."

After I finished, I stood on my tiptoes, my eyes welling up with tears of thanks, and gave him a peck on the cheek. "You're a good man, Professor Harris."

"Are you sure you don't want to come with me, Bonnie?"

"No, I'm not dressed properly, and besides, Jackson didn't want me to go. My dad will be there, and we're not on the best of terms."

"I'll have the interpretation of the tape from your last vision tomorrow. Can you be at my office at noon?"

"Yes, and won't that be interesting? It was the best vision yet."

"Excellent. See you then."

"Good luck!" I asserted, watching him stride over to the elevator.

I expected to receive a call from Jackson after the hearing, but I didn't, and of course, I started thinking the worst. Flea hadn't come home, so I spent the evening curled up on the couch, watching television. Few people knew at the time that if you had a colour television—which we had when most were still black and white—the test pattern at the close of transmission was the only thing broadcasted in colour. It wasn't until March 1975 that colour television was broadcast nationally. I used to get a kick out of waiting up for the test pattern to come on. Once it went off after about an hour, the screen came alive with hissing, swirling coloured pixels. I remember being high on acid one time, watching the colour pixels swirling around on the screen, thinking that some sort of alien force was trying to communicate with me.

The hissing white noise from the TV woke me with a start. It was 4 a.m., so I disconsolately dragged myself off to the comfort of my bed.

CHAPTER
IX

Totally out of character, I arrived at the meeting with Professor Harris twenty minutes early but knocked on his door anyway. It opened, and to my shock and horror, there was my father with Jackson and Professor Harris, having a meeting. I guess the expression on my face said it all because a shroud of guilt blanketed their conversation.

"So, what's going on here?" I growled reprovingly.

"Take a seat, Bonnie, and I'll explain," Professor Harris said cheerfully, trying to tame the undercurrent.

Careful to avoid eye contact with my dad, I sat in the spare chair, and the professor continued.

"Bonnie, we decided to call a meeting this morning because of the outcome of the hearing yesterday."

"A hearing that concerned me... so why wasn't I invited to this little get-together?"

"Please let me finish, Bonnie," Professor Harris asked politely. "The hearing resolved, given the evidence you provided, to allow Dr Jackson to continue practicing and to continue with your case under my supervision, on the proviso that we obtain a parent's consent. Your father accepted the verdict of the panel and requested to be shown the evidence we have accumulated to date, supporting Dr Jackson's hypothesis. We've been here for the last two hours going over it all."

His news lightened my mood. I cracked a smile at Jackson, and he reciprocated.

"Okay, so what do you think, Dad?"

He looked at me in that way only a parent can, to make you feel like a kid, and then said with a wry smile, "I guess I owe you an apology, love. I'm so sorry for doubting you." He stood and opened his arms, and I flew into his embrace, so happy to finally have his support. With tears welling in my eyes, I looked over his shoulder at Jackson, who was also misty-eyed. It was a very special moment, one I shall never forget.

"I can't believe what you must have been going through, my dear, having no one to support you, and us accusing you of being a drug addict. I am so thankful to Dr Bolt and Professor Harris for taking the initiative to show me the truth... which is quite amazing."

"There's no need for thanks, Mr Leigh. Bonnie is an exceptional person with an extraordinary gift," Jackson said solemnly.

"Hear! Hear! And from what I have learned from your last session, Bonnie, your case is now even more intriguing," the Professor said eagerly.

"Well, gentlemen, I should be getting along now. I will need to bring Bonnie's mum up to speed, though I must admit she never gave up on her daughter... that's to be expected from a Mum."

He shook hands with Professor Harris, then Jackson.

"I can see there is a certain chemistry between you and my daughter, Doctor, a little more than professional."

"Intuitive of you, sir. I hope you have no objection," Jackson said with more manners than I had witnessed before.

Dad looked at me, then back at Jackson, still holding his hand, and then shook it even harder.

"I'll tell Mum to be expecting you both for dinner soon then."

Now the tears were really flowing. I'd never had my dad's blessing like that before. I gave him a big hug and whispered, "I love you, Dad."

Once Dad had gone, Jackson gave me a hug. "If it hadn't been for your last-minute evidence, Bonnie, I would have been done like a dinner!" he admitted.

"The cavalry arrived just in the nick of time," Professor Harris added with a chuckle. "So, sit down, you two. We have a lot to talk about. Just wait till I find my notes... Ah! Here they are... Hmm, yes," he said, studying them. "Have you taken notes as we discussed, Bonnie?"

"Yes," I produced my notepad.

"Good. Do you recall when you were talking with Bran, he bestowed upon you a secret?"

"Yes."

"Well, because it was obviously Bran who was doing most of the talking, we don't know what the secret is. Your voice is the only one recorded, of course..."

"Okay, well first, I need to ask you guys, given that this was a person dying and passing on a request that resulted from his ultimate sacrifice, I need to understand the extent of what I divulge will be exposed, seeing it's of such a secret nature."

"It won't go any further than this room, Bo," Jackson said, looking puzzled by my statement.

"I think what Bonnie is referring to, Jackson, is if it will be published or passed on to any other person, in whatever form. Is that correct?" the Professor clarified.

"Yes. You see, at this stage, I don't know if my connection with Boudicca has a reason... though I suspect it does. What if she's trying to pass on a secret to me?"

"Like what?" Jackson asked.

"Like what if there is a big secret? I mean, a really big secret that is still relevant today? Maybe a secret people would die or kill for."

"I see what you mean. Professor, do you think that might be overestimating the significance of the secret?" Jackson questioned.

"No, not at all... you and I must be bound like a secret brotherhood to protect the information Bonnie grants us. How about we sign a non-disclosure agreement to that end. Agreed, Jackson?"

"Yes, will that work for you, Bonnie?"

"Yes, I think so."

"If anything at all is to be published, it will be with your consent, and you will be credited as the source," Professor Harris added. "Would you prefer to not discuss anything further until I have the papers drawn up, Bonnie?"

"No, I trust you both." I paused while we exchanged looks, aware that the three of us had just agreed to take an unfamiliar path together—a path of uncertainty as to where it might lead us.

"I've never seen anybody die before, especially a person I had bonded with, so the horror of it is still with me. He called the person Boudicca needs to find the sage. He said to bury the sage and his book... no gospel, that's right. I don't know whether Boudicca even knows the identity of the sage or anything about this gospel, but these were Bran's last words. So, I expect, given the passion of both Bran and Boudicca, the sage and the gospel must be very important. He also said the sage and his gospel are to be buried in separate locations but nearby, to make them harder for the Romans to find. I got the feeling the sage is very old and dying. Could he be the wizard Merlin?" I posited.

"I doubt it, Merlin appears to be a myth. However, in saying that, this entire experience with what you are revealing could well change that notion, so nothing is out of the question," the Professor admitted.

"One thing for sure, Boudicca has been handed a vital quest," Jackson added.

"And that's something new to our historical records, which is what makes this extra exciting," Harris chortled.

"Bran also said two other things, 'you will win at Londinium and Verulamium, and then before you become one with Andrasta, you must ensure that the dying sage does not fall into Roman hands nor his life's work.' How do you interpret that, professor?"

"Well, she does indeed win at Londinium and Verulamium, but eventually Suetonius Paulinus, returning from Mona, regroups with the XIV Gemina legion, some detachments of the XX Valeria Victrix legion, and all available auxiliaries to take on Boudicca and defeat her somewhere in the West Midlands. But, as I've mentioned before, that is the account of Publius Cornelius Tacitus, a Roman scribe or historian who accompanied Suetonius and is well known for exaggeration and glorifying Roman victories, consistently to the detriment of the opponent. So we can't be sure whether Boudicca was killed in that final confrontation or not. Tacitus states as her army fled, she rode her chariot at a huge oak tree and simply disappeared. The oak tree being the most sacred tree of the Druids, so we can assume his account to be bathed in myth. But when you say Bran predicted she will become one with Andrasta, well, that suggests magic because Andrasta was the Celtic Goddess of Battle, and Boudicca's very name means victory in Celtic. So Bran is saying she will leave the final fatal battle to fulfil the quest he has given her before she becomes one with Andrasta? This suggests the myth of the chariot and the oak tree may have some substance."

"That's amazing," Jackson said, agog.

"Professor, you would have seen in my notes that the visions appear to be linear," I said.

"Yes, I was intrigued by that. So you think yours and Boudicca's lives are running parallel in different times?"

"If that is the case, then we can't afford to waste time. These battles are imminent... we need to find out who the sage is and about his work. If she does bury him and his gospel, we need to know those locations, don't we?" Jackson said.

That thought threw a cat amongst the pigeons. The professor and Jackson looked to be frozen in time with the gravity of the concept. Finally, the Professor broke the pregnant pause.

"Goodness gracious me, if we were able to determine the location of a book, a gospel, or an account written about the early Britons from their perspective... well, it could change history!" He flopped back in his chair, amazed by the significance of what he had professed.

"It might debunk Tacitus once and for all!" I laughed.

But the Professor didn't find it humorous. Instead, he had a look of consternation on his wise old face.

"You look concerned, professor," Jackson said.

"I worry that such a discovery might not be well appreciated by some."

"The Church?" Jackson suggested.

"Them and others."

"Well, we can't let that worry us. We need to—"

"Yes, Bonnie, we need to get cracking... I agree... but we will need to be cautious. That's all I'm saying," Professor Harris said sternly.

"Okay, Bonnie, how about 4 p.m. today at my apartment?" Jackson said.

"Oh, I meant to say, you'll be pleased to know that the Uni has provided an office and facilities for you two for the term of the study... three years," the Professor beamed.

"That's fantastic news! Where is it?" Jackson asked.

"In the Quadrangle on Science Road, at the School of Philosophical and Historical Inquiry, Room 717, I believe."

I could tell by the beam in Jackson's eyes he was impressed. That pretty much confirmed the belief the University had in our project. On the other hand, I felt a little miffed... I was enjoying the shenanigans we got up to at Jackson's apartment. Anyhow, it didn't matter. What was more important was that our study now had the credibility of a university address. For someone who'd dropped out of school in the fourth year after getting an average school certificate pass, having an office at the prestigious University of Sydney gave me back some self-esteem. It's good to feel positive.

Later that afternoon, I was on the couch in our new offices with Jackson sitting opposite me, notebook and pen in hand, and the tape recorder rolling. His warm, hypnotic voice flooded over me, making my eyelids heavy, very heavy...

"Round up all the Roman women and take them to Andrasta's Grove. Wait there for my orders."

"Yes, my Queen," Domnall told me before striding off to issue the orders.

I called after him, "Torch every building, destroy every statue to

Claudius and any other Roman dictator or god—give no quarter."

The town square I was standing in was totally deserted of townspeople. Only my warriors darted in and out of buildings, their swords dripping with Roman blood and the spoils of victory. Unearthly screams were coming from people locked inside buildings that had been set alight, and the stench of burning human flesh spoiled the air. Unable to evacuate through fear of being cut down in the street and hacked to pieces, these people had chosen to be consumed by the flames. I looked down at the sword in my hand and my forearm caked with dried blood—I felt unclean—the aches and pains of battle fatigued me, but I needed to stay strong and resolute for my warriors—there was to be another battle after this, one that I expect to offer much more resistance. Many of the Romans had evacuated Londinium before our arrival, leaving their possessions behind. Helping themselves to the spoils brought cheer to my battle-weary warriors.

A Druid dressed in the obligatory white caftan, with hair and beard worn longer than others, walked towards me. He seemed unreal with the fires burning behind him. For a moment, I was reminded of Bran, but then recognised him as a lesser Druid, one who had chosen to stay with my army to escape the massacre at Mona.

"Boudicca, the day is yours again," he said with a raspy voice.

"Yes, Morgan, for this I thank Andrasta."

"You dwell in her light, great Queen."

"Walk with me, Morgan. There are things I need to know of you."

We walked from the screaming, burning, and looting towards the grove.

"You say there are things you need to know?"

"Before he passed over, Bran spoke to me... he is the reason we took Camulodunum and now Londinium, and soon we will sack Verulamium. It was his foresight."

"And did his vision see past these great victories?"

"To some extent, but that prophecy is not my need for today."

"How can I be of help then?"

"Who is the sage?"

CHAPTER
X

I could tell by his expression that my question had rocked him. I guessed that having the knowledge of the sage wasn't expected of me. He stopped abruptly.

"May I ask why you ask such a question of me?" he inquired.

"Because Bran bestowed upon me an undertaking I swore to tell no-one. This undertaking is to do with the sage, Morgan. Bran passed before divulging the name or the whereabouts of the sage."

He sighted an old oak tree near the edge of the grove and walked me in silence under it.

"You are ordained of the Druithin, so I have no compunction to give you the information you seek. What Archdruid Bran bestowed upon you was a vow he had inherited from his father King Arviragus, and that was to protect the sage and his writings from Rome. Bran expected to pass that responsibility to his son Caradoc before he died, but as you know, Caradoc, along with his family, was captured and taken as hostages to Rome. Caradoc, or Caractacus, as the Romans knew him, was married to Anna, the daughter of the sage. Bran's daughter, Gladys the Elder, Caradoc's sister, married the Roman commander-in-chief Aulus Platius and also settled in Rome... and so Bran had no choice but to pass the vow to you. The name of the sage—"

A haze suddenly came over me, and next, I was staring at Jackson.

"Are you with me, Bonnie?" he queried.

"No, quick, send me back... Morgan was just about to tell me the name!" I frantically insisted.

"What name?"

"The name of the sage... Jackson! You must send me back quickly, we need to know."

I realised I was right in his face and relaxed back on the couch to concentrate on his voice. But after a few minutes, I sat up and growled angrily, "It's no good, Jackson. It's just not happening. I'm not going under. What's wrong?"

"Your brain is too active... you're too emotional, Bonnie. You need to calm down. Come on, let's take a walk."

The warm and sunny afternoon showcased a new green carpet in the Quadrangle. The lawn had just been cut, leaving a heady scent in the air, almost powerful enough to distract one from the energy crisis, pollution, wars, and the rising crime rate. I mean, on a day such as this, things don't look nearly so bad. The vibes are good, and there's a spring in the step. The adrenaline flows—all the students in the Quadrangle looked cool and full of pleasant promise. Some of them were even smiling.

We found a spot and sat on the grass. I was beginning to calm down.

"Sorry, I reacted like that," I said warmly, taking Jackson's hand.

"Perfectly understandable. It would be frustrating being at my mercy, switching you on and off like a transistor radio."

We chuckled at the thought, but both knew he was right.

"I don't know, I guess I have this feeling that what I'm on is the cusp of finding out the point of it all... if that makes any sense?"

"Of course, it does. It's just that I have to keep your wellbeing in mind. You'll be no good to anyone if you suffer a mental relapse from an overdose of hypnosis."

"Can that happen?"

"Absolutely. It's called a rebound effect. Hypnosis has been known to stimulate previous conditions in some patients—depression, anxiety..."

"I see. So, doctor, what's your prognosis then?"

"That we only do it twice a day and in one-hour increments."

"Sounds sexy. Are you sure you've got the stamina?" I said, rolling my eyes at the innuendo.

"Are we talking about the same thing here?" he questioned with a joking arched eyebrow. I giggled playfully.

An hour or so of revitalising conversation, plenty of fresh air, and we were back at it. This time, his voice flooded my senses, and I easily drifted backward like a shooting star.

I was standing on a hilltop, looking down at the grove and the oak where I'd been talking with Morgan. A lot of Roman women were huddled together in the centre of the grove, dressed in basic stola and heavily guarded. Domnall and three of my warrior chiefs approached me.

"Three score of the most distinguished Roman women in Londinium, my Queen."

"Good, have their stola removed!" I ordered aggressively.

Domnall dispatched an adjutant to execute the task. Within minutes, the sixty women were standing huddled together, naked.

"Any more captives?"

"No, many Romans escaped, but all that remained have been put to the sword or burnt."

"No Britons?"

"No, as you ordered, they were secretly informed of our attack and given time to escape. Some have joined our ranks."

"Fine. I will speak with the Roman women now."

There was a cool breeze on my face as we walked down the hill into the grove. It was mid-afternoon, and the smoke rising from the burning city had darkened the sky. I felt contempt for these women—they embodied everything I found offensive about Roman occupation. I stopped short of them and then spoke out loud in my mediocre Latin.

"In all of your eyes, I recognise my persecutors. You watched my daughters raped and my brutal beating. You rallied Suetonius Paulinus and the legion Gemina, leaving Londinium to murder innocent Britons on the Isle of Mona!"

"Druid bitch!" came a spiteful counter from one of the women.

Then another screamed, "Pagan harlot!"

But their abuse only infuriated me further. I would show no mercy.

"Your lack of conscience leaves me devoid of any guilt in sentencing you. Your breasts will be slashed from your bodies and then sewn into your mouths. You will then be impaled on stakes. Each of you will endure hours of excruciating agony... you will be screaming for death, but no one will hear, and no one will care. I am Queen Boudicca... I tell you this because I want you to die with my name on your parched lips!"

My decree put rest to their abuse. I glared long and hard at their pale, terrified faces. Now their hysterical screams had changed from abusive to cries for mercy.

"Carry out my orders, Domnall!" I bellowed so the women could hear.

"Yes, my Queen!"

I turned my back on the screaming horde and started back up the hill, thinking to myself, how can I find this Joseph of Arimathea? I stopped at the top of the hill and looked back at the grove. Domnall and his warriors were busy carrying out my orders, mutilating the screaming women. I felt comfort in their torture. A runner approached me. Puffing, out of breath, he said, "Queen Boudicca, our scouts report Verulamium is evacuating, most Romans have abandoned the town!"

"Go to the grove and tell Ricon Domnall to summon the council immediately," I shouted with warring urgency. "Tell him what you told me. Then get some rest. We will need to break camp and mobilise before dawn."

"You're back... you're back, Bonnie..."

I slowly opened my eyes to Jackson's dulcet tones and was immediately overcome by the woe of being back. Oh, how I wished I could stay Boudicca.

"Are you all right?"

"Yes, but I would prefer not to feel like someone had pinched my lunch money."

"I think the depression is a side effect of the high emotional connection between you and Boudicca. With each visit, you're bonding more with her."

"We need to see Professor Harris urgently, Jackson. I have a name," I said gravely.

We were lucky to find Professor Harris in his office between lectures. He was amazed when I told him the name.

"This is some revelation, my dear... Joseph of Arimathea, extraordinary!" he said, holding his chin with his pale grey eyes locked on mine.

"What do we know about him?" I asked, wanting to know as much as he could tell me.

"It's not so much about Joseph as it is the gospel. That is indeed of incredible significance." He mumbled to himself, drifting off into deep thought.

"Joseph of Arimathea, Professor?" Jackson reminded him.

"Yes, yes, of course. He was mentioned by the Roman historian Cassius Dio as being the Minister for Mines at the time of King Aviragus, thought to be Bran's father. At that time, he could well have developed that relationship through trading for tin ore mined in Cornwall, which he took back to Rome. There has been speculation that, because he was the brother of the Virgin Mary, mother of Jesus, the missing years of Jesus' life were spent with Joseph on a trip to Britain, where he might have been exposed to Druidism. Some even suggest that this exposure may have led to the similarity between Druidism and the religious philosophy of the Essenes... Jesus and Joseph being Essenes, of course. It is also widely speculated that after the crucifixion of Jesus, Joseph brought his wife, Mary Magdalene, either to Britain or to the south of France for safekeeping. Evidence is derived from the Glastonbury Thorn, a tree that grew from Joseph planting his staff in the ground—a tree that still stands today and is native to Syria in the Middle East."

"Wow, that's amazing!" I said excitedly. I was beginning to feel that my mission with the visions was taking shape, and the magnitude of it could have incredible significance.

"So let me get this straight, Professor," Jackson said. "If this gospel that was sacred to the Druids existed, then it could well be an account of the life of Jesus Christ."

"Exactly. Moreover, it could be the only written historical record from the perspective of the Britons during the Roman occupation. This is incredibly significant, Bonnie... and incredibly dangerous."

"Dangerous... but why, Professor?" I pleaded, thinking it a negative statement.

Professor Harris gazed long and hard at us, as though concocting the easiest way to elaborate on his gloomy warning.

"Well, let's say that through your visions, you manage to determine the location of the sacred gospel and, for that matter, the burial place of Joseph. Then there are those who would do almost anything to obtain that information."

"Are you suggesting the Catholic Church?" Jackson posed.

"Any one of many religious sects... you must understand, archaeology and history have been tampered with for hundreds of years by religious orders intent on protecting the myths they have perpetuated. They, above anyone else, have a vested interest in keeping certain historical facts from public knowledge."

"What do you propose then?" I asked.

"Well, for a start, all information must be reserved for those we consider privileged enough to have it."

"That sounds like the beginnings of a secret Order!" Jackson said with a mischievous squint, met by an all-knowing smile of endorsement from the Professor.

And so First Light was born, our very own secret society. Those who wanted to join would first have to seek the endorsement of two of us. Only then would our secrets be shared. To kick things off, Professor Harris asked us to study the credentials of two of his colleagues in England for admittance. Dr Mike Roberts, Professor of Ancient Linguistics, and Dr Moore, Professor of Bronze Age and Iron Age Archaeology in Britain, both residents of the Department of Archaeology at Cambridge. He handed us a dossier on them, and we called it a day. As always, I was mad keen to be hypnotised again, but Jackson thought better of it, wanting me to have a good night's rest. We agreed to continue the next day.

As I got out of a taxi at Flea's apartment, Jackson looked at me oddly and said, "I've been summoned to a meeting with Gibson-Smith tomorrow, so I'll meet you at the office around 11 a.m."

I realised the gravity of the statement. "What do you think that's about?"

"I expect he wouldn't be too happy about the outcome of the hearing."

I leaned into the cab and gave him a kiss. "Good luck, don't take any wooden nickels."

He smiled, and I watched the taxi drive off. Deep down inside, I felt apprehensive—a burning, intuitive feeling that things weren't going quite right.

The next morning, I was sitting at reception in our offices, waiting for Jackson, staring vacantly at the teak-panelled door, bored out of my skull. I didn't like the office much—it was a small reception area annexed to a larger room. It felt more like the library of an exclusive gentlemen's club than an office. A leather-topped desk in the reception and another in the main room, with leather-upholstered chairs and a matching leather lounge, gave it a dank odour, like you smell in old people's houses. The springs on the lounge protested angrily when sat upon. There was a knock at the door, and I called, "Come in." Professor Harris strolled in with a grim look on his face, far from his usual exuberance.

"Hi, I was just about to make a coffee. Want one?" I said.

"I hope it'll be a better brew than what I get at my hole in the wall," he said, taking a seat. "You've tarted up the rooms a little," he went on. "It looks good. Are you going to get a secretary? It's in the budget, you know."

"Not for now... How do you take your coffee?"

"Just black, thanks. No sugar."

"Sweet enough without?" I joked, trying to lighten the mood. But as I handed him his coffee, I could tell by the look in his eyes he was about to deliver some bad news. I sat in my chair behind the desk, sipping my coffee, preparing for whatever he was about to say.

CHAPTER
XI

"Bonnie, we have a problem," Professor Harris said with furrowed eyebrows.

"I had a feeling something was brewing, what's happened now?"

"Jackson called me half an hour ago from the offices of Dr Gibson-Smith. He has agreed to withdraw charges provided he can monitor all the research undertaken with you."

"What! All of our notes! No way, that's ridiculous!" I reacted.

"Wait, hear me out. For Jackson's sake, we need to find a way to make this work, otherwise the consequences for his career could be dire and frankly endangering our research."

"But that would mean a breach of security," I argued. "We can't have him in First Light.."

"He wouldn't be a security risk if we censor what we give him."

"I don't know, professor, I don't trust him."

"I understand that, dear, but we don't really have any choice, do we?"

I knew he was right. We were caught between a rock and a hard place.

"Did Jackson agree to it?"

"We didn't debate it over the phone, I expect he'll be here soon enough to discuss it. I first wanted to run it past you."

Just then, Jackson arrived. It was obvious from his demeanour that his morning with Gibson-Smith had been an ordeal. Deep down inside, I couldn't help but suspect my dad of conniving the whole affair, he and his Machiavellian ways.

After a lengthy summary of his meeting with Gibson-Smith, Jackson agreed with censoring the information we pass on to him. None of us were happy about it because it meant a lot more work, double bookkeeping so to speak, but there was little else we could do. Gibson-Smith had us over a barrel. It was the thought of giving the cretin access to the tape recordings on a weekly basis that bothered me most. But when Professor Harris suggested the tapes would be of no use to him because they were in a dead language, it provided some relief. We agreed it was vital to keep the transcript of each session to ourselves, as it carried my detailed account of the experience. The professor guaranteed that his interpretation transcript of the tapes would also remain our secret.

Harris left us and we prepared for a hypnosis session.

The thundering of hooves, I looked over my shoulder and found a Roman soldier of rank on my tail, his horses whipped and galled their flanks and backs bloody. He had a javelin poised and hurled it at me. I watched it leave his hand and fly like an arrow. I flinched instinctively when it slammed into the floorboards of my chariot right beside my right foot.

"Pull!" I heard him scream. "Pull, or I'll take the hide off your backs." And his long lash sang. We raced together as though an invisible rope linked our chariots. I watched him seize another javelin. As he swung his arm back to throw, I judged the moment and flicked the reins. With the javelin in the air, I swerved just enough for it to fly past my shoulder. But the turn had cost me ground, and the Roman snatched his last javelin from the bin. He was close now, too close for comfort.

I watched him with a feeling of desperation, gathering in a firm rein to anticipate his next move. The moment he swivelled his right shoulder forward to throw, I swung my team back the other way, jinking their run at full gallop. But the javelin hadn't left his hand: he had feigned the throw. He raised the javelin again into the throwing position. This time he aimed not at me but my lead horse. The javelin took her high in the shoulder. It cut through hide and muscle, then struck bone but didn't penetrate her vitals. It wasn't a mortal blow, but a crippling one, for the javelin head was barbed and it dangled down her flank, hampering each stride she took. She tried with all her heart, but she couldn't keep the pace. Blood ran back along her flank and splattered on my legs. I could feel the chariot slowing under me, the javelin tangling in her forelegs.

The Roman drew his chariot level with mine and with a coarse voice yelled in triumph.

"It's all over, Boudicca, I have you now!"

I glared at him. His lips were drawn back in a horrible rictus, like that of a corpse who had died of lockjaw. He had thrown his last javelin but had drawn his Gladius. I could see my forces were winning the battle. The only person that stood in the way of victory was this Legati, who fancied his chances of killing me and having my forces capitulate. Verulamium would be mine, as would his head. The first javelin he'd thrown was still stuck in the floorboard of my chariot. I twisted and jerked it free. I held it like a spear and looked across at my adversary. His eyes narrowed when he saw the weapon and he took guard position with the sword. We were slowing down... he drew up beside me and lunged. The two chariots swerved apart then came together and struck so hard the collision almost threw me over the side, I had to clutch wildly at the reins to steady myself. He sliced with the blade but missed only just. Now the two vehicles were wheel-to-wheel, hub-to-hub. His blade slashed again, this time across my upper arm. I felt the sting of its razor-sharp edge and the warm blood tickling down my arm. But I felt no pain. I thrust the javelin at his face, which forced him to swerve away. We were heading towards a thicket and would soon have to turn and double back. He came at me again and our wheels locked, I knew if we were to go much further the superior Roman chariot would snap my axle. He leaned over, slashing at me with his sword, and I blocked each blow with the javelin. The gods were with me, the javelin slipped off his sword and with a second thrust, I stabbed him in the eye. I pulled hard on the reins to halt my chariot before the thicket, he couldn't do the same and his four horses plunged into the dense growth. His chariot hit a fallen branch and flipped up into the air—his horses screamed as they were impaled on branches—he was cast into the air. I jumped out and ran over to him with my sword in hand. He was on his knees on the ground with his face in his hands. A mixture of slimy black ooze and blood seeping through his fingers from his punctured eye. His good eye suddenly peered up at me. With death imminent and he lowered his head. With my heart pounding adrenaline surging through my veins, I raised my sword and with one almighty blow, decapitated him. The day was mine. I grasped the severed head by the hair and carried it back onto my chariot to go and join my warriors. Skewering the head on the end of the javelin, I drove into the melee parading my trophy held victoriously aloft. A resounding cheer erupted from my warriors, and that caused the remaining legionnaires to throw down their weapons and capitulate. Domnall appeared from out of the fray, his blue-tattooed body caked with the blood of his victims.

He raised his sword in the air and yelled with his distinctive gravel voice. "Boudicca, our Queen triumphant!"

I held the Roman severed head on the javelin aloft for all to see and yelled at the top of my voice, "Round up all the prisoners, Domnall, take their heads, for tonight we make an offering to the goddess Andrasta and feast to our victory to the songs of the bard."

A thunderous cheer exploded from my army.

I thought the surrendered Roman legionnaires looked remarkably passive considering I'd just ordered their execution. A thought intruded: I couldn't help but wonder if soldiers in the 20th century facing beheading after surrendering would act so compliant.

My wounded lead horse was being unhitched from the other three. She would have to be put down. I left the head in my chariot, walked over, and patted her goodbye... she had been a good warhorse, she had saved me from many an enemy and had never backed down from a fight.

"After you put her down, butcher her for the feast tonight," I ordered my groom. A new lead horse was hitched to the harness. I boarded the chariot and drove it along Watling Street to the top of a hill to view my prize: Verulamium.

Most of the buildings, with the exception of the great hall, were ablaze. The River Ver, named after the river goddess Verbela, sparkled in the noonday sun, a tribute to our victory. I remembered the town from when I was a child, called Uerulāmion then. Since those days, the Romans had given the citizens municipium status or Latin rights, stripping them of their real identity, and they had changed the name of the town to Verulamium. For now, Roman tyranny and its laws lay in the smouldering ashes of its buildings, vanquished. I noticed a group of my warriors outside the Great Hall, so I drove down the hill to check preparations for the victory feast. Stepping off the chariot, I saw a familiar face among them.

"Morgan, will you beautify the feast at sundown?"

"No, Boudicca, I will join Domnall now at the beheadings for dedication to Andrasta. Afterwards, I will journey two days to Glenlyon to find the sage, as we agreed."

"Good, we meet then on Cadbury Hill at Giamonios under the Mother's Moon. You know what to do should I fail to be at the rendezvous."

"Yes," he acknowledged.

I watched him walk off alone, collected the head of my Roman victim from my chariot, and entered the Grand Hall to place it on a spike. I couldn't help thinking what a doleful character Morgan had, his unfriendly demeanour made him difficult to trust, which wasn't at all consistent with the Druid manner.

It was the first time I'd arrived back thankful to be home. When I told Jackson about the chariot encounter and the executions, the colour drained from his cheeks, understandably so, it was pretty gruesome. But the exciting part was the scheduled rendezvous with Morgan and the sage, whom we expected to be Joseph of Arimathea. It was now a matter of getting Professor Harris to fill in the gaps, such as the date of the meeting at Cadbury Hill.

After lunch at the University canteen, we made our way to the professor's office. From our chairs opposite him, we watched intently while he scoured his library for the appropriate reference books. Then, with an armful of his treasures, he flopped back into his big old squeaky leather chair, thumbed through the pages of the first book, and then read from it excitedly.

"Ah, Giamonios... right, the Druid year is divided into a dark half and a light half. The dark half is Samonius, which is October to May, and the light half is Giamonios from May to October. The beginning and end of the year is Samhain, it falls on the last full moon of October. In that time, there are five days of ritual feasting called Uenicar. This is the in-between, a time of chaos and change. Now, as for Mother's Moon," he flicked through more pages. "Yes, here... the Mother's Moon is the full moon in May, Giamonios. So there you have it, they will meet on the first full moon of May in 61 AD. We need to determine exactly when that is in our time, to ensure you join the rendezvous with precision. Now, as for Cadbury Hill." He selected another book and quickly flicked through it. "Ah, here we are... Cadbury Hill is a place of ritual significance to the Druids. It is the site of an Iron Age hill fort." He peered over his glasses at us approvingly. "That we can expect to still be there when Boudicca, Morgan, and the sage meet. The name is derived from the Celtic god Sulis, a deity worshipped at the thermal springs in nearby Bath. Cadbury Hill and Solsbury Hill, another hill fort, are in Somerset, not far from the town of Glastonbury."

"Oh, I know where that is," I said.

"Yep, that's the venue of Glastonbury Fayre, isn't it?" Jackson chimed in.

"Yeah, in '71, they had Bowie, Joan Baez, Traffic, and Fairport Convention. I don't think there's been another concert since. Wasn't the first one the day after Jimmy Hendrix died in 1970?" I queried.

"Yes, I think you're right," Jackson agreed.

"Let's get back on track, shall we?" the professor grumbled curtly, annoyed at all the talk about rock concerts. "So, to recap, we have established that Boudicca will meet Joseph and Morgan. This is vital because it might, as we believe, lead to one of the greatest discoveries of the modern era."

"The whereabouts of the Gospel of Joseph of Arimathea," Jackson added.

Professor Harris sank back into his chair with his chin in hand, deep in thought. "Yes, but I do have one reservation."

"And what's that?" I asked.

He stood up, reached for a book in his library, opened it, and read out loud. "Suetonius Paulinus regrouped with the XIV Gemina, some detachments of the XX Valeria Victrix, and all available auxiliaries and marched along Watling Street to meet Boudicca somewhere in the Midlands. It was a resounding victory for Suetonius Paulinus, with Boudicca reportedly having either committed suicide after the defeat or fallen ill and died. So if history, as quoted by Tacitus and some years later by Cassius Dio, is correct, Boudicca died before ever going to Cadbury Hill to meet Joseph and Morgan."

CHAPTER
XII

"Oops," Cleo said, checking her watch. "It's hospital visiting time."

"Oh, shit! I jumped up. "I'm not even ready... I'll just put on my face... Meet me at the car, love."

We continued chatting all the way into town.

"I can't wait to find out what happened with Boudicca. Why haven't you or Uncle Jackson written a book about this? It would be a bestseller," Cleo proposed enthusiastically.

"Oh, you'll find out why soon enough," I said with a taciturn roll of my eyes.

Cleo waited at reception while I visited Jackson. He was looking much better, with a healthy skin tone, and that signature sparkle had returned to his eyes. After a warm hug, I sat on the edge of the bed and held his hand.

"So, how are you doing, big fella?"

"They're kicking me out tomorrow morning, said I'd given them enough lip."

"I don't blame them, you can be a nag when you want to be," I joked.

"This place is for the sick, I only tell sick jokes."

"Hopefully, they fixed that too."

"Not likely, only got a grease and oil change. So how's it going with Cleo?"

"Fine, we're getting to the scary part."

"Do you think she'll work out? She is, after all, the only option we have left."

"We just have to hope she's got the genes... anyhow, we'll soon know enough. By the time you get home and settled, provided you're up to it, you can try her out."

"Oh, I wouldn't miss that for the world. And I certainly still have the stamina... Herculean by nature," he grinned cheekily.

"We nearly lost you, darling. Can't have that," I muttered with a teary sniffle.

"Can't cash your chips if you don't have any, love. No, I'm going nowhere... we made a commitment, remember?"

"First light?" I said, drying my eyes.

With teary eyes, he took my hand and repeated, "First light."

That night, while Cleo was taking a bath, I entered the bathroom with a fresh towel for her, and seeing her nubile naked body made me feel date-stamped. Oh, how wonderful it would be to be her age again.

"Are you sexually active, Cleo?" I asked gently.

"Oh, I've had a few lovers, but I don't think I've experienced anything like you did at my age."

I sat on the edge of the bathtub.

"Yes, I was just thinking what I'd do if I had my time over again."

"Anything different?"

"No, I'd just pay more attention to the things that were enjoyable, knowing life is over so quick. When you get old you begin to realise how long forever would be. But then again," I said flippantly, "you're always wiser in retrospect."

"I suppose that's true. But it is a lovely thought. I'll make sure I make the most of those special moments from now on. I suppose recognising them as important at the time is the most difficult thing."

"Yes, that's true, they become more important after the event, unfortunately. Lean forward, love, and I'll scrub your back."

I took the loofah and gave her porcelain back a gentle rub.

"Did it feel the same for you when Boudicca had sex?"

"Yes. It's an odd thing, you know, as time went on, I bonded more with her every emotion, her every feeling."

"Did you feel her pain, like when her arm was cut in the chariot fight?"

"That's a funny one because when I got home that night after that lengthy rave with Professor Harris, I was taking a bath when I noticed a red mark on my shoulder exactly where Boudicca had been wounded. It faded the next day, but I swear overnight I could feel the throbbing of it healing. No, it didn't hurt at the time, probably because it didn't hurt Boudicca either. Her adrenaline was pumping so hard she was probably oblivious to the pain."

"Maybe they felt different about pain than we do."

I thought about that before answering; they certainly had more tolerance for pain back then.

"You know, Cleo, you're probably right. They felt differently about a lot of things. Like taking heads, for one thing... I can still remember Boudicca's excitement when she decapitated that Roman. His head was her prize, a trophy... and the way he simply accepted his fate was uncanny."

"Do you want to continue tonight?"

"Yes, why not? We might have less time once we bring Jackson home tomorrow... he'll need some attention, the poor dear."

"True, and I can only stay another two days, at any rate. I'll need to head back to Canberra on Sunday. Uni starts next Monday."

"Well, we'd better get on with it then, hadn't we?" I said happily, leaving her to finish her bath.

I went into the office, half expecting to find my darling husband behind his desk, sporting his standard gracious smile, but alas, that wasn't to be.

After a while, Cleo came in looking for me. She was wearing a man's shirt, barefoot, and had her hair wrapped in a towel. "Oh, there you are," she said with a gleam in her eye.

"Sit down, love. I thought we could continue in the comfort of the office."

"Just let me check my email before we get started."

After a moment, her face turned ashen grey. It wasn't difficult to sense that something was terribly wrong. "What's up, love? Bad news?"

She handed over the iPad. I read the email; it said: Vel pati in consequatur, iam desine and was signed Gaius.

"My guess is it's Italian or Latin," I said disquietly.

I entered Latin to English into Google, then typed the phrase into the window. To my shock, I got, "cease now or suffer the consequences." I showed it to Cleo, who was taken aback. She took the iPad from me and stared at the transcription, trying to make sense of it.

"What the hell does it mean? And who the fuck is this Gaius?"

"Have you spoken to anyone about my story?"

"No, why?"

"So you haven't posted anything on social media or anything?"

"No, I don't understand." She was getting upset.

"What about research? Have you been to any websites related to the subject?"

"Yes, loads of them. Referencing is important. Can you tell me what it means, you're freaking me out, Bo?"

"Yes, in a moment. But first, show me those references, please," I said sternly.

She opened a file on her iPad and showed me. I checked the long list of URLs.

"My, you have been busy," I said light-heartedly, deep down inside in a panic. Then I found it. "That's it, www.druidawakening.com. I should have warned you. Can you remember what you referenced on that website?"

"Warned me about what?" she said all flustered. "Um, wait, let me think. Yes, that's right, I entered General Gaius Suetonius Paulinus into Google, and it came up with a bunch of websites mentioning him, including Wikipedia, of course. I checked them all and eventually opened that one."

"And then?" I said, handing back her iPad.

"I found Gaius Suetonius Paulinus highlighted and clicked on it to find out more."

"That probably did it. Okay, I'll need to explain more when I have Jackson here to help me, but for now, please don't go to any more websites, and don't post anything on social media," I said vigorously. "If you get another email from this Gaius character, do not answer it... just show it to me. Okay, love?"

"Yes, but—"

"I'll tell you this much, love, so that you understand. There are people out there, such as Gaius, who don't want my story told."

"But what about when I publish it?"

"We won't continue tonight. Let's get some rest, and we'll talk about it all tomorrow with Jackson, okay?"

"If you say so, Bo," she said dispiritedly.

I had a restless night, knowing the enemy had been alerted. First thing in the morning, I drove alone to the hospital and collected Jackson. I explained to him on the way back home what had happened.

"That would be right," he agreed. "They would have tracked her through the IP address to her computer as soon as she clicked on the highlighted name. So we can assume they're onto us again, and they have our home address. You know what has to happen now, love?" Jackson said gravely.

"It's starting all over again," I answered soberly.

"Yes, but at least this time we have the benefit of hindsight: experience."

"Yes, but this time you're not in the best of health."

"Granted, but that's just another obstacle. We've been there before. We both knew it would only be a matter of time before they found us again."

"How much do you think we should tell Cleo?" I said worriedly.

"We should be honest with her, love... morally, we can't let her continue ignorant of the risks. I warned you it would eventually come to this, didn't I?"

"Yes, I know, I know, but we had no alternative. It has to be her," I said, trying to concentrate on driving while a thousand scenarios were running through my mind.

"I still believe it would have been prudent to have told her from the beginning."

"Maybe, but I chose not to, okay? What's done is done. I first needed her to buy into it first," I said defensively.

"Yes, I understand that, but we can't forget what they did to you, love, Professor Harris and the others."

"Of course, and that's why I need her to commit to it."

"Mo wouldn't have sent her to us if she didn't think she was ready."

"I just wish my sister had had a boy. It's so much tougher for a girl to deal with this, I can attest to that."

"Yes, you sure can, love. But I don't think a boy would have had the same genetic link to Boudicca. Look, we know what we have to do. We need to bite the bullet and do it. Everything is set up ready to go," Jackson said assuredly.

"Everything except us, that is," I corrected.

"Don't worry, we'll get by. We have till now."

"Yes, love, I know, but we weren't sixty-year-old geriatrics then!"

"Just another brick in the wall, my love," he said with a warm, as ever, positive smile. "Where are you up to?"

"We're just getting to the meeting of Boudicca and the sage."

"Well, the timing is right then. We would have had to make a move soon, at any rate."

"You're not wrong, my love."

Oh, how vital it is to have Jackson. I don't know what I'd do without him.

Once at home, we sat down in the office with Cleo to explain everything. It was obvious by the dark circles under her eyes that the email had kept her up all night, like me. I let Jackson do the talking.

"Cleo, the time has come to explain a few things to you about the whole Boudicca saga. We have been engaged in it since 1974, and it has totally consumed our lives. In fact, from that time on, more than once, it nearly took our lives. Do you remember Bo telling you that we formed a secret society with Professor Harris?"

"Yes, First Light," Cleo said.

"Well, since forming First Light, it has remained the cloak of secrecy under which we have operated. Your mother is a member, and around the world, there are now two hundred and fifty dedicated members, all sworn to secrecy and all with the single objective: to protect the information Bonnie received from Boudicca."

"I understand that... but protect it from whom or what?"

"He'll get to that, Cleo," I added, nodding for Jackson to continue.

"Today, we would like you to become member two hundred and fifty-one," he said proudly.

"Me? But why?" Cleo said astonished.

"We have waited for you to reach twenty-four years of age, Cleo. You see, we believe you have the special DNA needed to contact Boudicca, the same special DNA as Bonnie," Jackson explained.

"But how? Why?"

"Bonnie lost contact when Boudicca died. We believe it was only possible to make the connection with her while she was twenty-four. She died that same year. We don't exactly know why it happened, but we're hoping we are right with you having the right DNA."

"So, wait a minute... you think I will be able to contact her now that I am twenty-four?"

"Yes, we hope so, love," I said. "You know how we're up to when Boudicca was soon to meet the sage?"

"Yes."

"Well, soon after that comes a very important moment. When it happened, circumstances beyond my control prevented me from learning a most vital clue: the object of why I had been connected with Boudicca in the first place."

"And now you expect me to reconnect with her to find that clue?"

"Yes," I asserted.

"It will happen on a specific day, and it's approaching fast," Jackson added.

"Sort of like Mother's Moon, huh?"

"Yes, just like that," I affirmed.

"But we need to warn you of the dangers connected with it before you agree," Jackson said dutifully.

"Cleo, I couldn't have children after an injury I sustained from being physically attacked. Your mum bred you for this moment, to take over the quest from me. But you must first understand the risks involved before you agree. I promised that to your mother."

"I suppose I could feel set up, but in a way, I've always felt I was destined to do something special in life, and I guess this is it."

"That's right, Cleo," Jackson said excitedly. "But it means giving up a lot and putting yourself in serious danger, as demonstrated by the email you received."

"Okay, define danger."

"While we're driving to Sydney... we have to leave here within the hour because they're onto us. Tomorrow, we'll fly to London," Jackson said with a smirk. He knew that would tickle Cleo's fancy.

"London!" Cleo repeated with surprise. "But—"

"If you agree to join First Light and take on the responsibility, then I'm afraid your university degree will need to go on hold," I said delicately.

"Okay, I'll wait to hear the story in the car, but tell me first, why the threat?"

"These people already killed Professor Harris and three other First Light members. They injured Bonnie so badly," Jackson said, taking my hand and looking into my eyes with love. "They made it impossible for us to ever have children."

"They tried to kill me, Cleo, and when they failed, they sterilized me."

"They did that to ensure the special gene that was allowing Bonnie to channel Boudicca could never be inherited," Jackson added.

"But they didn't know about you, Cleo," I said, taking her hand and looking into her eyes. "For twenty-four years, you have been our secret."

CHAPTER
XIII

It took us longer than an hour to ready the house to leave, as we had no idea how long we'd be gone. We locked Cleo's car in the garage and convinced her to leave her iPad and iPhone with it to prevent her from being tracked. Jackson loaned her his iPad, and we transferred all her data to it. We promised to buy her a new iPhone in Sydney, and she considered that acceptable. It took a few more minutes for her to transfer her address book to a data chip. By 9 p.m., we were on the Princes Highway bound for Sydney. Cleo quickly piped up from the back seat.

"So, tell me about this bloke Gaius then?"

"We've got a five-hour drive to Sydney, so maybe it would be better if we continued with the interview. I think it will explain it all much better."

Cleo prepared the iPad. "Okay, whenever you're ready, Bo."

"I won't go into as much detail, Cleo. Some facts are more relevant now than they were before. I stayed at Jackson's apartment that night, and that's when I noticed the mark on my shoulder. Remember that, love?"

"Yes, and oh what a night that was," Jackson added boldly.

"So it was."

Anyhow, the next morning, we were at our office bright and early, keen to get started when Gibson-Smith came barging in with his feathers all ruffled.

"I've just come from Harris' office, and I'm far from satisfied," he bellowed at me.

"Oh, and good morning to you too, Doctor," I snapped facetiously.

"Where are the transcripts that were promised?" he demanded.

"Professor Harris is compiling them for you, what did he say?" I asked brusquely.

"He said he's been busy," he snarled.

"Then that would be the case," Jackson stressed.

"What's your rush anyway, Doctor?" I probed.

"It's not a matter of rushing, young lady. It's a matter of what was unconditionally agreed to."

"Well, it seems to me that you are neglecting the fact that this is all about me, and that being the case, I have a say in matters. So, why don't you just crawl back into your shell and accept the fact that you'll get the transcript when I'm good and ready? If it weren't for my personal admiration for the exceptional work of my colleague here, you would be getting nothing. Now get out of our office before I call security."

He turned on his heel and thundered out the door.

"Now that might trigger some repercussions," Jackson said circumspectly.

"Who cares? He's just an old bully."

The phone rang. It was the professor. Jackson filled him in on what had just happened, and they agreed to get a doctored transcript to Gibson-Smith by the end of the day to shut him up. Otherwise, the professor feared Gibson-Smith might try to stir trouble with the University board members he has in his pocket. With all that out of the way, we got on with the hypnosis session.

We progressed with sessions over the next few days, with nothing really startling happening. Gibson-Smith was satisfied with the transcripts, or so it seemed. He hadn't said anything to the contrary. I took Jackson to meet my folks for dinner, and that went well. There wasn't anything my parents could find to dislike about him. He is, after all, the perfect gentleman.

According to the professor's calculations, Mother's Moon in Giamonios in 61 AD would be on the same day for us in 1974, Monday, May 6th. Sydney is nine hours ahead of London, so we would have to start the session at 2 p.m. our time, which would be 5 a.m. for Boudicca. A couple of times that I'd been regressed, I found Boudicca asleep, so we eventually worked out the best times to avoid that from happening. The rule of thumb was that no-one other than Jackson and I would be in attendance at the sessions, but this particular session was potentially so significant that we made an exception for the professor. We also made an exception for two academic colleagues of his, new First Light recruits who had flown in from London for the event. Professor Mike Roberts, whose field is ancient linguistics, and Professor Judith Moore, archaeology. They were both young compared to Professor Harris, in their early thirties, and lovely people. They had been involved with our study from when Professor Harris first came on board, so they were up to speed on everything. In fact, they had some interesting things to add before we got started.

This was all covert stuff. Our office doors were locked from the inside, phones were taken off the hook, tape machines were set up ready to roll. Everything was kept hush-hush, on a need-to-know basis. Professor Harris chaired the meeting.

"Now that the introductions are out of the way, both Judith and Mike would like to brief you on their research in London," he said, nodding to Judith.

She looked and spoke like a headmistress and fitted in perfectly with the university decor. Her demeanour was patient, precise, and most pleasant, even if a smidgen conservative for my liking. Her hair was pulled back loosely across her head and tied in a knot at the nape of her neck. Her wide grey-green eyes looked highly intelligent, her nose was aristocratically straight, and her broad mouth was very self-assured. She was wearing a deceptively simple-looking beige linen dress with a wide collar and hexagonal bronze buttons all the way down the front. It was unusual to see someone look both completely feminine and completely efficient at the same time. She was certainly the archetype of a Cambridge Doctor of Archaeology, well, to me anyway.

"I feel I know you so well, Bonnie," she said in a contralto London posh accent. "After spending hours upon hours listening intently to your voice on those fascinating tape recordings and then reading Mike's translations. I have a rudimentary knowledge of Celt, you know, though I must admit Boudicca's dialect exposed the limits of my linguistic prowess."

That gave us cause for a scholarly chuckle.

Judith continued with a wry smile. "I just wanted to say that I'm very proud to be accepted into First Light, and I strongly believe that this project could lead to one of the most archaeologically significant finds of the century. Now, one question has been concerning us, and that is regarding Boudicca's death. Historians have relied on the biased written records of Roman historians Tacitus and Cassius Dio for years. The proposed rendezvous between Boudicca, Druid Morgan, and the sage defies academic convention because it is believed that Boudicca led her army directly from the battle of Verulamium along Watling Road to confront Gaius Suetonius Paulinus and his XIV Gemina legion and others. This supposedly occurred near High Cross in Leicestershire, close to the modern town of Atherstone in Warwickshire, though that is a hotly contested theory. Today, with the wonder of your connection to Boudicca, Bonnie, we might find evidence to support changing that convention, changing history, and that is very significant for me."

She nodded for Mike to speak up.

Mike, a handsome man in an academic sort of way, stood up and took a deep draw of his cigarette before speaking. He exhaled the smoke like a dragon, his voice carrying a hint of a Scottish accent. He had a charismatic presence, with smiling eyes and a few laughing lines under them.

"First of all, I too am honoured to be on board. I have little to add to what Judith said, except to say that thus far, this has been an amazing journey. It is the first time I have heard this dialect of Celt spoken, and I expect it is the first time it has been spoken since the second century AD when Latin superseded it. We have learned much from studying the recordings, more than I will speak of now, but hearing the voice of Boudicca speaking in her native Iceni to Domnall has been incredible, to say the least. It has given us an understanding of native Iron Age Briton far beyond anything known previously, and for that, the world is indebted to you, Bonnie."

"Thank you, guys. Terrific to have you on board," I confirmed.

Jackson spoke up. "If I might, we're expecting this to be the longest session we've had so far because there was no exact time for the rendezvous. So please make yourselves comfortable. There's a fresh pot of coffee on the sideboard and a box of fresh donuts to keep the belly growling at bay."

I took up my position on the couch before the live audience, feeling a little like a time traveller about to be dispatched on some kind of science fiction experiment.

Jackson began to speak in a drone-like manner, and then suddenly, I was on a white horse, riding like the wind towards the rising sun. It was exhilarating, with a cool breeze streaming my long red hair out behind me. The pounding of hooves on the cobblestone road, the clatter of my sword against my dress, and the lush green rolling hills and dales speeding by created a stunning scene. Soon, I came over a ridge and sighted a massive wooden hill fort ahead. There was a high rampart surrounded by a deep ditch embedded with long sharp posts to deter invaders. Columns of smoke rose from the round houses beyond the ramparts. I slowed my horse to trot up to the big wooden gates and then stopped at them.

"I am Boudicca, Queen of the Iceni. I come alone, and I come in peace," I called to the guards.

After a few moments, the gates opened, and I rode through. Inside, it was a different world. The market would soon open, and people were bringing their produce to sell. They paid little attention to me, as there were so many of them milling about. I had to dismount to lead my horse through the crowd. A guard quickly approached and led me to the entrance of the Great Hall, where a regal-looking rotund man awaited me.

"I bid you welcome, Queen Boudicca. Your great victories and reputation for fairness precede you. I am Tyree of Avon, Ricon of Cadbury. Please enter my Great Hall and carry with you your sword and shield," he said.

"Thank you, Tyree of Avon. Your hill fort is impressive, far from the Crannog I was expecting. I am here to meet the Druid Morgan," I replied.

"Well, enter then and await Morgan's arrival in comfort, Boudicca. You look like you could do with a feed," Tyree said.

I entered the grand timber building. Inside, the walls were decorated with shields, weapons, and the heads of prisoners taken. There was a long rectangular table that could seat at least fifty people, and at the end of the large room, beside a hearth well alight, were large chairs. Tyree offered me one of the chairs, and we both sat to warm our hands by the fire. He suddenly clapped his hands, and a maid appeared from a room off to one side, likely the kitchen.

"Bring us eggs, pork, and a flagon of warm mead, Zelda," he ordered.

Tyree's face bore the signs of many battles, with a deep scar down the left side that had blinded his eye, leaving it white and lifeless. He was made to look even larger than he was by the bear fur he was garbed in.

"I see by your eye and the limp that you have been the victor of great battles yourself, Tyree of Avon," I remarked.

"Yes, but none so fierce as yours and what you will soon face," he replied.

"Ah, word does travel fast for you to know of what lies ahead of me, or are you as prophetic as a Druid?" I asked.

"No, nothing so mystical. I heard of what happened on Mona from a visiting Druid, brethren of Morgan, whom you await. They are both men of Cadbury, you know?" Tyree said.

"Ah, now I understand. You have learned of my battles from the Druids that remain. It was a terrible attack on innocent people by the Romans, for which I will have retribution," I stated.

"And more so for the Roman atrocities against you and your family," Tyree affirmed.

"For their tyranny, good chief," I said.

"I bear the scars of a Roman Gladius," he pointed at his face. "And thirty of those trophy Roman heads on my wall are not payment enough for the loss of my eye. I support you, Boudicca, and I pledge my men to you if you need them for your coming battle against the rogue General Gaius Suetonius Paulinus. Oh, how I want his head in pride of place on my wall."

I felt comfortable in the company of a supporter of the rebellion. There had been a moment when the thought crossed my mind that he might be in league with Rome like many Britons who had chosen the riches of the Roman way of life. But I hadn't noticed any signs of Roman influence in the hill fort. One positive sign was when he ordered mead instead of wine. The Romans had introduced wine, and I blamed it for the seduction of many Britons.

After we finished an excellent breakfast, a warrior came and asked Tyree if he would receive two unarmed visitors. I guessed it was Morgan and the sage. We stood to receive them.

Two silhouetted figures appeared in the doorway, backlit by the morning light. One helped the other towards us, and I rushed to assist.

"Morgan, is this— ?" I started, helping him hold the old man.

"Yes, Boudicca, this is Joseph. He has struggled to make the journey to meet you, and I fear he will soon leave us," Morgan replied.

We helped the old man into a chair, and Tyree placed a jug of mead in front of him. Joseph was frail, with long white hair down to the middle of his back and a long white beard. He was wearing the blue and white striped caftan of the Judaic people. I filled a cup from the jug and put it up to his wrinkled lips. He glanced at me with soft blue eyes, managed a friendly smile, and wet his lips but didn't drink. I noticed he was grasping a book to his chest.

"Try to drink, Joseph. You need some sustenance after such a long journey," I said warmly.

He shook frail fingers at me as if to say there were things of more importance, and then whispered to me in Latin with a strong accent. His voice was weak, and I had to place my ear close to his mouth to hear. I repeated his words out loud.

"He is happy to see me and is now ready to pass over. His wish is to be buried beneath a sacred oak in the manner of the Druithin. He recognises that I too am a servant of the truth. Morgan knows the place. The gospel he carries is to be buried in a secure place separate from him. It is of importance for another time. Both burial places are never to be divulged. She who is destined to find them will, in time, of her own accord through destiny."

He stared deeply and knowingly into my eyes, and then handed me the leather-bound book. Then, just as with Bran, I watched the very essence of life drain from his eyes forever. He drew a breath, then gently exhaled a long sigh.

"He has left us," I solemnly stated, a tear of loss traversing my cheek. Oh, how I wished I hadn't been denied the opportunity of spending time talking with this beautiful old man. I could tell by his wise old eyes and his aura that he had seen and interpreted many wonders of life and beyond. My hope was that he had documented his wisdom in the gospel. I looked down at it in my hands, then at Morgan, who showed no emotion.

"We will do the burials at first light," Morgan said.

"At first light, then," I agreed.

CHAPTER
XIV

r Roberts had signalled Jackson, and he had awakened me. I was groggy for a few minutes, and then, looking out of the office window, I noticed it was dark. "How long have I been under?" I asked.

"Exactly six hours," Judith replied, checking her watch. "How are you feeling, dear?"

"I'm fine, thanks, just a little hungry."

"Wasn't your breakfast substantial enough?" Mike joked, lighting up a Rothmans cigarette.

"It was great, but more nourishing for Boudicca than me," I replied, returning the banter with a giggle.

Professor Harris announced, "Then I would like to invite you all for dinner tonight in celebration of an excellent day's research for First Light."

"Hear! Hear!" we agreed in unison.

"We won't forget that night in a hurry, will we, Jackson?" I said, noticing a faraway look in his eyes. Suddenly, I realised he might not be able to cope with driving. I hadn't given his condition a thought. It was dreadful of me, after all, he had just gotten out of the hospital a few hours ago, and here I was expecting him to drive five hours to Sydney.

"All of this chaos has made me neglectful, darling. Please pull over at the next petrol station so I can take over. You shouldn't be driving," I said.

"No, no, I'm okay," he argued.

"Rubbish!" Cleo piped up from the back seat. "I'll drive. Jackson can rest on the back seat, and you can keep talking, Bo. I've done this trip plenty of times. I know the road like the back of my hand."

I spotted a petrol station up ahead. "There, Jackson, pull in."

We stopped and topped up the tank. Cleo took over the wheel, and we headed into the night for Sydney. After a few minutes, I hit record on the iPad and continued my story.

The reason I said we'd never forget that night is horrible to even try and recall now. Jackson picked me up in a cab from outside Flea's apartment, and we drove on to Newtown to collect Professor Harris. Mike and Judith were to meet us at the agreed downtown restaurant. We pulled up outside the professor's terraced house in Bucknell Street, and Jackson waited in the cab while I went to the front door. It was open when I knocked, so I went inside.

"Professor, it's Bonnie," I called out. "Are you ready?"

There was no sign of him anywhere in the dark. I tried the light switch, but nothing happened. I sensed something was wrong and started upstairs. Each creak from the old wooden staircase underfoot sent a chill up my spine.

"Professor? Are you there?" My voice was shaky.

I reached the landing and looked tentatively about, my heart pounding in my chest. I questioned whether to fetch Jackson, but something drove me, perhaps the strength I had acquired from Boudicca or something else, and I entered the main bedroom. To my shock, I found the professor spread-eagled on the floor. I kneeled beside him and felt for a pulse. He was alive, but it was faint. The phone was on the floor off the hook. I dialled an ambulance. Once assured it was on the way, I rushed outside to tell Jackson. He paid the taxi fare, and we went back inside to call the restaurant and relay the message that we wouldn't make it.

When the ambulance arrived, the paramedics diagnosed head trauma. We went with them in the ambulance to nearby St. Vincent's Hospital and stayed there most of the night, waiting for positive news. At 4 a.m., a police detective inspector and a uniformed cop arrived and asked us to accompany them to Darlinghurst police station to make a statement. Jackson asked why but received no answer.

In an interview room at the station, we learned that the professor had been attacked, and it was regarded as an assault. At 6 a.m., we were finally released, and we found a café on Oxford Street to order coffees and wake ourselves up.

"What do you think?" I asked Jackson.

Sipping his espresso, he thought carefully before answering. "Someone wants to put an end to our research."

"But why... and why attack the professor?" I whispered

conspiratorially.

"I think we need to discuss this with Mike and Judith, but not at our office. It might be bugged," I suggested.

"They're staying at the Barker Lodge in Kensington, right next to the University of New South Wales. Why don't I give them a call and arrange to meet up there?" I suggested.

I used the café phone and scheduled breakfast with them in an hour.

They were waiting for us in the motel restaurant when we arrived. After helping ourselves to the buffet, we sat down in a quiet corner to talk. I gave them a rundown of the events, and we waited for their reaction.

"Who would want to attack the professor?" Mike queried.

"Someone who wants our research stopped," Jackson replied sharply.

"But why the professor? Surely, they would try to get Bonnie?" Mike countered.

"You're right," I agreed.

"What if it's not related to First Light research and it's something else?" Judith posed.

"It's hard to imagine what that could be. He has no enemies," Jackson said.

"I think we need to wait for him to tell us himself. Otherwise, we're only guessing," I suggested.

"You're right, Bonnie, but even so, we still need to consider that someone made an attempt on his life, and we have to assume it is related to First Light," Judith said gravely.

"Considering that, we need to seriously consider our position and our safety," Mike said resolutely.

We all sat back, pondering the situation.

"The professor once said there would be factions who wouldn't want our findings made public. Remember that, Jackson?" I said.

"Yes, I think he was referring to religious factions," he recalled.

"What religion is Gibson-Smith?" I asked.

"He's a practicing Catholic, of that I'm certain. His religious beliefs often got in the way of theory," Jackson said adamantly.

"What if he contacted some radical wing of the Catholic Church and told them about our project? Would that be enough to cause them to react?" I proposed.

"Who is Gibson-Smith?" Mike asked.

Jackson filled them in on the problems we'd had with Gibson-

Smith, and we all agreed that he was the most likely contender—if not himself, then someone he had contacted.

"Well, let me tell you a little of what I know about clandestine fanatical religious orders," Mike said, always keen to profess his inside information. "There are three orders created to protect the Catholic Church: the Opus Dei, The Knights of Malta, and The Jesuit Order, inside of which are several even more fanatical militant orders. I'll start with the Opus Dei: it is a devious, antidemocratic, reactionary, semi-fascist institution, desperately hungry for absolute power in the Church and quite possibly very close now to having that power. It is capable of doing an enormous amount of harm to anyone or anything deemed to oppose the Church. The Knights of Malta dates back to the time of the Crusades; its present members are reported to include some of the world's most prominent Catholics. The Knights are committed to defending the Church. Only the most devout and obedient are invited to join the Knights and Opus Dei, which its detractors have compared to mind-controlling cults. The Jesuits, a 500-year-old covert patriarchal society, geo-political, structured as a secret military operation: demanding secret oaths and complete obedience to each direct superior, which is ultimately the Superior General—often nicknamed as the Black Pope, since he dresses in black and 'stands in the shadow' of the white Pope. The 'Society of Jesus'—as they are officially known—was originally used by the Vatican to counter the various Reformation movements in Europe, to which the Vatican lost much of its religious and political power. My money would be on a faction of the Jesuits."

"Wow, now I understand what the professor was warning us about," I said.

"That's precisely why he was all for First Light," Jackson added.

"And obviously why he was worried about Gibson-Smith," I proposed.

"But why would Gibson-Smith suspect our research of being dangerous enough to warrant contacting one of these militant factions?" Judith asked.

"Maybe there was something in the doctored transcripts we gave him," Jackson considered.

"Wait, we might be missing the obvious here, we don't know if the professor's office or his home was ransacked. Maybe Gibson-Smith suspected something, told whoever, and they went looking for evidence and found it," I submitted.

"Mmm, what could they have found?" Jackson inquired.

I thought about it for a moment, then suddenly the penny dropped.

"The last tape recording transcript!" I bellowed.

"Yes, you're absolutely right. When he collected us from the airport, he mentioned that he'd only just finished the transcript of the battle of Verulamium tape, where Boudicca meets Morgan and talks about the sage. Do you remember, Judith?" Mike asked her.

"Yes, he said he was anxious for us to read it," she agreed.

"So that means he might have had it ready to show us at dinner last night instead of keeping it in the safe," Jackson speculated.

"He wouldn't be worried about Gibson-Smith because we'd delivered his doctored transcripts of previous sessions the day before," I said.

"I doubt he'd have a reason to suspect him anyway," Jackson figured.

We all knew we were simply shooting the breeze. What we needed was to speak with the professor. Only he could put our suspicions to rest.

Later that morning, I rang the hospital and learned the professor was out of danger. He was conscious, and we could visit him. We caught a cab to St. Vincent's Hospital.

It was great to find the Professor sitting up in bed in good spirits. After making sure no one was eavesdropping, he told us his story. When he left his office at the University, he was conscious of someone following him. A big man dressed in a black suit, sporting short-cropped military-style hair—he said he looked like a cop. It took him half an hour to walk from Sydney Uni to his terraced house in Newtown. Under his arm, he was carrying a folder containing the transcript of the Verulamium tape recording.

The four of us exchanged a knowing look: our suspicions were looking like being on the money.

When he arrived home, it became apparent the man in black had tailed him all the way. After entering the house, he made his way upstairs. The phone rang, so he went to the bedroom extension to answer. Before he could speak, he was hit from behind, and the lights went out.

"We need to go to your home to see if the folder is there," I said excitedly.

"There could be no other reason for the attack, Bonnie. I have no enemies," Harris conceded.

"We suspect Gibson-Smith has something to do with it. What do you think of that, Professor?" Jackson asked.

"Well, it is funny you should suspect him because I received a phone call from him just prior to leaving my office. He was unsatisfied with the transcripts he'd been given and demanded the actual tape recordings, arguing that he didn't believe the transcripts to be accurate. I reminded him that providing the tape recordings wasn't part of the arrangement and that they were the property of the University. I also ensured him that we had provided exactly what the hearing requested of us: a copy of the regression session transcripts. He cussed at me and slammed the phone down."

"The guy's a drag," I growled, "and that certainly points the fickle finger of fate at him, doesn't it?"

Everybody nodded in silent agreement.

"So, where do we go from here?" Mike said, looking a little unhinged and fumbling for a cigarette. "Let's put all this into perspective. Our research was stolen," he said.

"We presume," Judith added and snatched the cigarette out of Mike's hand. "You can't have that here!" she squawked like a headmistress.

Mike simply shrugged his shoulders, conditioned to Judith's imperious behaviour.

"I think we can safely assume the manuscript was the object of the attack, and the only person with motive is Gibson-Smith," Harris said.

"So we must assume that as a practicing Catholic with a grudge, he has contacted one of the militant arms of the Church, the Opus Dei, Knights of Malta, or the Jesuits, so that now they have become our adversary, unless he acted on his own accord," Mike proposed vehemently.

Jackson pointed out, "No, he's incapable of that, though he could have hired someone to do his dirty work, and he's waging a personal vendetta on me. We do have serious history, you know."

"Either way, with the transcript in his possession, he or they or both now know about the planned meeting between Boudicca and Joseph of Arimathea and the existence of his gospel," Harris concluded.

The thought of our security having been breached soured everything. We decided to go to our offices to make a plan. Besides, it was nearing the critical time for my next session—probably the most vital of all: the disclosure of the burial locations of Joseph and the gospel. We resolved to collect Professor Harris once he was discharged from the hospital later in the day.

It was a mad rush to the University. We couldn't afford to miss the all-important burial, and we would only have one chance.

Harris had given Mike the key to his house to search for the transcript folder and any other evidence. He and Judith took a cab there while Jackson and I went to our office at Uni. To our horror, when we arrived, we found University security waiting for us at the door, and he promptly marched us off to the office of the Dean.

Time was ticking away. It was now 2 p.m. Boudicca and Morgan had agreed to meet at first light. Nine hours behind us, that was about now... but here we were stuck, waiting outside the Dean's office. Finally, we were ushered inside.

We were shocked to find several board members and Gibson-Smith in attendance. After delivering him the most contemptible stare I could muster, Dean Holloway, a tall man with a regal countenance, asked us to be seated.

"Miss Leigh and Dr Bolt, it has been brought to the attention of the University board of directors that you have contravened a tribunal dictum by falsifying transcripts of your research. What do you have to say to that allegation?"

"Dean Holloway, that's a strong accusation—the hearing, as opposed to a tribunal, requested me to share our research with Dr Gibson-Smith, and that is exactly what we have done. Is that not correct, Dr Gibson-Smith?"

The pompous man puffed himself up and bellowed, "Yes, you did, but I have proof those reports were censored."

"Excuse me, but did I hear you correctly? You said we did deliver you the transcripts in accordance with the agreement, so what seems to be the problem?" Jackson countered.

"The reports were falsified, you know that!" he angrily contested.

"And exactly how do you draw that conclusion, Dr Gibson-Smith?" Jackson returned fire with interest.

I'd had enough of Gibson-Smith's self-important crap and added a dose of sarcasm to the discussion.

"You need to see a psychiatrist, doctor," I quipped in a half mumble.

His face soured as he glared at me contemptuously. When he had no comeback, Jackson went in for the kill.

"Gentlemen, are you aware that last night a folder of transcripts was stolen from Professor Harris when an attempt was made on his life?" He paused for effect, glaring at each individual, one at a time, and then ending with Gibson-Smith. "The Professor is in St. Vincent's hospital right now. He had been in ER all night... Dr Gibson-Smith. I rest my case, Dean Holloway. Please permit us to return to our work," Jackson said passionately.

Dean Holloway rose from his chair, a sign of acquiescence. "Thank you, Dr Bolt and Miss Leigh."

On our way out, we both glared at Gibson-Smith, whose face was glowing red, poised to explode.

CHAPTER
XV

He glared at me.

"It has been a hard day of work already, my friend, and I fear there is more to come," I added in a mock-serious voice.

Most Druids were renowned for their distaste of physical labour, anything beyond walking. I think Bran was the exception to that tradition.

"Was that your first time in Buddekaulegh?" he asked.

"Yes, I was told of the sacred place when I was a girl, but I didn't think I would ever visit. Is Fosse Way near?"

"Yes, it has been said the Romans will soon pave the Fosse Way."

"I pray they don't desecrate the sacred sites along it like they have done elsewhere. They build their temples over them and then adopt the names of our gods to appease the clans."

"Yes, it is the means to convert them while at the same time occupying the land."

"Yes, religion, wine, and wealth are mightier Roman weapons than the sword, chariot, and spear."

"Indeed, Boudicca, indeed... but I think their brutality reigns supreme."

"What do you suppose the sage scribed in the gospel?"

"I believe a wondrous account of the life and times of Joseph and of his nephew who he brought to our shores some years ago, to learn from the Druithin. It was then Bran first met Joseph and his nephew."

"I didn't know that," I said.

"Yes, it is known that because of the close relationship between Joseph, his nephew, and Bran, twenty years ago Arviragus Caractacus, son of Cunobelinus before he was captured by Vespasian and taken prisoner with his family to Rome to Emperor Claudius, he gave Joseph the land of Twelve Hides. The place we were today."

"Why had Joseph come here from his country?"

"Years ago, Joseph was Nobilis Decurio of Rome, minister for mines... he traded in tin ore from Tintagel and doing so had to deal with Cunobelinus and then Caractacus," Morgan said.

"Oh, I understand now."

I suddenly noticed a column of smoke.

"Look, smoke on the horizon is coming from Cadbury," I said urgently.

"Maybe they are preparing a feast," Morgan said.

"No, I do not think so, that is too much smoke."

Fearing the worst, I stepped up the pace, and before long, we were ashore where my horse was hitched. The two of us mounted up and rode at speed toward Cadbury.

I approached the hill fort from the cover of the forest. We dismounted to reconnoitre. I had a gut feeling something was wrong. It only took a few minutes for my fear to be realised. A party of twenty warriors debouched from the hill fort. I could tell they were on the side of Rome.

"They're a Numerus, and they are looking for me. Someone has informed on me," I whispered in a resigned voice.

"A Numerus?" Morgan questioned.

"Britons now serving Rome: mostly deserters. Lay low while they pass."

We got down out of sight. They were so close I could see blood spatter on their faces, forearms, and tunics. I feared the carnage we might find within the ramparts of Cadbury.

After they had passed, I left my horse, and we quickly made our way in through the gates. Most of the thatched roofs of the round houses were ablaze. There were dead, dying, and wounded all around. The townspeople were easy pickings because they had assembled for market day and were unarmed.

While Morgan went to the aid of the wounded, I drew my sword and made for the Great Hall, ready to strike at the enemy should they emerge from within. I stopped at the entrance and listened. I could hear voices inside. I peeked in and sighted two warriors standing over Tyree, tied in a chair. They were cutting him with daggers. He was taking the torture in silence, a brave warrior.

"Are you looking for me?" I shouted angrily, and the two warriors turned sharply to face me.

"You call yourselves Britons, but you side with the enemy and murder your own innocent people. You're nothing but scum. Fight me! I fear you not."

"Boudicca!" bellowed the bigger of the two.

"At least I have a name, and I am proud of it. Who am I about to kill so that I can condemn his name to Andrasta?"

"I am Blair, and he is Edan. We will take your head to Gaius Suetonius Paulinus."

"Well, come and get it then!" I said, kicking a table out of my way and raising my sword ready to do battle.

Edan ran at me with his Gladius aimed to stab. Though the Gladius is the stronger weapon, it is short, while mine is a long sword crafted to cut and slice, not to stab. Fighting with a Gladius without a shield is a disadvantage. I deflected his first lunge on the run and followed through with a vicious strike that cut deeply into his right shoulder, causing him to drop his sword. I whipped my sword back through his gut, and his steaming entrails spilled out onto the floor at his feet. He crumbled to his knees in agony, with one arm trying to hold his guts in. One swift blow took off his head.

With his face all bloody and torn, Tyree raised a smile at the ease by which I had dispatched Edan.

I confronted Blair. He moved towards me slowly, deliberately. The scars on his face and upper arms indicated he had fought many battles. His long sword was similar to mine, and that would make him a tougher opponent than Edan.

We circled one another, feigning a lunge, trying to unsettle each other.

"I've not fought a woman before," he said with a gravelly voice.

"And you will not live to fight another!" I spat back.

He slashed at me, and our swords clashed. I could feel his brute strength. I would need to out-finesse him with Andrasta's help—he was way too strong for me. I swivelled and struck at his thigh, but he was skilled enough to ward off the blow with his blade. If I were drawn into a close fight, he'd beat me.

In a surprise move, he rushed me. I quickly blocked a sweeping blow aimed to sever my sword hand at the wrist, and the hilts of our swords clashed and locked. At close quarters, he elbowed me in the bridge of the nose. I was stunned—warm blood flowed from my nose and dripped off my chin. I was lucky the punch had missed the target, my eye, for it would have blurred my vision.

I swivelled away sharply and pulled my sword free, but I was dizzy—stars flying about filled my vision. He recognised that and pushed his advantage, advancing with a salvo of fierce blows. All I could do was hold up my sword to fend them off, but my arms were aching—my sword had become very heavy—he was getting the better of me. Backing off, I collided with a large oak pillar holding up the roof and quickly ducked behind it to use as cover. It was good timing; he struck with all his might, thinking it would be the killing blow. But instead of his blade finding me, it sank into the stanchion. His blade was so sharp, and the blow so powerful that it wedged in the timber, and I saw him grimace, trying to tug it free. This was my big chance, and I took it. I whipped my sword with all the energy I had left and sliced open his exposed throat. The massive effort threw me off balance and onto the floor. I looked up at him—his eyes wide, grasping the blood gushing between his fingers from his cut throat. I struggled to my feet as he crumbled to his knees. After taking a deep breath, I took a grip of his long black hair and with a scream of triumph that seemed to echo repeatedly, I took his head with one almighty slash of my trusty sword. I held it high for Tyree to see.

"This is for you, Andrasta!" I shouted. "For you are within me!"

CHAPTER
XVI

verything was out of focus—then it cleared to reveal Mike, Judith, and Jackson—I was back. Mike had a look on his face as though he'd seen a ghost.

"That was the most amazing experience I've ever had," he admitted. "For a linguist to actually listen to someone fluently speaking a dead language... I... I'm lost for words." He wiped tears from his eyes.

"Are you all right, Bonnie?" Jackson said, taking hold of my hand and helping me sit up.

"Yes, I'm fine, but I'm afraid we missed the most important moment. We were too damn late. It was all Gibson-Smith's fault!" I said angrily.

"Don't worry, Bonnie. I think we learned plenty, maybe enough to narrow it down," Judith said confidently, with a genuine smile.

"Besides, if we missed out on the exact location like you say, there's still a chance she might still mention it to Morgan," Jackson suggested.

I felt let down, depressed—the object of all our work was to determine the burial place of Joseph and the gospel, and to that end, I had failed to deliver.

"You look disappointed," Judith said.

"I don't like failure. We've come too far to fail."

"She said the burial was near the settlement of Buddekaulegh at the place of the Twelve Hides, land given to Joseph by Cunobelinus. What does that mean to you, Judith?" Mike questioned.

She sat back in her chair with a confident gleam in her eyes. Today, with her shoulder-length brown hair tied back, she appeared a little matronly.

"Buddekaulegh is the ancient Celtic name for the town of Butleigh in Somerset, a short distance from Glastonbury. The place of the

Twelve Hides is fascinating because this is the site of one of the most productive archaeological digs in the UK—one that I spent many years on. The name Twelve Hides was presumed to be of Saxon origin, but it seems Bonnie might just have rendered that presumption fallacious. Basically, there were twelve hills, the most famous of them now is the Glastonbury Tor, named Wydr or Fort of Glass by the Celts, another name for the entrance to the otherworld of the Druids. Today's Glastonbury was originally surrounded by water, which explains why Boudicca and Morgan had taken a boat to bury Joseph. It was in that lake, a place known in legend as Pomparles or the Perilous Bridge, the place where Bedwyr, from the Arthurian legend, returned the sword Excalibur to the Lady of the Lake after the battle of Camlann."

"You say an entrance to the underworld," I submitted.

"Yes, in Celtic legend, Avalon was the underworld home of the god Afallach. Both these names refer to apples that once grew in Glastonbury. The Arthurian myth has it that the Twelve Hides were a sacred territory: an assembly of twelve tribes that upheld the local law. An Arviragus or pagan ruler in 60 CE was believed to grant Twelve Hides, or 120 acres of land, to twelve early Christian missionaries led by Joseph of Arimathea. Though no record exists, it is believed that the granting of the Twelve Hides was a tradition from an earlier time when Glastonbury was a Druid sanctuary. It has only been the Christian Church that has sought to tie early Christianity to Joseph of Arimathea and the building of the Glastonbury Abbey. It's a terrible misnomer, Church propaganda if you like, that Christianity began with Joseph arriving in Britain. I hesitate to say after today that the Twelve Hides of land were given to Joseph as Druid sacred burial ground. I expect that's where we would find Joseph and the gospel."

"But isn't that a large area?" Jackson asked.

"Yes, far too large. We need something more precise to recover the gospel," Judith said glibly.

"What about Cadbury Hill Fort?" Mike asked.

"It was destroyed by the Romans in A.D. 70 as part of their police action. It was excavated four years ago by Leslie Alcock, who uncovered evidence of a Roman massacre."

"So, it all ties in, but we still need a definitive location of the burial. Yes?" I asked.

Both Mike and Judith were nodding their heads.

"Then you better put me under again, Jackson. I think I should try to make her talk about it. I haven't tried that yet," I said.

Jackson checked his wristwatch. "I think we first need to plan what we're going to tell Matt," Jackson said.

"I agree, our priority must be to protect Quinn," Mike said.

"Quinn? Professor Harris?" I queried.

Mike nodded. "Yes, his first name Quinn translates to wise in Celtic."

They were right, of course... we first needed to get our house in order.

"I've got a question for you academics first: What would cause the Church to be so concerned about Joseph and the gospel?"

"I think I can answer that, Bonnie," Mike said, lighting up a cigarette. "Some scholars believe Jesus Christ didn't die on the cross. They assert he was taken down alive and stayed in the crypt of Joseph of Arimathea. After that, Joseph took Jesus and his wife, Mary Magdalene, to the South of France... Then, after ten or fifteen years, Joseph went to Britain where he stayed until he died sometime between 60 and 64 A.D. That would mean if Joseph kept a diary or a gospel as we now suspect, we could assume it would tell his version of those events, and that's something radical factions of the Church would do anything to suppress."

"I see," I said, quite stunned. "That makes sense."

We went to Jackson's apartment—it was safer than staying at the office, and besides, Matt Ryan was expected there later. I insisted on Jackson regressing me so I could try prompting Boudicca to talk about the burial. Mike and Judith watched Jackson put me under.

As I sank into a hypnotised state, I felt like two people instead of automatically becoming Boudicca. I opened my eyes. I was in a circular smoky room and figured it was a roundhouse. I was lying on a bed under furs. I felt she couldn't sleep and was staring at the ceiling, watching skeins of smoke from the hearth drifting upwards like spirits.

The bed suddenly rocked, and I looked beside me. I had company. A large hand suddenly wrapped around me.

"You're far better than I get from the village wenches," Tyree mumbled, puffing out of breath.

This was my chance to try promoting a conversation. I thought if I could implant a particular word in Boudicca's vocabulary, it would be proof I could intervene in her thinking process: a word that wouldn't be used at that time. I concentrated on the only word I could think of relevant to the conversation: scrummy.

"That was scrummy, Tyree," I said.

Success! Now that had worked, I needed to speak with Morgan. I sat up.

"I must collect Morgan and ride for my army."

"I fear I cannot offer you my warriors. My ranks were depleted by Blair's Numerus."

"Thank you for the offer, but we have a large enough force to take Gaius Suetonius Paulinus. Besides, I think once Edan and Blair fail to catch up with their men, there will be a reprisal. Best you prepare, Tyree."

"And you will need to be careful of them in riding for Watling Road. It would be safer for you to take the Fosse Way," he suggested.

"It was my presence that brought this upon Cadbury. I cannot take the Fosse Way—it will extend my journey. I will be able to make a detour around the Numerus when I find them. Then I will dispatch some of my men to rout them before they seek retribution on you."

"Thank you, my Queen."

I kissed his battered cheek and then slipped out of bed to dress.

I walked out into the noonday sun. Most of the village square had been cleared of dead and wounded, and the fires extinguished. I saw Morgan attending to an injured child and approached him.

"I ride for my army. Will you accompany me?" I asked.

"No, I am needed here."

I had no alternative but to try to get him talking about the burial.

"Come, walk with me to my horse," I said sternly.

It worked. We strolled over to my horse. He had been groomed, watered, and fed. I thought to raise the burial.

"Morgan, are you convinced that the sites where we buried Joseph and the gospel are safe from the Romans? I worry about the gospel. You know that one day it will need to be recovered," I cued him politely.

"Do not fear, it will be safe in the Otherworld, and the place will remain intact for centuries to come. I will see to that with the Culdees."

"There are few of you left after the massacre on Mona. You must promise me that your order will remain custodians of the secret."

"That will be done, Boudicca."

I mounted my white horse.

"I bid you farewell, Morgan."

"Your unity with the goddess awaits you, great Queen," he said sagaciously.

I rode out through the gates and headed north at a gallop.

Jackson's voice brought me out of the haze. He handed me a glass of water. I took it and sipped.

"How are you feeling?" he asked.

"Fine, thanks... it worked!" I said excitedly. "I could influence what Boudicca said. I wish I'd realised it earlier."

"We noticed," Mike laughed. "It was incredible. Out of the Celtic suddenly sprang the word 'scrummy,' rather English, I thought, and so we figured you had been successful. Well done, old girl."

"So, what did we learn? Are we any closer?" I prodded.

"We've been discussing it," Judith said. "You mentioned a couple of things that have narrowed the field a little. The Otherworld and the Culdees. The Otherworld is the sacred underworld of the Druids, and it had specific entrances. We already know the area of interest is within the Twelve Hides, so we need to research which of the Hides were considered entrances to the Otherworld."

"Is that good? I mean—"

"Yes, Bonnie, it is very useful... and it may help us narrow it down further knowing that the Culdees are the guardians of the burial place," she added.

"You said 'are.' Do the Culdees still exist?" Jackson asked.

"I believe that is entirely possible. Again, more research is needed there. But I do know from historical records that the Order of the Culdees was still operating in Somerset in the 18th century," Judith said confidently.

"I expect that once we have sorted out things here, it will be necessary for all of us to go to the UK," Mike proposed.

"Yes, we will only be able to conduct in-depth research there," Judith agreed.

Jackson and I exchanged an eager look.

"Now you're talking!" I exclaimed.

A few hours later, the intercom sounded, and Jackson made his way to answer it. After a short wait, he opened the door to a man wearing a suit that looked a size or two too small. This hulking man with the countenance of a perfect gentleman was Matt Ryan.

CHAPTER
XVII

After hearing a long explanation about our situation, Matt reclined in the lounge chair and gazed pensively out of the balcony window of Jackson's apartment at the Sydney skyline, silhouetted by the setting sun. We waited in anticipation of his opinion. Then, after it seemed to become intelligible to him, he grinned at Jackson, who was sitting opposite.

"What's a man got to do for a drink around here?" he said.

Jackson smiled and got up. "What will it be, Matt?"

"Scotch and scotch. You should remember that," he chortled.

"I do. Sometimes I have nightmares about the hangovers. Judith and Mike?"

"We're teetotallers. I'll make us a cuppa. What about you, Bonnie?" Judith asked.

"I'll have a drink with the boys, thanks, Judith. Need some help?"

"No, I'll be fine," she said as she wandered off to the kitchen.

Jackson went to the bar in the corner of the room to get the drinks.

"I have to say that if it wasn't for the fact that I know Jackson is brilliant in his field, I would never have believed what you have just told me," Matt admitted.

"It's difficult to accept, I know, but it is the truth and it is truly amazing," Mike said.

"It's obvious why it's fraught with danger... to certain parties, that knowledge would be sacrosanct," Matt said.

"That's precisely why we must find a way of protecting the knowledge and the members of First Light," Jackson said, bringing the drinks for us.

We raised our glasses. "Cheers to First Light," Matt said, then after a sip, "Ah, a single malt, the nectar of the gods."

"Tell us about yourself, Matt?" Mike inquired.

"Sure, I'm an officer in what was officially formed in 1956 as the International Criminal Police Commission, known today as Interpol. Our mission is to prevent and fight crime through enhanced cooperation and innovation on police and security matters."

"Cool, like 007!" I said.

"It's not quite as exciting as Mr Bond's world, but yes, we are mostly undercover," Matt admitted.

"Would what you've learned from us be of interest to Interpol?" Mike asked.

"Frankly, no. In general terms, there would need to be a murder before Interpol could officially become involved. But unofficially, yeah, it's just the sort of case that tickles my fancy... and besides, just like when we played rugby together, I will always stand by my mate here. He saved my arse on a number of occasions," he said, raising his glass to Jackson.

"How about joining up with First Light and handling our security?" Jackson suggested.

Judith returned from the kitchen with two cups of tea.

"That sounds like the way to go," Matt agreed. "But first, we need to bust the mighty Quinn out of the hospital and get him to a safe house."

"The mighty Quinn?" Mike questioned.

"The Manfred Mann song from 1968. It gave us the nickname for the professor when we were at Uni," Matt said with a chuckle.

"I prefer the Hollies version myself," Mike countered.

"It was written by Bob Dylan, you know?" Jackson perked up.

"Always chock-a-block with trivia, our Jackson. Yep, the mighty Quinn was our favourite tutor," Matt said with a grin.

"And of course, our rugby coach as well," Jackson reminded him.

By ten that night, we had the professor safely at Jackson's apartment. We all agreed that the next stop was London and made our travel plans accordingly. The first cab off the rank, however, was to get extra research funding approved by Dean Holloway, without alerting Gibson-Smith's spies on the university board, for while we were in Australia, we all agreed that Gibson-Smith was our nemesis.

Mike and Matt were burning the midnight oil that night, surrounded by reference books, debating which secret organisation was most likely our enemy, while I was busy helping Jackson pack. But I caught the gist of their discussion. Matt proposed a number of candidates: the Order of St. John, Jerusalem of Rhodes and of Malta, better known as the Sovereign Military Order of Malta or SMOM, the Jesuits, the Order of the Sword of Saint Jerome, the Crux Redemptoris, the Order of the Dragon, the Teutonic Knights, or the Order of the Holy Sepulchre. Finally, at about three in the morning, just as we were about to hit the sack, Mike asked Jackson if he could recall anything unusual about Gibson-Smith's personal office.

"Funny you should ask that. There was a weird painting on the wall behind his desk: a man holding a tiny lion's paw in the palm of one hand. Now wait a minute, I remember asking him about it, and he said it was a painting by... now who was it? That's it—Lotto, Lorenzo Lotto."

Mike dived for a reference book like a man possessed and quickly found out that Lotto was a Northern Italian painter born in 1480. He painted religious subjects and portraits. Mike showed Jackson a colour plate of Lotto's 1527 painting of a Gentleman Holding a Lion's Paw.

"Is this the one?"

"That's it, all right. So, what does that mean: a man holding a paw?" Jackson asked.

Mike flicked through a few pages of another book and then read aloud.

"The Order of the Sword of Saint Jerome developed an extensive network of contacts in all walks of life. These people don't know the true nature of the Order or their mission, but are devoted Catholics willing to help them out with information. Within the Order, these contacts are referred to as the Longa manus. That can be literally translated as the long arm, but the more colloquial translation is the cat's paw."

"The lion's paw, same difference... so we can presume this prick Gibson-Smith is a plant for The Order of the Sword of Saint Jerome," Matt said, standing and then pacing the room. "Though, I still wouldn't discount one of the militant factions of the Jesuits... they do use the same code names as the Order of Jerome."

"What does it all mean, Matt?" I asked.

The big man stopped pacing and eyeballed me. "It means, Bonnie, that this is bigger than all of us. We're up against the richest and most malevolent organisation on Earth: the Catholic Church."

"Is that a game-changer?" I inquired.

"For me, it is," Matt admitted vehemently.

My heart sank. For a while there, I was feeling safe with Matt involved, but now, I was getting nervous again.

"What are you saying, Matt?" Jackson queried.

"It means I'm going to need to involve others, and that weakens our control," he said.

I breathed a sigh of relief.

"Will you be coming to the UK with us?" Mike asked.

"No, but I'll have someone meet you there who is kosher. I'll coordinate the security side of things from here. Rest assured, if it gets hairy, I'll be there like a rat up a drainpipe. But for the time being, this guy can be trusted. Okay?" Matt said confidently.

"Do you think Quinn's up to it?" I asked in a resigned voice, knowing the answer.

"No, I don't," Matt chimed in. "But he'd be a bloody-side safer with you than staying here."

Two days later, we were aboard a London-bound Qantas Boeing 747. It was fortunate that Judith was born into a seriously wealthy British family, with the obligatory three-story 19th-century manor house nestled in the bucolic countryside of Buckinghamshire. After tragically losing her parents in a car crash and with no siblings, Judith inherited the house and family fortune ten years ago. Being a dedicated scholar and without plans to marry, she generously gave us the run of Moore Manor House. The house was isolated from the town of Milton Keynes, only ten minutes up the road, and we felt safe enough to set up several ground floor rooms as HQ for First Light.

I felt like a queen in the stately room that Judith had allocated to me. A giant four-poster bed, a fireplace, and all the privileged trimmings of English landed gentry. Jackson's room conveniently located next door. After we had settled in, we rang Matt in Canberra, and he arranged for a colleague from Interpol UK to call on us.

This time, with the brief background intelligence Matt gave us on him, I was expecting the real James Bond to turn up, and as it turned out, I wasn't disappointed.

A stunning white 1968 E-type Jaguar two-plus-two pulled up in the driveway, and a tall man dressed in an elegant, shiny grey suit stepped out of it. Judith and I, peering out the window, raised eyebrows. Yep, debonair Daniel Boyd had the full package: the look, the walk, the suave sophistication, the aristocratic intonation, the sexy little hint of arrogance. Daniel was the bee's knees—he had "cold-war spy" written all over him. When his cobalt blue eyes flirtatiously caught yours, if you were female, they said, "Do the wrong thing by me and I'll clout you." Yep, Mr Boyd was every inch of what Matt had warned us to expect.

It was the end of spring there, and I'll never forget the pungent aroma that engulfed me when I walked out the front door of the manor. Mike told me it was the fragrance of the reddish-purple flowers of Admiral Avellan. Isn't it odd how a scent can linger in one's memory?

It had been three days since I'd been regressed, the longest span to date. So, for the benefit of Daniel Boyd, whom we felt needed a little convincing to assure him he wasn't dealing with crackpots, Jackson put me under.

I became conscious of being in a battle by the din of war cries, screams of agony, and the clashing of weapons. My vision was blurred—I wiped my face and looked at my hand, blood. Was it mine? I thought not, seeing my sword in the other hand, drenched with blood. I was stopped in my chariot, surrounded by Roman legionnaires hacking and thrusting at me with sword and spear. It wasn't going well. Thoughts were running through my head. There's a large number of Romans in Testudo formation, and they're marching right over the top of my forces. We had them outnumbered ten to one, but that didn't matter. They were a superior fighting force, and they had us trapped in a valley surrounded by heavy woods. I looked up to the high ground and saw the sun reflect off the golden armour of a man on horseback. I knew it had to be General Gaius Suetonius Paulinus. If only I could reach him—I'd kill him, even if his best warriors were surrounding him. The thunderous war cry of the Iceni sounded, and I immediately recognised it as Domnall. He was speeding towards me in his chariot, slicing through the fray with half a dozen chariots in support. He reached me just in time as I was struggling to fend off my attackers.

"Our army is deserting, only the Iceni and Trinovantes warriors stand and fight," he yelled.

"Look up at the hillside, Domnall. It's Gaius Suetonius Paulinus. I need to get to him; it's our only hope."

"But he is too well protected, my Queen. Look to his flank, Tacitus, his scribe, keeping his version of the battle."

"What have I got to lose, my friend?"

"No matter the outcome of this battle today, your story of valour, Boudicca, will be recited by bards forevermore. We will give you support. Side up, flank Boudicca!" he growled loudly, and three chariots took up each of my flanks. I raised my sword and bellowed for all to hear.

"It is victory or death! This is my resolve, as a woman—follow me or submit to the Roman yoke!"

We charged into the fray and fought our way up the hill towards

Gaius Suetonius Paulinus. Halfway up, Romans on horseback halted our progress. I glanced down at my blue-painted body. It was cut and torn, but I felt no pain.

I looked across at my old friend Domnall and could only recognise him by his shock of auburn hair. The rest of him was a mass of bleeding lacerations, his kilt soaked with blood. Instinctively, I knew this would be our last hurrah. There was a raven in the sky overhead—I knew Andrasta awaited me.

"Talk to me, Andrasta. Is it time for me to join you?"

I smiled at Domnall, and he returned a toothless grin. What a great warrior he is.

"You are the pillar of my strength, my friend... take many with you, great warrior!"

CHAPTER
XVIII

I sat up, freaked out. It was like waking from a horrific nightmare. My heart was pounding like a drum, and I was struggling to draw a breath. Jackson's voice called in the distance, "Get her some water!" Then his hand grasped mine and calmed me down. A few deep breaths and a sip of water, and I was back to normal—well, sort of—in a state of shock, really.

"Bonnie, Bonnie, look at me," Jackson said.

I peered into his eyes. I knew he was checking to see if my pupils were dilated or not.

"Is she all right?" Judith asked, worriedly.

"It's finished," I murmured with regret.

"What has finished, Bonnie?" Mike queried.

"The connection, it has gone... broken," I said, tears streaming down my cheeks. "It was so heavy—"

Jackson handed me his handkerchief, and I tried to wipe away the tears, but they just kept coming. The feeling of loss was all-encompassing.

"If someone had told me about this, I wouldn't have believed them, but my God, that was absolutely amazing," Daniel said in awe.

"So that was the Battle of Watling Street, when Boudicca was defeated?" Quinn said.

Mike had a book in his hands and read to us.

"I have here the description from the Roman historian Tacitus that Bonnie mentioned was beside Gaius Suetonius Paulinus at the battle. The Britons arrived to battle in unprecedented numbers. Their confidence was such that they brought their wives with them to see the victory, installing them in carts stationed at the edge of the battlefield. Both leaders are said to have encouraged and inspired their troops, and then Suetonius gave the signal for battle, and the infantry moved forward to throw their javelins. Boudicca's superior numbers were of no advantage. In the narrow field Suetonius had chosen and, in fact, worked against her as the mass of men pushed together provided easy marks for the Romans. The Britons fell back before the javelin assault, and then the advancing wedge formation cut through their ranks. Suetonius ordered in his auxiliary infantry and then his cavalry, and the Britons turned to flee the field. The supply train they had arranged at their rear prevented their escape, and the rout turned into a massacre. The remaining Britons fled with difficulty since their ring of wagons blocked the outlets. The Romans did not spare even the women. Baggage animals too, transfixed with weapons, added to the heaps of dead. Seventy thousand Britons were slain with the loss of only four hundred Roman soldiers. Boudicca poisoned herself. The Greek historian Dio Cassius, also with the legion, wrote that Boudicca fell ill and died. No-one knows the truth."

"And we still don't!" I said truthfully. "She must have been killed; she was at one with Andrasta."

"Are you saying she just disappeared? I find that a little hard to take," Daniel said mockingly.

"Far out, man, don't you have any idea?" I angrily rebuffed him.

"I think Mr Boyd has a little catching up to do before he can accept some of the more fantastic things you have experienced, Bonnie," Mike suggested diplomatically.

I knew he was right; I was still emotional.

"You're right, Mike. I'm sorry, Daniel."

"Think nothing of it, Bonnie. So," he said, standing. "Where do we go from here?"

We all exchanged blank expressions. Now that the connection with Boudicca was severed, we were left on our own to figure out the map to the maze.

The car slowed to enter a small highway town. Jackson leaned from the back seat and said, "I need to take a leak."

"Cool, I'll stop at this petrol station," Cleo said, turning on the indicator and turning into the forecourt.

While Jackson went to the bathroom, Cleo and I sat in silence, both of us thinking about Boudicca's death. Then we both spoke at the same time.

"You go ahead," Cleo said.

"It's a bit numbing, even when I recall the connection being broken. It was like I had lost a close friend or a relative."

"I can imagine. So, let me get this straight... you guys believe that with me being twenty-four, the same age you were when you contacted Boudicca, who was also twenty-four, I might have the same special nucleotide, that original strand of DNA—same as yours—so that under regression hypnosis, I might be able to tune into Boudicca at the time she and Morgan were burying Joseph and his gospel, so we can determine the exact location. Is that it?" Cleo asked.

"Yep, you got it, that's the story, love."

"And when will that be?"

"Giamonios... the first full moon in May, and that's on the 18th," I said with a resigned voice.

"Shit, that's not far away!" Cleo erupted.

"And don't we know it! We've waited forty-one long years for this."

"My goodness... Well, I know it'll make you feel better to know I'm in. This like ...has to be my destiny," Cleo said happily.

"Thank you, Cleo, but you should first hear the downside of the story. It might change your mind."

Jackson climbed into the back seat. "Thanks, ladies," he said cheerfully.

"Cleo has agreed to join First Light," I told him.

"Good news," he said, affectionately tapping Cleo on the back of the head with the flat of his hand.

"I told her she needs to hear the rest of the story before totally committing, though."

"Two hours more to Sydney, so she may as well. You're getting to a heavy part," he said, settling back into the seat.

As Cleo pulled the car out onto the highway, I hit record on her iPad and then continued the story.

At the manor, Mike and Judith had come up with a plan. Daniel wasn't there that day; he was working on a case in France, I think.

"Yes, he was," Jackson confirmed.

"We called a meeting because we had finished analysing the transcripts. Judith and I agreed that all we could do with the limited knowledge we possessed was to visit each of the sacred sites of the Glaston Twelve Hides, to try and eliminate the least likely of them."

"Is there any archaeology on the Twelve Hides we can analyse, Judith?" Quinn asked.

She had anticipated the question and held up a large book.

"This contains the study of seven Glaston Twelve Hides digs completed in the 19th and 20th centuries. I've been through the lot but found nothing relevant," she said discouragingly.

"How about the Culdees?" Jackson asked.

"I've made contact with the Grand Master and set up a meeting at Druids Lodge House in Salisbury for noon tomorrow," Mike said adroitly.

I felt like a sardine in a can on the back seat of Judith's P6 Rover, sandwiched between Jackson and Quinn. After a two-hour drive along the A34, we arrived in Salisbury, the location of the infamous Stonehenge. It then took directions from a local at the main bar of The King's Head Inn before we managed to find the Druids Lodge House, on time, which was surprising.

The old house was a B&B, with the Druids Lodge Polo Club annexed—obviously the preferred place to stay for visiting polo players.

We went to the front desk, and Mike inquired about Don Eastwood. We were then directed inside. The room was what you'd expect of an English Gentleman's Club: dull incandescent lighting, wood-panelled walls, cracked old leather chairs positioned around tables to seat maybe twenty or so guests. A big fireplace occupied the far corner. The room smelled ancient, musky, like a library. There was only one person in the room, and he was hidden behind an open broadsheet newspaper. Smoke was rising above the paper in coils. He lowered the newspaper, grinned past the pipe in his mouth, got to his feet, and said, "Dr Roberts, I presume?"

We organised enough chairs to sit while Mike made the introductions. Don's thick black hair was almost down to his shoulders, and the luxuriant moustache had a sleek, insolent look. Maybe he gave it a hundred strokes of the hairbrush every night before going to bed. His welcoming smile was mirrored in his expressive green eyes.

"Are you a member of the Polo Club, Mr Eastwood?" I asked.

"No, I'm the owner of the establishment," he replied with a twinkle of sarcasm in his eye.

"Mr Eastwood, we have come to discuss a sensitive subject that we thought you might be able to help us with in your capacity as Grand Master," Mike elaborated.

"Well, as you would know, we are a secretive lodge, but please ask your questions, and we'll see what I can answer."

"Have you heard of the Twelve Hides?" Mike asked.

"Yes, I believe so. They were formerly hills around Glastonbury, weren't they?"

"Yes, indeed... from our research on Iron-Age Druidism, we

determined the Culdees were the custodians of information about the Twelve Hides," Mike continued. "Would that still be the case?"

"I'm not quite sure that I understand the question, Doctor."

"Put it this way," Judith chipped in, "each of the twelve hides was sacred to the druids, and some of them more sacred than others. Without compromising your lodge, can you tell us which of the Hides were and are the most sacred?"

Don Eastwood sat back in his comfy leather chair and drew on his pipe contemplatively. I found the pungent aroma of his tobacco quite pleasant.

After giving the question plenty of thought, he removed the pipe and pointed it at Judith.

"Very well put, miss, quite diplomatic of you."

"Doctor, Mr Eastwood, I am a Doctor of archaeology," she replied courteously.

"Well, doctor, let me put it this way—the Culdees may have originally been custodians of this secret in the past, but sometime between the Dark Ages and the 17th century, I think that covenant might have lapsed. These days, the Culdees is what I'd call a cosmetic lodge only, with few secrets, funny handshakes—and not too detached from Freemasonry. On Mayday, we garb up in druid smocks and enact a recently contrived ritual at Stonehenge for the benefit of tourists. So, in admitting that, I don't really think I can help you with the information you seek."

Mike stood, and we all followed him. We could tell by the conversation and the look on Mr Eastwood's face that he was terminating the interview. We all said our thanks, shook his hand, and filed out. I reached the car last and, feeling quite dejected, looked back at the lodge to see Mr Eastwood walking towards me. I stopped and waited for him. He whispered to me and slipped me a note. "Goodbye, Miss Leigh, lovely to meet you," he said and then walked off toward the Polo Club, puffing his pipe like a steam engine.

We piled into the car and drove off.

"What was that all about, Bonnie?" Jackson asked me.

"He blew my mind. He said, 'Bran would have wished me to tell you that five of the twelve, including the Tor, were the most sacred.' And then he put this note in my hand. It's a telephone number with the name Broin."

Judith almost drove off the road; she was so shocked.

"Bran? How would he know about him? Did you mention the name on the phone, Mike?"

"No, I certainly did not... I told him nothing, actually," Mike replied, as shocked as we all were. "And Broin is a Celt or Druid name for Raven."

"I think we'd better continue on to Glastonbury, don't you?" Quinn urged.

It was all serious cloak and dagger stuff. We suspected Eastwood was afraid of someone; otherwise, he wouldn't have gone to those lengths to pass on the message. And we debated—why me? Did he have some sort of inherited Druidistic psychic perception that allowed him to identify me as having known Bran, one thousand nine hundred and fifty-four years ago? We were baffled and hoped this person Broin—the Raven—would provide some answers.

CHAPTER XIX

We checked in to The George and Pilgrims Hotel in Glastonbury. Built between 1455 and 1475 by Abbot John de Selwood for pilgrims, it boasted the medieval charms of a world-famous old inn. It was very spooky. In fact, my room had a four-poster bed, and I knew I was bound to see a ghost in it come nightfall.

We met in the downstairs bar for a happy hour drink, and I took the opportunity to use the house phone to call the phone number Eastwood had given me. I was surprised to find it was a local Glastonbury number. It was as though Eastwood knew we'd be coming here. A woman answered the phone, and when I asked for Broin, the phone went dead. I imagined her putting her hand over the receiver while speaking to someone there, perhaps Broin. When a man spoke, I asked if he was Broin. He said he might be and then asked me to identify myself. I told him, and at the mention of Mr Eastwood, the harshness in his voice disappeared, and he agreed to meet me in the morning at the inn for breakfast.

After dinner in the hotel restaurant that night, Judith told Jackson and me that it was a necessity for us to climb the Glastonbury Tor at midnight. We were, after all, as she put it, in the Isle of Avalon and should experience its mystery.

I will never forget that night. It was cold enough to freeze the spots off a Dalmatian dog. There we were, all rugged up, so much so you couldn't even see my face, and off we went trudging up a huge grassy hill towards this strange-looking edifice on the top. There was steam coming out of Jackson's nose and mouth in great puffs like he was a dragon. The overcast skies made everything pitch black, so much so you could hardly see your hand in front of your face and only just make out the eerie Tor silhouetted against the night sky.

When we reached the Tor, the view below was quite breathtaking. Jackson laid a blanket he'd carried, and we sat down to take it in. Jackson had also committed the facts about the Tor to memory.

"The Tor is five hundred and twenty-five feet above sea level. It was built in the 14th century and is all that is left of St. Michael's Chapel. It is now National Trust. There you go, that's the first serving of my trivia feast for this evening."

"Hmm, can't wait for the next instalment. You can really feel something magical about this place, can't you?"

"Yes, it's pretty special."

It was nice to be alone on the hill that night. It allowed us to kiss and cuddle a bit in those icy conditions. Suddenly, the skies cleared, and an entirely new enchantment revealed itself to us: an incredible canopy of stars. With the lights of the villages below and the stars above, it felt like we were caught between two worlds. Then the most extraordinary thing happened—a white mist rolled in and, over the course of a couple of minutes, had blanketed the countryside below us. Now we certainly felt like we were at the entrance to another world or dimension.

"Ah, great timing. Now for my second serving of mystery trivia this evening... if you look into the sky, you can see small clouds that look like they've been made by ripple sole shoes. They are, in fact, footprints in the sky made by the Star Lord."

I could clearly see the footprints and imagined the mystical force that made them. All of a sudden, while I was staring at the heavens, a huge full moon began to rise. I looked back at the mist, and the light of the moon was making it glow ever so slightly.

"We sit at the entrance to the pagan otherworld. So magical is it that the Church built this structure to close it off, to counter its power. At the time of Boudicca, where you see the mist was water... these hills were surrounded by lakes. And you can see the hills appearing from out of the mist now. Count them, and you'll find there are twelve. Look there, that hill over there is Cadbury, you've been there. Now gaze carefully at the space in between the hills filled by the mist and tell me what you see?"

I peered long and hard, and then all of a sudden, I began to recognise shapes—shapes were appearing out of the mist! Then it suddenly dawned on me exactly what I was looking at.

"I think I can see the shape of a bird."

"Yes, it's a phoenix, the ancient sign of Aquarius."

"The zodiac... but how can that be?" I questioned... it was blowing my mind.

"There are twelve signs of the zodiac, twelve hills—the Twelve Hides, in fact. So now does it make sense to you?"

"Yes, but how?"

"Apparently, the ancients placed certain rocks in the ground in shapes of the zodiac. The rocks heat up through the day and then hold the heat into the night. Then, when conditions are perfect, like tonight—lucky for us—the heat from the stones prints the shapes of the zodiac in the low-lying cool mist."

"Unbelievable," I said with tears in my eyes. "How brilliant were the people who created this marvel of nature."

"The same people who built Avebury and Stonehenge, the forefathers of your Queen Boudicca, I expect."

"Star Lord, are your footprints in the sky. Take me, show us peace of mind, far away to a distant galaxy, Star Lord, you and me."

"That was beautiful, Bonnie."

"What?" I asked, mesmerized by the whole experience.

"That poem."

"Oh, that just came to mind—I made it up," I said, and he kissed me. There are few experiences in life that simply steal your breath away, and this I can truly say topped them all for me. Until now, it still brings tears to my eyes just thinking about it. Ah, the majesty of nature... the magic of nature: sometimes it just has to be seen to be believed.

Later that night, I was sound asleep alone in my big four-poster bed when I was awakened abruptly by the presence of someone in my room. The wind was howling outside, the old hotel was creaking, and the shutters flapping in the wind—all signs of a haunting. I sat up in bed, freaked out of my skin, and watched the silhouette of a person, a ghostly apparition, open the door and leave my room. I eventually went back to sleep but not without the ominous feeling I had been visited by the George Hotel ghost.

I was the first of our group to arrive for the buffet breakfast. Soon after, Jackson arrived with Quinn, followed shortly by Mike and Judith. Broin wasn't expected for another twenty minutes or so.

Before recounting our experience on Glastonbury Tor, I told them about my ghostly encounter. Oddly enough, Jackson and Mike had the same experience.

"I don't think it was a ghost," Mike said confidently. "Ghosts don't open and close doors."

"Mine was locked, so how did he get in?" I said.

"Mine too," Jackson admitted.

"I think someone was letting us know they're onto us," Mike said.

"What do you mean, like the Jesuits or someone?" Jackson protested.

"Shhh!" I insisted, looking around at the other twenty or so people now in the breakfast room. Several of them looked awfully suspicious. "Whoever it was might be here," I said in a harsh whisper.

"Whoever it was, we better be on guard," Quinn warned.

"Yes, we can ill afford another attack like in Sydney," Judith added.

"Should we call Daniel?" I proposed.

"Yes, I'll try him after we've spoken with Broin," Jackson concluded.

Just then, an odd-looking man entered the breakfast room, obviously looking for someone. It was difficult to conclude whether it was Broin, but he did look like an out-of-work Druid. I stood and beckoned him.

"Broin?"

He cracked a toothless smile through his ginger beard and took a seat at our table. I made the introductions, and we began chatting. His long, red hair and dark, mysterious eyes gave him an earthly and pagan aura. He spoke gruffly with a Cornish accent, and I felt a deep connection to his soul.

"It's an unusual name you have, Broin. My field is ancient linguistics... I recognise it as Celtic. It means 'the Raven,'" Mike probed.

"Ah, so I've been told. I don't know, it was the name my father gave me, and I've never questioned it. You said Don Eastwood gave you my contact. Why was that?"

"He hasn't called you then?" Jackson asked.

"No, should he have?" Broin replied.

"Not really, just thought he might have told you about us, that's all," Jackson answered.

"We met with Mr Eastwood yesterday at Druid's Lodge," I said. "We are researching the Glaston Twelve Hides, and we thought the Culdees might be able to help us. He passed us on to you."

"Ah, I see. We go a wee bit back, Don and I, but I'm not of his clan."

"Understood. Is there anything you can tell us about the Twelve Hides? We're keen to learn the significance of them to the Druids," Jackson questioned.

Broin leaned back in his chair and fixed his gaze on me, examining me contemplatively. His eyes penetrated deep into my soul, sending chills down my spine.

"She knows," he growled sharply.

"Who? Bonnie?" Judith asked sharply.

"Aye, she knows which of the twelve are sacred. More than me, she knows."

"And just how would Bonnie know that, Mr Broin? She's from Australia, and she's not a Druid," Judith queried.

"Don't matter where you're from, if it's in your blood—and it's in hers. Can't you tell?"

"If she knew the answer, Mr Broin, we wouldn't be asking you, now would we?" Judith said impatiently.

"All I can say is they're not the Glaston Twelve Hides—just the Twelve Hides. And they're far more significant than a grant of land to the Church—that's just religious propaganda. There are three real entrances to the otherworld. I gather that's what you really want to know. One of them is the Tor, the other two are unknown to me. But in saying that, it is likely they could be found by studying the zodiac in the mist."

He stood up to leave.

"Won't you stay for some breakfast, Broin?" I asked.

"Had it at dawn, thanks. I can't help you any more, lassie. That's all I can say... but I will say this: be plurry careful, because there are those who value the pagan way less than we do—as has always been the case. And they will stop at nothing to preserve their religious control."

He maintained a solemn stare at us and then glided out of the room as if he had been nothing more than an illusion.

We all sat aghast, lost for words. Eventually, Quinn broke the silence.

"Well, Broin taught us quite a bit, didn't he?"

"If you mean that I know more than I realise, yes. If you mean to be wary, well, your experience bears testimony to that," I said with unease.

It was all getting a bit too much for Jackson, so he went to phone Daniel.

"Do you think your experience last night on the Tor enlightened you, Bonnie?" Judith asked.

"If I search deep down inside myself, I think I felt we were sitting on a portal that had been capped. It was as though the magic within the hill was being blocked from connecting with the surrounding landscape. If that makes any sense?"

"It makes a lot of sense, Bonnie," Judith said warmly.

"But irrespective of what Broin said, I don't have any answers to our questions," I added remorsefully.

"Perhaps it's something spiritual, Bonnie," Mike suggested.

"Yes, you might have to visit the other eleven hides to see if you make a connection," Quinn proposed.

Jackson returned, sporting a solemn look. He sat down and growled, "Daniel is still out of the country. I'll have to contact Matt. It's hardly security when there's no one to enforce it."

"Let's finish breakfast and then visit the other eleven hides, shall we? It's a lovely day, and, like you said, Quinn, we won't know if Bonnie will be able to connect unless we try," Mike said, attempting to lift our collective spirits.

We went back to our rooms to collect our things in preparation for checking out. When I entered my room and went to the bed to retrieve my packed bag, the door closed behind me. I immediately felt a presence and turned back to the door. A man was standing there, hidden behind the door when I entered.

"You must have the wrong room," I said courteously.

"No, I have the correct room. Sit down, Miss Leigh," he ordered sharply. His voice bristled with suspicion. In the dim light, I could make out his sharp features, dark tailored suit and tie, and military short-cropped blond hair. I detected a Latin accent in his resonant voice.

"You know my name, so who are you and what do you want?" I said blandly.

His thin lips tightened. "I said to sit, Miss Leigh."

"I don't think so. Either identify yourself or I'll call for help," I challenged.

The cold grey eyes became watchful, then he quickly reached inside his coat, pulled out a pistol, aimed it at me, and rasped, "Take a seat, Miss Leigh."

There was no arguing with that. I obliged and sat on the edge of the bed.

"You can call me Gaius. I'm here to personally deliver you a very serious message—so listen to me very carefully, huh? You will leave the UK in two days and return to Australia. You will discontinue researching the gospel of Joseph. Do I make myself clear?"

I looked into his eyes, which were set a little wider apart than average. A scar parted his left eyebrow, adding to his menacing presence. He had me scared.

"Yes, I understand," I stammered nervously. "What happens if I don't comply?"

"The consequences for you will be life-threatening, and for the other members of First Light."

"That's heavy. What gives you the right to make threats like that?"

He gestured towards the gun in his hand. "This... You have two days, Miss Leigh. If you fail to leave, I promise I will find you and use this."

He stood up. He wasn't as tall as his bravado had suggested, maybe five-nine. In a flash, he concealed the gun and slipped stealthily out the door. With my heart beating rapidly, I cautiously approached the door, opened it, and took a sly peek outside. There was no sign of him. I rushed to the next room and frantically knocked on Jackson's door. When he opened it, the shock of the encounter hit me like a ton of bricks, and I collapsed into his arms, shaking like a leaf.

The context of his visitation had cast a gloomy light on everything we were doing. Jackson informed the others once we had gathered in the lobby, ready to leave. Judith reacted unexpectedly, flopping into a chair and fanning herself with a leaflet as though she was about to pass out.

"I can't believe this is happening!" she groaned in despair.

"I don't know what you're panicking about, Judith. It wasn't you Gaius ambushed," Quinn observed in his customary unflappable manner.

"It doesn't matter!" she growled indifferently. "He threatened us all by naming First Light. How on earth did he know about it? Answer me that!"

"I'd imagine it was mentioned in the transcript notes stolen from me in Sydney. This is no different than what happened in Sydney, Judith, except that Bonnie didn't get attacked, and this time the assassin took the time to speak to her. I, of course, wasn't afforded that luxury," Quinn said flippantly.

"It's a very serious threat, Quinn," Mike added gloomily.

"All the more reason why we need security! I'm going to try Matt again," Jackson said crisply, then strode off to the reception to make the call.

CHAPTER
XX

Later that morning, we were on the road, maps on our knees, navigating towards Solsbury Hill. Though occupied with driving with Mike navigating, Judith was still noticeably unsettled by the Gaius incident.

"With Matt arriving tomorrow, Judith, we'll be able to proceed with less concern," Jackson said, trying to reassure her.

"I appreciate that, Jackson, but Gaius gave us only two days to leave. That's cutting it a bit close, don't you think? Look, I'm just as eager as all of you to continue, but not if it means risking my life," Judith argued.

"Look, guys, I understand if you want to back out, but I'm committed. I can't just walk away. So instead of arguing, let's decide now, once and for all, who wants to leave," I proposed.

"This is Upper Swainswick. Take the next left turn, Judith," Mike instructed.

Judith turned the car off the A46 onto a dirt track signposted to Solsbury Hill. The debate was put on hold as we navigated the rough ride to the base of the hill and parked. As we got out of the car, a chilly wind greeted us. I sensed something peculiar about the place, a feeling of déjà vu perhaps, but I kept it to myself. While climbing the hill, the debate resumed.

"I'm not saying I want to quit, Bonnie," Judith insisted. "I'm just saying we need to ensure our safety, that's all."

"We can't guarantee that, Judith," Quinn stated.

"Yes, only Matt can provide that assurance," Jackson pointed out.

As we neared the summit, I started feeling dizzy. I stumbled, and Jackson caught me.

"Are you all right, love?" he asked, concerned.

"There's something here," I mumbled vaguely.

Two standing rocks marked the northeast corner of the hilltop, and long lines in the ground indicated remnants of hill fort ramparts. I staggered over to the standing stones, and when I touched one, I instantly felt better. It was as though the stone had energised me.

"You're connecting with this place, aren't you, Bonnie?" Judith said.

"Yes, I felt it as soon as we started climbing. It was as though all this energy was building inside me, and when I touched this stone, it was discharged, grounded," I claimed.

"Look at that view. That's the River Avon in the southeast, and there's Bath in the southwest," Mike observed.

"This has to be a portal to the underworld. Not as potent as the Tor, perhaps, but just as significant, I'd say. If there is an entrance here, where would it be, Judith?" I asked.

"Either on the eastern side where the sun rises or the west where it sets. Both are special to Druids," she said.

I walked over to the eastern edge of the hill, focusing on my inner feelings. "It's weaker here," I said and then walked west, in the direction of the setting sun. I stopped. "Stronger here."

"That's the northeast... What if the alignment was to the moon and not the sun?" Mike speculated.

"It would depend. The Druids favoured the sun, but the Neolithic Celts favoured the moon, and the Druids were heavily influenced by them, especially in the early days. Didn't the Druids have a calendar based on lunar cycles?" Quinn asked Judith.

"Yes, the Coligny Calendar," she confirmed.

While they were talking, I walked to the northeast edge of the hill.

"The feeling is definitely strongest here," I called to the others.

"Okay, that's two down, ten to go," Jackson said with a chuckle.

In the car, on our way to the next contender, Deerleap Standing Stones near Mendip, Judith spoke up, "Am I the only one with reservations, then?"

"No, I think we all feel threatened, Judith," Jackson replied curtly.

"So, are we all still in this together? All for one, one for all, so to speak?" I proposed.

There was an indefinite nod from them.

"Are all these sites under the National Trust?" Jackson asked, changing the subject.

"Yes," Judith replied hesitantly.

"Then, if we determine the most likely portal, could we get a permit to excavate it?" he further inquired.

"We would need to obtain official approval," Judith answered.

"Judith is the most likely person in the UK to get a permit for a dig," Quinn said respectfully.

"This being England, not exactly known for its expediency but famous for its bureaucracy... How long do you think it would take, Judith?" Jackson questioned.

"Up to ten years," she said casually.

"Thought so," Quinn grumbled with disdain.

"Wait, are you saying that even if we find an entrance to the underworld, we would effectively be barred from opening it?" Jackson said.

"More than likely," Judith said blandly. "But we're used to dealing with such circumstances. You know, someone finds an artefact on their farm, we are permitted to inspect the location but we can't touch anything. It's frustrating, to say the least."

"What if the farmer wants to dig for more buried treasure himself?" I asked.

"If it's his land and not under the National Trust, then he can. But generally, if there's a find of any value or significance, the Trust would be there very quickly to secure it and prevent desecration," Judith clarified.

It was starting to feel like we were automatically backed into a corner. Then Mike added some more thoughts.

"Look, correct me if I'm wrong, but isn't the objective of this exercise to try and ascertain the location of the burials? Once we have narrowed it down, we can focus on the process of obtaining permits. This was never going to be a swift process. Everything in the academic world moves at a snail's pace. Isn't that right, Quinn?"

"True, and speaking of that, we're not getting any younger. Let's get to the next site," Quinn added facetiously.

By late afternoon, I had felt the energy at Solsbury Hill, Burrow Mump, and now we had one last place to check before sunset: Wearyall Hill, closer to Glastonbury. It had been a long day, but at least we felt that we were making progress by eliminating some of the sacred sites. As we approached Wearyall Hill, I began to feel its magnetism. This was the strongest since Glastonbury Tor.

"Boy, this place sure has a vibe," I exclaimed.

"Are you already feeling something, Bonnie?" Judith asked.

"You bet, and it's strong," I confirmed.

"Well, we did save the best for last. According to your account, when Boudicca and Morgan rowed across the lake, it could have been either here or the Tor, but it was unlikely to have been as far as any of the others, including Solsbury Hill, in relation to Cadbury. Let me explain," Mike continued, lecturing us from the book he was holding, the true academic.

"Legend has it that Joseph of Arimathea landed here and rested on his staff, and it sprouted branches and leaves. It is clear that the legend of Joseph was used to extend a shamanic message into modern times, namely that this was yet another important, sacred site for the Church. John of Glastonbury stated that on Wearyall Hill, there was a monastery of holy virgins—the first reference to a women's community in the area. So, Wearyall Hill, also known as the Glastonbury Thorn, was considered by the Church a most sacred site."

"That translates to it being a most sacred pagan site. So, the Church would have capped it," Quinn observed.

"Exactly," Mike agreed.

"I have a gut feeling that Joseph planted his staff on Wearyall Hill because this was where he wanted to be buried or where he wanted to bury his gospel," I said emphatically.

We turned off the Roman Way and parked at the forecourt of the Wearyall Hill House Bed and Breakfast. From there, it was only a short stroll to the hill. As I stepped out of the car and headed towards the track to the hill, the magnetism grew stronger. Climbing the hill became a struggle against passing out; the energy had become overpowering. Jackson noticed I was having trouble and held onto my arm. There was no need to ask if I wanted to stop; he knew I wouldn't.

When we reached the peak, the dizziness ceased and was replaced by a sense of euphoria. The view was absolutely spectacular. In the distance, we could see the town of Glastonbury and the Abbey. Several of the other sacred hills we had visited—the Tor, Chalice Hill, St Edmund's Hill—were also visible in the panorama.

"That is Avalon," Quinn said in awe. "We're looking at Avalon."

In three directions, I could see the flat Moors, once water and marshes. And there, standing tall at the peak of the low hill, about twenty feet tall, was the Holy Thorn—a Hawthorn tree.

"So, this tree supposedly grew from Joseph's staff?" I queried.

"Well, that's what the myth claims. The original tree was destroyed in the 16th century, but this is apparently a cultivar. Every year, since the reign of King James I, it has been a Christmas custom for a sprig of its flowers to be sent to the Sovereign for the decoration of the Royal Family's dinner table," Mike informed us.

"Is that so?" Jackson exclaimed, astounded by the trivia.

I reached out and touched a branch. "I don't feel anything from it." Then I noticed a shape on the ground. "What's that?"

Judith came over, attracted by my pointing. "The remains of a well, I'd expect. Probably originally placed there by monks for the Abbey."

"Maybe, but the Celts often dug a cootie well, thinking that the May tree, as they called it, had healing properties and that the water in the well would be an elixir. Which, incidentally, has been found to be quite true," Mike mentioned casually. "The tree does have healing properties."

The five of us stood in the failing light, looking down at the circular shape in the ground.

"The ancients often placed ritual items in a well," Quinn suggested.

"Who knows what might be in there if it were excavated," Jackson considered.

"You'd never get permission to excavate this in a million years," Judith concluded.

"Great! So why are we bloody-well wasting our time here, then?" I snarled, annoyed. No matter what I believed to be there, we'd never get permission to dig for it—ridiculous.

"Do you feel anything from the well, Bonnie?" Quinn asked.

I reached down and touched the centre of the circular impression in the soil.

"I get a tingling sensation... It travels up my fingers like I'm touching something of low voltage."

"That's a hell of a lot more than you got from any other place!" Jackson declared.

As the sun sank, the bite of the night was felt. We decided to head back to Moore Manor to discuss our findings and our predicament now that we had been threatened by Gaius. Matt was due in tomorrow, so we also wanted to have our facts straight to inform him.

Deep down inside, I was excited by our discoveries. Jackson, Quinn, and I were convinced that there were portals to the underworld in three places—Solsbury Hill, Wearyall Hill, and Glastonbury Tor. I was certain that the gospel was buried at either Glastonbury Tor or Wearyall Hill and leaned toward the Tor for Joseph's remains. When we discussed it further that night around the central hearth in the library at Moore Manor, I couldn't definitively explain why I felt so certain about those locations, other than the mystic connection I seemed to have with them and an intuitive gut feeling. Quinn believed it might be because I had visited them before as Boudicca, and I was experiencing déjà vu. However, Jackson thought that because I had missed witnessing the burials, it had to be something else. Nonetheless, the most pressing question to resolve for now was how to proceed. We all agreed to stick with it despite the threat from Gaius, and we put our security in the capable hands of Matt. The challenge now was determining our next steps. Without a more definitive lead on the whereabouts of the gospel, Judith and Mike wouldn't be able to make a deposition to Cambridge and the National Trust for a permit to conduct an archaeological dig. It seemed we had hit a roadblock.

After dinner, we sat in front of the fire in the drawing room, enjoying a snifter of brandy, when Quinn took the floor, sucking on a cigar.

"We have narrowed the search down to three places, all of them most sacred and all under the protection of the National Trust. Until we have more information, we cannot proceed with uncovering the gospel. However, we now know it is probably in one of those three locations. I suggest we proceed with Judith preparing a deposition to present to the Cambridge Archaeology Department and the National Trust anyway."

"I don't mean to appear negative, but wouldn't that mean exposing our secret?" I countered.

"You're probably right, Bonnie," Quinn said, realising his oversight.

"I think we should have a clandestine dig," Jackson announced.

Mike, who had consumed more brandy than the rest of us and was looking visibly affected, reacted with anger. "That's just not on, Jackson! I didn't join this group to put my reputation at risk!" he slurred.

"Why not?" I said slowly.

"Because it's all I've got, and I'm not about to throw it away on a furtive, illegal endeavour. You three can simply return to your country with your reputations intact, but it's not the same for Judith and myself."

"It was only a thought, Mike. There's no need to get upset," Jackson said, trying to placate him.

"I'm sorry," Mike said, regretful. "I just want to proceed legally, that's all. We already have enough problems with this Gaius character without breaking the law as well."

"I agree with you, Mike," Judith said. "But I have an alternative idea. How about we keep the gospel our secret and only reveal that we wish to search for the remains of Joseph of Arimathea?"

"And the Holy Grail," Quinn added.

"The Holy Grail! What does that have to do with anything?" Mike mumbled.

"That's brilliant!" Judith exclaimed. "You know, I read in the newspaper yesterday at the George Hotel that a comedy group called Monty Python is shooting a movie about the search for the Holy Grail, to be released next year. That's sure to attract plenty of interest in the subject."

"Yes, I see your point. I read a book by Jean Michel Angebert earlier this year entitled The Mystical Origins of Nazism and the Search for the Holy Grail—try saying that after six brandies! Ha! Anyhow, it seems to have struck a chord with a large audience," Mike said, now more positive.

"So we could use all the publicity about the search for the Holy Grail as a cover for our actual search," Quinn said with a sly grin.

"Absolutely!" Judith agreed excitedly.

"I like it," I said.

It seemed we had found a solution to our problem.

CHAPTER
XXI

I had a special smile on my face the next morning at the Moore Manor buffet breakfast. Jackson had surreptitiously slipped into my room during the night, and we'd slept together.

After breakfast, Judith, Mike, and Quinn—the academics—went to work on compiling the submission to Cambridge University for a dig at the three sites in search of the remains of Joseph of Arimathea and/or the Holy Grail. Jackson confided in me that he wasn't confident and still favoured the idea of a covert dig. By mid-afternoon, the academics had come up with a promotional plan to support their submission. Mike and Judith would go to the press and BBC radio with the cover story: the search for the Grail. They figured this would generate public and media attention and provide more substance to the submission. Though we agreed, it meant Jackson and I would be spending more time in the UK, and that wasn't our preferred option. The question was what to use as evidence to support the dig. Jackson had the answer—me.

"Why not tell the story of the regression hypnotherapy but with a slight alteration? Instead of the gospel, we'll call it the grail," he told us.

It seemed like a good idea, but Judith raised a valid point that Gaius would most likely react poorly to me going public. We decided to leave the final decision until we could involve Matt in the discussion, so Jackson and I left to collect him from Heathrow airport.

The deadline Gaius had given me was up, and from now on, we would need to be on high alert. In reality, Gaius could be anywhere, tailing us, stalking us, staking out the manor—it would be up to Matt to provide us protection.

On the way back to the Manor after collecting Matt from

Heathrow, he filled us in on his research. He was convinced Gaius is a member of a secret radical militant branch of the Catholic Church called the Crux Redemptoris. He read us a brief he'd compiled on the order.

"To become a member of the Crux was to bear the heavy cross—to bear the suffering and punishment in order to have a chance to save mankind. They understood that once they vowed to fight the good fight against the evil forces of the Mythos, they realised the heavy physical and mental toll it would take on them. A hideous future of death, suffering, and insanity would befall many of its hardened champions. The society is small and secretive. Although the Vatican has been aware of their existence for centuries, the Holy See has not made any public moves to purge the order. The activities of the Crux Redemptoris have remained discrete enough that the Vatican does not see them as a significant threat or subversion of more Orthodox Church teachings. The Crux, on the other hand, makes every effort so that their activities will not embarrass or openly contradict the Vatican. The Crux is a secret anti-Mythos order originally established by Benedictine abbots of Melk in Austria along with the Benedictine abbey of Montserrat in Spain during the late 18th century. During that time, the leadership of both monasteries came to realise the existence of the Mythos threat. The two abbots had been close friends, and upon revealing their findings to each other, decided to pool their efforts together and establish a clandestine sub-order that would delve into the mysteries of the Mythos threat. Each monastery would train and indoctrinate a dozen or so of its best and brightest, and these men would be sworn to the secret order. The Crux Redemptoris is Latin for Cross of the Redeemer; the name is symbolic. The Crux Redemptoris exists today. The society remains small and secretive, a small network numbering no more than three-dozen clerics at any given time. Even in the sprawling Montserrat monastery, the majority of its monks are not even aware of the existence of this secret order that is right under their nose. Only the head abbots and a few select chosen monastics are sworn into service. They are sworn to protect Catholic ideology at any cost."

"That would explain why I thought Gaius was Latin. He's probably Spanish," I suggested.

"Big chance. They mainly recruit from the Mando de Operaciones Especiales, the Spanish equivalent of the SAS," Matt said.

"So, how do you rate them as adversaries?" Jackson inquired.

"Can't speak from experience, Jacko, but put it this way: anyone that highly trained would be a worry... and with the money and the power of the Catholic Church behind him, this Gaius could well have a God complex."

I don't think that by the time we reached Moore Manor, I was feeling any safer than I had before Matt arrived, now knowing about the Crux Redemptoris and all.

After Matt had informed the rest of the guys about Crux Redemptoris—which, I might add, left Judith looking even more distraught than she had before—we filled him in on our trip to Glastonbury and our subsequent plans.

"Look, I can protect you, but there are no guarantees. This guy would be a trained assassin, and he's already provided us with an exhibition of his ability to track you down. So, if I were you, I'd be seriously weighing up the value of calling his bluff," Matt said grimly.

Well, that certainly threw the cat among the pigeons. Mike started downing brandies like they were going out of style, Judith was transfixed on the fireplace gone with the pixies, Quinn was pacing the floor contemplatively, while Jackson and I sat together on the lounge, watching the whole production.

Quinn suddenly stopped pacing with a look on his wise old face like he'd had a revelation. "Daniel and the lion's den!" he said prophetically. We all stared at him bemused. "You two young ones, along with Matt, should go to Montserrat Abbey in Spain and confront the grand master of the Crux Redemptoris."

"To what end?" Matt questioned.

"Well, no matter what, this is the Order of Saint Benedict, the Black monks. They are governed by the Benedictine Vow, which revolves around five practices of Prayer, work, study, hospitality, and renewal. I know this because I wrote a thesis on the order some years back. I even have a contact for them."

"But Quinn, what would you hope to achieve by meeting them?" Mike asked.

"To call off their bloody dogs! Look, if you enter into a game of cat and mouse, eventually the mouse will get eaten. My philosophy is to take the bull by the tail, and what better place to do that than in Barcelona? In all seriousness, what have we got to lose? They're not going to harm you there," Quinn concluded.

"Ah, there you go—the Mighty Quinn has the answer," Matt said with a huge grin, clearly liking the idea of a few days in sunny Spain.

"It's ridiculous," Mike disputed. "It would be the same as putting your head on the chopping block."

"So do you have an alternative, Mike?" Matt enquired.

Judith was standing in the window bay with her back to us.

"I don't have one, it's just too dangerous," Mike said incredulously.

Judith turned sharply and then slowly delivered her thoughts. "I think it's the only option we have. It's either that or quit altogether. Let's vote on it?"

Mike pulled a disgruntled face and then waved at Wilson, Judith's longstanding butler, for a top-up. Wilson was in his mid-seventies and looked and dressed like an extra from a Hammer horror film. He hobbled around freshening up the drinks in a kind of somnambulistic glide.

We took a vote, and though Mike raised a hesitant finger, we were all in agreement with Quinn's plan.

"I'd feel better about it if Quinn was going. It doesn't make sense that all his knowledge of the Benedictine Order should be left behind," Mike tendered.

"You're absolutely right, Mike. How stupid of me to ignore the obvious. Of course, I'll go... As a matter of fact, if you're fine with leaving tomorrow, I'll begin making contacts. There is a branch of the order here in London," Quinn said.

"Wait, does that mean we're going to expose the truth to them?" I queried.

"I think we have to assume they, I mean Gaius, knows about the gospel because it was mentioned in the transcript stolen from me."

"But that means they don't want it found, doesn't it?" I said.

"That's true, Bonnie. If we open discussions about the gospel, it will surely be about them taking possession of it," Judith said, holding her chin in a contemplative pose.

"Lie to them," Matt growled. "These bastards have threatened you, so two can play that game. You're not going to give up, are you? So the idea is to get them off your back, so promise them anything, use what they can offer..."

"And then rip them off?" Jackson questioned.

"All of my instincts tell me that would be fatal, Matt," Judith said tightly. "One minute you're telling us we're up against a fearful foe that would stop at nothing to achieve its ends, and the next you're suggesting we challenge them."

"I'll take no part in that!" Mike demanded.

"No-one said anything about challenging them or Gaius. Why do you panic at any opportunity? Maybe you should ease up on your alcohol consumption, Mike," Jackson responded curtly, quite out of character.

It was getting hard to get a word in edgewise. It was heating up so much that I just stood with my hands on my hips and scolded them all. "Listen here, we'll get nowhere bickering! I agree with Jackson. Perhaps we should limit the booze talk and get on with addressing the facts."

That took Mike over the top, and he stormed angrily out of the room, slamming the door behind him. There was a pregnant pause while we all considered his actions.

"Now you've done it," Judith said. "I've seen him like this before. Once he gets his feelings hurt, he'll just walk away from the project and hit the bottle."

"So be it," Matt growled. "A man of his age should know when he's had enough."

"I'll go and speak with him," I offered.

"No, Bonnie. I think Mike needs some time alone to come to terms with his own actions. We should continue our discussions," Quinn said in a resigned voice.

We resolved that afternoon for Quinn, Jackson, Matt, and me to fly to Spain to propose a deal with the Abbot Primate for him to pass on to the Crux Redemptoris. We would use the bluff that we are searching for the Holy Grail, but should we find anything else, they would be the first to know. It was a risk we agreed was worth taking. It would all come down to the Abbot Primate's reaction to the proposal. In the meantime, Judith would prepare a media campaign. It would be double-edged in that she would academically validate Jackson's regression hypnotherapy technique with me, the subject, showing that experts had documented my ability to contact Queen Boudicca in 61 A.D. We knew the story was so outrageous it would easily generate the publicity we were after. Then, once we had created enough public groundswell, Judith would submit the application to the Department of Archaeology at Cambridge for a dig at three sites: Glastonbury Tor, Solsbury Hill, and Wearyall Hill. It was then expected that Cambridge Archaeology would present their endorsement of the proposal to the National Trust. If all went according to plan, the media campaign would assist in prompting a positive decision from the National Trust. At last, we had a strategy.

That evening, Jackson drove me into the nearby town of Milton Keynes on a mission to find Mike. Old Wilson said he'd seen him walk off towards town while we were still having our meeting. That was three hours ago, and it was now dark, so I thought of going on a search and rescue mission.

On our way to Milton Keynes, driving along the High Street of Stony Stratford village, I noticed an old Tudor-style pub called The Old George Inn and figured it looked like the perfect place for Mike. We pulled up and went inside for a look-see.

It was happy hour, and the main bar was filled with boisterous locals. I scanned the crowd, but there was no sign of Mike. Jackson led me into the lounge with its white walls and rough, dark, square-cut wooden columns holding up the 16th-century exposed beam ceiling. There, in the corner of the room, alone at a table, sat Mike, his head in his hands. We fought our way through the plethora of patrons, and when we reached him, Jackson offered him a cigarette. He took it and returned a wry smile. I sat next to him while Jackson went to get drinks. I was surprised that he was sober. Before I could say a word, he held up a hand in a "don't say anything" gesture.

"I need to apologise, Bonnie," he said with conviction. "This isn't the first time the spirit in the bottle has seen fit to tangle my senses, and I guess it won't be the last. We all have our demons," he admitted dispiritedly.

I felt sympathy for him. He was alone. All he had was his work, a smoke, and a drink.

"You're not wrong, mate," I said warmly. "And recognising those demons is half the battle. It seems to me, to your credit, you've done that."

"I'm no good for anyone, Bonnie. I turn to the bottle the moment I'm confronted by a big issue... I... I—"

I could see tears welling up in his eyes, so I took his hand and held it. "It's all right, mate. I can see how being a dedicated scholar would take an emotional toll on anyone. Is there something troubling you deep down inside? you can talk to me."

With his other hand, he cupped my hand that was holding his. I could feel it quivering like a captured bird. He fixed his troubled eyes on mine.

"Bonnie, I don't know if I'm camp or not."

The disclosure hit me hard, and I wasn't sure how to respond. I hadn't dealt with someone coming out of the closet before, although there was plenty of it going on at the time, from both sexes.

"Is there something you feel with a man that is different from being with a woman?" I asked delicately.

"I don't know. I've rarely been with a woman... mostly, I just masturbate three or four times a day, and that satisfies me sexually but not mentally."

"That many!" I said, surprised.

"Oh, it used to be a lot more when I was younger."

It wasn't what I meant... I thought it was a bit excessive. "Um, I see," I said awkwardly. "Have you been with a man?"

"Only when I was a boy at public school when the headmaster abused me."

"He what?"

"Oh, boarding school, you know, when I was sent to him for punishment, the cane... he made me remove my pants, and then he masturbated me before the caning, or sometimes he'd make me masturbate while he caned me."

"Christ, that would seriously twist anyone's head, Mike. Have you been with a girl?"

"Um, no, I... I—."

Just then, Jackson arrived with our drinks, causing Mike to immediately clam up. But as a psychologist and being incredibly perceptive, Jackson knew instinctively that we had been in a deep discussion, and his arrival had created an awkward moment. So he sat down and placed his hand over mine, still holding Mike's.

"Mike, there's nothing we can't talk about, mate. We are both here because we care about you," Jackson said warmly.

Mike instantly burst into tears, jumped up, and rushed to the bathroom. I quickly filled Jackson in, and surprisingly, he had suspected Mike's problem. After a couple of minutes, Mike returned, all freshened up. We talked at length about his problem, and he agreed to let Jackson help him. He knew he needed to decide whether to be openly gay or heterosexual. We didn't know it then, but that night would provide an opportunity to put his sexuality to the test. After an hour or so explaining the outcome of the meeting to Mike, we decided to head back to the manor. Mike agreed with our plan to go to Spain and work with Judith on the media campaign and the Cambridge submission.

The three of us walked happily arm in arm out of the pub, bound for the car park. When we reached the car, Jackson unlocked my door and then went to the driver's side to get in. I was inside, Mike was in the back seat, but Jackson didn't get in. Instead, I heard a loud thump, and his face smacked into the driver's side window. Then he slid down the window, leaving a trail of blood behind. I screamed. Mike jumped out of the car, and I noticed someone running off into the darkness.

"Bonnie, quick!" Mike cried.

I got out of the car and rushed around to find Mike sitting on the ground, cradling Jackson's head in his lap, blood gushing from an ugly gash next to his right ear. He had been struck with something.

CHAPTER
XXII

Mike and I helped Jackson, with a bandaged head, through the big oak front doors of Moore Manor. We were greeted with surprise, shock, and horror. Everyone knew it was a warning from Gaius. Aside from being angry at being blindsided, Jackson was okay. It was actually Matt who was most annoyed. He felt it had been remiss of him to allow us to go to the village without his protection, and he was right. Once again, the event had reduced Judith to a blubbering mess. Mike helped her upstairs for a rest.

An hour later, Mike came back down to the drawing room, and I noticed something different about him. Jackson had also gone upstairs for a rest, so Mike sat beside me on the lounge and whispered in my ear.

"I just made love to Judith, and it was quite wonderful."

The news shocked me. I hadn't expected him to say that at all. "Um, good one Mike. Does that help clear things up for you?"

"Well, put it this way, it was better than doing it with myself, but I think I might still need to experience a man to be certain."

"Hmm, might I suggest you avoid approaching this like researching a theory and instead just enjoy what turns you on?"

"Yes, yes, you're probably quite right Bonnie. Thank you. I think I'll take your advice and go back upstairs for seconds." He got up to leave.

"Just stay out of Jackson's room, please. He's off-limits!" I joked.

Just after Mike left, Matt got up from his chair, went over, and leaned forlornly against the fireplace.

"I think I need to deal with this Gaius character first," Matt mumbled angrily to himself but loud enough for us to hear.

Quinn looked up from the book he was reading. "What, before we leave for Spain tomorrow?" he said.

"No, but you can be sure as hell he'll follow us there. I need to draw him out so I can teach the bastard a bloody-good lesson," Mike growled, bristling with anger.

Remembering the physique of Gaius, I thought a showdown between him and Matt would be a mismatch, but he had it coming after what he'd done to my darling Jackson. Speaking of my man, in the morning, I replaced his bandage with a plaster, so he at least looked like he'd been in a fight as opposed to a war. Mike and Judith dropped us off at Heathrow, and we said our goodbyes. It was a delicate, almost awkward moment. We all knew what we were up against, but even so, Judith had worry written all over her face.

We arrived in Barcelona at noon and checked into the majestic Hotel Casa Fuster. An hour later, we were sitting under a big umbrella on the beautiful Blue View Terrace overlooking the swimming pool, sipping cocktails. This was a life I could easily handle. There's a lot to be said for hotel living. There was music playing, and I recognised the tune.

"That's the song that just won the Eurovision Song Contest."

"It was held at Brighton... who won?" Jackson asked.

"It was a band from Sweden called ABBA. The song is 'Waterloo'."

"Didn't Australia have an entry?" the Professor queried.

"Yes, Olivia Newton John, but she represented the UK... came 4th," I said.

"How's that?" Matt complained.

"She was born in England," I said.

"I didn't know she was a Pom," Jackson said, surprised.

We had no idea at the time of the pop phenomenon that ABBA would become massive over the next decade.

"I'll have to phone Dean Holloway tonight," Quinn said, putting on his sunnies. "Get him to wire us some more funds. We're getting a little short."

"You should get one of those Diners Club credit cards. They're all the rage," I said.

"Yes, I've noticed since we've been in Europe how they have a propensity to accept plastic over cash," Quinn chuckled.

"I've got one. It's great and seriously handy," Matt said. "There'll come a time when it will be too dangerous to carry cash at all, and we'll all be carrying plastic."

"How Orwellian," Jackson growled, squinting in the sun's glare but enjoying its heat.

"'1984' is only ten years away... Soon we'll be merely a numeral in a binary system," Quinn said despondently.

"So, what's the plan, man?" I asked Quinn.

"We'll meet with Monsignor Sergio Wolfe, Abbot Primate of the Benedictine Confederation, at his office in Montserrat Abbey at ten in the morning," Quinn said.

"Is it far?" I asked.

"About an hour's drive up in the mountains. We'll need to take a taxi. The view should be extraordinary," Quinn acknowledged.

"Good. Now I can spend the afternoon floating in the pool and soaking up rays." With that, I slipped out of my white terry-towel hotel robe and dived into the cool azure waters of the pool. Don't ask me why I'd brought a bikini with me to the UK in wintertime, but Jackson would probably tell you I packed everything bar the kitchen sink.

After dinner, we went to our rooms. As a safety precaution, we had doubles. Jackson and I shared one room, Matt and Quinn the other. Matt was optimistic that Gaius wouldn't strike again before our meeting with the Abbot Primate, which resulted in us having a peaceful night.

But it wasn't so peaceful the next morning navigating the hairpin bends and curves leading up to the summit of Mount Montserrat. We had to stop halfway to the summit for me to throw up. Way too many bends for my delicate stomach. It was a terrible waste of a fantastic breakfast. However, once we had arrived, it was well worth it. The panoramic view of Barcelona with the blue Mediterranean as the backdrop, all framed in a clear blue sky, was simply breathtaking.

A monk met us at the entrance of the huge complex and introduced himself as Father Gabriel. If you were to look up the word "monk" in the dictionary, I'm sure you'd find the guy's photograph—he was the classic Friar Tuck. He led us across the plaza, past the entrance to the basilica, all the while giving us a heavily accented tourist spiel so slick I figured he must have been delivering it since the place was built. I did learn, however, that it was originally a pagan Roman temple dedicated to Venus and then built into a Christian Abbey by hermit monks in the eighth century, only to be destroyed in 1811 by Napoleonic cannons. After that, it was rebuilt as the Benedictine monastery we see today.

Father Gabriel led us up three flights of ancient stairs. Quinn was struggling. It was stiflingly hot and a difficult climb for the old fella. I took his arm, and we ascended the final flight of stairs, arriving at a pair of regal-looking mahogany doors. Quinn and I exchanged surprised looks, knowing we had been led deep into the secret bowels of the monastery few others would ever experience.

Friar Tuck knocked three times on the big red doors and then, after a sharp nod to us, took flight back down the stairs with his cape streaming out behind him like a huge bat. The doors opened, and we were greeted by an ordinary-looking priest in a black habit, wearing a large silver cross on a chain around his neck.

He looked directly at Quinn and said with a thick German accent, "Professor Harris, I presume?"

They shook hands. "Monsignor Wolfe, I'd be happy to sit down after climbing that stairway to heaven," Quinn said with a wry smile.

I chuckled at his reference to the Led Zeppelin hit of three years ago, not sure that the Monsignor got the joke. After introductions, the Monsignor led the way to a simple cane lounge setting in his austere office. He looked about the same age as Quinn and just as alert. The room was decorated frugally, no paintings, nothing lavish. I expected it to be in the puritanical tradition of the Benedictine order. But the view out of the big bay windows was to die for.

We sat down and waited for him to open the discussion.

"Can I offer you something to drink, perhaps?" he asked politely.

"No, we'll be fine, thank you. We very much appreciate you taking the time to meet us today, Monsignor," Quinn said.

"I'm honoured by your presence, Professor. Your paper on the history of our order holds pride of place in my personal library."

"I'm flattered, Your Worship."

"Now," he looked at me, "how can I be of help?"

"Dr Bolt here has been using hypnotic regression to study the dreams or the subconscious mind of our Bonnie Leigh here," Quinn said.

"How interesting," the Monsignor exclaimed, sitting back in his comfy chair with the tips of his fingers formed into a steeple.

Harris continued to explain, "Yes, a number of academics, including myself, have been monitoring the study with interest. Under hypnosis, Bonnie was Queen Boudicca of Britain in 61 A.D. The content of the transcripts of recordings made of Bonnie while under hypnosis have been validated by experts, so we have no doubt as to the authenticity of the experience."

"I didn't know that was possible," the Monsignor said, obviously impressed. "I have, of course, read how spiritual possession has occurred in the past, but this is quite fascinating. Please, continue."

"I won't bore you with the details, but the long and short of the research revealed that Joseph of Arimathea did, as the Church has maintained, see out his days in England and was interred there with the Holy Grail. We know this because Boudicca was at the burial, and therefore Bonnie witnessed it."

Monsignor Wolfe was goggle-eyed. He shook his head in amazement and said, "Absolutely extraordinary, but I don't see how I can be of help."

Matt spoke up, "We came to you, sir, because both Miss Leigh and Dr Jackson have been told to discontinue their research under a threat from a person we believe to be a member of the Order of the Crux Redemptoris."

"The Crux Redemptoris? Why would they take exception to your research?" Monsignor Wolfe said, his attitude now blatantly defensive.

"We can't answer that, sir, but you can see by the bandage on Dr Bolt's face that the threat is real." He paused for the Monsignor to observe Jackson. "We want the threats and the violence to stop, and we're here to ask for your help in that regard," Matt said sternly.

The Monsignor stood and, still holding his fingers in an apex, paced the room contemplatively. He stopped.

"Mr. Ryan, I assume you are a bodyguard?"

"No, I'm an Interpol agent, sir."

"Is this an Interpol matter?"

"No, I have taken a personal interest."

"The Crux Redemptoris is sworn to protect the Church against mythos. In saying that, they do not employ violence as a means to censor research, so I find your claim surprising, though I, of course, have no reason to doubt you. I can only assume the Crux Redemptoris believe there is something in your research they regard extremely provocative for them to react in the manner you have outlined."

"Wouldn't it be more in keeping with the values of the Church for the Crux Redemptoris to raise this with us before issuing threats?" Quinn asked.

"A valid consideration, Professor, one that I will definitely take up with the Crux Redemptoris... but I will first need some assurances from you."

The mood had changed. We exchanged looks. There was an awkward unease.

"We are here to resolve this matter, Your Reverence," Quinn added politely.

The Monsignor took his seat but kept his fingers in an apex. "Are you certain you are telling me everything about your research,

Professor?" His bushy eyebrows sneered.

"There is much I could tell you, Your Reverence, but it is mostly academic. Anything specific?" Quinn asked.

"Well, there are certain reservations the Church has long had in relation to Joseph of Arimathea. For instance, it is believed he left the Holy Land for France after the resurrection of our Lord, with the Magdalene."

"I understand, but Miss Leigh was seeing Britain in 61 A.D. through the eyes of Queen Boudicca, not Joseph of Arimathea. Our research is limited to her view only."

"Yes, Professor, but the Church would prefer, shall we say, to contain any presumed history of Joseph of Arimathea so as not to confuse its doctrine."

"Our interest is only to corroborate a historical connection between Queen Boudicca and Joseph of Arimathea and then, perhaps, to uncover the Holy Grail. The only historical reference to Boudicca to date is that of Tacitus, and we know how biased that can be."

"And there is also Dio Cassius as a cross-reference," the Monsignor said knowingly.

"I see you are up on your knowledge of the Roman occupation," Quinn smiled.

"My intent is to legitimise my experience under hypnosis, Monsignor," I said.

He fixed his dark, beady eyes through his bushy eyebrows on me. They were brooding, all-seeing eyes, and I could feel them penetrate right down to my very soul. I needed to hold his stare. I knew he was judging whether I was speaking the truth. We were all detouring around the real truth, including him, but it was necessary for us to hold our ground. After what felt like an eternity, he lowered his hands and glanced at Quinn. With a big imitation smile, he slowly rose to his feet and held out a hand.

"Leave it with me, Professor Harris. Where are you staying and for how long?"

"We will be at the Hotel Casa Fuster until we have clearance from you to resume our work," Quinn replied truthfully.

"Ah, a lovely hotel... well, I hope so. There may be a caveat or two, but we shall see. Please enjoy your stay, Miss Leigh, Dr Bolt, Professor Harris, and indeed, Mr Ryan."

We didn't stay to take in the Gregorian choir or the other marvels of the basilica. We were keen to get out of there, so we took the cable car down the mountain, then the train back to Barcelona. Quinn wasn't confident we would get the result we were after. He felt Monsignor Wolfe was being way too cagey. It was obvious everything to do with Joseph of Arimathea was under Church scrutiny. They feared the gospel being unearthed and its contents revealed to the world. Matt was in full agreement with Quinn. He didn't believe the meeting went well at all. Jackson and I were a little more optimistic.

CHAPTER
XXIII

We took lunch by the hotel pool. I was keen to get into the water out of the heat of the day. Matt was adamant that we needed to stay together after we had exposed our intentions to the Monsignor and the Crux Redemptoris, so the three of them had to sit under an umbrella while I frolicked about in the water. After my swim, I suggested a trip to the Picasso Museum. I had read in the hotel tourist guide that there were 4,251 Picasso works on exhibit there—the largest collection in the world.

That evening, by the time we finished dinner, it was near 10 p.m., and we were beat—it had been a long day. Before going up to our rooms, Matt checked the front desk for messages and found one for Quinn. It was confirmation from Dean Holloway that funds had been wired to Quinn's account. We would have preferred to have heard from Monsignor Wolfe, but at least our budget had been topped up.

On the way to our respective rooms, Matt and I were walking along the hotel corridor together when he took hold of my arm and stopped me.

"Bonnie, I want you to stay with Jackson and Quinn tonight. I'll take your room."

"Why? Are you expecting trouble?"

"Just a precaution."

"You sure it's not that sixth sense of yours?" I asked knowingly.

"Let's just say I'm uneasy since letting the cat out of the bag."

Jackson and I collected our things and left Matt in our room. Quinn's room was on the next floor up. With Matt on high alert, we double-latched our door and then hit the hay. I knew Matt felt that if there was going to be any violent repercussions to our meeting, me being the conduit between the past and present made me the obvious target.

In the morning, we waited at Café Vienés for Matt to have the buffet breakfast with us, but he failed to show. Jackson figured he was probably on the phone to his office. We decided to take breakfast, thinking he'd eventually turn up. After we finished and he still hadn't shown, we decided to check his room—I still had a key.

When we got there, we found a 'do not disturb' sign hanging on the door handle. Thinking he'd slept in, we opened the door and went in. The curtains were drawn, and in the dim light, we could see him sitting in a chair with his head down, asleep, with a pistol in his hands rested on his lap. Jackson switched on the light, and then the picture became gruesomely clear. The front of his shirt was drenched with blood. Jackson rushed over and lifted his head—his throat had been cut from ear to ear—he was dead—murdered.

The police were called, and we were taken to Saint Marti Police Station and questioned before statements were taken. We were numb. We had lost a good friend. Matt had read it right and taken the fall for Jackson and myself—it was supposed to be me slumped in that chair with my throat sliced open. We knew the identity of the perpetrator, but we couldn't say anything. Because of Matt's status as an Interpol agent, the investigation into his murder was intense. A member of the Australian Consulate turned up at the police station. It was a terrible state of affairs. We hadn't had time to get our stories straight, there were just so many discrepancies—and that dragged it out even longer.

After an entire day of interrogation, we were released to return to our hotel, but they retained our passports. The agent from the Australian consulate drove us to the hotel, and we talked more candidly with him in the hotel's Café Vienés over a coffee. He had run checks on us and was satisfied with our stories. He promised to have our passports returned in the morning.

Once he'd gone, we went to our room, and Quinn telephoned Monsignor Wolfe. But it was to no avail: he was informed in no uncertain terms that the Abbey Primate had left Barcelona for his main office at the Vatican. We knew right then and there we had made the wrong decision in exposing ourselves to the Crux Redemptoris. It had been a setup. Quinn was distraught, blaming himself for Matt's death. The phone rang—it was Daniel Boyd. He had just returned from a mission abroad and learned about Matt. He told us to sit tight tonight, our passports would be returned in the morning, and for us to take the first flight back to London once we had them. We agreed to call him back with our flight details. He told Jackson he'd collect us from Heathrow. We tossed around whether to phone Judith and Mike, but finally agreed it would be best not to panic them.

"Sydney up ahead, ETA twenty minutes," Cleo announced.

On the other side of the darkness that was the expanse of Heathcote National Park, twinkled the many diamonds that made up the lights of Sydney. The highway cut a four-lane swathe through the 26.79 square kilometres of parkland towards the metropolis. Cleo slowed the car according to the speed limit from 100 km/h to sixty.

"Did Gaius kill Matt?" Cleo asked.

"We never found that out," Jackson said from behind us.

"After we got back to London, Daniel told us it was in our best interests to desist with our research. Judith and Mike, now an item, both agreed. We returned to Australia to surreptitiously continue our research and to expand First Light to what it is today."

"And what about Quinn?"

"Sadly, our old friend and mentor passed away back in 1999, but just like us, he never gave up on the quest," I assured Cleo.

"It meant that much to him... and what about Mike and Judith?"

"Still members... they, like us, have been waiting all this time for you to come of age," I said.

"Wow, it's a bit like I'm the second coming."

"More so to us, Cleo. You're everything we've lived for all this time. You represent any hope of ever justifying the loss of Matt, and the years we've invested into believing our interpretation of the legend of Boudicca," Jackson said.

The thought of all the loss and the passion it had taken—the self-doubt and the fear—had tears welling up in my tired old eyes. I felt the gentle touch of Jackson's fingers on my shoulder, and I knew he was feeling the same.

Silence prevailed in the car for the last twenty minutes it took us to cruise through Sans Souci, Pagewood, Maroubra Junction, to finally reach Mo's home in Kingsford.

We pulled into the driveway, and Cleo honked the horn. Mo came rushing out from inside and threw her arms around her daughter and then us. I then helped Jackson cart our bags inside the house.

Mo had lost her husband, Graham, to cancer years ago but continued living in the family home. Cleo was her only child, except for Ralph, a twelve-year-old Doberman.

Mo, who everybody claimed looked like me only with blonde hair, something I've always vigorously refuted, was happy we had told Cleo the entire story, including the nasty bits. Being understandably possessive of her daughter, she had stressed about her taking over from me, but over time she had come to terms with the inevitability of it. After we lost Mum and Dad within a year of each other, then Mo lost Graham, we'd bonded closer than we'd ever been. I think that helped things no end. Jackson and Mo got on like a house on fire, which helped as well—but then again, there was nothing to dislike about my darling man. It was odd that we lost Mum, Dad, Graham, and Quinn all in the same year: a bad year, 1999. We hoped that the turn of the century would bring us more positivity, and I suppose it did. Maybe now that Cleo is the right age and we are only days away from making contact with Boudicca again, it's right to feel we have finally caught sight of the light at the end of the tunnel.

I was checking my email on an iPad when I came across a message from Mike and Judith. They seemed anxious to know if Cleo had agreed to join First Light. Sending them an affirmative response would surely make their day. Over the years, Mike had become a computer expert. By the time he and Judith got married in 1979, Mike had reached the limit of his progress in ancient linguistics and decided to switch careers, delving into writing computer code. By the 1990s, he had gained a reputation as an expert programmer. When the Internet revolution hit full swing in the mid-1990s, he built a secret website for First Light and had been administering it ever since. Normally, we would chat daily on the website forum because it's secure, and I, being old-fashioned, haven't yet succumbed to social media like Facebook, Instagram, Messenger, Skype, or Facetime. I just don't feel comfortable talking to someone on a screen. However, I must admit that the Internet has revolutionised international communications. It used to cost the university a fortune in long-distance telephone and fax bills each month just to stay in touch with London, but now communication is free. It just goes to show how much money telcos had been making all those years by charging us for nothing but hot air. As soon as Mike and Judith received my affirmative response about Cleo, we had already planned for them to be on standby for a potential visit.

The next morning, we all woke up early, eager to embark on the venture. Cleo was thrilled by the prospect of regression, and I must say her enthusiasm was contagious. Jackson and I felt a bit nervous since there was a chance she might not establish a connection. There was no guarantee that Cleo had the same genes as mine or that she would be able to home in on Boudicca in 61 A.D. Jackson's hypnotic suggestions would assist, but success was never guaranteed; it was all part of the experiment. That's why Mike and Judith were put on standby. If we were successful, we had planned to catch the next flight to London, with a two-day buffer before the 61 A.D. burial of Joseph and the gospel. With Gaius having made contact, it was even more crucial for us to be in London. Once we learned the exact location of the burials, we would need to act swiftly. Judith had secured the official permits and prepared the necessary equipment, despite the strict limitations imposed by the National Trust. We knew we would have to find a way on the day.

Mo had arranged the office with a couch and three chairs specifically for the hypnosis session. The lighting was dimmed to Jackson's satisfaction, and all extraneous noise was silenced. We had chosen not to use our offices at Sydney University since it was crucial to keep our research with Cleo completely confidential. I held Cleo's iPad, ready to record the event. Mo was nervously chewing on what remained of her fingernails while seated in a chair. Jackson took his place in front of the couch, embodying the archetypal psychoanalyst, and Cleo lay stretched out on the couch, the ideal patient. We were prepared to attempt making contact with Boudicca.

I worried that, unlike me, Cleo hadn't experienced any nightmares—or at least she couldn't recall any. For the past twelve months, she had been living alone in Canberra, so there was no one to confirm whether she had spoken in a foreign language during her sleep or not. Jackson had always maintained, even before he hypnotised me, that I had already established a direct channel to Boudicca through my dreams. However, the question remained: would that make a difference with Cleo? Jackson was sceptical, unconvinced that the ability to connect with Boudicca was an inherited trait. Unfortunately, we never had the chance to test sister Mo to verify that hypothesis. When Jackson, Quinn, and I returned to Australia in June 1974, one of our first tasks was to try and locate Mo. Given that she was a year younger than me, we thought that if we regressed her at the right time, she might possess the necessary genes to connect with Boudicca. Perhaps she could have witnessed the burial of Joseph. However, Mo was on a surfing safari in Queensland and impossible to reach. I had informed my parents to let her know that I needed to speak with her urgently. But when she did call, they forgot. Well, I've always assumed that Dad didn't want her involved in what he considered my futile pursuits, so it conveniently slipped his mind. Therefore, we'll never know whether Mo could have reached Boudicca or not. However, I do know that she has never experienced the vivid nightmares that I have had. I'm certain that her numerous bed partners would have mentioned it if she had suddenly begun speaking in some strange language in her sleep, as I have.

In any case, when Jackson began regressing Cleo, his voice almost hypnotised me. My vision became blurry, and I struggled to stay awake. Mo noticed my drowsiness and grasped my hand, grounding me and preventing me from slipping under. It made me wonder what would happen if we both went under at the same time—could we meet? It took Jackson six attempts to induce hypnosis in Cleo, likely due to her heightened excitement.

CHAPTER
XXIV

It was a relief when Cleo finally went under and began speaking in what Jackson and I immediately recognised as Celtic. It brought tears to my eyes, and I tightly gripped Mo's hand as we sat transfixed, listening to Cleo speaking for the next two hours in a language we couldn't understand.

Eventually, Jackson gently woke her. "Cleo, you're back. Are you feeling okay?" he asked.

She sat up and rubbed her eyes. I knew all too well the bewildering feeling she was experiencing—a sense of disorientation upon awakening from a deep sleep. I had jokingly referred to it as the Rip Van Winkle Effect or RVW for short. Jackson took it seriously and began using the term as an acronym for "reviving from hypnosis" in his academic papers.

"Wow, what a trip!" Cleo exclaimed excitedly.

"Just stay calm and try to recount what happened from the beginning," Jackson softly advised her.

Cleo relaxed back onto the couch and took a deep breath. "Well, the first thing I saw was a man in brown armour running away from me—he was afraid. So, I chased him with my sword, wanting to kill him. I caught up to him and sliced at his ankles, cutting his tendons. He fell and rolled onto his back, surrendering like a dog. He looked up at me with pleading eyes, which only fuelled my anger. I slashed with my blade and cut his throat open. He frantically grabbed at the wound, but blood gushed through his fingers. It was over for him. I left him rolling on the ground, making choking sounds, and went after another man who was running from the fight. There was fighting all around me... my warriors were fierce and wild, attacking Roman soldiers dressed in red skirts, brown leather armour, and helmets. It was chaotic. Then, a wild-looking man approached me, his blue-painted skin caked with dried blood, his long red hair matted with blood."

"Boudicca!" he bellowed above the clamour. "Verulamium is yours!"

"It had to be Domnall, " Cleo said, "after hearing so much about him, I couldn't wait to meet him. He looked exactly as I had imagined."

It was a complete success. Cleo had connected with Boudicca. She was fighting alongside Domnall in the Battle of Verulamium and would meet Morgan later that day. Jackson, Mo, and I were absolutely thrilled. The long wait and hard work had paid off.

Later, on the back porch, as we lounged in big comfy chairs overlooking the swimming pool, I raised a glass of wine to Jackson. "Cheers, my love. It was all worth the wait."

We clinked glasses, and Jackson peered at me over his sunglasses. "I just wish Quinn was here to witness it."

The sun was shining brightly, and the gentle hum of Sydney's ambiance underscored our excitement.

"He would be proud of us," I said happily. "Oh, I sent the sound file of the session to Mike."

"They'll be over the moon," Jackson chuckled. "Cleo did exceptionally well."

Just then, Mo joined us, carrying a tray of snacks. "I'm so proud of her," she beamed.

"You have every right to be, Mo. The contribution she's about to make to mankind will be immeasurable. She was born for this," I assured her.

"I know you're right, Jackson, but I can't help worrying about her safety..." Mo admitted, her tendency to worry surfacing.

"Her safety is our number one priority, Mo," I reassured her.

Mo informed us, "Your e-tickets arrived. Your flight to London is at 7 p.m. I wish I could go with you."

"Don't worry, Mo. We'll be back before you know it," I said, affectionately squeezing her hand.

"Dad used to say that—'before you know it,'" she mumbled with a sad smile, holding back tears.

"Sit down and have a glass of wine with us, love," I suggested.

Just then, Cleo emerged from the house, her face pale as if she had seen a ghost.

"Are you alright, Cleo?" I asked, concerned.

She sat down in a chair and crossed her long, sexy legs, wearing shorts, a small singlet top, and bare feet. Her long, bushy red hair was tousled from being in bed, and she still had sleep in her eyes.

"I know you told me not to, but I forgot and checked my email. There was another message from Gaius," she said, biting her bottom lip.

Mo's normally sun-tanned face turned ashen grey at the mention of his name. "What did he say?" I inquired.

"He said, 'See you in London.' How does he know?" Cleo whined.

"You have to put it out of your mind, Cleo. Don't log on again. We don't want him to know our location," I advised.

"Oh no, does he know where I live?" Mo reacted. "You have to cancel everything!"

"No, Mo, he's just trying to scare us. There's no way he can trace us unless we use a cellphone, social media, or a website he has bugged," Jackson assured her.

"But you can't go with—" she was getting worked up.

"Hush, Mo. There's no turning back now, you know that," I urged her. "We're flying out tonight at 7 p.m., so you have plenty of time to pack," I said.

Cleo stood up and put her hand on her mother's shoulder. "It's alright, Mom. This is what I want to do," she said, giving her mom a peck on the cheek.

Mo nodded, and I squeezed her hand a little tighter. Cleo then slipped off her shorts and top, revealing a string bikini underneath. Her gorgeous, youthful body caught our attention.

"It's time for a quick dip, then," she said with a playful smile, her colour returning, and she dived into the pool.

"You must be so proud of her, Maureen. It must be comforting to see her grow into the stunning young lady you must have imagined when she was little," Jackson remarked.

"Yes, there was a time after I lost Graham when I could have given up on her. She loved her dad so much. It was a huge loss for a ten-year-old. But look at her now, I couldn't be happier with her, Jackson," Mo replied.

"She's bright, loving, caring, and beautiful, Mo. A mother couldn't ask for more," I sincerely added.

"I don't want her to go," Mo emphasised, keeping her voice down so Cleo couldn't hear.

Jackson and I exchanged a worried glance. He had predicted this might happen. I reached out to take her hand, but she pulled away. I could tell that it was eating her up inside, and she couldn't even look at me.

"I never believed she would be able to channel the past like you. I still don't... I think she's imagining all of this with images you've both planted in her head," Mo stated.

I was about to respond when Jackson nodded at me. He knew best how to handle the situation.

"You don't really think that, Mo. She's—" he began, but she cut him off, jumping up and glaring at us with contempt in her eyes.

"Don't try your psychiatric trickery on me!" she snarled.

"That's unfair, Mo!" I retorted.

She turned her anger towards me. "You're the witch behind all of this... you couldn't have a child of your own, so like everything else in our lives, you're trying to take mine. Dad always said you were the black sheep of the family, and now you've proved it. After all I've been through—"

She burst into tears and stormed inside the house.

"Holy-moly, didn't see that coming. She has a lot of pent-up emotions," I said, staring at the sliding doors she had stormed through. I was visibly shaking—her outburst had unnerved me. Jackson put a sympathetic arm around my shoulders.

"It's a positive reaction, Bo. Mo loves her daughter, and it's natural for her to have last-minute doubts and show her anxiety," Jackson reassured me, taking my hand and looking warmly into my eyes. "She can't come with us, and as a result, she's relying on us to keep Cleo safe. It's difficult for us to give her comfort considering all that has happened in the past, which she's aware of. Her claiming that you're taking everything from her comes from her childhood, when you probably took one of her toys or something."

That triggered my emotions, and I buried my head in Jackson's chest, bursting into tears. "I once took her doll," I whimpered.

Jackson straightened me up, holding my shoulders and looking empathetically into my teary eyes. "Go and tell her what really happened. Did you give the doll back?"

"Yes, but I ripped its hair off. It was blonde. I wanted blonde hair instead of red... everyone called me Ginger Megs."

Jackson's warm eyes smiled, and he chuckled. "Go tell her that. She'll understand it now."

Just then, Cleo came over, towelling herself down. "Are you alright, Bo?"

I nodded and wiped away my tears. "Your mom and I just had a little spat."

Cleo wrapped a towel around her head like a turban and sat down. "I was expecting that. She gets possessive when I'm going anywhere.

Should have seen her when I was leaving for Canberra. You'd think I was running away or something... and, might I add, it was her who suggested going to Uni there!"

"Affairs of the heart rarely make sense, Cleo. All you need to know is that she loves you a great deal, and that's what causes her anxiety."

I got up. "I'll go and talk to her."

"If we hear things being smashed, do you want us to rescue you? She does that," Cleo said.

"I know, she has a worse temper than mine. I got good at ducking when I was a kid. No, love, I can handle her."

When I entered the living room, I was greeted by a loud smash from the kitchen. She's up to her old tricks again.

"Mo, it's me. Just sit down at the kitchen table... don't throw anything. We need to talk."

"Go to buggery!" came the spiteful response. A saucer flew out through the kitchen door and shattered on the parquet floor.

"A flying saucer, hey? What next?" I said, chuckling. "I took your doll because I wanted her hair... I hated mine. I loved your beautiful hair... I was jealous of it... I still am!"

Silence filled the room, and in that silence, there was rumination. Then, a door closed—softly, not slammed shut. I knew she had gone to her bedroom. She was feeling guilt for her outburst. I went to her bedroom door and gently knocked.

"I'm coming in," I said sternly but calmly.

"Go away!" she snarled angrily.

My instincts told me she meant the opposite. So, I took a deep breath, prepared myself to dodge missiles, and opened the door. Mo was sitting on the bed, cradling a doll. It was the same doll I had stripped of its hair over half a century ago. I sat on the edge of the queen-size bed.

"You've kept her all this time," I observed.

She nodded, sniffling sadly. In that moment, she still looked like the eight-year-old little blue-eyed, blonde-haired girl from our childhood—upset and in need of soothing.

"Is it true, what you said?" she asked, her voice trembling.

"Yes, sis," I replied.

She looked up from the doll, her eyes filled with tears. "I'm sorry I said that."

I reached out my hand, and she took it.

"I only wish you and Jackson could have had—" Her sentence trailed off as her emotions overwhelmed her.

We hugged, and I gave her a peck on the cheek. "It's alright, sis. That just wasn't meant to be. Don't worry, I'll look after Cleo." I held her at arm's length and looked into her eyes. "You know I'd take a bullet for her."

She nodded. "Yes, I know. I'm just scared, that's all."

"Well, I hope that wasn't one of the saucers from your good dinner set."

"No, I have a special pile in the kitchen for throwing."

We both laughed and hugged.

"I love you, sis," I said, tearing up again.

"Me too, Bo."

The battle was over. Mo had vented her fears, and I had placated them. All was well, hopefully.

A little later, in our guest room while packing, Jackson sat on the edge of the bed, wearing a concerned expression.

"What's up, love?" I asked.

"That last message from Gaius has me worried," he confessed.

I sat down beside him and rested my face on his broad shoulder. "It was to be expected, don't you think?"

"I suppose so, but after what he did to Matt, you, and Reagan, and after having to dodge the bastard for so many years—"

"I know, I know. Sometimes it feels like I'm always looking over my shoulder for Moriarty," I agreed.

"Trouble is, we're a lot older now, and—" he began, but I cut him off.

"And so is he, darling. Don't forget that," I said, giving him a peck on the cheek. "It made me think of that day when Mo had mentioned—"

"Me too," he agreed.

"Look, if it'll make you feel any better, call Danny Boyd at Interpol and ask him to provide us with a bodyguard while we're there," I suggested.

"Good idea. Better safe than sorry. You're so clever, mon cheri."

"Darling," I said excitedly, "You spoke French!"

It was a game we always played, originating from the 1960s television series "The Addams Family." Whenever Gomez Addams' wife, Trish, uttered a word in French, he would become instantly aroused and attack her with kisses. So it was for us, and this time, since we were already on the bed, well—

Though I enjoyed making love with my darling, I couldn't get the question out of my mind: How is it that no-one has been able to catch

Gaius? Staring up at the ceiling, spent from the rapture of lovemaking, Jackson could tell something was weighing on my mind.

He playfully poked his finger in my ear and grinned. "Okay, what is it?"

"Oh, I don't know... the same question that has bothered me since Matt was murdered, the accident with Reagan—why was nothing ever done about it? Why does Gaius still walk free to stalk us? Boyd should have thrown the book at him years ago. It makes me angry to think about it."

"You have every right to be angry, love. So am I. But we both know it's because Gaius, one, is protected by the Church, and two, is way too smart for Interpol and the cops... he has always been one step ahead of them and us, for that matter."

"Ditto ditto the email to Cleo," I added.

"Exactly. He's a cunning adversary, and we've been lucky to avoid him as much as we have all this time." He raised himself up onto one elbow and looked lovingly into my eyes. "The only way to catch an animal is to snare it. I promised on Matt's grave that I would get even, and one day, I will."

I hugged him warmly but with a sense of fear. "Now you're scaring me. You're a writer, not a fighter... though you're still my knight in shining armour."

"Don't worry, my love... the pen is mightier than the sword. With what we have to do now, ensuring Cleo can link with Boudicca, a confrontation with Gaius is inevitable. If we want that to come out in our favour, then we need to prepare for it," Jackson reassured me.

"You're right," I agreed. "I know you are, but it's still very scary. It's hard enough without having to deal with bloody Gaius and the damn Crux Redemptoris."

"It has become an occupational hazard, love," he said.

Lying on my back, I looked self-consciously along my naked body, noticing how it had aged. A sense of loss washed over me as I visualised how it was when I was young. But then Jackson broke my introspection.

"You know, I've always figured we handled the meeting in Spain with Abbot Primate Sergio Wolfe badly," Jackson admitted.

I flashed back to swimming in the Hotel Casa Fuster pool, with Jackson, Matt, and Quinn admiring my body as I emerged from the water. "You think we could've done it differently?" I asked vaguely.

"Whatever we did, it resulted in Matt's death," he replied.

"I guess you're right. So do you blame Wolfe for that?"

"You know, I debated that with Quinn over the years... I think you have to blame him."

"But didn't Quinn resolve that?"

"No, he wrote letters to Wolfe, and then remember that confrontation with Gibson-Smith? Now, that was a doozy."

"How can I forget it?" I said slowly.

"I know," he said, then kissed me on the lips and got up. "Forget Mo mentioned it. Forget I mentioned it. Now, you be a good girl while I take a shower. I love you."

"I love you too," I beamed back at him and watched him walk naked to the bathroom. He was still in great shape, a little leaner in parts, but overall, he looked great for a man in his mid-sixties.

Another picture suddenly flashed in my mind. I was sitting at the front desk of our university office when the door burst open and Gibson-Smith stormed in, angry as a cut snake. He rallied up to me, waving a sheet of paper furiously under my nose.

"Where are bloody Harris and Jackson? I want to speak to them both right now!"

I took a deep breath and decided to play his game. "Do you have an appointment with Professor Harris, Doctor?"

He leaned on my desk, his knuckles white, and yelled angrily. "I know they're in there... tell them I demand to see them! Now!"

"Why don't you take a seat, Doctor, and I'll see if I can arrange an appointment at such late notice. You know how busy they are," I said calmly, hoping to further irritate him.

He retired to a chair, fuming. I picked up the phone and buzzed Jackson in the annexed office.

"Sorry to interrupt, but I have Dr Gibson-Smith here wanting an appointment with you."

"Oh, really!" Jackson exclaimed.

"Yes, I know he doesn't have an appointment. I don't know... I'll ask. Just a moment. Doctor Gibson-Smith, how long do you expect it will take?"

He glared at me with daggers in his eyes and growled, "Ten minutes!"

"He said ten minutes."

"Boy, are you rubbing it into him, having fun?" Jackson said with a giggle.

"Yes, I'll just check," I said, looking at a blank page in the appointment book. "Yes, you have lunch in half an hour at the Glebe Café... with me. Yes, apparently there's a special on today..." I glanced at Gibson-Smith. His face was bright red... he was boiling over with my rebuff of his arrogance. "Okay, I'll send him in." I hung up the phone and then deliberately took my time before telling him. He had overheard me talking to Jackson and stood ready to go in, but I wanted to rub it in a little more. So, I opened my desk drawer, took out a mirror, and checked my lipstick. He coughed to alert me. I put the mirror away and scowled at him. "You can go in now."

Later at lunch, Jackson told me that the sheet of paper Gibson-Smith had been waving about like trying to flag a taxi was a letter from the Benedictine Order. In one of Quinn's many letters of complaint to the Abbot since Matt's death, he had mentioned Gibson-Smith's attempts to obstruct our research. The response denied any relationship with Dr Gibson-Smith and any knowledge of our research other than what had been discussed with Abbot Wolfe. Incensed by the accusation and his loss of face, Gibson-Smith had fired off a barrage of threats, which resulted in Quinn, for the first time in Jackson's experience, losing his temper. He physically manhandled Gibson-Smith out of the office, warning him in no uncertain terms to keep his opinions and threats to himself. I remember the feeling of accomplishment from seeing Gibson-Smith with his feathers all ruffled, getting the bum's rush from a man in his mid-seventies.

It was 9 p.m. that night when it happened. It was 1979, a Monday—I remember that because I was listening to "I Don't Like Mondays" by The Boomtown Rats on the car radio. Jackson and Quinn were at a meeting with Dean Holloway, so I was taking Jackson's car home. He would follow later in a cab. It was winter, raining, and gloomy. I was living with Jackson after Flea had moved to Los Angeles to pursue a career in acting.

I had just turned from Victoria Street into Liverpool Street when everything went black. I woke up in St. Vincent's Hospital three days later, hooked up to all sorts of beeping machines. It wasn't until the next time I regained consciousness that I saw Jackson sitting beside me, holding my hand, and began to understand the gravity of my condition. He was pale, drawn, and it was evident he hadn't slept in days. I tried to speak, but my mouth and throat were parched, and I had a tube hanging out of my mouth.

Jackson's eyes lit up. "Darling, are you with me?"

It reminded me of what he used to say during the Rip Van Winkle Effect after a hypnosis session. I nodded my head. A tear ran down his cheek, and that told me this was serious.

I had been broadsided while turning into Liverpool Street. A witness reported to the police that the car that hit me had accelerated to deliberately collide with me and then sped off. The impact was so great that the steering wheel collapsed and jammed down on my pelvis. I was lucky my vertebrae hadn't been crushed. It took the Jaws of Life to extract me from the crumpled car. Jackson showed me a photo of the wreckage, and it was hard to believe I could've survived. The injuries put an end to our hopes of ever having a family. I knew Gaius was driving that car—it just had to be. It was his style. Gibson-Smith didn't have the guts to do it. Jackson and Quinn agreed with me later— the accident came as a direct response to Gibson-Smith's humiliation earlier that day. It couldn't have been a mere coincidence. The police were inept as usual when it came to Gaius. It was always our word against theirs, just as it was with Matt's murder and Quinn's assault.

I spent the next three months learning how to walk again due to horrendous nerve damage. But I had to be thankful that I was alive.

CHAPTER
XXV

The emotional recovery was the toughest part of my rehabilitation. Not having anyone to blame and no memory of the incident left me without closure. The door to the incident was left ajar for paranoia to creep through. I found myself constantly looking over my shoulder and withdrawn from my relationship. But Jackson did the right thing and gave me the time and space to get over it. We had been talking about getting married, but now having a family was out of the question. It didn't seem as relevant anymore. It took me a year to get my head back together.

Jackson came out of the bathroom, drying himself.

"Tripping down old memory lane, are we, love?" he asked.

"Yeah, I guess Mo mentioning the accident and Gaius rearing his ugly head again triggered some distasteful memories," I replied.

He sat on the edge of the bed, leaned over, and gently kissed me. Then, in a sexy whisper, he sang, "Always look on the bright side of life..."

He loves Python.

It was an emotional affair at the airport. Knowing what Cleo was leaving to do had Mo almost hysterical with worry. All the guarantees of Cleo's safety we could muster had little effect in calming her. A "best we get going" nod from Jackson and the three of us making a break for the departure gate was the best option. I turned just before entering and waved at Mo, who, overcome by the inevitable, had calmed down.

We were in business class. I had Cleo next to me, and Jackson was in the seat in front, next to a very large man. As we climbed towards the setting sun, below us the city of Sydney was cast in a wonderful golden sheen. It was as smooth as silk. I love the exhilaration of take-off in an Airbus A380. And that feeling once she reaches the point where she's flying, and the power is backed off, the flaps are retracted, and you get that moment of weightlessness before she whispers into her ascent. Cleo had flown before, but never in an A380. And just like me, I could see she was enjoying every nuance. No white-knuckled fear of flying for us gals.

"Bo, why hasn't Gaius been arrested and put away for all he's done?" Cleo asked.

The seat belt sign went off with a ding.

"Good question, after what happened to Matt and then later the car crash I had," I replied.

"Oh, I didn't know you had an accident. Was it bad?"

"Can't really call it an accident, love. Yes, it was. It was the year after we got back from the first stay in the UK. We'd had a run-in with Dr Gibson-Smith, and later that evening, a car broadsided me and then sped off."

"Gosh, were you hurt?"

"Yep, the steering wheel crushed my pelvis. Another half an inch, and it would have shattered my spine, and I would have lost the use of my legs. As it turned out, I was okay but unable to ever have children."

"Oh, I'm so sorry, Bo. So do you blame Gibson-Smith for the hit and run?"

"No, not him personally. He didn't have the guts. It was Gaius for sure. But like always, he seems to just vanish into the ether like a phantom, and we can never prove anything."

"Surely Interpol would want him for murdering Matt."

"Again, there was no proof. He's that clever."

"Wouldn't he be old now? You'd reckon he'd give up on you?"

"He'd be in his mid-fifties, but don't forget the Crux Redemptoris will have recruited more soldiers since those days. He's just been laying low, waiting for us to make the next move."

"How did he anticipate you're making it with me... now?"

"Remember the files that were taken from Quinn?"

"Yes."

"He knows we missed out on finding the location—"

"So your diversion to find the Holy Grail didn't work, then?"

"No, Judith went on the radio and spoke to the media. She got a lot of press, but though Cambridge supported the dig submission, it was eventually rejected by the National Trust. They weren't going to have anyone digging up those sites."

"And the Church?"

"Well, we believe it was the Church that put pressure on the National Trust. They wouldn't even give us permission to try GPR at the sites."

"What's GPR?"

"Ground penetrating radar. Not as sophisticated as what we have today, but effective enough. It can reveal signs of a burial or objects buried up to a certain depth."

"So after the car crash, did Gaius make any other heavy moves on you?"

"Funny, there was an instance where I met him. None of the others believe me, but it was an uncanny feeling," I said.

"Well, you're the one that saw him at Glastonbury, so you'd expect you'd recognise him, wouldn't you?"

"Um, I don't know. It was dark in that hotel room, and anyhow, this was some years later."

"Tell me about it. I'd rather listen to you than watch a movie, and we have got 21 hours to kill."

"Okay, it was our first trip back to the UK since Matt died. We went there primarily to attend Judith's and Mike's wedding. It was no big deal to them, but for us, an old married couple since 1980... well, we just wanted to be there. Even Quinn came. By then we had more First Light UK members, and they were invited to the reception at Moore Manor, soon to be changed to the Roberts Manor. Not quite as regal-sounding, we thought.

Little had changed there: the manor looked just the same, and Judith and Mike had aged gently, as had we all. Mike had quit smoking and was looking much better for it.

The following day after we arrived, with only Quinn, Jackson, and myself in attendance, celebrant Druid Don Eastwood, whom you might remember we met at Salisbury, married Judith and Mike by an old oak tree in Bernwood Forest, Buckinghamshire, just walking distance from the Manor. It was a mystical ceremony that seemed to take me right back to Boudicca when nature seemed to play such a vital role in the very heart and soul of the people and their belief system. Garbed in Gothic white caftans with wreaths in their hair and barefooted, Judith and Mike entered the circle in the forest to be greeted by old Don with his long grey beard and hair that draped in a ponytail down to the arch of his back, dressed in obligatory Druid garb. Holding an Athame, a ceremonial dagger, across his chest, the Grand Druid bellowed words of magic in the tongue of the ancients that prompted the forest to fall silent and listen.

The sunlight was blinding after the gloom of the library as I stepped out through the double glass doors onto the wide flagstone terrace at the back of the manor. A small group of people had gathered under a giant striped umbrella at one end of the terrace, so I headed towards them. They resolved into Judith, flanked by Quinn and Jackson, as I got closer. We had changed out of our pagan clobber into casual dress appropriate for the occasion.

"Bonnie, darling," Judith smiled gaily. "Come join the party. This is Peter Wilson," she said, beckoning a tall man in a grey suit grasping a champagne flute. At the mention of his name, he approached me, sporting a huge grin.

"Peter, may I introduce Dr Bonnie Bolt," Judith said. By then, I had a Ph.D. in Ancient History.

"At last, I finally get to meet the infamous Dr Bo. What a pleasure," Peter said with a strong Irish accent.

He was around average height, with a sinewy body, and a handshake that was firm without him being muscular. His long flaxen-coloured hair was thinning a little up top. I expect he was around forty.

Over the course of the next half an hour, four more members of First Light UK arrived: Rebecca Tynes, Ahmed Rashid, Brigitte Yates, and a boisterous, overweight old professor archetype with great bushy eyebrows and a strong German accent, Dr Hugo Von Schmidt. And what a character he turned out to be. A little later, a much older Daniel Boyd from Interpol arrived with a young sidekick, Rick Molloy. All was going well with us reacquainting ourselves with Daniel and learning that Rick had been designated our new point person at Interpol. Though I was a little concerned that he looked like he'd just graduated high school, Daniel assured us he was in his mid-twenties and had graduated detective school with honours.

Rebecca was about the same age as Rick and quite a vivacious flirt. She was tall, brunette, and had the slender, almost emaciated body of a fashion model. The sharp planes of her facial bone structure emphasised her enormous green-flecked hazel eyes, which had their own special quality of melting liquidity that had obviously seduced many of her colleagues. Brigitte, on the other hand, was plain, demure, and very French. She appeared to be a socialist academic and, like Flea, had a penchant for her own gender.

Ahmed, from Pakistan, was a studious-looking young man in his early thirties. He had a dependable appearance and an intellect that bordered on eccentricity. But Dr Hugo, now this was a character one would never forget. His love of food and wine was evident in his girth. He looked as though he would have been better suited to the opulence of the 19th century. Dr Hugo had a big round face with heavy jowls framed with woolly ginger mutton-chop sideburns that made his round wire-rimmed glasses, over which flowed his great red, bushy eyebrows, appear far too small for his face. He was as bald as a badger and dressed as if he were on a safari in the colonies. Quinn claimed that Dr Hugo was a virtual walking encyclopedia on archaeology.

After dinner, we found ourselves in the library, standing in front of the fireplace, thawing out from the cool autumn air. The Butler alerted Judith to the arrival of a latecomer. Ahmed quickly announced that it would be his colleague visiting London who desperately wanted to meet Professor Harris. Judith explained that Ahmed had phoned ahead to get her permission for him to attend.

Ahmed accompanied the Butler to greet his friend. Hugo had planted his bulk in a chair from which he was unlikely to be able to extract himself, and I was pointing this out to Jackson when Jackson's voice suddenly trailed away into nothing. I became conscious of light footsteps approaching from behind us. Jackson looked over his shoulder for a moment, his lips parted in a pallid imitation of a smile.

Ahmed's colleague had stopped upon entering the library, observing us all with the scrutiny of a buyer at an antique auction.

"Everybody," Ahmed announced. "This is my friend Paul Sicario. He is from Spain."

" Vell we von't hold zat against him!!" Hugo chortled loudly at his own joke. We entertained his joke to keep him from feeling embarrassed, not that he would, given his parched sense of humour.

"I met Paul two months ago on a dig in Morocco. He was doing research for the University of Madrid. I noticed at the time he was reading Professor Harris' book, 'The Romanisation of Britain,' and when I told him that I knew the Professor and that he would be visiting the UK soon, he organised a visit here in the hope of meeting him," Ahmed said.

Sicario snapped to attention and bowed stiffly. His sober grey suit and plain white shirt with a thin black necktie wouldn't fool anyone. He looked like he'd be more at home wielding a machete than a pen. He was a tall, bull-necked guy with short greying brown hair. Cold realism showed in the taut lines running from the corners of his slate grey eyes. A jagged white scar through his left eyebrow bore witness to perhaps a small error of judgment he might have made in his life.

He didn't look at all like a scholar to me; he looked more like a soldier. I noticed that both Daniel and Rick were eyeballing him with the same sort of scepticism. Quinn made his way over to Ahmed.

"Professor Harris, please allow me to introduce my colleague, Paul Sicario."

"Please to meet you, Paul," Quinn said cheerfully, extending a hand to shake.

"The pleasure is all mine, Professor," Sicario replied with a Latin-accented voice, taking Quinn's hand.

Mike ambled over to us and said in a guarded tone, "Not sure about this guy."

"It's not like Judith to invite someone without first clearing it with us," Jackson said, equally guarded.

CHAPTER XXVI

"There's something about him..." I said before being interrupted by Peter Wilson, who by now had had a few too many and had ambled over to glare at me like a dog on heat.

"I've heard so much about you, Bo, but I didn't expect you to be such a dish," he slurred.

"Thanks, Peter, but if it's a lay you're after, I'm out of commission—already taken." That set him back a few years. He wasn't prepared for my notorious sharp riposte.

"Why not try Miss Tynes over there? She looks more your style and age group."

"No, she's only interested in more mature men, such as your husband..."

I noticed Rebecca was busy fluttering her eyelids at Jackson, deep in conversation.

"How about Brigitte then? Look, she's standing there all alone beside Hugo, who is about to nod off."

"No, I've been on a dig with her. She's too aloof."

"She's French, darling. They're born that way. Look, I know this is England and you're used to just walking up to a chick in a pub and putting the hard word on her... and that a knockback is acceptable... but the French are different. They thrive on romance. You'll need to woo her."

Quinn brought Paul over to meet me.

"Dr Bolt, meet Paul," Quinn said.

His knife-slash lips tightened until they practically disappeared. "It is a pleasure to meet you, Dr Bolt. Are you an Australian as well?" he asked.

"Yes," I assured him, feeling the smile tighten on my lips until they ached.

He took a quick step toward me and held out his hand to shake. I took it cautiously. It was as hard as a rock, certainly not the hand of a scholar.

"You appear nervous, Dr Bolt. I am sorry if I have that effect on you?" he remarked.

"Have we met before?" I asked uncertainly.

Daniel stepped into the conversation.

"Agent Daniel Boyd, this is Paul Sicario," I said.

"Agent? Are you with the CIA, MI5, or something, Mr Boyd?" Sicario asked.

"Interpol. And you're with?" Boyd inquired with a professional police stare that could melt steel.

"I'm a freelance researcher of antiquities, Mr Boyd. Mostly, I work with the University of Madrid."

"Ah, the Universidad Autonoma. I know it well," Quinn said with a smile. "Which department are you doing research with?" Quinn asked.

"The Faculty of Archaeology, Professor," he answered.

"So, are you on holidays here?" Boyd asked.

"You could say that, and I will be taking in as much as I can of what your country has to offer."

"So you've not been here before?" I asked.

"Yes, but it was back in the early seventies. Much has changed since."

A loud slap broke the train of conversation, and I immediately found the source. Brigitte was striding off in a huff towards the balcony, leaving Peter holding his cheek.

"She must be impressed with whatever he said," Quinn chortled.

"Why's that?" Boyd asked.

"She's French. A slap is as good as a yes," I said.

We all nodded our heads in good-humoured agreement.

I excused myself and wandered off to the ground floor ladies' bathroom.

While in the cubicle, I heard the door open, and someone entered. I looked down under the door at a pair of men's shoes. Whoever it was, he was facing my door.

"I expect you will be leaving tomorrow, Dr Bolt?"

I recognised the voice. "And what makes you think that, Mr. Sicario?" I replied, trying to steady my voice.

"Oh, I don't think it, I know it."

His answer worried me. Suddenly, a hand pushed through the gap under the door to my cubicle and fastened around my left ankle. I struggled against it, trying to pull my leg free from his vice-like grip. I kicked at his hand with my other foot and tried to stab it with the high heel. His other hand appeared under the door, holding a knife, and I watched in terror as he stabbed the blade into the calf of my leg. The pain was excruciating. I froze, not wanting to move my leg while the knife was still stuck in it. He slowly twisted the blade.

"I think this demonstrates your need to leave tomorrow, Dr Bolt. With a simple move while my knife is in your leg, I can easily sever the peroneus longus ligament. And though it can be repaired, you would never walk the same again. So, what will it be, Doctor?" Sicario's voice dripped with menace.

My body went into shock. I was shaking, tears were tracking down my cheeks, and my mind was clouded by pain.

"If I scream... Agent Boyd will come running," I said through clenched teeth.

"By the time he gets here, I will have gone, and you will be bleeding to death because, along with the peroneus longus ligament, I will have cut your peroneal artery. So, your answer or a scream, what will it be? And I remind you of what happened to your friend in Barcelona if you decide to ignore me. I will find you," he said slowly and deliberately.

"You fucking bastard Gaius, you're nothing but a murderer... you tried to kill me in the car..." I choked on my words as he pushed the knife deeper into my leg. The pain propelled me backwards. "Argh! All right! All right!" I pleaded—and with a sudden jerk, he withdrew the blade. I heard the door to the ladies' close behind him. I slowly stood and shakily pulled up my panties. I was going to pass out. There was a puddle of blood on the floor. My leg was throbbing, and my shoe had filled with blood. I couldn't move, or I'd throw up, so I decided to stay put and just scream my lungs out.

Judith was the first to arrive. In a panic, she helped me out of the cubicle into the waiting arms of Jackson. One look at the pool of blood on the floor and the cut on my leg, and both Daniel and Rick darted out in pursuit of my assailant.

Quinn looked at the wound and said, "It was Gaius, wasn't it?"

Still seeing stars and biting my bottom lip, I nodded.

"Did you guess?" Jackson asked him.

"Only when I remembered there is no Faculty of Archaeology at Universidad Autonoma, but by then, it was too late," Quinn admitted.

"I should have guessed it as soon as I heard his name. Sicario means assassin in Latin," Mike cursed, shaking his head.

"What did he want, Bonnie?" Judith asked, gripping my arm in case I collapsed, though she looked like she was about to pass out herself.

"He told me to leave the UK tomorrow, or the same fate would befall me as Matt."

"Let's get you to the hospital. That'll need stitches," Jackson said, picking me up in his arms.

"This whole quest is about as impossible as walking to the horizon. You never get there," Quinn said prophetically, and I will never forget that saying as long as I live.

"So it was Gaius disguised as Paul Sicario," Cleo asked with keen interest.

"Well, he almost admitted to killing Matt, though he never confirmed he was Gaius when I mentioned it."

"Didn't you recognise him from the last time at Glastonbury?"

"Too much water under the bridge, love."

"Obviously, the Interpol guys failed to run him down. Did you leave the next day?"

"We sure did."

"Was Judith upset about breaking the security?"

"You bet she was. Ahmed was so upset he wanted to leave First Light, but we couldn't have that. We beefed up our security measures after that incident."

"Why do you think he wanted you to leave?" Cleo inquired.

"Paranoia, I've always reckoned. You'd think that after all the noise Judith made about searching for the Holy Grail years before that amounted to nothing, they, the Crux, might have dropped their vigilance, but no. They're so freaked out we might actually uncover the gospel."

As we continued talking, Jackson leaned over from the aisle to join our conversation.

"Have you got Bo telling stories again, Cleo?" he said in a low voice.

"Love, can you remember when we went to that weird convention in San Diego? What was it?" I asked.

"The Holistic Psychic Expo in 2005, and we stayed with the medium who invited us," Jackson recalled.

"Sharlene," I said.

"Ah yes, Sharlene Cayce," Jackson said, remembering.

"She tracked us down through Quinn's research paper on Regressive Hypnotherapy after it was published on the Internet," I explained.

"It was really Jackson's work, but Gibson-Smith had him gagged from publishing any of his research back then. Now, of course, things have changed since Gibson-Smith kicked the bucket in 2010," I added, leaning across Cleo."How's it going sitting next to the monument?" I whispered to Jackson.

"I'll never look at sardines the same way again," he said light-heartedly.

Suddenly, we hit some CAT, clear air turbulence, and the safety belt sign lit up with a disturbing ding. The intercom sprang to life, and the captain asked passengers to take their seats, warning that we were encountering a few bumps while changing cruising height. As Jackson returned to his seat, and we fastened our seatbelts, I peered out of my window at the rich red sunburnt expanse below in the shadowy sunset of Australia. Wispy skeins of cloud were whipping by, likely causing the CAT.

"So what happened with Sharlene Cayce then?" Cleo asked, bringing us back to our conversation.

"Yes, sorry, I got distracted... well, that was an adventure to archive. Sharlene is the granddaughter of the great medium Edgar Cayce and daughter of Hugh Lynne Cayce. She lives on a small farm about fifteen minutes from San Diego, California. It's a beautiful little place, very comfy. She lives alone and grows all her own food. She is vegetarian, of course, not vegan, and keeps chickens. Not only is she a legitimate clairvoyant but also quite an accomplished academic in the school of Peace Studies at the University of San Diego. She's an old hippie at heart, really, though at the time only in her forties. She dresses in the most outrageous colourful African clothing I think I've ever seen."

"I remember we were surprised at how effective the publicity had been. When we arrived, we saw Jackson's name plastered all over San Diego airport. It was also in magazines, newspapers. He was a local celebrity," I continued.

"Sharlene collected us from the airport and then took us to half a dozen different radio stations for on-air interviews. By the time we got to her farm, we were exhausted, and I'd also become an instant local celebrity as Jackson's regression subject. I, of course, never mentioned First Light secrets, but I was adept at talking about my seventies Boudicca channelling experience without giving too much away. I was actually more vocal about it in America, where I found people much more receptive. It was quite refreshing, actually. I remember saying to Jackson, 'How long has this been going on? We should have brought our studies to America years before. It would have made a massive difference to our progress.'"

"There were a few USA members of First Light by then, but mostly on the East Coast, academics brought on board via Quinn's scholarly connections," I explained.

Jackson and I were sitting in deck chairs on the back veranda of Sharlene's log cabin, admiring the golden sunset and savouring a fine 2002 Napa Valley Cabernet Sauvignon. Sharlene, whom we thought had gone inside to get some cheese and biscuits, strolled out totally naked and slipped into the Jacuzzi built into the decking. I was taken aback by her effrontery. She certainly wasn't shy. After she called us to join her, as though it was to be expected, we stripped down and followed suit. A couple of joints later, a few more glasses of wine, and with the motion of the soft spa bubbles caressing our tired bodies, we felt like we were in hippie heaven.

The next day was the convention, and what a turnout that was. The auditorium was packed to the rafters with three thousand fans. Backstage, Jackson was more nervous than a cat on a hot tin roof. He'd given plenty of small talks before, but nothing like this. Sharlene took him aside for a couple of minutes, and when he returned, he was a changed man, full of confidence and ready to go. When I asked what had brought about the radical change in him, he mentioned a sniff of white powder Sharlene had given him from a little plastic apparatus. Now, I'm no prude when it comes to recreational drugs, but that stuff certainly fired Jackson up like never before. It was the best oration I'd ever seen him give, and he's unlikely to ever eclipse it.

After Jackson's speech, we wandered around the exhibit hall, chatting with people Sharlene introduced us to and taking in the various displays. Sharlene then took us to a smaller one-thousand-seat auditorium and stopped us at the entrance.

"You know what? With all I know about your research, I think you will both appreciate what my friend here has to say," Sharlene said, as if she had seen it in our stars.

We both looked at the poster at the entrance that read: "Psychic researcher Reagan Spears speaks out about Why Christianity is a Lie."

People were filing in, and the lecture was just about to begin.

"Well, the topic certainly has me intrigued," Jackson admitted.

"I'm with you. Let's go in," I agreed excitedly.

Sharlene gave us a knowing glance and led us inside the packed auditorium to three seats at the front reserved especially for us. The house lights dimmed, and a spotlight illuminated a lectern stage left. A tall, lanky man, dressed in a black t-shirt, black jeans, and red Converse sneakers, with a blond bob and wearing round John Lennon glasses, walked out on stage. After five minutes, Jackson and I were sitting riveted, our mouths gaping in awe of what he had to say. He told us that he had channelled an Iron-age Druid from 61 A.D. named Morgan, who claimed to have known Joseph of Arimathea, the uncle of Jesus Christ. This was the very same Morgan I knew. As the lecture went on, it became clearer that this man was on a similar mission to ours. And then, I noticed something. When a projector came on from the rear of the theatre to show slides Spears had taken on a recent visit to Glastonbury to authenticate Morgan, I caught sight of a person sitting in the aisle across from us who looked like Gaius. I yelped when I recognised him.

"What is it, love?" Jackson asked, concerned. "You look like you've seen a ghost."

"Slowly, look to your left... at the aisle parallel with ours. Count six people in, and who do you see?"

When Jackson looked back at me, his eyes were the size of dinner plates.

"Paul Sicario," he croaked in a harsh whisper. "It's Gaius!"

CHAPTER XXVII

Gaius looked older, his hair grey and thinning, and he was less athletic, but no less sinister. We listened to Spears for the next hour, keeping one eye on him and the other on Gaius. After a standing ovation, the house lights came on as Spears left the stage. When we looked for Gaius, he had vanished, and that was far worse than seeing him in the first place. Knowing that he was even in the same country was enough to give us the creeps, and he had to know we were there because Jackson's name and image were plastered everywhere.

Sharlene took us backstage to meet Spears, a very eccentric man with a distracted manner of communication. We were uncertain whether he was in it for fame, money, or, like us, a passion for uncovering the truth. We were pleasantly surprised to learn that he knew of our work.

As the backstage area became overcrowded, Sharlene pulled us aside. "Hope you guys don't mind, but I invited Reagan for dinner at my place tonight. It's so goddamn difficult to get to know someone when there's so much hyper-shit going on. He's not normally as distracted as this," Sharlene said.

"That was lovely of you, Sharlene. Thank you," Jackson replied, appreciative of the invitation.

Just then, a woman pushed through in a desperate bid to get an autograph from Jackson. I raised an eyebrow mockingly at Jackson, who responded with a comical, conceited smirk. The woman, young and pretty, seemed to want more than just an autograph. A man standing nearby noticed Jackson giving the autograph and approached him.

"Dr Bolt, I enjoyed your lecture. What did you think of what Mr

Spears had to say? Is there a correlation with your work?" the man asked.

"Yes, we've certainly followed similar lines of research and reached corresponding conclusions," Jackson replied.

"Which are?" the man inquired.

"Oh, a little complicated to go into right now... um, who do I make the—" Jackson began, pen ready to sign the program.

"Just put 'CR,' a fellow researcher," the man replied, an odd look on his sullen face. As Jackson signed the program, the man stared at me, making me feel uncomfortable. I tugged on Jackson's coat sleeve and whispered, "Let's move on."

In the car on the way back to Sharlene's farm, I voiced my concerns.

"That guy you gave the autograph to gave me the creeps. Did you see the way he was staring at me?" I said, feeling unsettled.

"Plenty of weirdos there, honey. This is America," Sharlene chuckled.

"Yes, I was picking up a weird vibe from him as well. I preferred the fan before him," Jackson added, smirking.

"CR... Crux Redemptoris. I wonder if that's just a coincidence?" I pondered.

"God, what's that? Sounds like some sort of infectious disease!" Sharlene laughed.

"You're not wrong, Sharlene," Jackson replied, his tone serious.

Later, at sunset, we were once again on the veranda, enjoying the view of the rolling hills, the trees, and the Pacific Ocean beyond, when a car pulled up in front of the house. Sharlene went to greet her guest and brought him out to join us. It was evident from the way Sharlene and Reagan interacted that they were lovers. It was quite a unique experience to be in the company of a clairvoyant and a psychic. We had a lovely afternoon, and Reagan proved to be a completely different person than our first impression had suggested. We found that we had a lot in common, though we remained cautious about sharing all our research.

At one point, Sharlene took my hand, closed her eyes, and concentrated. Then, she said, "You will hand over your quest to another within a decade, and then together, you will find the answers to the questions you have long been denied."

She then took Jackson's hand and said, "You will author a book next year that will be very successful and make you a lot of money. It will have a three-word title, and the third word will be... 'self.'"

"I've been thinking of writing a new book. As a matter of fact, the young lady who approached me for an autograph today gave me her card," Jackson said, producing the card from his pocket and handing it to me.

"Phoenix Publications—Editor, Kylie De Soto, Los Angeles. And along the bottom of the card, it states: 'We dare to venture where angels fear to tread.' Ooo, sounds out there," I chuckled, handing the card back to Jackson.

"She's my publisher. That's why she was there, and I thoroughly recommend her. Only a small outfit, but boy, she has one hell of a work ethic," Reagan said, blinking rapidly.

"Thanks for the recommendation, Reagan. I appreciate it," Jackson expressed his gratitude.

"She's a bit of a character," I commented without thinking.

"No need to worry yourself, Bonnie. She's gay," Reagan smiled.

"God wouldn't have picked that one," Sharlene chuckled.

"How's your book doing, Reagan?" Jackson asked, curious.

"The new one isn't out yet. To be honest, I haven't finished it. But the last one, 'Our Alien Ancestry,' sold four hundred and ten thousand copies over two years here. Kylie is still getting releases for it in other countries. It made me a millionaire," Reagan replied.

Jackson and I exchanged enthusiastic glances.

"Put in a good word for us, Reagan. I like the idea of having loads of money for a change," I said, warmth in my voice.

"Hey, Sharlene, what lies in the future for me? Maybe my new book will be an even bigger seller. I'm pretty sold on the title 'Why Christianity is a Lie.' It got a nice response at the convention today."

"Just be careful, Reagan. There are militant religious forces charged with keeping a lid on exposing Church doctrine. We've had first hand experience," Jackson cautioned.

"Don't worry... I've also had my share," Reagan replied dismissively. "Only yesterday, I got a goddamned threat from some extremist religious sect."

I was about to ask him who it was when Sharlene took his hand and slipped into a trance. Suddenly, her eyes opened wide, and with a frightened look, she dropped his hand as if it were a dead fish.

"Oh no, don't tell me my book is going to be a fucking failure!" Reagan joked.

Sharlene hurried inside without saying a word, and I followed her, concerned.

"Sharlene... Sharlene," I called out as she stopped in the kitchen and opened the fridge. I could see she was crying, trying to disguise it. I grabbed her shoulders and turned her to face me.

"What's the matter, love? You saw something, didn't you?" I asked, worried.

She nodded, but the words wouldn't come out, only tears.

"What did you see?" I pressed.

"Nothing," she finally said, her voice slow and strained.

"So, what's—?"

"Nothing means no future. I think he might be ill and doesn't know it yet," Sharlene confessed.

"Oh, my goodness! What, like a tumour or something?" I gasped.

"I can't be sure, but maybe. I don't think he's got long," Sharlene whispered, her voice filled with sadness.

"Can he change his destiny?" I asked, desperately searching for a glimmer of hope.

"That's out of my understanding, Bo. I just catch glimpses into what's coming and sometimes what's been, but a healer I'm not," Sharlene replied.

I gave her a hug. "Come on, off with our clothes, and let's see if we can coax our fellas into the Jacuzzi," I suggested, hoping to lift her spirits.

She smiled and nodded, a mischievous gleam returning to her eyes. We disrobed and walked out onto the veranda, surprised to find the guys already waiting for us, stark naked in the Jacuzzi.

"What took you so long, girls?" Reagan quipped audaciously.

Reagan didn't stay the night because he had an early appointment with Kylie scheduled at his hotel. We agreed to meet up the next day for happy hour drinks at the Waterfront Bar on Kettner Boulevard.

The last day of the conference was spent meeting people, checking out bookstands, and exploring the exhibits. Sharlene had her own booth, offering free readings as the Oracle of Diego. She looked vibrant in her gypsy attire, though the absence of a crystal ball was noted. At one of the stands, we ran into Kylie, who mentioned that she had breakfast with Reagan. Funny how knowing someone's sexual orientation can change how you perceive their actions. Now, instead of interpreting her behaviour towards Jackson as flirtatious, I couldn't help but think she might be interested in me. Drawing from my experience with Flea, I knew how to handle such situations. But if I were inclined differently, Kylie would certainly be on my short list. Speaking of Flea, when Jackson mentioned to Kylie that we would be staying a few days in LA to visit a friend before heading back to

Sydney, she insisted on meeting up there to discuss a book deal. So we set a date.

Happy hour at the Waterfront Bar came and went, but Reagan didn't show up. Sharlene tried calling him multiple times but only reached his voicemail. The atmosphere in the car on the way to San Diego airport was sombre, and just as Sharlene pulled into the parking lot, we heard a newsflash on the car radio—prominent author Reagan Spears found murdered in his hotel room.

We sat frozen in disbelief. Sharlene's words from the previous night echoed in my mind—she had seen nothing. She had seen his death. With teary eyes, I looked at Jackson, and we suspected we knew the identity of the murderer.

Flying to LA that day was out of the question. We called Flea to inform her of the circumstances and that we would catch the same flight the next day. Distraught as she was, Sharlene managed to drive us to San Diego Police Headquarters on Broadway. There, we learned the gruesome details of Reagan's murder—his throat had been cut, mirroring the manner of Matt's murder.

It took a few hours of explaining before the police allowed us to leave. We provided them with as much information as we could about Gaius and how we had seen him at the lecture, as well as the strange person called CR who had asked for Jackson's autograph. But even as we told the story, it sounded too much like an episode from the X-Files. The police took our details and instructed us not to leave the USA until given clearance, but they approved our flight to LA.

The night ahead was going to be tough, with Sharlene feeling upset and guilty for not acting on her premonition. Then, Sharlene's cell phone rang. It was Kylie, who had been on the road to LA when she heard about Reagan on the radio. She immediately turned back and had just left the police station. Kylie was afraid, so Sharlene invited her to stay with us at the farm. About an hour later, Kylie arrived in a white BMW 325Ci cabriolet.

We sat on the veranda, and Kylie shared with us that Reagan's laptop was missing, along with the master copy of his forthcoming book. Our suspicions leaned even more towards Gaius, although the police were reluctant to believe that he might have been killed by a fanatical religious order determined to silence him.

We talked into the night, consuming our fair share of wine. The more Kylie learned from us, the more she hesitated about publishing anything that might attract the attention of the Crux Redemptoris. After Sharlene lightened the mood by stripping down and taking to the Jacuzzi, we joined her, and Kylie began to calm down. I remember sitting next to her in the Jacuzzi—a well-endowed young lady with an attractive figure. When her hand discreetly wandered underwater to touch me intimately, I had no choice but to lie back, look up at the starry sky, and indulge. Jackson didn't notice, but when he stepped out of the Jacuzzi, I noticed he was partially aroused, making me wonder if Sharlene had also experienced wandering hands. It turned out that she had. At least it provided a distraction from an otherwise horrendous day.

Instead of flying to LA the following night, Kylie offered us a ride. It was difficult saying goodbye to Sharlene. We had become close friends over those few days, so we made a pact to see each other again soon. When Sharlene hugged me goodbye, she whispered in my ear that we would meet again in exactly two years. And she was right—I flew to LA with Jackson in 2007 for the launch of his first book with Phoenix Publishing. To Sharlene's delight, the book was titled "The Divided Self," a word she had prophesied but had ironically slipped Jackson's mind. It was only when she reminded us that we recalled her prediction. Both Sharlene and Reagan were mentioned in the foreword, particularly due to what happened when we arrived in LA.

Kylie dropped us off at Flea's apartment in Hollywood around 10 p.m., and we agreed to meet for dinner the following night. When Flea brought us inside, she broke down in tears. Jackson came to her rescue, and we quickly learned that her longstanding girlfriend had just ended their relationship that day. It was a heartbreaking situation for a woman of her age, with her looks and body no longer fitting the ideal of the romance market, especially in a town like Hollywood. Not that Flea was unattractive—she looked like she was in her late thirties, stunning—but she was out of touch with the singles scene. It was too late for her to return home; she had been living in LA longer than she had in Australia. Though her acting career hadn't taken off, she had become a moderately successful talent agent. But a twenty-year relationship meant she had no understanding of the dating world and the thought of having to navigate it again terrified her.

In his usual fashion, Jackson brought some hope into Flea's life, and by 3 a.m., with the assistance of two bottles of Jack Daniels, he had stopped her tears and sent her off to bed.

The next morning, with hangovers in full swing, we enjoyed bacon, eggs, and coffee on the balcony, each wearing mandatory dark glasses. Conversation was avoided, sudden movements were discouraged. However, the day could only get better, and once we were able to talk,

Flea suggested going on a sightseeing tour. We had a fantastic time.

That night, we took Flea with us to meet Kylie for dinner at Le Dome on Sunset Boulevard, a celebrity hotspot that didn't disappoint. Familiar faces were everywhere. After dinner, Kylie handed Jackson a flash drive.

"Reagan would have wanted you to have this, Jackson. It's his book, unedited, but it will never be published," she said sadly.

"Why not?" Jackson exclaimed as he accepted the drive.

"His family won't give consent. He was about to divorce his wife, you know... and now that he's gone, she has control over the estate. She stands to gain millions from the insurance. So, she called me today," Kylie explained, wiping away a tear. "She told me I couldn't publish the book. She wouldn't give her consent, so that's that."

"How low. You'd think she would want the work he died for to be his legacy," I said, expressing my frustration.

"She sounds like a real bitch to me," Flea growled.

"I'm with you, honey," Kylie said with a warm smile.

"What can I do with it?" Jackson asked, referring to the book.

"Take what you need from it... Reagan researched a similar hypothesis to yours, didn't he?" Kylie inquired.

"Yes, but—"

"It's not plagiarism, Jackson," Kylie interrupted, raising her eyebrows. "I'll give you written consent as his editor to use whatever you need. Just make sure to credit him, as I know you will. He would want this, believe me."

"That's a noble gesture, Kylie, and we will honour it. Thank you," I said sincerely.

I studied her lovely face, appreciating her commitment to ensuring Reagan's work would be recognised. By the end of the evening, I had seen as many stars as I had while sitting naked in Sharlene's Jacuzzi, and Jackson had received a publishing offer. Flea, on the other hand, had a date with Kylie. All seemed well in Hollywood.

The flight attendant handed me a tray of food, and Cleo, the detective, initiated a recap. I confirmed that the events I had just recounted were the last known interactions with or sightings of Gaius. She asked if I believed Gaius was the one who had murdered Reagan and if any further evidence had been discovered. I handed her a book from my carry-on bag.

"Here, it's a good read. You'll finish it by the time we reach London," I suggested.

She looked at the title.

"The Divided Self, excellent," she said with a smile.

"Pay particular attention to the last time Reagan channels Morgan with Boudicca present. He mentions a box that we believe contains the gospel," I advised.

"By the way, how did things turn out between Kylie and Flea?" Cleo inquired.

"They're still together," I replied.

CHAPTER
XXVIII

After dinner, I made myself comfortable and left Cleo reading Jackson's book. I found flying relaxing and had no trouble falling asleep. Giving her the book got me thinking about Reagan's work. The fascinating part was how he continued to channel Morgan until his execution at the Hod Hill massacre in 63 A.D. I recalled Reagan quoting Morgan's description of Boudicca's fate to Carrick, the Ricon of the Dumnonii clan at Kersek, now Exeter.

According to Morgan's account, Boudicca drove her chariot, pulled by six white horses with coats stained in Roman blood, at full speed toward General Gaius Suetonius Paulinus. He stood on a hill with his officers, observing the battle below. The battle had been won, but this fiery red-headed woman, her body painted blue and caked in Roman blood, dared to charge at them. They had no idea of her bravery and determination.

Suetonius ordered his men to stop her, forming a human barricade to prevent her from reaching him. However, with fury burning in her eyes, she deftly manoeuvred her chariot past them and raced toward a large old oak tree. When the chariot emerged from behind the tree, much to the astonishment of Gaius Suetonius Paulinus and his men, Boudicca had vanished. All they saw was a lone raven taking flight from a branch on the oak tree. Gaius Suetonius Paulinus turned to his scribe Tacitus and ordered him not to write about what they had witnessed, instead detailing Boudicca's death as a great Roman victory.

I found comfort in the manner of her passing described by Morgan. It was how one would expect the Queen of the Druids to depart. Unfortunately, Reagan never channelled Morgan or Boudicca burying Joseph. His focus was different from ours. Still, much of what he saw through Morgan's eyes turned out to be beneficial for our studies, especially the mention of Joseph's secret book being kept in a box.

We arrived at Heathrow at 7 a.m. on a cold, dreary, and wet Monday. It was heartwarming to see Judith and Mike waiting for us in the arrivals area. We hadn't seen them in over a decade, but it felt as if it had been only yesterday. They treated Cleo as if she were their long-lost daughter, showing just how much she meant to them.

About an hour later, we entered the beautiful old Moore Manor, which I still couldn't bring myself to call Roberts Manor. After settling into our rooms, we gathered in the library for an update. With only two days until the full moon at Giamonios, we wanted to ensure we were fully prepared—we couldn't afford to miss this one and only opportunity. Before Judith joined us, Mike informed us that she had been diagnosed with early signs of type-two diabetes two weeks ago. She had been experiencing fatigue, blurred vision, headaches, and weight loss, prompting Mike to take her to the doctor. Now that it had been diagnosed, it was important to manage her blood sugar levels to avoid hypoglycemia. Mike was overseeing her diet and lifestyle.

"These are the joys of aging, I'm afraid," Judith said, settling into a comfortable chair as she realised she was the topic of conversation. "But it won't stop this old iron horse from seeing the quest through."

"That's the spirit, Judith," I said with a smile.

"Come, Cleo, sit beside me... Mike and I have been waiting years for you to be here with us. And look at you now, such a lovely creature," Judith said warmly.

"If you're up for it, Cleo, we thought I might regress you soon so we can closely track Boudicca in the two days leading up to Giamonios," Jackson proposed.

"Absolutely no problem, Jackson," Cleo responded eagerly.

"I've been brushing up on my Celtic for this moment, Cleo," Mike added.

"Cleo, you have a distinct advantage over my own ventures into the unknown. You have the benefit of hindsight. You know almost everything I've experienced—the people, the towns, the events. You have the benefit of travelling into the past fully briefed. There, you will meet a Boudicca you already know, in a sense. After reading Reagan's book, you should also have valuable knowledge from Morgan's perspective. One important thing to consider is something I learned, though perhaps too late. I discovered I could influence Boudicca by planting thoughts in her head. This can be helpful, but it can also hinder the objective. We must allow events to unfold as we expect, so you can't divert her from her task. I know this sounds like a speech from Richard III with the winter of discontent, but you understand how much this means to us. Our life's work is now in your hands. And remember, you're doing this for those who have given up their lives for the quest—Quinn, Matt, and Reagan. All of us who believe in the quest believe in you, Cleo," I said, feeling a surge of emotion. Tears welled up in my eyes as I spoke passionately. The room fell into a pregnant pause as we all contemplated the mission and its significance. I took a seat, allowing Jackson to continue.

"When I first regressed Bo, the sessions often lasted up to six hours, which was incredibly draining for her. We did that because we were on a learning curve, and we didn't know what was coming up in Boudicca's life. We wanted to miss nothing. But with you, Cleo, we have the benefit of hindsight, as Bo mentioned. So we'll have three two-hour sessions per day, with breaks in between for debriefing, recuperation, and sustenance. I won't schedule specific starting and finishing times yet, as we'll need you to inform us of Boudicca's current downtime for sleep. Any questions?" Jackson explained.

"If I sense danger that she doesn't... what should I do?" Cleo asked, raising a valid concern.

"That's a good question. I'll let Bo answer that," Jackson replied.

"We believe that we shouldn't tamper with history, to borrow a concept from Star Trek. The Temporal Prime Directive is intended to prevent time travelers, whether from the past or future, from interfering in the natural development of a timeline," I explained, trying to lighten the mood. We all chuckled.

"What about the fact that I can understand what is said without knowing the language?" Cleo asked, another thoughtful question.

"Another good question, Cleo. I'll let Mike tackle that one," I said, passing the baton.

"We believe that under hypnosis and connected to Boudicca, you are actually occupying her conscious mind. In that state, you understand what she understands, if you get my drift," Mike answered.

"And if I may add, Mike," Jackson interjected, "I'm quite certain, after years of conjecture, that your DNA, like Bo's, is somehow connected to Boudicca's. It could be through a transposon, a small strand of unique DNA that inserts itself into another place in the genome and is passed on through successive generations. However, we can't be certain."

"So, we're somehow related?" Cleo asked, intrigued.

"That's the most likely scenario, but without a sample of Boudicca's

DNA, we'll never know for sure," I added.

"Hey, wouldn't it be a trip if we knew where she was buried and could get a DNA sample?" Cleo pondered.

"Not possible, I'm afraid, Cleo. Once Boudicca dies, you will lose contact with her, and you'll never witness her burial," Judith explained.

"But surely, Sharlene Cayce, being a clairvoyant, could contact Morgan, just as Reagan did, and find out," Cleo countered, her mind racing.

I was awestruck by her idea. I hadn't considered that possibility.

"That's why having you on board is so important Cleo. We never would have thought of that. It's so bloody obvious, yet we overlooked it. We could have tried Sharlene channelling Boudicca," I said, mentally scolding myself.

"But let's not get distracted from the objective for now. We should certainly explore that idea later," Judith interjected, sounding like a strict schoolmistress.

"Okay," Cleo said, reclining on the lounge. "I'm ready whenever you are, Jackson. Countdown to ecstasy."

Jackson assumed his position, and Mike closed the curtains, dimming the lights. Notebooks and pens were at the ready. We settled back into our chairs, eagerly anticipating Boudicca's voice once again.

An hour later, Jackson woke Cleo. She wore a disgruntled look on her face.

"Cleo, are you with us?" Jackson asked warmly.

She slowly sat up and rubbed her eyes. "Hmm, yeah, but I'd rather be there. How long have I been out?"

I smiled knowingly. "Only an hour," I said.

"But you said it would be three," she complained.

"Mike deduced from what you were saying that you were going to take a rest, so I woke you," I added.

"I see... yes, yes, you were right," she said dispiritedly.

"Cleo, while it's still fresh in your mind, can you share your experience?" Mike asked.

"Okay... I was at Cadbury finishing up breakfast with Tyree... Ha! He's such a cool dude... then he was told there were guests. I guessed it must be Morgan and Joseph."

"I remember that," I said.

"They appeared in the doorway, one helping the other. I could see Morgan was struggling, so I went to give him a hand. 'Morgan, is this Joseph?' I asked, grabbing hold of the old man. 'Yes,' he said, 'this is Joseph...' and then he went on about how it was a tough journey for the old guy. We sat Joseph in a chair, and Tyree brought a jug of mead. Joseph had long white hair down to the middle of his back and a long white beard—I thought he looked like God. He was wearing a blue and white striped caftan. I gave him a sip of beer. He looked at me with striking blue eyes, and even though he was stressed out, he managed a tired smile but didn't drink. He was clutching a book to his chest. 'Try to drink some, Joseph,' I told him. 'You need sustenance after your journey.' He pointed at me and then whispered in Latin. His voice was so weak I had to get really close to his mouth to hear."

"He said he is happy to see me and is now ready to pass over," I told the others. "His wish is to be buried in the manner of the Druithin... he recognises that I, too, am a servant of the truth and says Morgan knows the place. The gospel he carries is to be buried in a secure place but separate from his body. It is of critical importance to another time. Both burial places are never to be divulged. She who is destined to find the gospel will do so in her own good time, or words to that effect—he was talking about me now, I reckon." Then he stared into my eyes and handed over his life's work. As he did so, he took a last noble breath, and then life left his eyes forever. I looked at the book in my hands, and my mind, well, Boudicca's mind, was cast to Bran when I watched life leave him... there was no exhale, and I thought to myself: Do people always die inhaling, or do some die exhaling? I wonder if it makes a difference?"

"Anyhow, I told them he had left us... I was crying. I wished I'd had more time with him... he was a paragon of wisdom, and I wondered if he had documented all of that immense knowledge in the gospel I was holding. If he had, it would be one of the most seminal books ever written."

I glanced at Morgan, and without displaying any emotion at all, he said, "We will do the burials at first light."

"I thought, 'First Light'—yeah, the name of the society—and then agreed."

"That was when the session finished for me, Cleo. I remember," I said.

"Yes, I remember that as well Bo... it was where you got the name 'First Light,'" Mike said.

"Go on, Cleo," Judith pressed.

"Morgan picked Joseph up in his frail arms, slung him over his shoulder, and dutifully carried him out of the building. Tyree finished off the pitcher of beer.

'I will need to make an offering to Andrasta tonight,' I urgently told him. 'Giamonios has started... tomorrow the moon will be full. Where is the nearest sacred spring?'

'I will have one of my men point the way from the front gates... it is quite near. In the meantime, you should rest. I will have a maiden take you to your quarters. She will bathe you... or would you prefer a boy or a warrior?'

'There will be no sex before honouring Andrasta tonight... so I won't be needing a young buck; a maiden will suffice.' I thought that was a pretty strange thing for her to say but went with the flow. Tyree called for a maiden, and a pretty, skinny little blonde thing in her teens trotted out. I looked down at the book in my hands; it felt like I was holding the whole world. The temptation was too great, so I opened it. I couldn't recognise the language of the text, but it was beautifully neat. It was a large book, heavy, loose-leaf parchment bound in skin. I closed it and then handed it to Tyree.

'Guard this with your life, old man... I will collect it from you at dawn.'

'It will be safe with me.'

The maiden led me out of the great hall. There was plenty of activity outside as preparations were being made for market day. A bulked-up hunk came running over and told me Tyree had ordered him to show me the way to the sacred spring. He led us to the front gates, out, and then he stopped and pointed at the road that led down the hill.

'Take the first fork on the left. It stops at the grove... the spring is beyond. Would you like me to accompany you?' he asked with a sparkle in his eyes.

On any other day, I wouldn't have hesitated to take him along to have my way with him, but not at the spring; that would be sacrilegious. We went back into the compound, the hunk trotted off, and little miss prissy led me over to a small, thatched-roof roundhouse. Once inside, she undressed me and herself, took some hot water from the hearth, topped up the wooden bathtub, and then bathed me. It was the first time I'd seen my body naked. Wow, I had great tits, a big bushy mop of red pubes, hairy armpits, and battle scars all over me. Looking at my feet, I couldn't believe the size of them—I could have done with a manicure and some nail polish. The naked little chick did a great job... she cleaned under my fingernails and toenails, scrubbed the grime off my back and neck, bum, and washed my amazing flock of curly red hair. I felt like a new woman when I stepped out of the tub of filthy water. I told her I needed to pee, so she brought me a wooden bowl. I squatted over it and relieved myself. She tipped it into the bathwater, then threw in my clothes and jumped in to wash them. Sounds gross, but not really; my leather clothes would be softened by the urine in the bathwater; otherwise, they'd be as hard as a rock when they dried. Don't ask me how I know that. It was probably the first bath she'd had in a year. Anyhow, the bed looked inviting and comfortable with at least three big bear furs to snuggle up to. Then I heard Jackson's voice. Great timing. I figure she'll sleep for two or three hours before her moonwalk—wouldn't want to miss out on that."

CHAPTER
XXIX

We were totally enthralled by Cleo's summary; her attention to detail was as assiduous as mine. Mike had recorded the session using a digital camera and would later write up a direct English translation of Cleo's Celtic.

"You held the book," I said awestruck.

"And you opened it and saw the contents, amazing!" Mike said.

"Do you know how many UK members of First Light would have given their right arm to be here today to witness this momentous occasion, Cleo?" Judith said.

Cleo smiled. "I wouldn't have minded, the more the merrier."

"No, Cleo, in our secret society, you are its biggest secret. First Light knows nothing about you except that you're a new member," Mike said.

"And that's how it will stay until we have the location," I affirmed.

"Don't think of us as paranoid, Cleo," Judith said cynically in a small voice.

After all we had been through, I wasn't about to stand for that.

"It was obviously not you whose life was threatened, Judith, otherwise you might think differently. I think we'll stick with the security measures," I scowled at her.

Jackson sensed tension brewing between us and chose to lighten the mood. "Cleo, take a rest now, and we'll have another session in two hours. The one good thing about being in England is we don't have to account for the time difference."

"I didn't realise that..." Cleo said, getting up from the sofa. "I might take a stroll outside. Want to come, Bo?"

Spring was a lovely time of year to be in England, and the grounds of Moore Manor typified everything English about a country garden.

All of the plants were flowering, and the air was rich with the scent of blossoms. We ambled arm in arm along the path that led through the rose garden.

"Seemed a bit stressed in there between you and Judith?" Cleo said casually.

"Oh, she can be an old fuddy-duddy at times. I don't think she ever got over allowing Gaius in the guise of Paul Sicario to infiltrate our First Light meeting last time we were here."

"You'd reckon she'd feel guilty about it and want more security, not just knock it."

"No, that's not her form. She's got a little of that conservative old-school-tie British public school snobbery about her, you know. Sometimes I feel like she's addressing me like I'm a pupil and she's the headmistress."

"Yeah, I can get that. You had sex as Boudicca, what was that like?"

There was a bench beside the path, so we sat down.

"I don't know that you'll get the opportunity to try it yourself, but let me tell you, I've always been faithful to Jackson except for when I was Boudicca, and I don't think I've ever experienced anything quite like it. Every emotion I felt was real."

"Even the sensation... you know, the feeling of having him inside you?"

"Yes, and you know that total body sensation you get just before you're about to sneeze?"

"Far out! Oh, what a bummer that I'll miss out on a super orgasm like that," she said like a spoiled little girl.

I looked into her lovely eyes and then delicately brushed a strand of hair away.

"I did mention you might be able to encourage Boudicca to think certain thoughts, didn't I?"

"Yes, I remember that... what are you thinking?" she said slowly with a devious gleam in her sparkling young eyes.

"Well, remember that hunk?"

We got back to the Manor at lunchtime, in time to find a magnificent spread Judith had prepared. As we sat down to eat, I couldn't help but feel there was something amiss between Judith and Mike, as though they were separated by a great distance even though sitting together. Judith didn't really seem the same to me since the run-in with Gaius. I wondered if it was a symptom of her diabetes or whether she might have a guilt complex or something, so I thought to raise it at an appropriate moment after lunch. With Jackson seated beside me at the long beautifully dressed dinner table in the main dining room, and Judith, Cleo, and Mike deeply engaged in conversation, I seized the opportunity to run my sentiments by Jackson.

"Have you noticed anything odd about Judith?" I said furtively in a low tone.

"Yes, she seems introverted. Perhaps it's her age or the diabetes."

"I'm more inclined to think it's something else. She seems withdrawn from Mike and quarrelsome whenever I talk to her."

"Two different things, I suspect. I'd say their relationship is a bit rocky, and she's got a problem with you about something."

"Should I raise it?"

"Absolutely. With a day as important as tomorrow promises to be, perhaps the beginning of an entirely new line of investigation, we all need to be on the same page. Save it for the library after we have finished here."

It was the sort of sound advice I expected from my man.

Later in the library, after we'd all settled into comfy chairs to discuss the coming session with Cleo.

"Judith, I feel I need to raise a question with you," I said slowly.

"Yes, Bonnie, do go ahead," she said curtly.

"I am concerned that your attitude towards me has changed and would like to know if I have offended you in some way?"

She appeared to be taken aback by my presumption.

"I think you're being oversensitive," she said defensively.

"Be that as it may, perhaps that is your perception of me while not others."

"That's pathetic!" she snapped irritably. "You come over here after living in Australia for years with a siege mentality, expecting us to simply adopt your stance on everything."

"That is completely uncalled for, Judith. What you're saying does not reflect my sentiments," Mike said adamantly.

"I don't give a hoot about your sentiments, Mike," she snapped.

The statement really hurt Mike; you could see it in his eyes.

"I think it might be best, Judith, if you qualify what you mean by 'siege mentality,'" Jackson asked calmly.

"All right... since Quinn died, you two have just shut us out. If it wasn't for the webpage Mike created, we'd be totally in the dark. I expect it's all to do with Gaius' attack on Bonnie," she proclaimed.

"Okay, that is what I suspected. You have a problem with me after I was attacked here by Gaius, don't you? I suspect you still feel guilty for breaking the security protocol and letting him into our meeting," I growled.

"That's preposterous! It wasn't me who invited him in; it was Ahmed!" she scowled.

"But he asked your permission, and you gave it," I countered.

She jumped up aggressively and strode out of the room fuming. After a contemplative moment, Mike spoke up.

"I apologise for her behaviour, Bonnie, Jackson, and Cleo, but she hasn't been herself since her condition was diagnosed six months ago." He was close to tears, and then he uncharacteristically put his head in his hands and wept.

Jackson went to his side and warmly placed a comforting hand on his shoulder.

"What condition, my friend? You told us about the diabetes."

"She said she had told you," he whimpered. "There's more than that..."

"No, she's told us nothing," I said.

"She has breast cancer. They want to give her a mastectomy."

I found myself hugging poor Mike, and now it was all very clear.

"Oh, the poor dear... God, why didn't she say something?" I grumbled, in tears.

"Too proud, probably, plus she's getting old and cranky," he said with a wry smile. "The problem is she's had it for so long without knowing. It only came up after she had been diagnosed with diabetes, which was bad enough. At her age, breast cancer is really dangerous—life-threatening. She has less than a fifty-fifty chance of survival even after a modified radical mastectomy."

"What's that?" Cleo asked.

"The surgeon removes the entire breast..." Jackson said.

"Both in her case," Mike added. "And the underarm lymph nodes as well."

I flopped back into my chair, shattered by the revelation.

"Oh dear, oh dear, that explains her moods," I said, getting up. "I need to speak with her."

"Wait, Bonnie," Mike warned. "You should know that she believes this is going to kill her, and it makes her angry because she has important things to accomplish, especially with First Light. So time has become more precious to her than it ever was. I believe the only thing that will motivate her to defeat this is Cleo determining the location of the gospel, and us going after it."

"That explains her urgency to get on with things," I said.

"What you're saying, Mike, makes a whole lot of sense," Jackson said. "A goal. I think it might be best to allow Judith to keep her secret for the time being. If I were you, Bonnie, I'd go and smooth things over with her but keep mum about the cancer."

"Let me go with you, Bo. I think she puts a fair bit of faith in what I'm going to do, and she'll listen to me," Cleo said wholeheartedly.

We clasped hands and left Jackson and Mike behind to go and find Judith.

After checking a few rooms in the ten-bedroom stately manor, I knocked on the study door and then opened it. Judith was seated behind her desk, looking at her computer. She glared at me, her face displaying annoyance at the disturbance. We barged in and flopped into a couple of chairs opposite her desk, acting like a couple of teenagers.

"Bo wanted to come and apologise to you, but I said no, there was no need for that... I said let's go find her and talk about what we're going to do once I find where that bloomin' gospel is hidden," Cleo barked with youthful enthusiasm.

Judith's face lit up from sour to sweet in an instant. It was so clever of Cleo. She'd put an end to the drama and placed a positive spin on the mood in one sentence.

"Yes, well, that does warrant some discussion, doesn't it?" she muttered with a waggish smile.

By sundown, we were all friends again, and Jackson was busy delivering a mesmerizing spiel to Cleo.

An hour later, after witnessing an incredible display of sensual body contortions from Cleo, we could hardly wait for her to reiterate the experience. We were sitting around like students waiting for a much-anticipated lecture.

"It was perfect timing," Cleo said enthusiastically. "When I joined her, Boudicca was standing in front of a body-length copper mirror, anointing her naked body with a pungent oil or animal fat, not sure which... but at any rate, it was seriously arousing. The long pink nipples of her large, firm breasts were erect, and her muscular body glistened in the flickering firelight like a gleaming bronze statue. It was time Boudicca and I became as one. As barefooted, naked to the world, I slipped out of the roundhouse into the dark of the night. It was cold, but it didn't bother me. There were only a few people in the market enclosure, and they didn't notice me scoot by. I ran like an Olympian, the breeze stroking my body like mystical fingers as I sped down the hill towards the fork in the road. In no time flat, I had entered the dark forest. It was then I realised I was carrying something in my hand. I stopped to locate the path to the spring, which was hard to see in the darkness. I looked down at the small wooden statue in my hand. It was female with massive breasts and a huge oversized backside. To me it seemed to symbolise Mother Nature... or in Boudicca's case, Andrasta. Staring at the effigy in silence, I closed my eyes and then heard the distant babble of a brook. I opened my eyes, confident Andrasta was ready to show me the way. The near full moon rose huge in the sky and sent yellow rays slicing through the canopy of trees like a scythe... and that helped me make out a small hollow ahead, and in it, the brook with its otherworldly mystical ambience. When I reached it, I knelt down and kissed the effigy, ready for sacrifice. Holding it reverently in both hands out in front of me, I closed my eyes and said, 'I will soon be at one with you, my goddess. Protect me until that time comes. I ask you to give a place of honour beside Bran to my friend Joseph, who entered your underworld this morn. They know each other and will have much to discuss. I am excited to join them in a matter of days.'

"I was suddenly alerted to a twig snapping behind me. There was someone watching me. I dropped the effigy into the brook to complete the ritual, then slowly rose up and turned sharply to face my voyeur. I called out, 'I know you're there... show yourself—I am unarmed.' The bushes parted, and the form of a well-built man appeared silhouetted by the moonlight—I didn't recognise him.

'I am sorry, my Queen,' he said plaintively. 'I was sent by Tyree to ensure your safety. It is I, Ansgar.'

'Step into the light so I might see you, Ansgar. Your name means warrior, does it not?'

'Aye,' he said.

I immediately recognised him as the hunk... Andrasta had sent me a man to nourish my desires, and she'd selected a fine specimen for the task.

'Come, but first remove your clothing in this hallowed place.'

He did as I ordered... his body as delicious to the eye as I had anticipated. It was also quite obvious by his thick sword standing erect and proud that my sensuous body had aroused him. I took his hand and lay him on the damp earth and then straddled his hulk and slipped his sword into my moist sheath. We made love. In the grove of my goddess, I was impassioned—but even after such intense lovemaking, he was still not spent... he was more than just a hunk, he was Adonis. If we did it again, I feared I'd never make it back to Cadbury—

especially with what I knew was ahead of me. Oh, how I could have just lived forever safe in his comforting arms. I helped him dress—he had brought me a robe. I took him by the hand, and we walked slowly and silently back to the hill fort. At the door to my roundhouse, I stole a parting kiss, knowing it would be our last. I also knew it was likely to be the last time I would ever make love in this life. And then you called me back."

We were astounded.

CHAPTER
XXX

At dinner that evening, there was excitement in the air for the next session. Jackson stood and raised his glass.

"Judith, Mike, Cleo, and my wonderful wife Bonnie, I'd like to propose a toast to what we have collectively achieved to date and whatever may lie ahead of us tomorrow. With that toast goes many heartfelt thanks to you, Judith and Mike, for once again being such marvellous hosts... and in addition, I'd like to mention those who cannot be with us for their contribution to our objective: Graham, Quinn, Matt, Reagan, and Bonnie's parents. To our success!"

We all repeated those words and took a sip of champagne.

"Do you expect to contact Daniel at Interpol after tomorrow, Jackson?" Mike asked.

"Surely not after the mess they made of it last time," I grumbled.

Jackson sat back in his seat. "Unfortunately, we don't have much choice, do we?"

"Rick Molloy is probably in charge now. Boyd would be retired, wouldn't he?" Mike queried.

"I've got no time for either of them, and I haven't heard or seen anything that would give me cause to be concerned. Gaius is probably retired himself these days," Judith snarled.

"Sadly, I have to report that we recently heard from him," I said.

"I got a threatening e-mail from him," Cleo said sternly.

"How on earth did he find out about you?" Mike submitted, startled.

"I was checking a website about Boudicca when I was interviewing Aunt Bo, and I must have triggered an alert that captured my IP address," Cleo explained.

"Yes, that would certainly do it," Mike agreed. "I found a number of traps set by our Benedictine friends on the net."

"Yes, didn't um... now what's her name?" Judith struggled for her name.

"Brigitte... Brigitte Yates, you remember her, Bo and Jackson?" Mike said.

"Wasn't she the French lass Peter Wilson was hitting on?" Jackson said with a smile.

"If I remember rightly, it was Brigitte doing the hitting," I joked.

We all had a chuckle, remembering the slapping incident.

"She was doing some net research on Tacitus when she clicked on a link that took her to a spurious religious webpage. She opted out but then received a very strange threatening e-mail the next day. It wasn't signed, but when she sent it to me, I managed to trace the source code to an IT centre at the Vatican. I tried to dig deeper but smacked into an impenetrable firewall," Mike explained.

"That sounds suspicious. When was that, Mike?" Jackson queried.

"Last week, wasn't it, Judith?" Mike asked.

"Yes, I think it was," she answered vaguely.

That made me nervous. What with the e-mail to Cleo, it was all too much and too recent to simply brush aside as mere coincidence.

"I'm going to give Interpol a call. There's way too much at stake here," Jackson said assertively.

"I think you're right," Mike agreed.

"We're not overreacting, are we?" Judith questioned.

"We have nothing to lose by covering our bases, Judith," Jackson said, drawing his cell phone from his pocket. He left the room to make the call.

"The big question for me is... if it is Gaius rearing his ugly head again—put yourself in his shoes—is it better for him to stop us from determining the location of the gospel or to simply wait and then take it once we've got it? I, for one, have always wondered why he didn't simply kill me and end it all. Could that be the reason?" I submitted.

Mike stood, went to the bureau, and poured himself a fresh slug of brandy. "I believe the latter, Bonnie. He has had forty years to find and murder you and hasn't. He's simply kept the pressure on... however, he has killed others with no real bearing on uncovering the gospel. That tells us something, surely?"

"Sure, he has been biding his time, just like us, waiting to pounce once we've got the prize?" Judith asserted.

"That's logical," Mike concluded.

"If that is the case, he or his cohorts could be nearby, you know, watching us," Cleo affirmed.

Simultaneously, we all glanced at the windows, speculating whether Gaius was lurking in the shadows outside, watching and waiting. The thought made the little hairs on my forearms stand on end.

"Ooo, it just felt like someone walked on my grave," I said gloomily.

Jackson returned.

"I spoke with Interpol... you were right, Judith. Daniel Boyd retired a few years back, and Rick Molloy is no longer in the force. It was difficult because I had to explain their involvement from the beginning. Anyhow, they found a file on their database and offered to send out an agent. I agreed, and, I hope you don't mind, Judith, I said he or she could stay here with us for a couple of days."

"No, that's fine, Jackson. You did the right thing," Judith said soberly.

I handed Jackson a brandy. "When will he arrive, love?"

"He's driving up from London..."

"Two hours, give or take," Mike said.

I looked at my watch. "So around eleven tonight... you obviously didn't speak to the actual person, otherwise you'd have known for sure whether it's a he or she?"

"Yes, I admit I found that a bit odd. I was told they'd have to select someone and then brief them... they weren't sure who yet," Jackson added.

"By the time they do all that, it could be after midnight before they turn up," Cleo said. "I've had it, we'll have to be up before dawn tomorrow. I think I'll hit the hay."

I went over to Judith and whispered, "Can you move Cleo to the most secure bedroom you have?"

She nodded in agreement to my reasoning.

"Cleo, let Mike show you to the Bryson room. It's between Bo and Jackson's room and the room for the Interpol agent. There are adjoining doors, so we can be sure you're safe."

Just as Mike and Cleo got up to leave, Jackson's mobile rang. We all waited while he went out of the room to take the call. He came back a moment later, looking miffed to the extreme.

"What's wrong, love?" I asked.

"I can't believe these people. They said they can't have someone here until tomorrow or the day after," he snapped irritably, totally unlike him. Always an even-tempered man, hardly anything ruffles his feathers, but in this instance, with so much at stake and such a potential threat, he was showing his frustration.

"We were just saying that it doesn't seem logical Gaius would want to hurt us. He's had ample opportunity to do that over the years. It makes more sense that he's planning on taking the gospel once we have it," I told Jackson.

"And all the intimidation?" he queried.

"I'd reckon that was to keep the pressure on us. I admit, it would have been smarter for him or the Crux to just sit it out and wait, but for some reason, we must have posed a threat early on," Mike considered.

"I can understand why they killed Matt. They would have considered him a real threat, but why your friend Reagan?" Judith asked.

"It could only be to prevent him from publishing his book," Jackson reasoned.

"Yes, and remember what happened with Henry Lincoln's book 'The Holy Blood, the Holy Grail'," Mike said. "It caused an avalanche of detrimental publicity for the Church."

"And spawned more books, bestsellers to boot..." I said.

"Don't forget the blockbuster movies like 'The Da Vinci Code'," Cleo added.

"Okay, if we accept your scenario that he's unlikely to strike before we find the gospel, we need to prepare for the eventuality," Jackson said sternly.

"Let's look at the facts—we have to assume he wouldn't know Cleo is the link to the past now," I presumed.

"No wait, that doesn't seem logical—if you were still the contact, Bonnie, why would we have waited this long?" Judith assessed.

"Because Boudicca died, and we missed out on getting the location... or we haven't been able to obtain permission to dig for it... I don't know, I'm only guessing," I stammered.

"No, I think he must know more than we're giving him credit for. He has to know what we're up to... he's been letting us know that with the emails to Cleo and Brigitte," Jackson surmised.

"Well, I tell you what I'm doing... I'm going to bed," Cleo said with an exhausted grimace.

Mike wrapped an arm around her shoulders and said, "Come on then, I'll show you your room, miss."

"Good night, everyone. I'll see you in the a.m. Aunt Bo, will you give me a wake-up call?"

She gave me a peck on the cheek.

"You bet-cha!" I said.

After they had gone, I opened up more candidly.

"I have to admit, guys, no matter what way we judge his next move, the thought that Gaius has been in contact gives me the heebie-jeebies. I promised Cleo's mom her safety wouldn't be compromised... and now with no Interpol support, I feel I'm letting her down," I admitted.

"You've got every right to feel that way, love, but I don't know what more we can do to improve the situation other than being vigilant," Jackson said mildly.

"Perhaps we need more people in the house?" Judith proposed.

We thought about it for a minute, and suddenly the idea began to make sense.

"You're right, Judith! We should have First Light members here on guard," I exclaimed, as if I had just found something I'd lost.

Judith jumped to her feet with fire in her eyes, the first I'd seen in a long time.

"I'll get on it right away!" she said, heading for the phone.

In a little over a couple of hours, we had six First Light members warming their hands by the fire in the library. Two of them I already knew, Brigitte and Ahmed, the others were younger new recruits—all of them with impeccable academic credentials. Brigitte and Ahmed were now in their fifties and professors of archaeology at Cambridge. The others were their pupils. We had agreed not to explain to the younger ones about Cleo any more than she was part of our Australian team. It was however important to tell Brigitte and Ahmed the truth; they had experienced the serious breach of security twenty-seven years ago in 1988, and so little explanation was needed. Looking at them now made it obvious to me how much time had flown by.

Ahmed agreed to take control of the team and to keep a watchful eye on everything overnight.

We bid goodnight to everyone, and Jackson, Judith, and I made our way upstairs. As we were walking along the corridor to our rooms, Judith said crabbily, "Now that you've got us all wound up, I, for one, won't be getting any rest tonight."

I stopped and said, "You go ahead, Jackson. I want a word with Judith."

"Okay, good night, Judith," Jackson said warmly.

I watched him enter our room and turned to Judith.

"Your trouble," I said earnestly, "is that you won't allow yourself or anyone else, for that matter, to relax."

"And that's bad?" she questioned scornfully.

"You just need to let everybody do their thing. No good being a control freak, Judith."

"Wrong!" she said firmly. "With some things, one just can't rely on others," she corrected.

"That doesn't mean you should worry—out loud. We're all in this together," I insisted.

"What are you trying to say, Bonnie?" she said calmly.

"I know about your medical condition, Judith," I said soberly. "And I just want to hug you and say that it will be all right, that's all."

"So, what's holding you back then?" she said with a choked voice.

We embraced and both wept... I could feel her angst evaporating and welcomed the old Judith back in my arms.

"Hugging is a great way to hide your face," she whispered in my ear.

"There's no need to hide it, love," I said warmly. "We're in this with you."

"Oh Bonnie, it can be a wee bit rough getting old, love. Sometimes the only excitement left in your life is when you get angry."

I entered the bedroom on tiptoes and found Jackson flat on his back on the bed, still wearing his reading glasses and snoring soundly with an open book on his chest. I expected him to be asleep but didn't realise I'd been so long in the corridor talking with Judith.

A few minutes later, I was under the doona beside my man, listening to the ravages of the wild night outside. A storm had moved in and was making its windy presence felt with a tumult of lightning cracks, thunder, and torrential rain. Each lightning flash illuminated the room briefly, casting ghoulish shadows that my mind insisted on morphing into Gaius. I was still awake at 4 a.m. when Jackson's phone alarm sounded.

CHAPTER
XXXI

Making our way downstairs, the excitement and lack of sleep had gifted me a belly full of butterflies.

"I badly need a coffee fix," I confessed to Jackson.

"You look like death, love. Didn't you sleep at all?"

"Not a wink."

"Oh dear, I'll get one of the kids to make up a brew," he said, rubbing his hands together in an attempt to warm them.

When we entered the library, we found the six First Light members all very much awake in front of the fireplace, engaged in what seemed to be an intense philosophical debate.

"Good morning, everyone," I said, jostling through them to get as close to the blazing fireplace as humanly possible. "Blimey, it's cold."

"Don't be ridiculous, Bonnie. Spring is in the air," Ahmed said with a wry smile.

"Not the sort of spring I'm used to, Ahmed," I grumbled. I hate the cold.

"Who's on coffee duty?" Jackson said, enquiringly.

Jane Mayweather, a pretty little blonde, jumped up as though Jackson had issued an official edict.

"Me, sir... I'll just go brew us a fresh pot, yeah?" she said timidly with a real Londoner accent.

Cleo joined us, yawning with sleepy eyes, looking very much like she'd only seconds ago managed to extract herself from the warmth of a comfy bed.

"Good morning, Cleo," I said.

A shocked expression took over her tired face—she wasn't at all expecting to find all these people.

"Oh, good morning... everyone," she said conscientiously, touching up her unruly hair.

"Everybody, meet my niece Cleo. That's Jane leaving to brew us some coffee, this is Professor Ahmed Rashid, and Professor Brigitte Yates... this is... I'm sorry," I said, motioning to the remaining two lads.

The older of the two, Cleo's age, stood. Tall, clean-cut, well-dressed, and glowing with gentlemanly manners, he smiled.

"Wayne Richmond," his announcement came with a public school accent.

The other lad had the look of a scallywag with a shock of unkempt shoulder-length mousy blonde hair, old blue jeans, a checked shirt, and vest. He stayed seated on the ground in front of the fireplace and gave Cleo a wave.

"Yo, Dylan Scott at your service," he said in a Cornish accent with a twist of the Bronx.

I could tell by the look on Cleo's face she was impressed with both boys.

"Cripes, it's cold!" she protested and tried to pinch grid position at the fire.

"You with First Light Australia, I haven't seen you online?" Wayne remarked.

"I'm only a new member," Cleo said with the hint of a blush.

"How do you select your members in Oz then, Dr Jackson?" Dylan asked.

"Oh, we stretch yellow crime scene tape about ten feet in length between two members about waist-high. I'm sure you've seen the stuff on CSI or whatever. Then we ask the two new recruits to step under it simultaneously. If one or both lift the tape, then that tells us one thing, and if they duck under it tells us another."

"Fascinating, Doctor. So if you lift it?" Wayne asked.

"A lifter is dominant and considered arrogant, whereas a ducker is careful and decisive," Jackson said with a poker face.

"So, who gets in then?" Dylan asked.

"Oh, the ducker, of course... the lifter misses out," Jackson said abruptly.

"You can't be serious?" Dylan scoffed.

Jane returned with a tray of coffees.

"Terrific, Jane. You are the bringer of welcomed insomnia," I chuckled.

I could tell by the puzzled look on Dylan's face that he was still struggling with Jackson's initiation ritual. He wasn't sure if he was taking the Mickey or if it was indeed some sort of peculiar psychological test reserved for the antipodes.

Jackson checked his watch. "It's now 4.15, we'll get underway at 4.30, okay?"

Just then, Judith and Mike arrived and helped themselves to a mug of coffee. Dylan joined them and spooned cream into his coffee with a compulsive hand.

"You're as crafty as a barnyard rooster, Doctor Jackson," Dylan said comically out of the corner of his mouth. "There's no way you'd have an initiation ceremony like that in Oz."

"I guess you're right, Dylan. To be honest, it's the same as yours here," Jackson said flatly.

I immediately took a liking to them all, each with a special quality, and according to Mike and Judith, exceptional individual skills to boot.

Dylan cruised over to Cleo, sipping his coffee. "That looks more like a cup of cream than coffee," Cleo jested.

"I like things rich and sweet, just like you, darling," he replied smoothly.

"Look out, Cleo," Wayne warned cynically in jest. "I think Dylan just used one of his best lines on you."

"Well, he'd better have some better ones in reserve because that one had very little impact," Cleo said with a wry grin.

Dylan's face looked like he was just out of a week-old coffin. The mood was just getting to be fun when Mike, who had whipped back to the study to light the fireplace, returned.

"Shall we?" Mike requested.

I turned to Judith and said softly, "What about Ahmed and Brigitte?"

"I think so," she replied equally hushed and then spoke up like a schoolmistress. "Ahmed, you and Brigitte can join us if you wish. Wayne, Dylan, and Jane should get some rest. But keep an eye out for strangers... don't let anybody in. Understood?"

They nodded.

As we filed into the warm study, I said to Ahmed, "Dylan's a real card."

"Yes, but to be honest with you, Bonnie, he is one of my brightest students. You know, last year he sold 5.4 million Facebook likes for thirty US cents each."

"Good grief, that's... 1.6 million dollars! That's a heck of a lot of work and money," I exclaimed, astonished.

"No, not really a lot of work. You see, he wrote an algorithm that generates Facebook likes. He confided in me in his first year that he wanted to come up with a way to make money while he was asleep, and he certainly did that. He's a technological genius, Bonnie, I tell you," Ahmed said proudly.

We took a seat in the warm study while Jackson prepared Cleo. Then he turned and faced us.

"I feel the need to remind us this morning that we are about to embark on the most important session since Bonnie first contacted Boudicca through regression hypnosis back in 1974. This morning, Cleo will hopefully determine where Boudicca and Morgan buried Joseph of Arimathea and his gospel. Cleo is about to make history, and in doing so, will vindicate all of our work and our collective sacrifices. Does anyone have any questions?"

"Yes, Cleo, remember you do have the ability to subconsciously suggest to Boudicca what you may wish her to do or say. The thought will come to her as an inner thought, an idea if you like, but like having a little voice inside her head," I said.

"In that case, will Cleo have to speak to Boudicca in Celtic, so will she understand?" Brigitte asked.

"Excellent question, Brigitte. I only tried it once, and I believe somehow the message was translated for Boudicca to understand. Don't ask me how," I said.

"I get it, Bo. I know how important it is to get this right. We're only going to get one crack at it, aren't we?" Cleo said, obviously feeling the pressure.

"Blimey, I'm getting Goosebumps," Judith admitted with a shiver.

We all fell silent while Jackson put Cleo under.

This time, he revived her after what felt like the longest three hours of my life. We needed to make sure she had time to witness the burials, and I was certain that after three hours, Boudicca would be back at Cadbury.

There had been little physical movement from Cleo during the session, but she did speak in English a couple of times... and what she had said was fascinating. We couldn't wait to hear her recount of the session. By now, after four cups of coffee, I was wired, but if I hadn't had them, I would have certainly nodded off.

Cleo sat up and glared at us as though we were strangers she had difficulty recognising. Then, as she broke through the veil of reality, her expression softened.

"I'm parched," she complained with a grin.

I poured a glass of water and handed it to her.

"Thanks," she smiled. "Wow, that was really something."

"Where did you leave her?" I asked.

"She was with Tyree after that horrific fight..."

"Good," I smiled at Jackson. "I remember that fight very well."

"I think I'd like to go outside for some fresh air before I fill you all in. Is that okay?"

"Absolutely," I said for everyone. "I know how draining it can be."

"It's not just that, I want to collect my thoughts. A lot happened, and I want to be clear."

"Are you feeling okay, Cleo? Not dizzy or anything?" Jackson asked, concerned.

"Yes, Uncle Jack, I'm fine... like I said, I just need to clear my head. Just give me half an hour," she requested sweetly.

When we joined the others in the library, we found them in various positions, asleep. So, as not to disturb them, we crept out silently and went into the dining room. Judith took Brigitte to the kitchen to rustle up a tub of porridge for breakfast.

After fifteen minutes or so, we were hoeing into a bowl of porridge, milk, butter, and brown sugar—yum. Cleo joined us for a bowl, but we avoided talking about the session. We'd wait until she was good and ready. Our bellies full and a mug of coffee in hand, we returned to the study for Cleo's story. You could have cut the excitement in the air with a knife. We sat glued to her in suspense, anxious to hear what we've been waiting so long to learn.

"I was leaning over a wooden bowl, washing my face. And as I wiped the water away, I peered at my face in a small copper mirror. It was a little distorted but clear enough to make out the sharp features of Boudicca's proud face. It was then I decided to try and talk to her. I decided to tell her who I was. I said, "Hello, Boudicca, my name is Cleo, and I'm visiting your mind from a different time." She stopped wiping her face, a little startled, and then stared at the mirror suspiciously.

"I know it's difficult to believe this, but it is true. I am from another time, and my spirit has been sent back in time to be with you."

"'Andrasta, you have come to me," she murmured, a little stunned.

I realised it would make more sense to her if I became Andrasta to her. She would at least believe she was possessed by her and perhaps embrace the idea. It was great that my English was being converted somehow for her to understand me.

"Yes, Boudicca, it is I, Andrasta. I entered you at the sacred spring when you and Ansgar made love."

"Did I wrong you, goddess?"

"No, no, your sacrifice allowed me to enter you."

"What do you ask of me, goddess?"

"I ask nothing more of you, great Queen, than to accompany you and offer you advice at this important stage of your life."

"For that, I am thankful."

"Carry on as normal. I will stay with you. Speak to me whenever you feel the need."

I didn't say any more because Morgan called from outside that it was time to go.

The moon was still full in the night sky. It was an hour before dawn. Morgan led me to Tyree waiting by the gates with two horses. He was holding a gleaming metal vessel in his arms, which he handed to me.

"This receptacle has been in my family for generations," he said proudly. "It was made in Tintagel, a place Joseph visited many times. It accommodates the gospel as though it was constructed expressly for that purpose," he said sincerely. "I took the liberty of sealing the gospel inside it with Roman wax. I hope you don't mind."

"Very wise of you, Tyree. Thank you," I said, checking the red wax seal and then handing the container to Morgan.

"I noticed a lock of hair pressed between the pages of the book. I wonder to whom it belongs?" Tyree said, with his big, bushy eyebrows arched with a furrowed brow.

"Perhaps Joseph says so in the gospel," Morgan speculated.

Morgan and I mounted up, and we rode down the hill. After a short while, we came to a lake. On the bank, we found a wooden skiff, and beside it, the body of Joseph wrapped in linen. Tyree's men had left it there for us, along with the tools for digging a grave. We loaded everything on board, launched the boat, climbed aboard, and then Morgan rowed us out into the mist that was hanging in mystical skeins on the mirrored surface of the lake. I could make out very little—just the eerie mist parting magically as the bow cut through it. We were cloaked in the pitch black of night, with only an occasional glimpse of the full moon when it appeared from behind the thick cloud blanketing us. There was no breeze—the air chilled me to the bone—the only sounds came from the stroke of the oar slicing the water... the creaking of the boat and lapping water at the bow. Morgan, in his usual manner, was deathly silent in his paddling.

"How long?" I asked.

"We will know we are in the right place when the sun's first rays reveal it to us," he replied cryptically.

After what felt like an eternity, first light finally appeared as a bright horizontal streak on the eastern horizon.

"There," Morgan said gruffly.

I looked to the west, directly ahead, to see that not far from us, a hilly island was now lit up by the dawn. Beyond it, as we came closer, I could see two more hilly islands, with the first one by far the tallest.

"What is the name of this place?"

"It is known as Ynyns Witrin," he said.

"I pray we will not have to carry Joseph to its summit?"

"No, it is upon Ynyns Witrin Joseph requested the gospel to be buried."

CHAPTER
XXXII

As the first rays of the sun warmed my back, we struck shore. The sound of the hull grating against the rocks startled the fish, causing them to swirl in the water around us. The abundance of fish made sense of why Tyree and his tribe looked so healthy.

We stepped out into the shallows and hauled the boat up onto the bank. I collected the metal casket while Morgan took the digging tools, and we started up the hill. Unlike the next hill with a single tree at its summit, this one was bare.

We reached the top, out of breath, and found a flat sacred stone that had been positioned on the ground by Druids. Morgan expected it to be there and immediately began levering it open. When he had loosened it enough, he called me.

"Here, help me lift one end," he said, gasping for air. Druids don't do manual labor, so they're not used to it. I gripped the end with him, and on the count of three, we lifted it up. It was about the length of Morgan, head to toe, and heavy. Underneath, we found bones - human bones.

"Someone is buried here!" I exclaimed.

"Yes, it is a cairn. We need to work around the bones. They are ancient and fragile and must not be disturbed."

We dug a hole down about three body lengths to take the casket. Morgan produced a ball of knotted twine and measured the depth—the length of the twine was the sacred burial depth. We dug a little more to his satisfaction, then dropped the casket into the hole and carefully refilled half of the hole with rocks and then the remainder with soil. It was hot and sweaty work—we were so clammy that when we got back to the boat, we took a quick dip in the lake to wash away the grime and rejuvenate ourselves for the task ahead.

A breeze came up and cleared the air. In the distance, I could see a boat, realising they were only fishing and presented no threat.

Morgan found the strength to paddle us to the next hill and was glad to get a little assistance from the breeze. We hauled up onto the bank, took one end of Joseph's body each, and started up the hill. Even though it was a much smaller hill than Ynyns Witrin, it was steeper and a tough climb. Morgan said it was known locally as Thorn Tor. When we reached the summit, Morgan looked as though he was about to collapse, so we sat for a moment for him to regain his breath.

He pointed, "That tree grew from Joseph's staff when he plunged it into the soil."

I studied it, amazed. It was not a species I recognised.

"That is magic. Now I understand why he chose this place to enter the underworld," I said.

"Well," he groaned. "We had better get to work. This will be more difficult. It is a rocky hill, and we'll need to hurry as there is a storm coming. Let us fetch the tools."

I don't know how he knew there was a storm coming. I couldn't see any signs in the sky, but he was right about it being a difficult dig. The earth was very rocky, with not a lot of soil. We eventually excavated a hole to the prescribed depth, and after we had placed him in it, we backfilled it with rocks, soil, and then built a small cairn on top with bigger rocks.

Content with our work and looking like a pair of copper miners from Tintagel, we took another swim and then headed back across the lake for Cadbury.

"It will rain soon," Morgan said, puffing. "These waters can be treacherous if the wind gets up. Look, even the fishing boat has gone."

"I'll take the oar. You have a rest," I told him. Even though I was tired, I sat at the stern, took the oar, and began sweeping it from side to side.

"Thank you. It's not a priestly thing to toil so hard."

"It has been a hard day of work already, my friend, and I fear there's more to come," I said in a mock-serious voice.

Most Druids were renowned for their distaste of anything physical beyond walking. I think Bran might have been the exception to that.

"Is this your first time in Buddekaulegh?" he asked.

"Yes, though I do know of it. I was told of the sacred place when I was a girl, but I never expected I would one day visit it. Is the Fosse Way near here?"

"Yes, it has been said the Romans will soon pave it."

"I pray they don't desecrate the sacred sites here like they have done elsewhere in building their roads. They build their temples over ours and then adopt the names of our gods. It's terrible."

"Yes, it is their means to convert the people while at the same time occupying the land."

"My husband Prasutagus always said, religion, wine, and wealth are greater weapons of Rome than the sword, chariot, and spear."

"Indeed he was correct, Boudicca, indeed."

"What do you suppose was scribed in the gospel?"

"I believe the wondrous account of the life and times of Joseph and of the nephew he brought to our shores many years ago, to learn from the Druithin. It was then Bran first met Joseph and his nephew."

"I didn't know that," I said.

"Yes, it is known that because of the close relationship between Joseph, his nephew, and Bran, twenty years ago Arviragus Caractacus, son of Cunobelinus before he was captured by Vespasian and taken with his family to Rome as a prisoner to Emperor Claudius, gave Joseph the land of Twelve Hides. The place we are today."

"Why had Joseph come here from his country?"

"Joseph was formerly Nobilis Decurio to Rome, minister for mines... he traded in tin ore from Tintagel and, in doing so, dealt with Cunobelinus and then Caractacus," Morgan said.

"I understand."

I suddenly noticed a column of smoke rising on the horizon ahead.

"Look, there - that smoke is in the direction of Cadbury."

"Maybe they are preparing a feast in your honour," Morgan said.

"I don't think so. That is too much smoke for a feast."

I stepped up the pace rowing, and before long, we were ashore, where we found only one horse hitched. The other must have bolted. We mounted up and rode at speed for Cadbury.

I had a gut feeling all was not right, so we approached the hill fort from the cover of the forest and then dismounted to reconnoitre. It only took a minute before my feelings were realised. A party of twenty warriors had debouched from the hill fort and were heading toward us. I could tell they were on the side of Rome.

"It's a Numerus," I whispered to Morgan. "They're looking for me. Someone has informed on me."

He turned sharply from watching them, fear in his eyes. "A Numerus?"

"Britons, now servants of Rome—mostly deserters, mercenaries. Lay low for them to pass. If they find us, they will kill us."

We ducked down out of sight. They were so close I could see blood spatter on their faces, forearms, and tunics—they'd been in a fight. I feared the carnage we would find within the ramparts of Cadbury. And then I heard your voice, Jackson, coming at first from the distance, and then... I was back.

There wasn't a dry eye in the room. That's how emotional we were. Cleo had provided us the solution to a problem we had waited forty years to solve. Judith was sobbing so much I had to hug her. "Oh, Bonnie, we finally have the truth."

Cleo came over, took Judith's hand, looked into her teary eyes, and said rousingly, "Judith, the adventure now begins!"

She was dead right—we were about to embark on a most exciting new adventure, one we at times had doubted would ever eventuate.

"I can't believe you actually spoke to her, Cleo," Judith reminded us.

"It was a stroke of genius saying you were Andrasta. Not only did it make sense to Boudicca, but I think it motivated her," Jackson said.

"I thought that part was brilliant—hearing Cleo speaking in English and then answering in Celtic," Ahmed said.

"And what about those place names? What did you make of them, Mike?" Brigitte asked.

Mike had been sitting quietly, scribbling away on a notepad. He looked up, hearing his name. "Uh?"

"Brigitte asked what you thought of the place names," I said.

"Oh, yes, well, Buddekaulegh, as Judith has told us, is the county or district where Boudicca and Morgan were located. I believe it to be a corruption of her name. Buddeka is Boudicca, and Legh means area or place—so the translation of Buddekaulegh is: Boudicca's place—which makes a lot of sense given what we now know. Thorn Tor, the place Joseph's body was buried, we visited years ago... it was where Bonnie felt a special connection. It is known today as Wearyall Hill and was indeed the place Joseph originally planted his staff to grow into a tree and the location of the 6th Century Virgin's Convent. Then Ynyns Witrin, the direct translation is the island of glass. This is the location of the time capsule containing the gospel of Joseph of Arimathea and is better known to us as Glastonbury Tor."

I took Jackson's hand and squeezed it tightly. "I knew it!" It was such exciting news.

Cleo left the room to visit the ladies.

"I will commence the translation later on, but it's clear from what Cleo reported what we need to do next," Mike said, raising an eyebrow at Judith.

"In a way, now knowing the location makes it even more difficult," Judith said despondently.

"Why so?" I asked.

"Because we know it's impossible to excavate either location. We've tried to get permits before and failed, remember?" she said dispiritedly.

"Yes, we do. So where does that leave us?" Jackson questioned.

Judith's reality check had dulled the excitement. We sat like mourners at a funeral, hoping someone would come up with an answer.

Cleo returned with Dylan, Wayne, and Jane.

"I told the guys we've found the location of Joseph and the gospel. I thought we should include them in our plans."

"Good thinking, Cleo," I said gravely.

"Hey, what's up... did someone die?" Cleo said, picking up on the sombre mood.

"Both locations are under National Trust protection, Cleo. There's no way they will give us permission to dig them," Jackson said discouraged. "We need a backup plan."

"Can't we just go there in the dead of night and dig like gravediggers?" Cleo said, trying to lighten the mood.

"No, Cleo. They'd lock us up and throw away the key if we did that!" Judith chortled.

"But Cleo said the thing we're after, the box, is made of metal—probably bronze," Dylan declared, obviously onto something.

"That's right, Dylan. So what difference does that make?" Ahmed asked his favourite pupil.

"Plenty. We could use Radan ground penetrating radar to detect the metal box, then excavate it with a keyhole dig," he said, sitting back in a chair and folding his arms, sure of himself.

The idea had lifted the cloak of gloom from us. Even Judith was on the edge of her seat. We all knew about Dylan's technical genius from Ahmed's story and now were hoping he knew what he was talking about.

"How is Radan different than any of the other geophysical detectors we use in archaeology, Dylan?" Judith queried.

"Rad, Jude, this unit is the bee's knees of detectors. It can find metal, any metal, in rock, sand —almost anything down to thirty feet. If the metal box is still intact, it would find it, that's for sure."

"How? What makes it so different, young man?" Judith insisted.

"Okay, it was developed as the front-line unit for landmine

detection. It runs on a regular laptop and provides the user with powerful tools to clean up and view data in 3-D. Radan is an acronym for Radar Data Analyser."

"How do you know about it?" Judith inquired.

"My brother is an army bomb disposal officer and rated out on Radan. He used it in Afghanistan... says it's better than your bog-standard ground penetrating radar by a country mile... and he'd know... his bleeding life depended on it."

"And what about this keyhole excavating you mentioned?" I quizzed. "I've not heard of it."

Dylan grinned cheekily. "Yeah, well, it's a technique I only just read about. Archaeologists have been using it in Italy and Greece for when they find layered ruins, like a cake. They dig a keyhole through layers to get to the level they want without disturbing the other layers," he demonstrated by overlapping his hands. "You know what I mean?" By the look on his face, he thought his words had fallen on deaf ears, but he hadn't counted on us mulling it over in our minds. After a few minutes of silence, Judith glanced at me, and then a massive grin broke on her face.

"You know," she beamed. "I think the lad might be onto something there."

"Do you think the National Trust might buy it?" Mike questioned her excitedly.

Judith nodded slowly, then with all of us on the edge of our seats, said, "I think if we can assemble an ironclad case, one supported by strong precedents... with the army's use of Radan... and evidence of successful archaeological digs using keyhole excavation, we would be in with a definite chance."

"I don't think you'll need a permit for the Radan. It's no different than sitting on Glastonbury Tor with a laptop and a picnic basket. We could be searching for the metal box with it while you're busy getting a permit for a non-invasive keyhole dig," Dylan said.

"You're absolutely right, young man," Judith said excitedly. "And that is precisely what we'll do. Cleo, Bonnie—the adventure has definitely begun!"

CHAPTER XXXIII

"I'm intrigued by the lock of hair Tyree mentioned he found in the gospel," I said to Cleo in the back of the car.

"Yeah, that got me as well. Who do you think it belongs to?" she said.

"It might be Jesus," I said thoughtfully.

"Or it could be the Magdalene's?" Jackson added.

"Whoever it's from, if we recover it, we'll be able to get their DNA, wouldn't we?" Cleo proposed.

"Now there's a thought. You're full of little gems of wisdom, aren't you, darl?" I said with a chuckle.

"Maybe it's an age thing," Dylan said sarcastically, very much his nature.

"You'd better watch it, young man. We're into equality in this family," I jested.

We pulled into the car park of The Cross Keys in Milton Keynes, a beautiful 16th-century thatched roof pub. This was where Jackson had arranged to meet our assigned Interpol agent.

We went inside to the main bar, which surprisingly lacked patrons, and sat at the bar. The barman asked what we'd like.

"Always this quiet at lunchtime?" Jackson asked.

"No, you watch, in a blink of an eye, the place'll be packed," the big, full-bearded rotund bartender growled. We ordered drinks and took them to a window seat, ready for the invasion. The ceiling was low with rustic exposed beams, and the place smelled like a museum.

"Why didn't he or she just meet us at the manor?" Cleo asked.

"My bet is Chris Kelly is a she," I said.

"Logic doesn't enter into it when dealing with Interpol, Cleo. I've got no idea why we're going to such lengths and why I wasn't told whether we're meeting a he or a she," Jackson snapped.

Nothing ruffles Jackson more than bureaucratic absurdity. He's been that way since he dealt with the Gibson-Smith debacle in the mid-seventies.

Minutes later, a good-looking woman in her mid-thirties entered the pub, garbed in a chic three-quarter-length brown coat, with a grey knee-length skirt, a green blouse underneath, and a hat covering her bob-cut auburn hair. She peered over her sunglasses at us and, without altering the bland expression of her thin pale face, made a beeline for us.

"You win the money, Bonnie," Jackson said out of the corner of his mouth.

She stopped at our table, removed her sunglasses, and spoke with a thick Irish accent.

"Dr Jackson Bolt?" she purred, removing a brown kid glove from her right hand and extending her hand to shake. "Chris Kelly, pleased to meet you."

"May I introduce my wife, Dr Bonnie Bolt, our niece Cleo, and one of our students, Dylan Scott. Please take a seat. Can I get you a drink?"

She removed her hat and coat and sat. "I'll take a single malt on ice, thank you," she said, still unable to crack a smile.

"We've had agents appointed to us before, but you're the first female," I said.

"Yes, Matt Ryan, Daniel Boyd, and Rick Molloy," she rattled off smartly. "I'm up to speed on your case. It has been active since nineteen seventy-four and not without incident, to be sure."

"That's precisely why we requested an agent. We have been in similar situations before that have turned out bad, and we are expecting nothing less on this visit to the UK," I said doggedly.

"Tell me, Dr Bolt—"

"Call me Bonnie or Bo."

"What is it exactly that you are expecting?"

I detected cynicism in her tone. Just then Jackson arrived with her drink.

"We have reason to believe someone or an organisation means us harm," I said firmly.

She took a deep breath. "What is your rationale to believe that?" She picked up her drink and took a sip.

"Oh, the death of Matt Ryan and the attack on me personally in nineteen eighty-eight, the murder of Reagan Spears, a colleague in the USA, and, of late... threatening emails," I said flippantly. "Do I detect a note of scepticism from you, Agent Kelly?" I added cautiously.

"Call me Chris. No, not intentional," she said firmly in a lower voice.

Jackson detected the awkwardness of the conversation and jumped in.

"I called your office because there has been a history of attacks... the last one verified by two of your own field agents," Jackson said sternly.

"Yes, I've read the report, but there has never been any proof or evidence—"

"Listen, Miss Kelly, if I have to argue our case with you, then we're talking to the wrong person. Over the years, we've had enough proof to sink a battleship. My best friend had his throat cut from ear to ear, my wife had her leg stabbed by a man both your agents met and let escape. Do I need to go on?" he growled angrily.

"The assailant you reported in nineteen eighty-eight, Paul Sicario, doesn't exist..."

"Bad choice of words, Miss Kelly. I have an ugly scar on my leg as testimony to his bloody existence."

She was beginning to look rattled.

"I mean, there is no record of him," she countered.

"Look, his name is Gaius, and we can show you recent threatening emails from him. We know he is a member of the militant Benedictine order, the Crux Redemptoris. They are sworn to removing anyone or anything that demeans their religious ideology from circulation. Doing so is a victory against darkness for them. They have a papal bull from the Vatican to protect their actions. We have proof that Gaius is a member of the Crux Redemptoris," Jackson spelled out slowly and clearly.

"Sounds like the plot of a Dan Brown book," she returned serve.

Jackson stood up enraged. "I find that remark distasteful, young lady," he snapped.

"I'm sorry if I've offended you, Dr Bolt, but I'm only trying to do my job. You have to understand profiling is critical to dealing with a case."

He sat back down, still miffed, and growled, "I expect so, but you could go about it in a more congenial manner."

"It is how we are instructed. Look, Doctor, the reason agents have been unsuccessful before is that they failed to ask the hard questions. If they had, it would be in their case records, and apart from Matt Ryan's, it just isn't."

"So are you saying agents Daniel Boyd and Rick Molloy failed to complete a case report?"

"Yes, Matt Ryan did, but it's outdated... But I have read a comprehensive report from the San Diego police on the Reagan Spears murder. It was inconclusive."

"Both of those murders are cold cases. Why, for God's sake?" Jackson growled with a scowl.

"Whoever we are dealing with here, if it's the same person or, as you say, an organisation or an order, they are very clever. They are, in fact, professional assassins, formidable opponents. And you're expecting me to protect you from them."

"Okay, point taken," I said. "But rest assured, even with this formidable opponent, we're still sitting opposite you alive after forty years of harassment, while we can't say the same for your agents," I snarled.

"So what does that tell us, Dr Bolt?"

"Call me Bo or Bonnie, please. There are two Dr Bolts," I said soberly. "It tells us we're doing something right, does it not?"

"Okay, Bonnie... No, it tells you he or they don't want you dead," she said emphatically.

We knew she was right because we had come to the same conclusion. She could see that in our expressions.

For the first time, she cracked a tight, thin-lipped smile, took a sip of her scotch, and then said more civilly, "Okay, let's start over again, shall we? How about you tell me the truth about what Gaius and the Crux Redemptoris want from you."

We had never really disclosed the absolute truth to Interpol and felt guilty for that. I glanced at Jackson; we both knew it was time to come clean.

An hour later, patrons surrounded us as the barman had predicted. Despite the noise, Kelly had listened expressionless and intently to our story, and at the end, she was left sitting, staring transfixed at us with a perplexed gaze in her big green eyes. This was also the first time for Dylan to hear the whole story, and as a result, he had eyes the size of dinner plates.

"That is without a doubt the most extraordinary story I have ever heard. You're lucky I'm one of the only agnostic Kellys in Ireland," she admitted with a wry grin. "I think I need another Scotch."

Jackson went for refills.

"Now does it make sense, Chris?" Cleo asked.

"To be sure, Cleo... to be sure it does."

It was decided at the pub that Chris, whom we were now on better terms with, would stay with us at the manor. We would involve her in our every move as a member of the team—for all intents and purposes, she would appear to be a member of First Light.

By the time we got back to the manor, settled down in the library, introduced Chris to all and sundry, and explained the plan, it was late afternoon. Jane and Wayne had been busy most of the day making inquiries about hiring a Radan ground penetrating radar unit.

"We located a Radan unit, and we can get it tomorrow, but I need to go back and tell them how long we'll need it for," Wayne reported.

"What do you think, Ahmed?" Judith asked.

"A week... ten days, and the possibility of extending if need be," he said.

"Jane and I have been on the hunt for an operator, but so far, no luck," Brigitte said, a little downcast.

"I can do it!" Dylan said, raising his hand excitedly like a schoolboy. "Just get them to email me the manual right away, and I'll have it down in a flash."

"I wish I could be so confident," Mike mumbled under his breath.

"Don't worry, Mike, he means what he says. He can do it," Ahmed said confidently.

"Good, then that's settled," Judith said matronly. "I've spoken with the National Trust, and they will undertake some research on keyhole excavation... I'm expecting to do the same, and we will then present our collective findings at a meeting at the end of next week."

"Two questions: when will we go to Glastonbury, and who will be going?" I asked.

"All of you, except Brigitte and myself. We'll stay here to complete the research and make the presentation to the National Trust," Judith said.

"I should stay with you as well," Mike said.

"No, my dear, your expertise will be needed more in the field. Mike will be the team leader, agreed?"

We all agreed. With his academic knowledge and qualifications, he was the obvious choice. Wayne went to arrange for the Radan manual to be sent to Dylan, while Arthur, the new butler, served the rest of us afternoon tea. Money wasn't a problem for us anymore. We had sizable grants from the University of Sydney and Cambridge, as well as a very healthy endowment that Quinn had left First Light.

I'd just sat down with a cup of tea. Judith and Mike were standing nearby, and I overheard them talking.

"I have the appointment with the oncologist this week," Judith said disconsolately. The way she said it caused me to mist up. I watched Mike take hold of her hand and grip it warmly. I could tell from their body language that it was an appointment of special circumstances. Judith surreptitiously wiped away a tear.

"That's why I wanted to stay, to accompany you," Mike whispered.

"No, no—it won't be necessary, my dear. It is most important that you are with Bonnie and Jackson."

Cleo sidled over to me and interrupted my eavesdropping.

"Aunt Bo, I want to be regressed before she's gone. I need to be with her in the end as Andrasta, you understand?"

"I do, love." I called Jackson over. "Cleo wants to be with Boudicca at Wattle Street."

"You know, I was thinking exactly the same thing. Why not? When?" he asked.

"As soon as you've finished your tea. This is the day," she grimaced sadly.

Jackson and I recognised the importance of this for Cleo. I'd had the benefit of a longer relationship with Boudicca, but it seemed Cleo's was even closer than mine. I whispered to Judith what we were going to do, and she told Mike. I knew they wouldn't want to miss it for the world. We told the others to stay put and took Cleo to the study, along with Chris. We thought it would be important for her to experience the session.

Cleo sprawled out on the lounge, and we pulled up our chairs. Mike readied a recorder.

I took her hand. "Love, I remember the battle like it was yesterday. It was a terrifying experience, but one thing... I never found out what happened to her. Did she die by the sword? Was she captured and poisoned, as Cassius Dio wrote? You now have the chance of determining the truth."

"What happens when the person you're occupying dies, Jackson?" Cleo asked.

It was a good question, something we had never considered.

"I really can't answer that, Cleo," Jackson answered disconcertedly.

"Do you think it might be dangerous, like I might die as well?" Cleo said, concern showing on her face for the first time.

CHAPTER XXXIV

"Maybe we shouldn't—" I began before Cleo cut me off.

"I'll take the risk," she said bravely.

"Are you sure love?" Judith asked doubtfully.

"There are things we need to know and dangers connected with everything we're doing. So let's just go for it," Cleo said, resting back on the couch ready for Jackson's mellow tones.

"She's a brave lass," Judith said with a proud smile.

"As you are my dear friend, how are you feeling?" I whispered.

"I'm fine love but I'll be glad when I get my next oncologist appointment over and done with," she admitted. Concern was easy to detect in her powder blue eyes.

"What's so special about it?" I queried candidly.

"He'll have the results of tests to see if it's metastasized on not."

I grasped her hand and squeezed it knowing the fear that must be eating away at her. "I think Mike should be with you instead of with us. We can do without him, whereas I don't think you can."

With teary eyes she nodded slowly in agreement.

In a little under an hour Cleo woke of her own accord. She sat up and wiping tears from her eyes and declared emotionally, "She's gone." Then she sobbed as though she had lost her best friend. I comforted her with a hug.

"Shhh! Love, it's all right. I know how it feels."

Once again we had listened to her speaking in English and answering in Celtic. Mike was ecstatic at being able to record more bilingual conversation.

Cleo was settling down.

"Are you all right now love?" I asked.

She nodded, blew her nose on a tissue and then more composed sat back on the lounge ready to relate her experience.

"That was unbelievable!" Chris said totally astonished.

"Wait till you hear her account of it," I told her.

"It was a shock to find myself in the thick of a battle screaming like a mad woman," Cleo started. "I was in a chariot drawn by four beautiful white horses. Her heart was beating like a drum, all around were men and women fighting, bloody fighting—fighting to the death, there was chaos and confusion—screams, shouts and wails. I knew my army needed inspiration.

"It is victory or death!" I screamed out at the top of my voice. The battle seemed to stop abruptly as all eyes were cast in my direction—I roared fiercely for all to hear, "I thank thee, Andrasta, and call upon thee as woman speaking to woman; for I rule over no burden-bearing Egyptians as did Nitocris, nor over trafficking Assyrians as did Semiramis for we have by now gained thus much learning from the Romans! Much less over the Romans themselves as did Messalina once and afterwards Agrippina and now Nero who, though in name a man, is in fact a woman, as is proved by his singing, lyre-playing and beautification of his person; nay, those over whom I rule are Britons, men that know not how to till the soil or ply a trade, but are thoroughly versed in the art of war and hold all things in common, even children and wives, so that the latter possess the same valour as the men. As Queen, then, of such men and of such women, I supplicate and pray thee for victory, preservation of life, and liberty against men insolent, unjust, insatiable, impious,—if, indeed, we ought to term those people men who bathe in warm water, eat artificial dainties, drink unmixed wine, anoint themselves with myrrh, sleep on soft couches with boys for bedfellows—boys past their prime at that—and are slaves to a lyre-player and a poor one at that. Wherefore may this Mistress Domitia-Nero reign no longer over me or over you men; let the wench sing and lord it over Romans, for they surely deserve to be the slaves of such a woman after having submitted to her so long. But for us, Mistress, be thou alone ever our leader. This is my resolve as a woman—follow me or submit to the Roman yoke!" My warriors cheered loudly reenergised by my speech.

I charged into the fray and with support from three more chariots we fought our way up a hill towards their general and his officers poised at the summit watching, away from all the slaughter. It was Gaius Suetonius Paulinus I could see and I wanted his head. Half way up the hill Roman cavalry halted our progress. I glanced down at my body, it was cut and torn but I felt no pain. I looked beside me at my trusted old friend Domnall, his chariot at my right as always. He was only recognisable by his shock of auburn hair, the rest of his body was a mass of bleeding lacerations—his kilt caked with blood. This would be our last hurrah. I noticed a raven in the sky—it must be Andrasta—waiting for me.

"Talk to me Andrasta, is it time for me to join you?"

I'm here with you ...I said. I'm here.

"Give me strength for what I am about to do."

My arms are your arms, my body yours ...you have my power.

I grinned at Domnall and he returned a big toothless smile. What a great warrior he has been.

"You are the pillar of my strength my friend' I shouted. "Take many with you great warrior!"

"Andrasta!" I screamed as loud as I could and could hear the word echo throughout the valley. Then, I charged my chariot at Gaius Suetonius Paulinus. At speed I looked back over my shoulder and saw Domnall and the others plunge their chariots into the Romans, their warhorses reeling from the blades on the wheel hubs hacking and cutting at Roman legs. I saw Domnall wheeling his great sword, slicing through his attackers and the blood from the gaping wounds spraying in the air. And then I saw him overwhelmed by them. There were just too many. I looked away ...I wanted to remember him alive. Behind, I could see my army in retreat—I had been left alone. When I looked back ahead a path had opened to Gaius Suetonius Paulinus. Knowing it was a trap I bellowed at my horses pressing them to charge at speed. They laboured on the climb up the slope but were strong warhorses.

Your brethren await you in the underworld! I told her.

"I hear you Andrasta! I hear you!"

A wall of Roman legionnaires suddenly closed around Suetonius—my horses reared up—I was surrounded.

"Whoa!" I bellowed and I hacked with my sword at the Romans closest me. My horses reared from the stabs of Roman spears. Out of the corner of my eye I caught sight of a big old oak tree with a raven perched on a lower branch, watching me. All of a sudden time mystically began slowing—I was moving in slow motion—it was unworldly. I wheeled my chariot to face the oak tree and pulled away from the attacking Roman hoard. I shook the reins and we galloped with great effort but still in slow motion directly at the base of the huge oak tree. My white horses streaked red with blood grunted from the effort and the sound of their exertion overtook the thunderous roar of the battle. Froth was flying like snowflakes from the mouths of my horses as they pressed on hard going—and then in a blinding flash of light, I found myself watching the battle from above. It was over—I could see my army of dead piled high. Fleeing battle-watchers, wives, mothers, sisters and lovers along with their children were being mercilessly put to sword by the victorious Romans. The once crystal clear waters of the brook that meandered through the valley was now running red with the blood of Briton's ...and then I woke up."

"So we're none the wiser," Judith said, first to comment.

"Oh, I wouldn't say that Judith, I think we know what happened," I said.

"Enlighten me then Bonnie."

I looked at Cleo knowingly, "Boudicca joined her husband Prasutagus, Bran, Domnall and Joseph."

"She became one with Andrasta as symbolised by the raven," Cleo said.

"So she died in the chariot crash then," Judith posed.

"You could say that," Cleo agreed with a wry smile.

"It seems to me we are talking about something supernatural here rather than factual," Mike observed.

"I guess in our terms you could look at it in that way, Mike, but not in theirs," Jackson suggested.

"I see what you mean," Judith considered. "The spiritual world and nature, for that matter, meant a lot more to Britons then than it does today."

"Their belief system was based on Earthly and celestial spirituality, only later did Christianity destroy that," Mike said, affirming his resentment of organised religion. "Turned history on its head, buried truth under a morass of deceit that continues nowadays, appalling."

"Yes, organised religion, in particular Catholicism, has a lot to answer for," I agreed.

"It was noble of you to give Boudicca faith in her goddess during her final moments, Cleo," Mike said. "But what happened to you before or as Boudicca died?"

"Because I was both Boudicca and myself separately, it was easy to disconnect, I guess, and yeah, seeing the raven helped."

"Wow, you've got me gobsmacked, I'm lost for words!" Chris admitted.

The next day, a van delivered the Radan unit. Dylan had been locked away cramming the instruction manual and emerged bloated with confidence, ready to take delivery of the piece of expensive high-tech equipment. He and Wayne carried the two large boxes inside the manor, and we all stood around like fans at a football match at halftime, waiting for the gadget of doom to be exposed, as Cleo called it: the unveiling. It ended up a bit of an anticlimax: it was just a laptop and a metal detector. But you could tell by the excitement on Dylan's face that he knew looks were deceiving—he was like a kid in a candy store.

"Reminds me of getting my first Meccano set," Jackson said with a chuckle.

"What's a Meccano set?" Chris asked with a corrugated brow.

"A metal version of Lego," I said.

"Oh! Hardly," Jackson protested.

"So when are we off to Glastonbury then?" Chris probed, totally sold on the adventure after witnessing the session.

We all glared at Judith for an answer. "A rented Mercedes Vito van will arrive tomorrow at 8 a.m."

"How many does it seat?" Wayne asked.

"Nine, plus room for the Radan gizmo and a small bag each," Brigitte explained.

We left Wayne and Dylan fiddling with their toy and went back into the library to plan the Glastonbury trip.

That night there was more room hopping going on than in a brothel on The Reeperbahn. Jackson and I were in bed reading and giggling every time we heard the patter of feet in the corridor outside and a door being surreptitiously closed. Cleo was in the room next to ours; she had a visitor that we presumed to be Wayne not long after we'd retired. On the other side was Jane, and she had a visitor much later, around midnight. Jackson bet it was Dylan, but I reckoned it was Brigitte. That outraged Jackson; he couldn't visualise Jane being attracted to a woman in her fifties. But I assured him that age had little to do with it. The squeaking bed ratified my suspicion, but the bet between us still stood with Jackson remaining unconvinced.

Breakfast was early. When we arrived at the dining room, Chris was there alone. Brigitte and Jane arrived together last and then sat trading sly glances, as lovers do. I nudged Jackson under the table, and I knew by his expression that I'd won the bet. It was all fun and games, though I caught Cleo occasionally glimpsing at Wayne a little starry-eyed.

The Mercedes van arrived on schedule, and Jackson did a magnificent job of squeezing the luggage and the Radan equipment into the rear compartment. Then, after bidding goodbye to Judith,

Mike, and Brigitte, eight of us piled into the vehicle and hit the road with Wayne behind the wheel.

It was a fun three-and-a-half-hour drive to Glastonbury. We were singing, telling jokes, making confessions, and telling stories. Chris had the best stories, as the Irish do—some of her personal experiences were legendary—she was one tough lady. By the time we got to the Tor B&B, we knew each other much more intimately.

Brigitte had booked us three rooms for ten days. Three men, Ahmed, Dylan, and Wayne, were in one room. Next door were Jane, Chris, and Cleo. And beside them, Jackson and myself.

It was a lovely old house, hosted by a sweet elderly couple, the Temples, and it was close to the town—in fact, we could see the Tor in the distance from our window. We even had Wi-Fi, which was surprising, basically all the comforts of home, including a wonderful big living room with a massive fireplace. I phoned Judith on the mobile and told her we'd arrived safely and how lovely the accommodation was. We agreed to text every few hours as our main means of communicating, and I reminded her I was expecting a positive from her Harley Street appointment.

After lunch, we prepared the equipment for our first assault on the Tor. The batteries had been charged, and the software checked to be running perfectly. Dylan gave it all the thumbs up, so we loaded it into the metal, dustproof, field carry cases provided, packed it back in the van, and then boarded it for the short trip to the Tor.

Driving through the town of Glastonbury, I was happily taking in the sights when I noticed something.

"Wayne, stop the car!" I urged.

He pulled over to the curb. I opened the door and hopped out. Chris instinctively knew something was wrong, so she got out and stood beside me. I held my hand up to shade my eyes from the sunlight.

"What did you see, Bonnie?" Chris asked, intrigued.

"See those people outside Becket's pub there? I saw someone standing with them that looked like Gaius. He watched us drive past and stared like he recognised me."

"Did you say you saw Gaius?" Jackson said, joining us and looking where I was pointing.

"Do you want to take a look?" Chris asked.

"You get back in the car, Bonnie. I'll go with Chris," Jackson said.

"No, Jackson, I can recognise him. Come on, Chris. Are you armed?" I asked nervously.

"Yes."

We crossed the High Street and walked the hundred or so metres to the pub at a quick pace. We stopped amongst the group of what appeared to be students drinking on the footpath.

"He's not here," I said. "Let's check inside."

My heart was racing ten to the dozen. The last thing I wanted was to set off a false alarm to Chris... that would make me appear totally paranoid.

We pushed through the students to get inside and found the main bar packed to the rafters with more students. I wasn't tall enough to get a good view.

"They must be rugby players," I said. "They're all huge!" Then I saw him on the far side of the room. He was alone, he'd aged, but it was Gaius all right. I could never forget those piercing unblinking grey eyes. I avoided eye contact and quickly turned my back to face Chris, hoping he didn't see me. She was taller than I and would have a better view of him.

"Chris," I had to raise my voice to get above the racket. "It's Gaius all right... he's standing directly behind me on the far side of the room. He's alone. Crew-cut blondish hair—a suntanned face—piercing grey eyes. He's wearing an expensive-looking dark brown leather jacket."

"I can see him." She drew closer to me. "Now, listen to me very carefully, Bonnie. Walk slowly back out the way we came in. Leave me here like you don't know me. Wait outside for me. Have you got that?"

"Roger," I said and immediately started for the front door.

CHAPTER XXXV

When I got outside, I found Jackson standing next to the van, waiting for us. They'd backed the van up closer to the pub.

"He's inside," I said, puffing more from panic than effort.

"Where's Chris?"

"I pointed him out to her, she told me to get out and wait for her."

Five minutes passed, then ten, and still no sign of her.

"I'm getting worried," I told Jackson.

Dylan joined us.

"Is Chris still inside?" he asked casually.

"Yes," I said, concerned.

"I'll go in. The dude she's chasing doesn't know me," he said. "And I look like any other student."

"Good thinking, but watch yourself. The guy's a killer," I warned him.

He quickly blended in with the other students and slipped inside the pub.

Another ten minutes passed, and we were just beginning to get worried when Dylan and Chris stormed out of the pub and climbed directly into the van without saying a word.

Dylan leaned out and called to us, "Get in quick!"

We jumped in and shut the sliding door. Chris was distressed, holding her stomach and wincing in pain.

"What's wrong?" I yelped.

"She's been stabbed. We need to get her to a hospital real quick. She's losing heaps of blood!" Dylan said urgently.

"Hit the Sat-Nav, Wayne. Find the nearest hospital!" Jackson said.

Within seconds, Wayne said, "It says for minor injuries, West

Menlip Hospital on Glastonbury road, but for emergencies, Musgrove Park in Taunton."

Chris lifted her hand, covering her stomach, to show Jackson the wound... it was bad.

"How far is Taunton?" he asked Richard.

"Twenty-two miles," he replied sharply.

Chris shook her head. Her face was pale.

"Ah, no! West Menlip and go for it, mate!" Jackson said pressingly.

Wayne put his foot down, and we sped to the hospital.

Two hours later, we were still in the hospital waiting for word on her condition. Fortunately, when we arrived, the duty doctor was qualified enough to handle her injury.

It was a nervous wait—the wound didn't look good. Dylan told us he'd gone inside the pub and couldn't find Chris anywhere. He'd pushed through the crowd toward the back of the room and into the corridor leading to the toilets. When he got there, he found a bunch of people hovering over someone writhing on the ground in a pool of blood. It was Chris.

Sitting on an uncomfortable bench, I rested my head on Jackson's shoulder.

"What are we going to do, darling?" I said plaintively. "This bastard is so dangerous."

He pinched between his eyes in an effort to relieve a headache.

"We can't lose Chris, love... I..."

The appearance of a doctor put an end to our conversation. Jackson stood up to greet him.

"Doctor, I'm Dr Jackson Bolt, and this is my wife. We're with Chris Kelly, your patient."

"Miss Kelly is in a stable condition now but has a nasty wound in her abdomen. We have called the police. Ethically, she shouldn't have been removed from the crime scene."

"Yes, but she would have bled to death!"

"Yes, Dr Bolt, I understand. You did the right thing to save her life. But the police won't be of the same opinion. Of that, you can be sure."

Well, he wasn't quite right about that. Once the police arrived and learned Chris was an Interpol agent, they were most appreciative of our effort. An APB had been issued based on Chris's description of Gaius. There was no point staying at the hospital; Chris would be kept overnight, and we'd be able to check on her condition in the morning. In the meantime, Dylan and I had to go to the local police station to give a statement.

We finally arrived back at the B&B in the dark. I had phoned Judith from the hospital and told her. She was understandably disturbed by the news.

Jackson called Interpol in London, and they reacted immediately by dispatching agent Edward Cronin to sort things out. We were to expect him at the B&B first thing in the morning. We were relieved, but with Gaius on the loose, we were all in a state of shock and worried. Sitting solemnly, warming ourselves by a blazing fire in the lounge room of the B&B, we talked over our options.

"We have to assume he knows we're staying here," Jackson submitted.

"You're right, but knowing that only makes it worse," I said.

"I don't think he will attack us here. We're all staying together. And besides, I think he only attacked Chris because she probably confronted him," Ahmed said.

"I'm with you," Wayne agreed.

"We only have to get through tonight, and then we'll have James Bond to watch over us, right?" Jane said chirpily.

"I just want to get up on the Tor with my mate Radan," Dylan growled.

"There will be plenty of time for that once we've met Agent Cronin and settled everything to do with Chris. We can refocus on the Tor then, Dylan," I told him sternly.

"Chris hasn't been able to give us her account of what happened yet," Jackson reminded us.

"That could be even more scary," Cleo said with a dour expression.

None of us got a decent sleep that night. We all slept with one eye open, looking for a sign of Gaius.

At breakfast, we all brandished the tell-tale dark circles under shift-worker's eyes.

"Wish we could've slept in. I'm buggered," Cleo yawned.

"I slept all right. What kept you up?" Dylan said cheekily.

"It's all right for you three blokes together, but it was only us two girls, and that damn branch kept scratching on the window in the breeze all bleedin' night," Jane sneered.

"Why didn't you give me a call? I would have looked after you," Dylan said, being comically wistful.

"I'm sure you would've, you cheeky bugger," Cleo chided him playfully.

We had just finished breakfast when we heard a car pull up

outside.

"This must be Cronin," Jackson said, standing up. "I'll go and check."

A few minutes later, he returned with a much younger man than I was expecting. Edward Cronin was tall, with modern-cut black hair on which he'd slapped too much product for my liking—it gave him a just-got-out-of-bed look fashionable these days. His eyes were gunmetal blue, serious-looking but sexy, and they were well contrasted with his sharp grey suit, white shirt, and blue pencil-thin necktie. He carried himself with confidence, not arrogance, but with a take-no-prisoners vibe. Jackson made the introductions, and he sat beside Cleo, who was clearly impressed by him. He had a mid-Atlantic accent in a low, sexy register. Wayne looked a little jealous of Edward sitting so close to Cleo.

"First, let me say I'm sorry for what has happened. It's never easy when a violent attack such as this invades your life. For us, it comes with the job."

I interrupted him, "Are you a senior agent like Chris?"

He smiled at me, "No, I just have different training than Agent Kelly. I've been with the force ten years, whereas she's been with us for six. Does that answer your question, Dr Bolt?"

"Yes, I was just expecting Sean Connery rather than Ricky Martin, no offence," I said in jest. It got a giggle from all and sundry.

"I have the tatts and the haircut but not the voice, sorry to disappoint you, Doctor," he said with a wry grin. He stood. "Dr Bolt?"

Both Jackson and I said yes at the same time, then I realised he was addressing Jackson.

"Call me Jackson, and my wife Bonnie, just to avoid confusion. We don't use the doctor tag amongst the team."

"Can you take me to Chris?"

"Bonnie will need to come as well."

"No problem," he said.

"Ahmed, can you call Judith and bring her up to speed? We'll be back soon," I said.

When we got to the hospital, we were ushered into Chris's room. She was sitting up in bed, with a sad smile on her pallid face. After giving her as much sympathy as possible, we settled down to listen to her version of what had happened.

"After I watched you fight your way back through the crowd, I turned to face Gaius, and he had gone. I pushed my way through into a corridor that led to the toilets and saw him disappear into the gents.

I decided to wait to ambush him. There were a few people in the corridor, and I stood out like a sore thumb, so I struck up a conversation with a guy. A few minutes later, Gaius came out of the Gents and came my way. I stopped him and asked if he was with Jonny Ferguson, a name I just made up. He didn't answer, just glared at me. Sorry, I said, didn't mean to be rude, just thought you were him, that's all. Just then, there was a surge of people, and he was pushed against me. I felt a sharp pain and looked down. I'd been knifed. He tore away from me and melted into the crowd. Next thing, I was in the hospital."

"So he stabbed you then?" Edward tried to confirm.

"I expect so. It was so quick," she said in a small voice.

"We still don't know if it was Gaius or not?" Jackson said.

"Well, there wouldn't be any logical reason why anyone else would stab her, would there?" I argued.

"I guess not," Jackson admitted.

"We have to assume it was him," Edward conceded.

"He fitted the profile given me by Bonnie," Chris said.

Just then, a nurse ushered two cops into the room. The superior was Detective Inspector Duff, who had taken our statements yesterday. Jackson introduced Edward, and Duff made it immediately obvious he didn't like him.

"I think it would be best if, once Miss Kelly here is well enough to move, you lot leave Glastonbury," Duff said snappishly.

"I'm sorry, Inspector Duff, but that won't be possible. We are here to undertake archaeological research," I said contritely.

"I don't care if you're here to dig up King Arthur himself. I think you will be safer out of here. We are talking about an attempted murder here."

"We are well aware of that, Detective Inspector, but running away from the assailant isn't the answer. Besides, these people have a job to do," Edward reasoned.

"And just who is going to guarantee their safety, you? I can see by the state of your officer here how effective you lot are," he countered smugly.

"That's my job, and if you need confirmation of that, I can have Police Commissioner Allen give you a call," Edward returned serve.

All puffed up with his self-importance, DI Duff rocked back and forth as though he was back in his Bobby uniform. He wasn't impressed with Cronin raising the stakes.

"All right then, be it on your conscience," he grumbled. Upon leaving, he stopped at the door, turned, and added, "If we are called for any indiscretion, I will personally speak to Commissioner Allen."

"No problem, good to know we have your complete support while we are here, DI Duff. I'll put that in my report," Edward said with a wry smile.

Edward had cleverly outwitted Duff, though I dreaded to think what would happen if we did need the help of the local constabulary. Oh well, we'd cross that bridge if we came to it.

Chris struggled to sit up straighter. "Nice pair of wankers those two. Didn't ask how I was, no question of them trying to catch the assailant," she said begrudgingly.

"I think it would be best to get you out of here and back to your flat in London," Edward said and then turned to us. "Can you give me a few minutes alone with Chris, please?"

"No problem," I said and gave Chris a peck on the cheek. "Glad you're recovering well, love."

We went out to reception to wait for Edward and found DI Duff talking to a nurse. When he saw us, he stopped talking and, with a guilty look on his face, without acknowledging us, strode out of the building.

"You know, I don't trust that guy," I admitted.

"You're not Robinson Crusoe, love. If I didn't know any better, I'd say he's in collusion with Gaius," Jackson said.

"Maybe he's one of the clan?"

"Or like old Gibson-Smith was. What did they call it, the cat's paw?"

"Longa manus or the long arm, but known colloquially as the cat's paw," I said, observing the dodgy body language of the nurse Duff had been whispering to.

"She looks sketchy as well," Jackson muttered so the nurse couldn't hear.

CHAPTER
XXXVI

hris had brought Edward up to speed on everything; now it was his turn to be agog with our story and the reason for us being in Glastonbury.

Back at the B & B we decided Ahmed would collect Chris from the hospital in an hour's time and drive her to the train station at Castle Cary, about twenty-five minutes away. There he'd put her on the train to London for her to be collected from Paddington Station by an assigned Interpol driver. Edward wasn't about to leave us out of his sight. While Ahmed was doing that we prepared everything for an assault on the Tor.

I took the time to phone Judith. She had an appointment with the National Trust in two days' time, and had nearly completed her research to present them. She was happy to have determined that keyhole excavations had been a huge success elsewhere, and was confident of that being a convincing precedent. Her experience in handling National Trust was unrivalled, so it was good to hear her brimming with confidence. Her Harley Street appointment was in a couple of hours and she was just getting ready. Mike would drive her. I promised to call her immediately upon our return from the Tor with our findings and for hers.

After I finished talking to Judith, Cleo approached me.

"Can I have a word Bo?" she asked with an anxious look.

"Sure," I said, put an arm around her and walked her outside away from the others.

"I want to talk with Sharlene about finding Boudicca's body for DNA testing."

"You're mad keen to prove or disprove a genetic link aren't you?" I said tightly.

Her head lifted quickly, "Well yeah, I want to write the story with scientific credibility ...without that, I'm not sure it would be taken seriously."

"Yes, that's something we've struggled with ourselves. Your poor old uncle has fought for years to have regression hypnosis accepted by the academic community but it's a bit like UFO abductees—after a few hoaxes were uncovered, they were all considered suspect. What do you have in mind?"

"Whatever happened to Boudicca at her death means there must be physical remains. I think the Romans would have found her corpse by the oak tree and I think that though her spirit had left her, she died when the chariot hit the tree. I can't prove it but I feel that's how it happened. If that was so it would have suited them to not record it because the last thing they wanted to do was have her seen a martyr, so I think they would have buried her with the bodies of Domnall and her generals, somewhere near the battlefield."

"That's clever thinking love but remember Cassius Dio wrote that she fell ill, died and was given a lavish burial. I prefer him to Tacitus who was prone to sensationalism, besides no-one really knows the location of the battle of Watling Street."

"Maybe by ill he meant she died from her wounds ...but the lavish burial surely means she was buried at the battlefield."

"So do you want Sharlene to what, try and channel Boudicca?"

"No, Gaius Suetonius Paulinus," Cleo said.

"What an interesting idea," I said, stunned by it.

I told Jackson and he reacted as I had, but agreed. We knew Judith and Mike would also be excited by the idea. I promised Cleo to phone Sharlene after dinner that night.

When Wayne returned with the van after dropping Chris off at the station, we headed off to the Tor.

Judith had produced a grid map of the Tor for us. The idea was to scan four-metre squared blocks at a time in a methodical order so that no mistakes would be made. As field co-ordinator Ahmed was familiar with using that method on his many previous digs. Jane and Wayne were to handle the metal detector, which would feed data wirelessly to the laptop for Dylan to interpret. We ran over our jobs on the way to the site as though it was a briefing before a dangerous wartime mission. Edward was impressed with the professionalism of the team. They were after all the best in their field the UK had to offer.

We parked under the trees in the car park of Berachah Guest

House and then made our way along Well House Lane up the hill to the Tor.

The Tor looked different by day, less imposing. Holding Jackson's hand as we huffed and puffed our way along the narrow track, we reminisced climbing it at midnight on that icy cold night forty years ago. It was a night we'd never forget for it was the night my destiny revealed itself.

"Star Lords are your footprints in the sky?" I whispered to Jackson.

"Ah yes, I remember your poem." And we both searched the blue sky for footprint clouds.

We stopped for Wayne and Dylan to catch their breaths—it was a hard climb carrying the Radan. Edward and Jackson took over from them and we set off again.

I was holding Cleo's arm when Dylan said all mysterious like, "You know there have been some strange things happen to people up here?"

"Oh do tell Dylan," Cleo said with a cynical chuckle.

"I'm serious, there was this woman, a tourist I think, came here one night and started up the hill, alone. When she was near the top she could make out someone standing beside the Tor dressed in a black hooded cloak. As she came closer she realised it was a woman, but the woman didn't appear to notice her—she just stood there—still. Suddenly, out of nowhere a mist began to roll in and just as she reached the Tor it like totally engulfed her ...she couldn't see a thing and had to reach out her arms like a blind person to try and feel for the Tor but instead her fingers found a face! Suddenly, the face appeared out of the mist and it was horrific—the gnarly, craggy, ugly face of a decrepit old witch. She snarled with rotten teeth and a stinking breath and then disappeared into the mist. A breeze suddenly sprang up and blew the mist away ...it was then the woman discovered she was alone on the Tor. She could see for miles around and there wasn't a soul to be seen. She learned later from locals that she had encountered Aganzoita Moonfrog—the 16th Century witch of Well House Lane who had been burnt at the stake on the Tor."

"Great story Dylan, did you make up her name?" Cleo asked.

"Yeah, Arganzoita Moonfrog was the name of a mate's metal band."

"Sounds like one, if you'd left out the Moonfrog surname it might have been more convincing," Cleo said rolling her eyes.

We reached the Tor.

"I don't know, I like the idea of a Moonfrog," Dylan said with a wrinkled-up nose.

"Get to work you silly wanker," Cleo joked.

We were lucky there was no-one else on the Tor. We set up the equipment and got stuck into it. Ahmed decided to start from the Tor itself.

Cleo, Jackson, Edward and I sat on the grass and took in the splendid view. It had turned cloudy but every now and then the sun peaked through.

"Looks like rain," Jackson suggested.

"Might get a shower but that's about all," I speculated.

"All those credentials and you're a weather girl as well," Edward quipped.

"No, but my granddad taught me, if there's enough blue in the sky to make a pair of sailor's pants then it will stay clear."

"Mine said something like that but about ants," Edward recollected.

Completely unexpectedly Dylan let out a loud excited squawk. "There we go, there's something down there manmade!"

Ahmed ordered Wayne and Jane to freeze and we rushed over to Dylan. He was wearing headphones listening to the audio response from the detector and ripped them off in a flurry.

"Wait, I'll replay it," he said eagerly.

It was an anxious moment. We all watched the monitor like we were hoping to win lotto.

"Okay, check out the 3-D graph," he advised us and then hit play. A line similar to that on a hospital brain activity monitor showed smooth and steady, then suddenly spiked.

"There!" he said sharply and handed me the headphones. "Listen, I'll play it again."

I put them on, and when he replayed it, I heard a loud beep.

"Hear it?" he asked.

"Yes, does that mean there's something there?" I took the headphones off.

"Much more than that, watch this."

We watched intently while he clicked the cursor at the peak of the spike, and it read out: CU-29-63.546 amu.

"CU is the chemical element symbol for copper, twenty-nine is its atomic number, and 63.546 is the atomic mass," Dylan explained.

"That's incredible!" Jackson said.

"So it's a copper object," Dylan said confidently.

"Okay, save that, Dylan. Now we need to cover it in four separate passes from four different points to verify it," Ahmed said.

Over the course of the next two hours, we identified and verified not one but seven occurrences or incidents, as Dylan called them. He was thrilled, but we were becoming less confident—there were just too many potential targets.

Ahmed came over to us after noticing our mood had sunk into dejection.

"Look, some of the incidents will be things buried, copper coins, wire, rubbish—but some may well be artefacts, who knows—but we must remember there is a lot of archaeology on this hill, and one of those incidents could very well be the casket."

"Thanks, Ahmed, it's easy to get despondent in going from the sublime to the ridiculous inside a couple of hours," I admitted.

"Bonnie, the first incident was the strongest, and it showed there is a copper object 5.0292 metres below the surface. Now, that is a significant number because the Druids measured in rods, and one rod is exactly 5.0292 metres. It could be it," Ahmed said.

That brightened us up.

"But it showed it was copper... wouldn't copper have degraded over time underground, you know, turned green and just rotted away?" I questioned.

"Not if it was bronze, that would last," Ahmed said reassuringly.

"Bronze is eighty-eight percent copper and twelve percent tin, so a bronze container would come up on the scanner as being copper," Dylan explained.

"Did it show the same reading on every pass?" I delved.

"It sure did. I could imagine Morgan measuring exactly one rod down for the casket, can't you?" Ahmed said confidently.

"I recall it was three body lengths," Cleo said.

"Yeah, well, that's about sixteen feet or five metres," Wayne confirmed.

"You couldn't be lucky enough to find the bloody thing on your first effort, surely?" Edward questioned.

"That's a bit like saying Elton John was an overnight success when it took him over ten years," Cleo said dismissively.

"What she's saying is it has taken us forty years to get to this point, and our research has been thorough, so yes, we could be that lucky, but I wouldn't be calling it luck," I said.

"I suggest we call it a day. There is further analysis Dylan can do on the incidents with different software, but he will need to do them at HQ."

Ahmed was right, so we packed it in for the day.

After dinner that night, I phoned Sharlene as promised. She was thrilled to hear what we were doing. I told her what Cleo had in mind, and she agreed to give it a try. I'd called her cell phone and was happy to learn she was in the South of France on vacation and would come to London to meet us once we got back there. Cleo was beside me and overjoyed with the plan. After I signed off from Sharlene, I told Cleo I was going to ring Judith.

"Oh, there's something I need to ask Mike," she said.

"Okay, I'll ring, and you can speak with him first."

I called and put it on speaker.

"Hi Bonnie, I hope you're ringing with good news," Judith said enthusiastically.

"I've got you on speaker, so Cleo can hear. We've found something that looks promising, but Dylan needs to run some more tests before we can declare a national holiday."

"That's exciting!" Judith said.

"What brilliant news, hi ladies," Mike said on speaker as well.

"Hi Mike, we've just spoken with Sharlene. She's in France and will visit us when we get back to the manor. Cleo wants her to try and channel Gaius Suetonius Paulinus."

"My goodness, what on earth for?" Mike said surprised.

"I want to determine where Boudicca is buried so we can try and exhume some hair for DNA testing. We need to know if there is a genetic link between us or not," Cleo said strongly.

"And you think Gaius Suetonius Paulinus would know where she is buried," Mike questioned.

"Well, didn't Cassius Dio state that Boudicca fell ill and died and was then given a lavish burial?" I said.

"You're quite correct, but of course, that's not what Tacitus recorded... but in saying that we know his habit of being inaccurate... so yes, I can see how you would make the assumption that Suetonius might have ordered her burial, especially if she died on the battlefield."

"Even if she didn't, there must have been a body; she couldn't have just disappeared... and it's logical they would have given her a decent burial. Pride would have prevented them from making it known to the Britons or mentioning it in their own records. I think he would have insisted on keeping all the glory for himself and had her buried in an undisclosed location," Cleo proposed.

"I think you might have something there, Cleo," Judith said. "What a coup it would be if we could find Boudicca's body and the site of the battle of Watling Street."

"Our learned colleagues cite Dunstable in Bedfordshire as the most likely location for the battle," Mike said.

"Anyhow, we're all for it at this end, Cleo," Judith said. "We understand how important it is for you to know what caused the connection between you, Bonnie, and Boudicca. It had to be more than something supernatural."

Cleo went into the living room, and I turned off the speaker to discuss the doctor's appointment in privacy.

"How did the appointment go, love?"

"It was positive news, Bonnie. It hasn't metastasized, and the surgeon thinks he has narrowed the tumors down to the breasts, and the lymph nodes are safe for now."

"Oh, that's excellent news, Judith. You must be relieved... and you too, Mike."

"Yes, Bonnie, we can't tell you how that makes us feel. He'll operate in six months' time," Mike said.

I was tearing up. I could hear the emotional tremor of relief in both their voices.

CHAPTER XXXVII

Later that night, Dylan wandered into the lounge room. Unable to hide his excitement, he held up a flash drive and announced proudly, "I think we've definitely found it."

I looked up at him sharply after having been staring contemplatively at the fireplace for ages.

"Tell us your thoughts, Dylan."

"I've checked and rechecked the data, and there's no doubt, a copper target the size of a shoebox is at 5.0292 metres. To confirm the data, I switched from ground scan to metal discrimination, then thermograph, and finally a 3-D thermo scan. All registered the copper object of the said proportions, and it's locked in with a GPS location so we can uncover it whenever we wish," Dylan said excitedly.

I leapt up and gave him an enormous hug. He playfully pushed me back and said, "Forget the hugs, where's the bleedin' champagne?"

Acting on sound advice from Edward, now that we had what we needed, we packed everything up the following morning and headed back to the manor in Buckinghamshire. I sent a text to Sharlene to say we were on our way.

On the road, I told Edward I hoped we'd left Gaius in our wake. But he remained unconvinced of that.

We reached the manor without any hiccups and immediately went into a meeting to bring Judith, Mike, and Brigitte up to speed. They needed to get to know Edward, but that was easy; he was most affable. Dylan took them through his findings, and Judith, always a difficult person to please on all things archaeological, was most receptive. She was now convinced she had a compelling case to put to the National Trust at the meeting the next morning.

Mike enlightened everybody on what was planned with Sharlene, and that caused a stir. Dylan was over the moon with the prospect of using the Radan to find Boudicca—she must have, he suggested, been buried with her sword, which would be detectable.

Mike had done some research on Gaius Suetonius Paulinus that he enlightened us with.

"Tacitus wrote of Suetonius addressing his legionaries: 'Ignore the racket made by these savages. There are more women than men in their ranks. They are not soldiers—they're not even properly equipped. We've beaten them before, and when they see our weapons and feel our spirit, they'll crack. Stick together. Throw the javelins, then push forward—knock them down with your shields and finish them off with your swords. Forget about plunder. Just win, and you'll have everything.' This, more than anything else, tells us Suetonius planned to annihilate Boudicca and her army. It was reported they killed not only the warriors but also the wives, children, and even pack animals. Tacitus claims 80,000 Britons to have fallen for the loss of only 400 Romans. Now, from descriptions of the terrain, many towns have claimed to be the location of the Watling Street final battle. Dunstable in Bedfordshire, Paulerspury in Northamptonshire, Kings Cross under platform 10—Mansetter in Warwickshire, and even places that have had post-mortem manifestations such as Epping Forest in Essex, where Boudicca was reported loitering in a park as a ghostly apparition. But for me, the most convincing site is Stanmore Common. As a matter of fact, the late Professor Quinn Harris, one of the founders of First Light, first postulated the Stanmore Common theory as the site of the battle in the late nineteen-sixties. Watling Street is a Roman road that runs directly from London to St. Albans. It passes Stanmore Common, and the topography there certainly fits the description by Tacitus... and the idea that Boudicca might have been killed in a chariot crash during the battle and then buried at the battleground makes perfect sense. I remember Quinn once saying that the Romans had seventy thousand plus dead to dispose of—they were experienced at dealing with the dead, they would simply stack the corpses in a pile and then incinerate them. But first, they would isolate the leaders of the vanquished to give them a secret but honourable burial. Had Boudicca died as Cleo suggests and Bonnie corroborates, Suetonius would almost certainly have buried her with her sword and shield, as was customary for pagan Romans of the pre-Christian era to honour the leaders of those they had defeated in burial. So we could indeed expect that the graves of Boudicca, Domnall, and other chiefs killed that day to be buried at Stanmore Common. Further to that, I found a local legend that claims a mound discovered in 2010 in the grounds of Limes House, on Wood Lane in Stanmore, is reputed to be the grave of Boudicca."

We were almost rejoicing; it was so exciting.

"So what did they find when they excavated the mound?" Wayne asked.

"It hasn't been excavated," Mike said.

"You're kidding, why not?" Dylan protested with a shrill voice of amazement.

"Maybe it's the National Trust," I suggested, looking at Judith.

"No, it's not. Maybe no-one has shown enough interest or raised the funds," Judith posed. "I'd hazard a guess that other sites would have priority."

Just then, Arthur the butler came in with Sharlene, and general mayhem erupted when I virtually flew across the room to hug her, with Jackson in hot pursuit.

After introductions, we all indulged in an afternoon aperitif and much debate about scanning Boudicca's gravesite with the Radan.

Sharlene, Cleo, and I took a stroll outside for a chat. I hadn't seen Sharlene for over ten years, but she still looked terrific. Though we were the same age, her organic diet had preserved her better than my carnivorous fare, and she looked still in her forties while I... well. Cleo and Sharlene got on like a house on fire. Though it could be considered a distraction from our main objective, we felt finding out if Boudicca was actually buried in Stanmore was vital, especially for Cleo and me.

When we came back inside, Jackson pulled me aside for a quiet word.

"Edward told me he has serious concerns about trying to excavate the casket. He's convinced Gaius would be planning on stealing it from us and wouldn't stop at killing someone to get his claws on it. With that in mind, and with so many of us involved, he believes it's almost impossible for him to protect us on his own."

"What does he want to do then?" I asked, concerned.

"He thinks we should discuss it with the principals and come up with a strategy."

"Okay, we'll leave Cleo and the others talking to Sharlene, while we take Mike, Judith, Ahmed, Brigitte, and Edward into the study to resolve it," I decided.

We did just that and came up with the idea of splitting the party into three groups. Group one, Sharlene and Cleo, to focus on determining Boudicca's burial site. Group two, the young ones with Ahmed in charge, to act on group one's findings, and hopefully, that will be to scan the Stanmore burial mound for Boudicca. And group three, the seniors along with Edward, to focus on the National Trust and unearthing the gospel.

In the morning, after Judith and Brigitte had departed for London to make the presentation to the National Trust, Edward asked for a few minutes with Jackson and me, so we went into the study.

"I thought about it overnight, and I believe we should create a diversion to bring Gaius out into the open. Then I will be able to deal with him," he ventured.

I looked at him blankly. "Wouldn't that be a little dangerous?" I questioned.

"That's the way I work, Bonnie."

"We had actually thought of that before, and it's basically what got my friend Matt Ryan killed back in nineteen seventy-four," Jackson said regretfully.

"Yes, I know about that, but I have a different scheme. Hear me out... We have to assume Gaius knows less than we think. Really, he's tapping us to be able to tail us, but that's about all—and that's all he wants—to keep close enough, in touch, so that when we find what he's after, he can simply take it."

"So you think he's watching us?" Jackson said.

"Perhaps not him, but someone would be, yes."

"Do you think he knows who you are?" I asked.

"No, but he will find out if we're not careful. After all, when he worked out who Chris was, he acted, didn't he?"

"Yes, so what's your plan?" I urged.

"We need a replica casket."

"Brilliant, so that he steals the wrong one," Jackson said.

"Yes, but more so that he tries to steal it from me. I'll be the bait."

"So are you expecting this to happen in Glastonbury if and when we exhume the real casket?" Jackson posed.

"I think we have to make it so. Otherwise, he'll continue the waiting game for the ideal moment, and that will play right into his hands."

"I'm not with you," I said.

"He emailed Cleo, right?" he questioned.

"Yes," I said.

"Well, you can be sure he's got your cell phone bugged."

"Oh my God! You think so? If that's true, he would have heard everything I told Judith from Glastonbury," I felt the blood draining from my face.

"That's probably how he knew who Chris was," he said matter-of-factly.

"You know, you're probably right. When Judith admitted on the phone that she was worried about us, I told her Chris was more than capable of protecting us," I said, shocked.

"There you go. So, we use your phone to bait him, but you can't stop using it, otherwise, he'll get wise. Just be careful what you say and tell everyone in the party that you'll be doing that. Okay?"

We nodded.

"Cool, I'll think over what to say and script it for you so that we leak to him only what we want him to know. In the meantime, I'll get you a clean phone."

We had a plan, and we felt confident Edward had the smarts to pull it off. We were just dubious about our own smarts.

While Ahmed, Wayne, and Judy were researching the battle of Watling Street, Dylan was fiddling with the Radan and studying the operating manual.

In the study, Mike, Jackson, Cleo, and I were talking with Sharlene about how she'd go about channelling Gaius Suetonius Paulinus.

"I use psychometry to channel a past life. Admittedly, the item only takes you back to the last time it was used, and sometimes that's not by the person you're seeking to channel. But that's a risk you have to take. If you use a body part, it's more accurate. Like, it will definitely be the right person, but it will only be the last time the body part was alive... and let me tell ya, sometimes that can be a bit confronting. So, I'll need something that belonged to this guy Paulinus," Sharlene said.

Well, that certainly threw the cat among the pigeons. We all exchanged bewildered looks.

Then Cleo sparked up brightly, "Hey, would they have something belonging to him at the British Museum?"

"You know, you might just be right," Mike said, holding his chin, thinking. "And I think I've got just the person to ask. The curator was one of my students. I'll call him now."

Five minutes later, Mike popped back in from outside with his cell phone in his hand and asked Sharlene, "Would his personal seal work?"

Sharlene shrugged, "If he touched it the most, then yeah, it damn well might."

"Well, it was found in his tomb in Pesaro, Italy, so it would have only been handled by archaeologists since, but wearing gloves, of course. So fine—I expect," he said pragmatically. "I'll arrange for Judith to collect it from museum archives while she's in London."

Jackson winked at Cleo, who was sitting with her mouth agape, amazed by what Mike had just pulled off. We, of course, knew how much influence Mike had within UK academic circles, but in this instance, he'd totally outdone himself.

"Hard to believe the seal of Gaius Suetonius Paulinus will be here this afternoon," I exclaimed.

It was shaping up to be an eventful day. Our hopes were high that Judith would have a successful meeting and return with good news along with the seal.

It was mid-afternoon when I heard Judith's car pull up outside, causing my heart to skip a beat. We had agreed, as a security measure, for her not to phone us with news, so we had been left on tenterhooks. We waited in the library, as excited as teenagers awaiting exam results.

Judith and Brigitte knew what this moment would mean to all of us and played it right down to the wire before we were about to explode from suspense. They sat in the vacated chairs we had left because we were standing, fidgety and nervous. Judith calmly reached into her coat pocket, withdrew a ring box, opened it, and displayed the ring inside.

"This is the ring seal of Gaius Suetonius Paulinus." She watched our collective mouths drop open, aghast. Then she produced an envelope from her inside pocket and said slowly, "And this is a permit for a keyhole excavation on Glastonbury Tor."

Well, you could have heard a pin drop. Then we erupted with tears of joy. I hugged Judith, who was weeping as well, and then I hugged Brigitte—and then we all hugged. Even Edward. It was such an emotional moment. We had done it!

CHAPTER XXXVIII

e all took turns marvelling over the golden seal of Gaius Suetonius Paulinus, and I, for one, couldn't wait for Sharlene to use it to channel him. But first, we decided to devise a plan for the dig, and to that end, it was critical for Edward to take the lead in strategising our deployment. He surprised us by having a PowerPoint presentation prepared. He used Bluetooth to connect his laptop to a wall-mounted fifty-five-inch flat-screen television in the theatrette next to the study, and we watched it with keen interest. A short question time followed, and then Edward stayed with the others to talk further while I took Sharlene to the study next door to make contact with the other side.

She was okay with all of us being present—Mike, Judith, Jackson, and Cleo. I waited while she entered a meditative trance, and then, as she had instructed, wearing gloves, I pressed the seal into her opened palm. We figured this could well be the inaugural use of psychometry in archaeology, and if it worked, it would open up many possibilities.

With her eyes closed, Sharlene spoke, "Who owns the item I hold?"

"Gaius Suetonius Paulinus," I said.

It was much spookier than a regression hypnosis session. In a similar way to hypnosis, Sharlene tuned into the vibration of the object in her hand. It is an ability she had perfected over time, along with something inherent, allowing her to connect with the object. Maybe akin to Cleo and myself having a genetic link to tune into Boudicca. Sharlene calls it "the gift," a term coined by her illustrious grandfather Edgar Cayce. It took about twenty minutes of silent meditation before she spoke again.

Then she said slowly, "I have found Gaius Suetonius Paulinus."

We sat amazed, listening to Sharlene talking to Gaius Suetonius

Paulinus. We could only understand her questions because Gaius answered in a foreign language. Mike was recording it on a digital movie camera.

A couple of times, we prompted her on what to say. Eventually, when she figured we had what we needed, she fell silent, as if in a deep sleep. I knew not to wake her. It was important for her to wake of her own accord. We waited anxiously for her to come around, and when she did, she was groggy.

"Do you remember much of the experience, Sharlene?" Jackson asked.

"No, a little comes back over time, but I've always believed it best to let sleeping dogs lie. I'll let you guys analyse the recording while I have a drink of water and then take a stroll outside—I need to reconnect with nature." She slipped her shoes off and walked barefoot out of the room.

Mike had scrolled back the tape and was listening to the recording through headphones, jotting down notes. After about fifteen minutes, he removed the headphones and said emphatically, "Quite literally amazing."

"What language was that?" Jackson asked.

"It was Latin," Edward said, surprising us.

"Yes, you're right. Though most educated Romans spoke Greek at the time, Latin was their formal language. I noted the conversation, and it was incredible. I'll read you the translation. Sharlene asked, 'Are you Gaius Suetonius Paulinus?'

He answered yes, and you must be a god to be talking inside my mind?

'Yes, I am a god, but I will not divulge my name.'

What is it you want of an old man on his deathbed?

'I ask if your memory serves you well?'

Not as good as it once had, but well enough. Go on.

'Do you recall the battle of Watling Street, in Britannia?'

My most triumphant victory, yes.

'Do you remember seeing Queen Boudicca die?'

Of course, a savage. Her four white horses all torn and smeared with blood. She drove them at a tree. She needed to die—the fight was over. I would have crucified her anyway.

'Did you bury her?'

Yes, of course, separate from the others but nevertheless in a common grave. I bestowed on her no honour, but to give her respect in death to appease the gods. My gods. Did I please you?

'Yes, I was pleased.'

Then why ask me this when you should already know?

'There has been some confusion.'

I understand.

'Where was she buried?'

On the battlefield, of course, at the base of the very oak tree she used to take her own life. Such as it was with those Druids—they worshipped the oak. She was buried with her torc, sword, and shield to take on her journey into the afterlife.

'When did you bury her?'

Soon after her death but in secret, so as not to risk spreading a rumour. There were some who saw her golden torc as a prize of victory. I didn't.

'Can you describe her, Boudicca?'

A crazy woman with a blue-painted body and wild red hair. Proud they were, these savages. A strong warrior, a worthy opponent, even though female—they had untamed women that fought like men. In fact, she fought like a score of men, and in the end, I'd say she died well. But the glory is mine...

"It was at that point I had an authentication question," Mike continued, "and I whispered it to Cleo to pass on to Sharlene. She asked, 'What was the name of your biographer uncle?'"

'Gaius Suetonius Tranquillus, of course. Why?'

I then whispered a second question to Sharlene, and she asked it.

"Who did you replace as governor of Britain?"

'Quintus Veranius. Silly man died in office.'

Mike glanced at Judith, impressed with the answers.

"The authentication answers were absolutely correct. It would be unlikely for Sharlene to have known them," Judith said sternly.

"Do you think she knows the history of Roman-occupied Britain?" Mike asked me.

"No, maybe a little of what Reagan had told her about his work. But if you're trying to make sense of it—"

"I wasn't doubting her, Bonnie. She was, after all, speaking conversational Latin fluently, and that would be impossible for her to know unless she had studied it for years. It was just so unbelievable, that's all," Mike muttered, a smidgen embarrassed.

"How on earth does she manage to walk around here in England, where there's so much history, without tuning into everything she touches?" Jackson asked, scratching his head.

"That's a good question. But she does have to enter a state of deep meditation before she can tune in ...and can't really walk around in that state," I suggested tactfully, punctuated with a wry smile.

They laughed at my joke.

"I tell you what, with a gift like that, she could be extremely valuable to the Cambridge Archaeology department," Judith said.

"I don't think she would do it, love. I remember her telling me that she did a stint for the cops in San Francisco some time ago, to help solve a murder, and it turned out bad for her."

"What happened?" Cleo asked.

"If I remember rightly, the detective in charge was convinced she was a charlatan and was determined to prove it. So he contradicted everything she came up with. It was an emotional case, a missing four-year-old girl from memory. The parents were ex-hippies and believed in Sharlene's psychic ability to locate their kidnapped daughter. You know the story: the detective disliked hippies and begrudged Sharlene's involvement with his case. Anyhow, a highway patrol cop found a necklace belonging to the little girl by the side of the highway. Sharlene used it to visualise where her body was hidden and saw it in a drain on the side of a highway near a bridge. The detective ignored it, but the hippie family pushed the highway patrol cop to search for the bridge, and he found the body. Then, in a massive turnaround, the detective wanted Sharlene to help find the killer, but after all the pain, she didn't have the heart ...and from that time on, she only used her gift for special circumstances."

"Wow, that's an amazing story... must have been terrible for her, and how privileged are we to have her helping us?" Cleo said. "Let's go tell the others."

There was excitement in the air when Cleo and Mike confirmed that Stanmore was a likely site for Boudicca's grave. Dylan was practically bursting with anticipation at the thought of scanning the location with Radan to find Boudicca's sword, shield, and especially her golden Torc. The newfound knowledge led us to revise our plans. It was decided that Wayne, Judith, Mike, Edward, Jackson, and I would go to Glastonbury to excavate the Tor. Meanwhile, Ahmed, Brigitte, Jane, Dylan, and Cleo would head to Stanmore to scan for Boudicca's grave. But first, Ahmed would create a grid map for the geophysical survey. Wayne got on the phone to rent the necessary equipment for the keyhole excavation. The mansion buzzed with activity—we were on the case.

In the morning, various items started arriving, mostly for Wayne, but there was one peculiar box addressed to Judith. When she received it from the courier, she handed over the seal, indicating that the box was from the British Museum. She called Mike, Edward, Jackson, and me into the study to show us what she had received. It was a replica of the gospel bronze casket, designed by Judith and Mike in collaboration with the museum's antiquities department. The replica looked entirely authentic.

"The question is, will it deceive Gaius?" Edward questioned.

"I believe so. It's made of bronze, not copper, but it would fool me, and I've probably examined more artefacts than he's had hot lunches. They did an excellent job of aging it... see how the copper is tarnished green," Judith remarked.

"Well done, guys! Let's hope we don't have to use it!" I said flatly.

"Yes, we could do without Gaius. Speaking of him, how is Chris?" Jackson asked Edward.

"They've given her extended paid leave to recover."

"Let's hope she's enjoying herself in Mykonos or some other equally exotic place," I joked.

"With you all set to embark on your respective tasks, I think I might head back to Saint-Tropez to continue with my own thing," Sharlene told me.

I grabbed her elbow and took her aside.

"Hmm, that sounds intriguing. So, what's his name?" I whispered discreetly.

"Maurice," she replied with a saucy smirk. "And tomorrow he turns twenty-five. He'll be the birthday boy in his birthday suit."

"Hmm, are there any tickets for sale?" I teased.

She playfully elbowed me in the ribs. "You don't need a ticket, honey."

I loved the mischievous sparkle in her eyes. Despite being fifty plus, she had a youthful spirit.

"I'll be at Le Yaca Hotel for the next month if you need me, honey... and you know you're welcome to come visit. You too, Cleo," she said as Cleo joined us.

"Who knows, darling? We might just take you up on that," I said, taking Cleo by the arm.

An hour later, dressed as though she had walked right out of a scene from Woodstock the Movie, Sharlene climbed into her rented Citroen, blew us a big kiss, and drove out of our lives but not out of our hearts. Standing next to Cleo, waving goodbye, a feeling of loss washed over me. At my age, there is something insecure and fatalistic about bidding farewell to an old friend whom you don't see very often.

It's as if the subconscious mind questions whether you'll ever see them again.

The manor felt quieter without Sharlene. It was as if someone had extinguished a radiant light. However, the subdued atmosphere worked well for our purposes. Everyone focused on their tasks to prepare for our early morning departures to our respective locations.

That night, the sound of little footsteps echoed persistently through the floor. Jackson and I sat in bed, speculating on the identities of the clandestine visitors. I had won the previous round, but this time we seemed to agree.

From the bedroom window, the dawn cast long, slender shadows on the ground from the trees. I could see the brightness, but I couldn't feel the warmth. It's different in England—the temperature seems to take much longer to rise compared to the corresponding season in Australia.

Within a few hours, both vans were packed and ready to go. Cleo was emotional, fearing for our safety and worried that Gaius was more likely to strike this time. When she said her goodbyes to Wayne, I realised her concern went deeper than I had presumed. This budding relationship confirmed that Jackson and I had been right about at least one of the nocturnal visitors last night.

The younger team set off for Stanmore while we, the older members, waited for Mike, who had to rush back inside to retrieve something he had forgotten. Eventually, we hit the road. This time, there was no singing or fooling around. We were a serious group, inwardly excited about the excavation but outwardly concerned about Gaius.

CHAPTER
XXXIX

We were booked into the same B&B in Glastonbury as before. I had bought a new prepaid SIM card as Edward had suggested, so once in my room, I phoned Ahmed. He said they had arrived at their B&B in Stanmore, dropped off their gear in their rooms, and then rushed down to Stanmore Common to start scanning the terrain. There was a huge area to cover, unlike at Glastonbury Tor. It was a big job and likely to take them several days, and to make matters worse, it was raining heavily. Luckily, in Glastonbury, it was sunny and almost warm. I ended the call with the promise to call later that night for an update.

Judith called the Council to inform them of our arrival, as they had requested. They wanted to see our permit before granting us authorisation to proceed with the excavation. Wayne drove us to the Town Hall on Magdalene Street to get the permit stamped.

Judith disappeared into the Council Chambers and emerged ten minutes later, waving the stamped document triumphantly, as if it were a winning lottery ticket. With our spirits lifted, we made our way to the Tor.

There wasn't much for us to do, apart from assisting Wayne in carrying the small amount of equipment up the Tor. Once he began digging, we could only relax in the shade of St. Michael's Tower and observe.

"Do you know the tower is a Grade 1 listed structure, designated as a scheduled monument?" Judith mentioned.

"And what does 'scheduled monument' mean?" I asked.

"It means it's protected," Mike grumbled.

"Why don't they just say 'protected' instead of 'scheduled monument'? It makes it sound like it hasn't happened yet," I replied with disappointment.

"It dates back to the Ancient Monuments Act of 1882," Mike added with a frown.

"Well, isn't it about time they changed it, then?" I muttered.

I glanced back at Wayne, who was about two metres away from us on the grassy slope. He was securing a small petrol motor on top of a drill tube.

"It looks like he's going to take a core sample," I joked to Jackson.

"Spot on. Wayne told me it's a similar process. The thing is actually a core drill. After reaching one metre, he'll pull it back up, open it, and examine the core. Look, he's almost down to the first metre already," Jackson explained.

"Will it damage the box if it hits it?" Edward asked.

"No, it won't touch it. He'll stop just centimetres from it. Once at the prescribed depth, he'll use a larger tube with a wider gauge to cover the box. And here's the interesting part—it has a device at the drill head that opens up like a claw to retrieve the target," Jackson happily shared.

We had to raise our voices to be heard over the sound of the drill motor.

"A smart machine... so do both drills use the coordinates provided by Radan?" Edward questioned.

"Apparently so," Jackson confirmed.

"That's why it's called keyhole excavation," Mike assured us, always the clever clogs.

"Will it work for Boudicca's grave?" I asked.

"No, we'll need to excavate that in a conventional manner. We wouldn't want to risk causing damage," Judith asserted, sounding like a headmistress again. Thankfully, she was back to normal, with her fears alleviated.

"We won't need to keyhole it because it's not a scheduled monument," Mike remarked facetiously.

Jackson was just finishing enclosing the dig area with crime scene-like tape when the noise of the drill motor abruptly ceased, and Wayne called him over.

"Guys, over here!" Jackson called out to us.

We ducked under the yellow tape and joined them.

"I've reached five metres, and the object is at 5.0292. It's time to bring out the big gun. Jackson and Edward, I'll need your help," Wayne said.

"It only took an hour to dig down five metres," I remarked to Mike.

"Yes, apparently they use the same core drill for polar research, sampling ice cores for dating and climate analysis. If there's no rock in the way, it's quick... Dylan's data indicated there wasn't any rock," Mike shared, a treasure trove of trivia.

I examined the two long core samples. "A lot can be determined from these, I suppose."

"Yes, I'll have them studied back at Cambridge. At the very least, we can learn about the weather during different periods from the seeds and pollen. A regular time capsule," Judith explained.

Jackson and Wayne struggled with the large core unit. Both of them had to turn the drill as if it were a massive tap. Once it had dug down and reached one and a half metres, they had to lock in the next length to go deeper. Edward lent a hand. Wayne worried that if they failed to position the drill precisely at the provided coordinates, it could cut right through the object. They perspired more from anxiety than effort.

"We're getting close!" Wayne shouted. "Hold!" They stopped abruptly. He stepped onto one of the carry cases positioned beside the drill and took hold of a lever at the top of the last core pipe.

"That must be the grabber controller. Exciting, isn't it?" Judith nervously murmured to me through gritted teeth.

I watched with wide eyes. Forty years of anticipation hinged on Dylan's accurate data and Wayne's precise drill positioning. I could hear my heart pounding in my chest.

"Okay, fellas, turn, but very slowly," Wayne commanded.

With beads of sweat dripping from their chins, Jackson and Edward carefully rotated the drill. Suddenly, we heard a scraping sound, like metal against metal.

"Stop!" Wayne shrieked. He checked the reading on the digital display. "We're right on top of it. I think that was the sound of the diamond head touching the sides of the casket. Now, very, very slowly, we'll lower it another two hundred and fifty millimetres."

He nodded, and the guys rotated the drill three super slow turns, hand-cranked. "That should do it! Stop!" Wayne called urgently. Then, with our eyes fixed on him, he closed his eyes and, with deep concentration, gripped the lever and slowly squeezed it. He froze, and we froze along with him, all of us holding our breaths.

Then his eyes snapped open. "I've got it!" he exclaimed.

We let out a collective sigh of relief.

Just when we thought we had succeeded, Wayne announced, "Now comes the risky part."

My shoulders slumped.

"Alright, guys, start turning slowly counter clockwise. We're coming out!"

It took twenty painstaking minutes for them to extract the drill from the hole.

"Stop, hold it right there," Wayne finally said, stepping down from the packing case. He wrapped his arms around the tube, as if giving it a big bear hug, and said, "Right, guys, grip it, and we'll gently lift it out of the hole and place it on the ground, okay? On three... One, two, three!"

It came out relatively easily, and they carefully laid the five-foot tube on the ground, as delicate as handling a baby. We all stood there for a minute or two, simply admiring it, each of us wondering what lay inside.

"Well, I suppose it's time to see what we've got," Wayne said cavalierly.

It felt like I had chewed my fingernails down to my elbows. Judith had her back turned—she couldn't bear to watch. Edward, Mike, and Jackson stood there like wide-eyed statues. Wayne knelt down, unfastened, and unscrewed the end section of the drill. Once undone, he opened the metal casing, and all of us, except Judith, stared at the large clump of black dirt in shock. As if she knew without even looking, Judith spun around, walked directly to Wayne, knelt down beside him, and took charge.

"Excuse me, Wayne. Bring me that bottle of water over there, quick smart," she ordered him.

She knew exactly what she was doing; she had the experience to warrant it. Wayne returned with the bottle, handed it to her, and she poured it over the clump of dirt. Slowly, she washed away the dirt, and a square shape began to emerge. Mike handed her a hand towel, and she lifted the box, stood up, and then towelled it down, all the time holding it as though it were a newborn baby.

"Tyree's cask is definitely bronze," Jackson said with teary eyes.

"First time it has seen the light of day in nineteen hundred and fifty-four years," Mike mumbled as if in a dream.

"To think the last person to touch this was Morgan," Judith said with reverence and then gently handed it to me.

I felt honoured—it was like I'd been handed the Holy Grail. "Oh, it's ...it's heavy... and before Morgan held it... Queen Boudicca held it in her hands," I said with a lump in my throat. We backfilled the excavation, and then on the way to the B & B, we called into council chambers for Judith to fill in an excavation termination form.

We gathered in the drawing room of the B & B to discuss the day. I took the floor.

"I think we should leave now for the manor. I don't feel comfortable here," I told the others.

There was no dispute from anyone, so we packed everything and were on the road within the hour.

Three hours later, we arrived at the manor. When we got out of the van, the night seemed to blanket us with an oily, sinister darkness that chilled me to the bone. I felt evil was nearby, and it probably was.

Clutching the casket wrapped in a towel, I told Judith, "Quick, let's get it inside. It's spooky out here."

Edward stopped us. "Wait, I'm not letting that thing out of my sight for a second. Jackson, can you and Mike give Wayne a hand with the rest of the gear?"

"No worries," Jackson confirmed.

The trickiest parts of the mission had arrived, and I say parts because there were two... the opening of the casket and hanging on to whatever it contained.

I reverently carried it into the study and then handed it over to Judith to lock it into the safe. Edward checked his watch. "I've made the call. It will arrive in exactly three hours, around midnight. We best prepare," he announced like a military commander.

Mike came in. "Have you locked it up?"

"Yes," Judith replied.

"Did I hear you say we've got three hours?" he said to Edward.

"Yes, why? Do you want to start on it?" Judith asked.

"I'll need to check its condition first, and then I'll photograph as many pages as I can in the time."

"I don't know if that's a good idea," Edward said sternly.

"Oh, sorry Edward, but we do," Judith growled.

"Okay then, Mike," he checked the windows were locked. "I'll lock you in here and hold the key. Phone us if you need to come out or when you're finished," Edward said.

"We'll need to stay here to help Mike open it... just to be sure," Judith all but ordered.

"We'll all stay," I said as Jackson and Wayne joined us.

It was a heady moment. The book could be dust or not even inside the container. Mike handed his HD digital video camera over for Wayne to operate.

"Here, you've got a steadier hand than I lad, film this, will you?"

Mike asked.

"No problem," Wayne said, taking the camera and then getting into position for the best light and angle. Mike laid a sheet of plastic on the desktop and then unravelled a sheet of leather containing archaeologist's tools.

Once again, we all took a deep, nervous breath while Judith slipped on a pair of diamond grip forensic latex gloves. She opened her palm, and Mike slapped a scalpel into it. It was like a delicate surgical operation.

She steadied her hand to cut through Tyree's seal. "It seems such a shame to lose Tyree's mark. Make sure you get a close-up of it, Wayne," Judith said.

"Yep, got it, looks great," Wayne said.

We took turns getting one last look at the wax seal before it would be broken forever. As old as it was, the colour had faded, but Tyree's mark was still visible. After positioning her body for Wayne to get a clear shot, Judith gently cut the seal and then, using the blunt end of the scalpel, delicately pried the lid open.

We couldn't help ourselves and crowded Judith for a closer look at the contents. "Give a lass some room, please," Judith asked politely. "There... Hmm, good. It looks intact."

The tremble in her voice emphasised the enormity of the moment. We had taken a step back to give her more space. Then, with the precision of a surgeon, Judith gently slipped her fingers underneath, lifted the book from the casket, and laid it ever so delicately on the plastic sheet laid out.

We were breathing again but still trapped in awe of the unveiling. Again, by using the blunt end of the scalpel, Judith pried open the dark brown leathery front cover of the thick book and then stepped back with both gloved hands up to her mouth in shock. "Oh, my Lord!" she gasped.

CHAPTER
XL

Judith's eyes shone with reflected lamplight as tears of astonishment welled up in them. Mike leaned over to take a look and then withdrew quickly. "Unbelievable!" he gulped.

"I've never seen anything so beautifully preserved. It's as though it was written yesterday," Judith said, flopping into a chair, nonplussed. The rest of us could only gape open-mouthed.

"What language is it written in, Mike?" I asked.

"It could be Essene, Hebrew, or Aramaic, but on first glance, it looks like Aramaic," he said, putting on a pair of latex gloves. "I'd better get started."

Judith got up and peeled her gloves off. "Yes, yes, let's leave Mike to it. It looks like there are about three hundred pages. Photographing them will take a while, and it's vital he gets it done, and we all know why."

We filed out of the study to let Mike get on with the work. Edward stopped me in the hall.

"Bonnie, it's time to make a call to Cleo on the old phone," he said.

"Alright," I smiled quickly and searched in my handbag for it. "Ah, there it is. Oh, I have a text. It's from Sharlene."

"She shouldn't be using that number!" he grunted angrily.

"Oh, I'm sorry... I forgot to tell her, I—"

He cut me off. "Read the message," he said flatly.

"She has decided to stay a few more days in London because her friend flew over. She's at the Mayfair Hotel and hopes we got the gospel," I grimaced. "Oh dear, I'm so sorry."

"Nothing we can do about it now but to go on high alert. Right, text Cleo that we've unearthed the casket and we are taking it to the British Museum tomorrow at noon to open it under their sterile supervision."

He waited while I sent the message and checked it was delivered. I looked into his eyes... he was worried.

"What do you think he will do?"

"It would be crazy to try and second-guess him. It's what we do that counts."

"It's a crazy world," I said softly.

"And don't I know it," he said with a sigh. "Come on, we need to tell the others in the library."

An hour later, we joined Wayne at the fireplace in the library and were still debating the plan when Judith's phone rang.

"Oh, it's Mike," she said, peering at Edward. He nodded. "Okay, take it."

"Hello love, what's up?" she answered.

"You what!" she looked at us wide-eyed. "Put it to one side... don't let it distract you for now. How many pages have you completed? Okay, do you need anything else? No, fine, call me later, bye."

"What's happened?" I asked her fearfully.

"He found a lock of hair pressed between the pages."

"So it was true then," I said easily.

"A lock of hair?" Edward said, confounded.

"Whose could it be?" Jackson mused.

"Ah, that's the burning question," Judith muttered with a chuckle.

"Joseph's? Mary Magdalene's?" I posed.

"Or his famous nephew?" Jackson added with raised eyebrows.

"Jesus!" Edward erupted.

"It could be." Judith eyed us all with a wry grin.

"You've got to be kidding!" Wayne said, goggle-eyed.

"Can we find out through DNA testing?" I asked.

"No," Judith shook her head. "We would need to have his DNA already to confirm the hair belongs to him, and I doubt even the Vatican has that."

"Speaking of the Vatican," Edward said, checking his watch. "ETA one hour fifty-eight minutes."

My pocket buzzed. It was my old mobile... no one was supposed to use that number. I held it up for Edward to see.

"A text on the bugged phone," I told him. We read the text and were shocked by it.

"What is it?" Jackson said, concerned by the look on our faces.

"The message says, 'I am prepared to trade the life of Sharlene Cayce for the gospel.'"

Stupefied would not adequately sum up how we suddenly felt.

"This is not good," Edward grumbled, pacing the library floor. "This is definitely not good."

"What if he's bluffing?" Jackson asked.

"What if he's not?" I snapped.

"He's got us... we're the proverbial meat in the sandwich—damned if we believe him— damned if we don't!" Judith said dispiritedly, removing her glasses and pinching the bridge of her nose with her fingers to relieve a sudden headache.

Edward stopped pacing, turned, and faced us. "We have no alternative but to see our plan through," he said unyieldingly. "I have to answer... don't I? We can't just risk her life—"

"Everybody just sit down and take a deep breath," Edward said, taking a seat himself. "Now, let's think this through rationally."

"I don't know about you, Edward, but you can't get any more rational than that—he's going to kill her if we don't give him what he wants. And what makes that even more threatening is, we know from experience that he bloody well means what he says," Jackson growled angrily. "I'm sorry, I'm not angry at you, Edward, I just don't want to lose another—"

"It's alright, Jackson, I understand. I think it would be best to offer him the casket," Edward said.

"Over my dead body!" Judith said soberly.

"The fake casket, Judith," Edward said sharply. "But we'll need to make the exchange cleverly so as not to put Sharlene at risk."

"I hope they taught you how to do that at spy school or whatever," I teased sourly.

"In fact, they did, Bonnie, and I was in the top three," Edward smiled.

"How many were in the class?" Judith said snidely.

"Three.." Edward mumbled with a wry grin.

He got a laugh out of us even with the severity of the situation.

We were still deliberating when Mike called to be let out of the study. Time had gotten away from us; it was eleven fifty-five already. Judith saw to Mike and brought him back with her.

"I've only managed to photograph half the gospel... and here's the lock of hair," he handed me a resealable plastic bag containing a lock of mousey brown hair. "I was thinking, we could immediately narrow it down by checking if it's male or female... the lock of hair... through DNA testing," Mike stuttered. "I have a contact at Scotland Yard Forensics... the ENFSI."

After we told Mike what had happened to Sharlene, he realised why we were not so responsive to the idea. Suddenly, we heard the sound of helicopter rotors.

"It's here, give me the gospel," Edward said.

It was all a bit of a rush and had taken us by surprise. Mike handed him the casket containing the book.

"Are you certain it will be safe?" I asked despairingly.

"It will be kept in the vault at the Manchester Interpol office, accessible by any two of us. You understand, if I've gone for whatever reason, then it will take two of you to get it released."

"Okay, we've got that," I agreed.

"Give me the lock of hair to go with it?" Edward asked.

We all looked at each other and shook our heads collectively.

"No, we'll have it tested," I said.

"But I can arrange that as well," he argued.

"I'll give you a few strands for testing; we'll keep the rest," Mike said, fumbling in his pocket and then producing another resealable plastic bag. He put a few strands in it and then handed it to Edward.

Edward raced out of the library, and a few minutes later, we heard the chopper lift off from the front lawn.

"Oh, I do hope that thing didn't damage my garden," Judith croaked.

"I have an odd feeling about what just happened," I confided in Jackson.

"Me too, perhaps it was letting go of the gospel after it only just arrived, fear of loss?" Jackson said with uncertainty.

"Did you manage to read any of it, Mike?" I asked.

"Very little, but one thing I can say is it's definitely a chronicle of Joseph's life, a memoir if you like. I can hardly wait to start on the transcript. Wait, I'll get the camera and read you some of it."

"Great idea!" I eagerly said, settling back in my chair, trying to get over my fear of loss.

Judith went to the bureau and poured us a round of Port to celebrate. Handing them out, she said, "This is a lovely drop. I didn't realise you Aussies produced such fine port. Thank you, my dear Bolts, for such a splendid gift."

"Thank you for sharing it with us, Judith. Para vintage Port is regarded as one of the best at home," Jackson said.

"I thought you only had port with a cigar," Wayne mused.

"It used to be so, Wayne, but now that smoking is politically incorrect, there's no cigar," Jackson chuckled at his own joke.

"Cheers, everyone, to finally achieving what we all believed was possible all those years ago!" Judith said.

We all raised our glasses in toast.

"Edward is taking his time, isn't he?" I muttered.

Suddenly, the mood changed when Mike appeared in the doorway, ashen-faced.

"What's wrong, dear?" Judith asked, concerned.

"It, it's ruddy-well gone!" he stammered.

"What's gone, Mike?" I asked.

"The camera... damn thing is nowhere to be found!" he said, scratching his head, perplexed.

"It might be just a senior moment, love. I'll help you check," Judith said.

All of a sudden, a loud shout from the back of Mike almost sent him through the roof.

"Surprise!"

He swivelled around sharply and yelped in shock, "Sharlene!"

She was the last person any of us expected to see. To our absolute astonishment, she wandered into the library in her happy-go-lucky manner, with a big cheeky grin on her face, and declared, "Well, I didn't expect to be back here so soon, and by chopper no less. So, what's up, kids?"

I found myself standing, staring at her in disbelief, with my mouth agape.

"What do you mean, 'what's up'? Where's Edward?" I managed to spit out.

"Oh, he went back with the chopper. Didn't he tell you, honey?" She said, enquiringly.

"He what?" I squealed. Now I was worried. I grabbed her shoulders and barked, "What did he say to you?"

"Just to tell you the crew thanks you, whatever that means. You know him."

"Guess we didn't," Jackson snapped.

"The what?" I cried out, shaken. "The crew? You mean the Crux, as in Crux Redemptoris!" I flopped into the nearest chair and stared at Jackson. "Oh my God... what have we done?"

"Did any of us check his ID?" Jackson said.

"No, and why should we?" I said, annoyed.

"I don't get it," Judith said, mystified by it all.

"Edward or whatever his real name is... is an accomplice of Gaius. He has taken the gospel, the camera, and some of the hair... he would have taken all of the hair if it hadn't been for Mike insisting on a second DNA test," I said dismally.

"Was it a set-up?" Sharlene exclaimed.

"Too bloody right, it was!" I replied angrily. "He left us with the replica casket—his bloody idea—it was just a diversion so he could take the original."

No words could aptly describe how we all felt—duped would come the closest. No matter how we looked at it, we had fallen for it, boots and all.

"He'd even given us a bloody hint when he said, 'Speaking of the Vatican, ETA in one hour fifty-eight minutes'—it was a Vatican chopper," I surmised.

"I should have said something," Mike admitted.

"Why? Did something make you suspect him?" Jackson asked.

"When Sharlene had finished channelling, and you asked me what language she had been speaking?"

"Yes, I remember," Jackson said.

"Well, Edward inadvertently jumped in with, 'It was Latin,' and I thought... how the hell would a cop know that? Now I know, he's bloody Crux Redemptoris, isn't he?"

We were all sitting with our heads in our hands—the signs had been there all along, and we'd totally ignored them. I felt like a fool, but there was nothing I could do about it. After all this time and all the effort, Gaius had finally won.

"Not all is lost," Mike announced. And when we looked up at him, he was holding the plastic bag containing the lock of hair and shaking it. "We still have this."

He was right; we might have lost the gospel, but we still had the hair, and there was much to be gained from the analysis of it.

"And we've got the Boudicca dig," Judith said dejectedly.

"And I have some pages from the middle section of the gospel I copied onto my laptop as a test, so we've got something," Mike said, trying to find a positive out of the quagmire of negativity.

"Where did you get the hair?" Sharlene asked.

"It was pressed between pages in the gospel," I told her.

"Whose is it?" she asked.

"It could belong to Joseph, Mary Magdalene, or even Jesus Christ," Judith said.

"I should be able to tell you that, I reckon," Sharlene said slowly, with a cheeky grin.

We suddenly realised she was right... she could use the hair to commune with the spirit of the owner. It seemed we had a lot more in our possession than we had initially thought. Though it was demoralising to have lost the gospel so revered by Boudicca and the Druids to a sect of religious fanatics no better than the Roman oppressors of the Britons, there was a positive—we at last had Gaius off our backs. However, I must say one doesn't easily let go of a forty-year quest that had already cost the lives of some of our colleagues.

CHAPTER
XLI

It was never going to be an early night after what had happened. I insisted on continuing the debate of events with Jackson, Wayne, and Judith. Sharlene was asleep in a chair in front of the fireplace. Mike had gone to the study to transcribe the few pages of the gospel he'd scanned on his computer.

"I feel responsible for this whole bloody mess," Jackson admitted.

"Why, because you were the point person with Interpol? Don't be ridiculous, love," I said, taking his hand.

"I'm going to call them. I know we can't chase after agent Cronin to get back the gospel, but they have a bloody obligation to do exactly that," he growled.

"I agree with you, Jackson," Wayne said. "That bastard can't get away with this."

"All right, then we are in agreement," Judith said, reverting to headmistress. "Jackson will call Interpol, Mike is transcribing and will have the hair DNA tested for gender through his contact at forensics... Wayne can drop the hair sample at Scotland Yard tomorrow. We'll have a session in the morning with Sharlene to see if she can use psychometry to identify the owner of the hair... and I expect we will eventually join the others at the site in Stanmore. Does that cover it?"

"It does, Judith, and I'm not going to waste any more time. I'm calling Interpol right now," Jackson said angrily.

I'd never seen him so angry. I'd hate to be whoever takes his call.

"But it's nearly one in the morning," Judith complained.

"I don't give a rat's arse!" Jackson growled, striding out of the room to make a call outside.

"Is it okay if I offer to give Mike a hand, Judith?"

"Yes, Wayne, he'll appreciate your assistance."

I phoned Cleo to explain what had happened; she was heartbroken. Losing the gospel to Gaius was bad enough, but not being able to keep the promise we'd both made to Joseph was unforgivable. In tears, I promised her that, as far as I was concerned, it wasn't over yet. I would find a way to get back what was rightfully ours.

Sitting in the hallway, elbows on my knees, head in hands, I was in a sombre mood when Jackson came in from talking on his mobile. He sat in a chair beside me and took my hand.

"Seems no one knows how this could have happened. Apparently, agent Edward Cronin was indeed the replacement for Chris Kelly, but he hasn't reported in or been heard of since he was dispatched to meet us in Glastonbury days ago. I think we have to assume the real agent Cronin has met his maker or indeed the Edward we know was for real but a turncoat. Anyhow, they're sending me his photograph to identify him."

His phone buzzed. "That'll be it." He opened the file and showed me. It was Edward all right.

"A turncoat, then," I groaned and rested my head on his shoulder.

"So it's phase two then," he said.

"What's phase two?"

"They'll put out an all-points bulletin on him. The senior agent I spoke to, Ronan Phillips, guaranteed they'll have him within twenty-four hours."

"It's not him we want."

"I know. Anyhow, it's something. You go up to bed; I'll text them back to initiate phase two."

I gave him a peck on the cheek and then dragged myself upstairs to bed.

The mood was brighter than I expected at breakfast. Mike and Wayne had burnt the midnight oil deciphering the few pages of the gospel Mike had saved and were eager to divulge the contents. Judith had packed half of the hair into a secure container ready for Wayne to deliver to the British Museum. Mike had called his contact at Scotland Yard forensics, and they told him they didn't have the budget to DNA test the hair sample. So he decided as a second measure to try his friend at the British Museum, the person who had loaned us the seal, and she agreed to have it done and to fund it.

"Lucky Mike has a good relationship with the BM. If we had to go to Cambridge for help or, God forbid, the National Trust, we'd be pushing up daisies before we got any results!" Judith scoffed.

"You look like you're bursting at the seams to tell us something about the gospel, Mike," I said light-heartedly.

"Oh, just before you tell us, Mike," Jackson said sternly. "I spoke with Interpol. Edward is a turncoat, probably planted years ago by Crux specifically for the task. A national hunt to run him down is underway."

"Well, let's hope they get the gospel before it's whisked away to a Vatican abyss, never to be heard of again," Judith moaned.

"Go on, Mike, I know Wayne has to get on the road," I said.

"We only had fifteen readable pages. Remember, they were only tests, so some were out of focus and unreadable,"

Just then, Sharlene joined us.

"Morning, folks. Now that's a better face than the one you were wearing last night, sweetheart," she said to me, taking a seat alongside me. I gave her a friendly hug.

"Mike is just about to tell us what he learned from the fifteen pages of the gospel he managed to hang on to and translate," I told her.

"As I said last night, the pages were roughly from the middle of the book. Joseph talks of a marriage and the new wife expecting a baby. The marriage is between Jesus Christ and Mary Magdalene, and he says expressly that the apostles are in full support of the union. In fact, he pays for the wedding feast as a gift to the couple. Later, he tells of warning Christ that the Pharisees are not to be trusted. They consider him a threat and that if he continues his militant rebellious ways, they will conspire to have him eliminated. He fears for Christ's life and, in trying to temper Christ's anger, reminds him of his stay in Britain and how Druidism had taught him not to fight with the sword but with words of wisdom."

"That's an incredible revelation," Judith said.

"Yes, but we can't authenticate it without the gospel," Mike complained.

He was right, of course. No matter what we learned, it needed to be backed up by hard supporting evidence. Getting the gospel back was absolutely essential. Jackson had faith in Interpol, but I didn't. I'd lost faith in them the moment Boyd and Molloy failed to run down Gaius when he attacked me with a knife.

Judith dispatched Wayne in the car to deliver strands of the hair to the British Museum for analysis. We finished our coffees and then moved to the study for Sharlene to attempt to contact the owner of the hair.

As the four of us walked the corridor to the study, we had no idea what we were heading into. So far, this forty-year rollercoaster ride had produced an obstacle around every corner, and I expected this venture to be no different. I could sense anxiety in Jackson and Judith, while Sharlene, who hadn't experienced our ride, remained her cheerful self. I wished right then and there that I could share her boldness.

Mike was already in the study, preparing everything, seating, and a recorder.

We took up our positions while Sharlene sat on the couch and began her meditation ritual. We knew the drill: she would open the palm of her hand when ready to receive the object of focus. Wearing white cotton gloves, Mike took a few locks of the hair and held it ready for Sharlene.

We were tense... we knew this moment had the potential to be epoch-making.

Sharlene opened her hand, and Mike placed the lock of hair on her palm. He quickly moved back to the desk and hit record on his iPad. Suddenly, Sharlene's eyes opened wide, and her face distorted. She let out a frightening, earth-shattering scream. Moving swiftly, Mike snatched the lock out of her hand. Her face was flushed, as though she was choking.

"Quick, Jackson!" I gasped.

He was already on his way to help her.

"Sharlene, Sharlene," he said in a calming tone. "Sit down... take a deep breath... you've had a fright... you're all right."

Her head snapped sharply to lock eyes with Jackson, glaring at him paranormally like the Regan MacNeil character in the movie The Exorcist. Then she collapsed, out cold. Luckily, Jackson caught her in his arms before she could hit the floor or, worse, hit her head on the edge of the desk on the way down. He gently placed her on the couch.

Judith went to fetch a glass of water for her. We waited for fifteen or so minutes for her to regain consciousness. When she opened her eyes, her signature devil-may-care look was absent. She slowly sat up and knuckled her eyes.

"Sharlene... are you all right, love?" I asked, offering her the glass of water.

She took a sip. "I'm sorry, Bonnie, but I've never experienced anything like that before... ever," she said, still very rattled.

"Do you want to tell us about it?" Jackson inquired gently.

"Look, to be honest, I'm not sure what I saw. It was only a flash... like lightning, but it held more meaning than anything I've ever felt before. More worry, anguish, sorrow, guilt... like every synonym known for the word regret."

"So you were overcome by this massive feeling... did you see anything?" I asked.

"In the flash, I was looking at someone."

"Could you see yourself? Were you male or female?" Judith asked slowly.

"Male, I think... I was looking at a woman... she was crying," she muttered vaguely.

"Can you describe her? What colour was her hair?" I asked, thinking it might have been Joseph looking at Boudicca when he died.

"She had long black hair, dark skin, big eyes... she's not old but not young."

"Well, if it's the moment of death you witnessed, that rules out Joseph because he was inside the Great Hall with Boudicca when he died, and she had red hair," I said.

"And being a male rules out Mary Magdalene. That only leaves Jesus," Mike said excitedly.

"That's a huge call, Mike," Judith growled. "It could have been anyone. A Druid, a chief... anyone... Joseph did live to a ripe old age, remember, and he had many friends."

"Sharlene, do you have any idea who it might have been?" I asked.

"No, but he was middle-aged and wasn't afraid of dying. I remember her more now... she was dressed in a blue and white robe."

"That doesn't tie in with Jesus. He wasn't old. He was thirty-two when he was crucified... though the blue and white robe is synonymous with Palestine," Mike suggested.

"He loved the woman crying for him," Sharlene added as if she just realised it.

"When you channel, do you have to go back to the last minutes of the person's life?" Judith asked Sharlene.

"Only when it's a physical part of their anatomy I'm using. If I was able to handle the tremendous emotion of that moment, I'd be able to explore memories... you know the saying: just before you die, your life flicks past you in a montage of images?"

"Yes," Judith said.

"Well, that's what I should be aiming for, that moment. But you see, going from meditation to hysteria is going from one extreme to another. There's just too much going on in the person's mind, and it makes it impossible not to get caught up in the emotion of it, like I did."

"Say I was to hypnotise you, and while you're under, we put the lock of hair in your hand?" Jackson proposed. "Would that work? You wouldn't be as emotionally attached?"

Slowly, a smile formed on her lips. "You know what, Doc? I reckon you might just have something there. I think I remember hearing about my dad using a similar method. Let's give it a try!"

We prepared ourselves like pioneers venturing into another dark, unknown dimension—a place where none of us had ever set foot—hypnotising a medium. Anything could happen. Sharlene relaxed back on the couch. Jackson pulled a chair up close to her and settled into it. Mike stood by with the hair.

This time, I was even more nervous than before—if that's humanly possible.

CHAPTER
XLII

ackson's melodious voice did the job, and Sharlene went under much faster than Cleo and I ever had. He gave Mike a sharp nod, and he unfurled the fingers on Sharlene's left hand and gently placed the lock of hair on her palm. Her hand closed around the hair. It took a long time before we saw any reaction from her, and it wasn't until Jackson prompted her that we got a result.

"Describe what you're seeing, Sharlene."

She didn't answer in English; she spoke in a foreign language. We turned to Mike for his hypothesis, and he mouthed the word "Aramaic."

An hour later, Jackson brought Sharlene out of the hypnotic trance. This time she had full recollection and was keen to share it with us.

"I need to tell you what I saw. He's dying of an illness. His wife is with him. He's reminding her of the place they came from years ago, and that he feels guilty for having left it. She assured him they had no choice but to leave for the sake of their children. She says that if it hadn't been for Joseph, they would have been imprisoned or worse, killed. That's about as much as I remember. I'm sorry... but I will probably recall bits and pieces over the next couple of hours."

"Don't concern yourself too much, Sharlene. I recorded everything you said. It will just take me a little while to translate," Mike said.

"Why do you have to translate it?"

"Because you were speaking Aramaic," Mike said.

"What's that?" Sharlene asked.

"The language Jesus spoke," Judith said.

"Are you saying I just channelled Jesus Christ?" she said, stunned. We all exchanged nods.

"Yes, we think there's a good chance that's exactly what you just did," Judith confirmed.

Sharlene was awestruck. I've never seen her so lost for words.

"Why don't you guys go and have a cuppa while I translate the recording? Perhaps we might get a definitive answer from it," Mike suggested.

"Good thinking, Mike," I said. "I could do with a brew."

A while later, when we were in the library, Mike came in carrying a notebook. He sat down, and we gathered around, anxious to hear what he had to say.

"There's no point in reading you a direct translation. It's better for me to paraphrase it. Most of what was discussed was personal, about the couple's three children: two boys and a girl. But I did learn they were in the south of France. At one point, he called her by name, Mariam, which, of course, translates in English to Mary. She never mentions his name. Now, it's here we need to consider the possibility that the couple is, in fact, Mary and Jesus. The Aramaic name for Jesus Christ is Eashoa' M'sheekha. If we accept this hypothesis, because that's what it is, we have no evidence, we must understand that historically it is likely Jesus didn't die on the cross and was not resurrected in the manner we have been led to believe. Being with Mary in France is testimony to that. So let's say, as has been proposed by others, that the crucifixion was a symbolic execution that Joseph of Arimathea had orchestrated. I say this because Joseph did go to Pilate to ask for the body of Jesus, which was contrary to Roman law, and when Pilate heard that Jesus was already dead, he was so surprised to hear he had died so quickly that he even dispatched a centurion to check.

Now, the Bible tells us that Jesus had been on the cross for two to three hours. When a person was crucified, they didn't die quickly but rather a slow, painful, morbid death, which took two to three days, possibly even a week! Next, the crucifixion took place in what seemed to be a private garden that was, in fact, owned by Joseph of Arimathea. The importance of this observation is that if there was any fraudulence associated with the crucifixion, then the public could be kept away from it in a private garden, and Jesus could be privately taken away, revived, tended, and ministered to."

"So you're suggesting it was fraudulent," Judith proposed.

"Only if these two people in the south of France are, in fact, Mary and Jesus, married with children. Also, it ties in with the gospel of Joseph, doesn't it? And why the Church was so desperate to take it. It stands to reason the lock of hair belonged to Jesus because Joseph played such an important role in setting the stage for Jesus to emulate the legend of the Hebrew messiah and thereby revolutionise a people and initiate a new religion. A new religion that was based on many of the principles of Druidism, right down to the clothes Jesus wore and how he wore his hair and beard—he looked like a Druid. Why? Because Joseph had brought him to England to educate him in Druidism. This has all been about Joseph fashioning a Messiah—a saviour."

We sat there, staring at Mike dumbfounded. He'd dropped a bombshell—the implications of what he was proposing were epic: that Joseph had virtually tailor-made Jesus... after staging his death and resurrection, he got him out of town quick smart to dodge his enemies—the Roman authorities and the Hebrew Pharisees. In doing so, he had bought him legendary status, martyrdom, among the people by fulfilling an ancient prophecy.

"If it is true, then Joseph was probably the most clever man in history," I said.

"You ain't kidding, sister!" Sharlene agreed.

Wayne walked in, surprised to find us sitting around flummoxed. "What's happened now?" he said.

We were quiet in the van on our way to Stanmore. There was just so much to think about, and it was giving me a headache trying to make sense of it. I had arranged for Cleo to meet us at the Three Crowns Pub in Bushey Heath, not far from Stanmore Common where they were working. The weather had turned ugly with rain, prematurely ending the scanning for the day.

It was mid-afternoon by the time we found them at the main bar. Other than our team, there were few others in the pub, so we commandeered a couple of tables and chairs to accommodate the eleven of us. Once we all had a drink, Dylan delivered his report.

"We've scanned nearly half the common and come up with diddlysquat... but, in saying that, we expected as much," he grinned cheekily. "We've been saving the best for last."

I looked across at Jackson. He had that characteristic hank of hair hanging over one eye and was wearing a broad smile. It struck me then that I'd been so preoccupied with recent events that I hadn't given him the time of day, and being such a great sport, he hadn't complained. I looked at Cleo, sitting up close to Wayne, and seeing that young love increased my guilt. I caught Jackson's eye across the table, and my lips formed a kiss blown towards him. He tapped his chest with his fingers to signify I was in his heart. God, I love that man. Sharlene brought the house down with her description of the chopper ride and then her channelling Jesus and Mary. For a while, the seriousness of it all had been forgotten, and we'd found time for each other and a good laugh. As expected, Dylan was convinced he was on the verge of locating Boudicca's tomb. He was certain he would detect her golden torc, sword, and shield if the weather permitted him tomorrow. No one wanted to thwart his enthusiasm... even though he might have been fantasising, it was still motivating.

Jackson's phone rang, and he stepped outside to take the call. When he returned, we quieted down to hear what he had to say.

"That was Interpol, they've got Edward."

A roar went up, and we all raised our glasses, but Jackson held up a hand to stop us; he hadn't finished.

"Hang on! Hang on... They didn't get the Gospel..."

The glasses were slowly lowered as we were once again cloaked in gloom.

"But there is good news... Mike, they got your camera... and yes, with the cassette intact."

The excitement erupted again, and Mike even shouted the next round. Jackson squeezed in beside me.

"As long as the data hasn't been erased, it might work out for the best," he whispered to me.

"How's that, love?"

"The Crux gets the original, we get the copy, and we all live happily ever after."

"Yes, I suppose you're right. They'd be comfortable; we wouldn't be able to publish the gospel without provenance, and that way, they keep control," I said.

"At least they'd be off our back. They asked if we wanted to press charges."

"We'd better discuss that with Judith and Mike, but not now," I leaned on his shoulder. "Let's play up for just a wee bit longer."

"Okay, but no dancing," he joked.

Mike leaned across the table to us. "When will we get the camera back, Jackson?" he asked.

"By courier tomorrow morning."

Cleo got up from the opposite side of the table and came to me. "Does Wayne have to go back with you guys?" she said covertly.

"Hmm, do I smell romance in the air? Who can replace the running around Wayne does for us?" I asked with a sardonic smirk.

"Jane," she said quickly. "She and Dylan are fighting all the time anyway."

"What about?"

"Oh, they just beg to differ on just about everything."

"All right, but you behave yourself young lady, promise?"

"You and I both know I have Andrasta looking over me," she giggled.

"No running naked through the forest anointed with oil, this is the 21st century. If you're caught doing that, they'll lock you up in a rehab centre," I joked.

"Thanks Bo," she smiled happily.

"Enjoy every minute love because we've only got two days left on the permit. Time and money is running out, if nothing is found we'll be heading back to Sydney real soon," I said watching the excitement drain from her eyes.

In the van on the way back to the manor we were collectively introspective, that is except for Jane who wouldn't stop jabbering. She had a story to tell about all of them, finally I had to put a plug in it. "Judith," I said loudly to get over Jane's prattling. "What are you going to tell National Trust?"

"Good question, I've been giving it a lot of thought."

"No point in beating about the bush, you have to tell them the truth," Mike chimed in.

"Yes, that's what I'd decided. I just wanted to determine if there was any chance of getting the gospel back first."

"If we hadn't made the report to the council that we found it—" Mike continued.

"We had to do that Mike, you know the backfill requirements—we had to leave the place as it was and report what we'd found," Judith said.

"True ...we still have the film," Mike said nonchalantly.

"That's right," Jackson erupted. "Isn't that provenance enough Judith?"

"As a matter of fact it is Jackson. You know I'd totally forgotten about the recording. It wasn't on the tape stolen with the camera was it Mike?"

"No, the unearthing is filed with all the hypnosis sessions and the tapes of Sharlene."

"Oo, I didn't realise I was in your cast?" Sharlene joked.

"I'll edit them over the next few weeks into documentary," Mike said.

"Can I have a copy?" Sharlene asked.

"Absolutely," I said.

"You'll have your work cut out for you Mike if the tape in the camera still contains the pages of gospel," Jackson speculated.

"Yes, it's a pity I didn't get all of it," Mike said dismally.

"How much did you get?" I asked.

"Well, I had to start from the back to the front, so along with the twenty test pages, well the fifteen in focus, I fell short of about a quarter."

"So you got three quarters of it missing out on the first quarter?" Judith clarified.

"Yes, and from what I've already transcribed I'd say the first quarter was his early years in Britain, Palestine and Judea."

"Will you be able to use any of what we learnt from it and the hair sample?" Sharlene asked.

"If you mean academically, probably not Sharlene," Judith said.

"But we could publish a historical fiction novel couldn't we?" I posed.

"I don't see why not." Judith said. "I also believe there would be value in publishing specific things we have uncovered that we have provenance for in academic archaeological journals.."

"We'll have years of work studying with all we have," Mike added.

"You have distinctive educational ethos my friend," Jackson quipped.

"Maybe it should it all remain the secret of First Light until we're ready to expose it?" I suggested.

"By it you mean the Jesus hypothesis, the story of Joseph and the Boudicca files?" Jackson asked.

"Yes, and the story of Gaius and the Crux Redemptoris," I snarled.

"You'd need to be brave," Mike said.

"I think Cleo has her sights set on writing a book and I don't think she'll pull any punches," I said.

"Fifty shades of hypnotism?" Jackson quipped.

CHAPTER
XLIII

The sun was edging up over the horizon, and the shadows of the leaves, moving in the breeze, dappled the white façade of the manor with a vaguely psychedelic pattern. Somewhere, a bird was singing. At this hour of the morning, I figured it had to be out of its tiny feathered mind. I hadn't slept a wink, but I wasn't bothered by it. Sitting on the garden bench, looking at the manor and smelling nature was revitalising.

The front door of the manor opened, and Sharlene emerged dressed as a dead-set Hippie. Walking along the path towards me, she blended in perfectly with the trippy backdrop.

"Aren't you a sight for sore eyes this morning?" I said with a smile.

We hugged, and she sat beside me.

"Judith gave me the pick of her wardrobe, and I found this from her protesting days in the sixties."

"It fits you well."

"I expect a tie-died psychedelic caftan would fit almost anyone."

"And the matching bandana."

"Yep, right down to the sandals, see?"

She showed off the sandals.

"You look amazing, Sharls. What keeps you young?"

"Screwing young guys, I reckon. And speaking of such, I've got to love you and leave you, darling."

I wrapped my arms around her. "I don't want to let you go! I can't thank you enough, Sharls."

"Hey, that's what I'm here for. At least with that lunatic Gaius out of your life, you'll be able to get on with living without having to look over your darn shoulder all the time. I only wish we could make him pay for Reagan."

"Don't worry, what goes around comes around. I'll get someone to drive you."

"Don't stress, Bo, it's all arranged. Jane will drive me to town."

"Better wear earplugs," I joked.

"Yeah, she could talk the spots off a Dalmatian, that one."

We strolled arm in arm along the path back to the manor with the warm rays of the sun on our backs. I was going to miss Sharlene. There was never a dull moment when she was around.

Later, while we were waving Sharlene off to London, a courier arrived on a motorbike and handed over a package to Jackson. It was Mike's camera. My phone rang.

"That's funny, it's the wrong phone." But it didn't seem to matter anymore, so I answered it.

"Hi Cleo, you rang the other phone—oh, it was in your auto-dial, no worries. Yes, we just got the camera, haven't checked the film yet, but we expect it to be intact." Jackson had the camera open and gave me a positive nod—the film was there. He took it inside for Mike. "No, Jackson is going to call Interpol later. Yeah, we're still in the dark as to how they ended up with the camera. Yep, Sharls just left... no, Jane took her... I know she'll have her ear chewed off all the way to London, poor dear. You spoke to Mo, great, how is she? Yes, I'm sure she misses you. Okay, love, I'll call you later for Dylan's results. Oh, how's things with Wayne?" I prompted cheekily. "Hmm, sounds serious. Okay, Darl, bye."

When I got to the study, Jackson was already filling Judith and Mike in on his conversation with Interpol.

"I'll need to get back to them to let them know if we're going to press charges on Edward. What are your thoughts?" he asked.

"Surely they'll charge him themselves," I chimed in.

"Yes, they said he would receive the police equivalent of a court martial," Jackson said sternly.

"Judith, what do you think about pressing charges on Edward?" I asked, sitting down.

She looked over the rim of her glasses at me and said passionately, "Robbery, kidnapping, impersonating a police officer, take your pick. In 1961, John F. Kennedy said, 'The only thing necessary for the triumph of evil is for good men to do nothing.' So, in that, you have my vote."

"And mine," Mike agreed.

"Think of it this way, if we don't threaten to press charges, they won't have much leverage on him to get Gaius. For the sake of our friends Matt and Reagan and indeed Chris Kelly, we have an obligation to have Gaius brought to justice," I said strongly.

"Okay, I think we're all in agreement. I'll call Interpol now, put it to them, and we'll see what they have to say," Jackson said sharply.

"Oh, the film is intact, by the way. Not erased," Mike said happily.

We had at least three-quarters of the gospel, even if only a copy.

Jackson went outside to phone Interpol, and Mike got to work transcribing the gospel, while Judith focused on writing a report for the National Trust. I started work documenting all we had on Sharlene's psychometry sessions.

Jackson returned a little while later, annoyed. "They're sending someone in a couple of hours to take statements from us. They said that after interrogating Edward, the gospel has left the country... Edward delivered it to a private jet at Luton airport, and it was whisked away. The camera was on the back seat of his car when the cops ambushed him. He had been ordered to destroy it, but fortunately for us, he hadn't gotten round to it. They warned me to expect Gaius will be coming after it."

"How would he know Edward didn't destroy it?" Mike asked.

"Because there were two men in the car when Interpol pulled it over, and one of them escaped."

"Gaius!" I groaned.

"So, we're lucky to have the film back, but we've still got Gaius on our backs," Mike stammered.

"But he doesn't know that we've got it, does he?" Judith said.

"Not yet," Jackson said.

"There's a lot at stake with what we now know... and having that knowledge obviously isn't in the best interests of Crux Redemptoris. We'll just have to go into stealth mode again," I summed up.

Later that day, I heard a car pull up in the forecourt of the manor. We were in the study when Arthur knocked on the door and announced we had a guest from Interpol. We were surprised to find it was Chris Kelly.

"We were told you were on leave?" I questioned.

"No such luck. A couple of days off to repair and then desk duties for a while. I'm so sorry for what happened with Edward," Chris said.

We were so happy to see her and that she was looking sprightly.

"Did you know him well?" Judith asked.

"Just another colleague. I'd never worked with him, but he was at Manchester HQ for a year, same as me. But I came from the Dublin office, whereas he came from Edinburgh."

"What happened?" I asked.

"Well, when you alerted us to the chopper and the theft of the gospel, I was on duty and assigned the coordination of pursuit. Luckily, we tracked the chopper to Luton Airport, and then it was a matter of monitoring his movements on the airport CCTV to set up a roadblock and catch him leaving. We missed stopping the private jet because it had a pre-clearance for take-off. It had been well-coordinated. The Beechcraft Premier was ready to fly as soon as the chopper landed."

"To whom was the jet registered?" Jackson asked.

"It had been hired by an office of the Vatican."

"How and when did Edward turn?" I asked.

"Now that's an interesting question. He's of extremely pious Catholic stock. In fact, his father was a Personal Prelate of Opus Dei in Edinburgh."

We exchanged "as you would expect" looks.

"Well, that about explains it, doesn't it? From Opus Dei to Crux Redemptoris, probably recruited by Gaius," I posed.

"How on earth does a person with a background such as that succeed in joining Interpol?" Mike asked.

"We can't discriminate, Mike, and he exhibited no allegiance to any religious order, so he was above suspicion."

"They must have taken some time to plan it?" Judith questioned.

"Yes, well, he first needed to graduate from police academy in Scotland, that's two years, then to join Interpol—an eleven-month course, then a year at the Manchester office. So that's four years."

"That tells me Gaius knew what we were planning with Cleo," I said.

"You're right, Bo. He had to have known, maybe not expressly that it was Cleo," Jackson said.

"I think he's had you guys bugged since the Reagan affair. Without a doubt, for the last fifteen or so years since the emergence of e-mail, he's been reading yours, Bonnie," Mike said.

"That would make absolute sense, Mike. Once he got an indication of when you'd be likely to make a move on the gospel, i.e., when Cleo turned twenty-four, he probably pulled all the strings to implement his plan with Edward," Chris said calmly.

"But why did he attack you?" Jackson asked her.

"The perfect introduction for Edward... the only way to ensure success was to have someone on the inside. I was the best way in—to win your confidence —you weren't going to question him—he was the saviour, wasn't he?" Chris said.

"Gaius must doubt his own ability now he's older," I said.

"Different times, Bonnie. It's no longer the Cold War days where he could kill and simply get away with it... there's just too much public surveillance nowadays. He needed an accomplice. That's why we're concerned for your safety. Without his accomplice and the mission in jeopardy, he might revert to his old, less sophisticated ways of getting things done," Chris explained.

"You talking murder?"

"Yes," she agreed. "He needs that film, and the longer you have it, the more duplicates you could produce."

"Are you suggesting an attack is imminent?" Judith said bitterly.

"To be sure," Chris said with dread in her tone.

"Well, what is Interpol going to do about it?" Judith demanded.

"First, I'm going to take a statement from each of you. Then I'll stay with you until I'm sure you are safe from Gaius. In the meantime, Edward will continue to be questioned, and I expect they will eventually uncover the lair of Gaius. So, who's first?"

We took turns giving Chris our statements over the course of the afternoon, but everything turned sour when Mike received a phone call. He assembled us in the library.

"I've had a call from my contact at the British Museum. They have the initial results on the follicle of hair tested. They found no match in the UK National Criminal Intelligence DNA Database, which was to be expected. However, they have determined the gender, and it turned out to be female, I'm afraid, which casts a rather dubious shadow over the result from the psychometry with Sharlene."

"That doesn't make any sense," I complained.

"I know. I asked if they could have made a mistake, and they said that though they were only preliminary results, they think not. I asked them to check another follicle, and they agreed."

We felt as though we'd been blanketed by negativity —everything was going pear-shaped.

Mike returned to the study to continue translating the gospel pages. We had decided for Chris to stay close to the work, seeing it was the target of the Crux.

Sitting around, dazed by Mike's news, I decided to call Cleo, and it rang out.

"What if Gaius has other accomplices?" I suddenly thought out loud.

"Should I check on Chris Kelly?" Jackson said worriedly.

"Better than making the same mistake twice," I figured.

"She is, after all, Irish, and we know they can be staunch Catholics," Judith mumbled without taking her eyes off the book she was reading.

Like a man on a mission, Jackson leapt out of his chair and stormed outside to make the call.

"What the hell would we do if she fails to come up kosher?" Judith posed.

By now, I was pacing the floor, wringing my hands.

"I have that feeling again, Judith, something is wrong. I got it last time when the chopper took off, remember?"

"A touch of anxiety, perhaps. Just take it easy, pet. We can't do anything until we've heard from Jackson."

CHAPTER
XLIV

It felt like ages for Jackson to come back from calling Interpol. "She's clear," he announced upon entering. I guess he could see the relief on our faces. "She's not Catholic and has a much higher security clearance than Edward had. I asked if anyone else is suspected of being in collusion with Edward and got a negative. They're satisfied with his cooperation so far—he is, after all, facing a minimum of twenty-five years in the can. He was warned that if anything happens to any one of us while Gaius is on the loose, he will face charges of collusion which will extend his stay a further ten years," he said acidly.

My good phone rang.

"Hello, oh, hi Wayne. What's that? She's not. Surely she'll be back soon. You've what? Tried her phone... Yes, I tried her an hour ago and got her voicemail. Why did she go on her own? I see. Okay, let me discuss it with the others, and I'll call you back. Okay, thanks for calling me, bye." I looked at Jackson concerned. "That was Wayne, he said Cleo took the van two hours ago to pick up some takeaway and hasn't returned. He's been calling her and only gets her voicemail. I tried her an hour ago and got the same."

"Do you think there's any cause for alarm?" he queried.

"Yes, I do. With this arsehole Gaius on the loose, anything could happen, and I've had that gut feeling again."

He could see I was teetering on the edge of panicking.

"Sit down, Bo. Take a few deep breaths and calm down. I'll go and get Chris."

Judith consoled me with a nip of scotch.

Jackson returned with Chris and Mike.

"Where was she going in the van, Bonnie?" Chris asked.

"To a Chinese takeaway in Bushey Heath, only a five-minute drive from Stanmore Common."

"Okay, first thing is to ring the Chinese restaurant to see if she picked it up," she said pragmatically.

"I'll do that," Jackson said, drawing his cell phone.

"What's the number plate of the van?" she asked.

"Oh, I've got that on my phone in a text," Judith said, fumbling for her phone to check. "Here it is, BD14SMR," her voice faltering with nerves.

"Good, now we'll just wait for Jackson."

Jackson finished the call and said, "She collected the order two hours ago."

"Right, that's not good. But let's not panic. She might have had an accident. I'll ring the local Police and check," Chris said calmly. She walked over to the window and rang Interpol, then had them put her through to Harrow Central, the nearest police station. We couldn't hear much of the conversation. After the call, she returned to us.

"Right, well, she hasn't been in an accident. No police were called, so I've put out an APB for the van. Give me Cleo's number so I can have it tracked. I'll also get CCTV for a five-mile radius around Stanmore Common up to Bushey. Maybe you should call Wayne back and get them to go back to their digs. There's nothing more we can do for now but wait."

I rang Wayne, and Ahmed answered. I was glad; he's more level-headed. I filled him in and then told him to catch a couple of minicabs back to the B & B and to stay put until further notice. He reported that Dylan had detected half a dozen targets, and analysing them would keep them occupied. When I finished talking, Jackson gave me another scotch, this one slightly more generous than Judith's, and well needed. He sat beside me and held my hand— we were worried.

Chris returned after a few minutes with some more news. The police had located the van not far from Stanmore Common. The takeaway was in the van and still warm, but there was no sign of Cleo. They were dusting the van for prints.

The news was far more disturbing than relieving. I was now convinced Gaius had abducted Cleo.

Chris got back on the phone to her office, this time to get a trace on Cleo's cell phone and to order the CCTV footage.

While she was doing that, I rang Cleo's number and again got her voicemail. I was going to leave her a plaintive message, but then thought better of it and just hung up. I knew that keeping control of my emotions underpinned the rational decision-making required of me.

My mouth was dry and foul—that's what the tension was like—you could almost taste it.

Suddenly, Chris came flying back into the room. "Okay, Bonnie and Jackson, come with me. You guys man the deck."

Judith sprung to her feet, all flustered. "Where are you going? You can't just leave us here unprotected. What if Gaius—"

"Okay, okay, then we all go," Chris said impatiently. "Where is the tape and hair, Mike?"

"Locked in the safe," he stammered.

"Judith, please tell Arthur to advise Jane to wait here when she gets back from dropping off Sharlene," Chris ordered.

"Have you backed up the gospel?" I whispered to Mike.

"Here," he handed me a flash drive. "You take this one, I've got one, and so does Judith—all copies. I've got the lock of hair in my pocket," he smiled slyly.

We squeezed into Chris's red Ford Fiesta.

"New car smell," Jackson said from the front passenger seat.

"Company car, brand new... if you need more legroom," Chris said, starting up.

"No, don't push back. I'm not a contortionist," I squealed.

"Where are we going, Chris?" Judith asked.

"Harrow Central police station. By the time we get there, they should have the CCTV to check. What's the best way from here?"

"Take the M1 through Luton, and then I'll direct you. It should take us under an hour," Mike advised.

"Isn't there a police station in Stanmore or Bushey Heath?" Jackson asked.

"No more Bobbies on the beat, mate. They started closing suburban stations in 2012," Mike said despairingly.

Chris found a park out front of the three-story red brick building.

Inside, we were met by a female officer and taken to a viewing room on the second floor. As I settled into a chair with Jackson sitting next to me, he whispered, "I don't like this, Bo. It isn't a win-win situation for Gaius at all. He'd know we would have made stacks of digital copies of the film. No matter what he does, he won't be able to get them all."

"Maybe he's only after the lock of hair?"

"That's a thought—but then again, we'd only need to keep a few strands. Besides, the British Museum already has some."

"So do you think it's purely vengeance, then?"

"I hope not," he said, looking troubled.

We were facing six monitors and the back of a single operator in civvies. Chris sat beside the operator. The video had obviously been preselected because monitor one showed the van being pulled over by a blue Volkswagen Golf Hatchback with a lone occupant obviously posing as a police officer. After a brief discussion between him and Cleo, she went with him of her own free will. The image froze, and Chris swivelled round to face us.

"Do you think that's Gaius? I can't tell," Chris asked.

"Nor can I," I said. "But it seems he's posing as a policeman and has conned her to go with him."

"Yes, I agree. Okay, there's no point in replaying the journey of the kidnapper's vehicle. We have an APB out on the Golf. The last vision we have is of it entering a housing estate in Watford. Show that, please, officer."

Monitor two showed the blue Golf enter the estate.

"There is no CCTV there, but it's a cul-de-sac, and it hasn't come out. We have to assume it's still there, so we've set up a roadblock."

"Seems a bit odd that someone as cunning as he is would drive into a cul-de-sac, don't you think?" Jackson posed.

"You're right, Jackson," Chris agreed.

"Chris, why don't you send the police in now?" I asked.

"It's normal procedure to wait for the kidnapper to make contact."

The desk phone rang, and the video operator answered. She immediately handed the phone to Chris.

After she hung up, she said, "No prints of any value on the van."

"That's bloomin' obvious. He never touched it," Mike growled intolerantly.

"Just bear with us, Mike," Chris said warmly, aware of his frustration. "Bonnie, I'll need your phone number. You're the most likely target for him to contact."

"I've got two—my old phone Edward figured Gaius had tapped and a new prepaid one that he couldn't," I said.

"Don't worry, both would be tapped," Chris said with arched eyebrows.

We're always wiser after the event. Edward had done a great job of setting me up, and I felt abused. But a tap on my knee from my caring husband absolved my guilt. I gave Chris the two numbers.

Three doors down from the viewing room was a briefing room. We were herded in there to chairs set out in front of an electronic whiteboard. We sat while Chris went to the board.

"I brought you here because we'll map out on the board what we know. It's synchronised with another whiteboard two doors up, being viewed by a Metropolitan Police flying squad trained in terrorism and kidnapping."

My phone rang. Chris heard it and held up her hand.

"Which phone is it, Bonnie?" she said quickly.

"Um," I fumbled for them both. "The new one."

"Okay, answer it and keep whoever it is on the line."

I answered, my heart beating like a drum.

Chris phoned through to have the call traced.

"Hello," my voice cracked. I pressed speaker.

"How is your leg? ... And of course, your injuries from the car accident? Shame you couldn't have kids—but you thought you'd be clever with Cleo here... I want everything," the voice demanded with a heavy Latin accent.

"Who is this?" I shrieked, emotion getting the better of me.

"You know who it is," the male voice said calmly, coldly. "I will phone again in two hours. In that time, you will collect every copy of the book and every follicle of the hair, including what you gave the Museum."

"Two hours isn't enough time to do that, the museum is in London," I complained.

Chris signalled me to keep him talking.

"Collect it, I will tell you what to do with it after two hours. If you don't comply, I will remove a piece of your niece's body every hour after that until I have what I want, is that clear?"

Suddenly, the horror of his threat overwhelmed me. I couldn't speak—I froze. Jackson immediately recognised the problem and waved at me to hand him the phone.

"I need to know Cleo is alive and in one piece, put her on!" Jackson demanded.

Chris nodded her assurance to Jackson. His resolute attitude was exactly what was needed.

"Dr Bolt, why, of course—I remind you of what happened to your friend in Barcelona."

The statement chilled every one of us to the bone.

"Uncle Jack?" Cleo's quivering voice cut the silence.

"Yes, love, are you all right?"

"Yes, but—"

There was a noise as the phone was obviously ripped away from her.

"That's enough! Two hours!" Gaius growled.

"You're a man of God, why are you doing this!" Jackson snarled. But it was all in vain... the call had been terminated.

Chris was still on the phone. She hung up and pocketed her phone.

"He timed it to perfection. We couldn't get a trace or triangulate the call. It wasn't made from a cell phone."

"So if it's a landline, he must be in a house in the cul-de-sac," Mike surmised.

"There's no point planning on the whiteboard; we simply haven't got time. I'm going to deploy a team to search the houses in the cul-de-sac. While that happens, you'll need to work on collecting everything he demanded," Chris said very deliberately. Then she made a call to initiate the plan.

Suddenly, the whiteboard lit up into four split screens. It was a live feed from cameras mounted on the helmets of Tactical Support Team (TST) officers in the cul-de-sac. A tag appeared below screen one—Red Team. Then three more screens came to life subtitled: Blue, Yellow, and Green. We were about to watch the house-to-house search live, like a reality TV show.

Mike got on the phone to the British Museum, while Judith phoned Jane at the manor and filled her in. In the meantime, I had calmed down enough to phone Ahmed at the B & B. Jackson and Chris sat glued to the whiteboard like it was a football grand final.

CHAPTER
XLV

We watched the TST teams progressively door knock each of the twenty houses in the cul-de-sac. When no one answered the door of the second last house, they forced it open with an enforcer: a battering ram. There was no one inside the house; it was completely empty, but the side garage had a front and rear roll-up door. The rear led to a dirt track through the backyard to a common area the house backed on to. It was obvious Gaius had escaped by entering the garage in his car and then driving through it onto the common.

"Told you he was bloody cunning," Jackson said, getting to his feet and pacing the floor, holding his chin. It took something very serious for Jackson to openly display his frustration like that.

"Come, everyone," Chris announced, standing. "Let's go to the canteen for a coffee and a think."

The coffee tasted as bad as they always made it out to be in BBC cop shows. The mood was dour. Chris ducked out for a moment only to return with a uniformed cop she immediately introduced.

"Everyone, this is Chief Superintendent Richards. He's in charge."

He was black, tall, skinny, with back hair greying at the sides and bushy eyebrows. There was an air of authority and confidence about him. His voice was deep, and his tone reassuring.

"I will address you all with a heads-up first, then questions. I've been brought up to speed on most everything to do with this case, thanks to the case file given to me by Agent Kelly here. There's no real need to tell you what we're up against here—he's a murderer, and you know that better than I. Our aim is to bring the perpetrator to justice without any harm to Cleo. This will be a delicate mission, and I ask for your full cooperation and your patience. Right now, a team is attempting to track the kidnapper's vehicle. The most important thing to remember in a case like this is that it isn't about a financial ransom. The kidnapper is driven by a fanatical obsession, which makes his moves extremely difficult to predict. He is not working according to a paradigm we've experienced previously. It's more akin to the sort of idealism connected with terrorism. The ultimate objective is to draw him out, but we need to locate him first, and we need to come up with the bait. Any questions?"

"Does that mean using a sniper?" Mike asked.

"If the situation presents itself, yes," he answered confidently.

"Can we keep this out of the press?" Judith asked.

"Always difficult to do, but we shall do our best. In these circumstances, we expect to have a twenty-four-hour window before they get hold of it, and that, of course, is dependent on police exposure to the public. Already, we have raided the cul-de-sac, and I'd expect some of the residents to have made contact with the press about it. We have designated Gatekeeper as the case code name and will maintain the cover story that it is terrorist-driven. That will cloak it for the time being."

"Where did he make the telephone call from if it was from a landline?" Jackson asked.

"No confirmation, but it seems likely he made it from inside the house," Richards suggested.

"He would have had to get out of the car with Cleo, go inside the house, make the phone call, then get them both back into the car and drive out of the other side of the garage," I said.

"I suppose so, but I don't get your point, Dr Bolt."

"She is suggesting he couldn't have gone too far by the time the TST team broke into the house and discovered it empty. Have you put up a chopper for surveillance?" Jackson explained angrily.

"No, but—"

"Why not?" he demanded.

"It takes paperwork to get the authority."

"If Cleo was a politician, I expect there wouldn't be any paperwork, would there?" Jackson growled.

"Probably not, sir... Please calm down. I understand your frustration, but anger will not help anything."

While Jackson continued staring down Superintendent Richards, Chris got on the phone to Interpol to request aerial surveillance.

"Now, if there are no more questions?" Richards paused for a few seconds. "None? Good," Richards said, keen to make an exit.

"I've cleared a chopper through Interpol," Chris announced.

"Well done," Jackson said grumpily and went back to drinking his coffee.

Mike's phone rang, and he walked outside to take the call.

Superintendent Richards wished us luck and left. The only consolation was we had a chopper on the lookout for the Volkswagen Golf.

"I told Ahmed to get everyone back to the manor. Under the circumstances, it's best to forgo the day we have to go on the dig," I told Judith.

"Definitely the right move. Should I ring Jane and let her know they're coming?"

"Just send her a text," Jackson told her. "Everything else is on a need-to-know basis for now."

"Yes, you're right," Judith said, texting.

Mike came back in, beaming a big smile. "Well, things are looking up at last. That was Sharon at the British Museum. They received more data from the hair test. Firstly, it shows a diet with specific markers from the South of France."

"Well, that probably confirms it belonged to Mary," Judith said.

"Ah, but here's the exciting part. It seems the hair is, in fact, from two people, a male and a female," Mike said, with a huge grin. "Well, that means we might have the DNA of both Jesus and Mary!"

"Now you're talking!" Judith said excitedly. "You should tell Sharlene, Bonnie."

"It's great news, but I'm not really in the mood right now, Judith. Besides, I never doubted her psychometry," I admitted dispiritedly.

"What does that mean?" Chris asked Mike.

"It means the hair samples we have, which were pressed between the pages of the Gospel of Joseph of Arimathea, could belong to Jesus Christ and Mary Magdalene."

"Wow, and that proves what?"

"Well, it ties in with the Gospel, in that Joseph wrote that he took Jesus and Mary, who were husband and wife, to the South of France after the crucifixion."

"So Jesus didn't die on the cross, then?"

"No, it was a symbolic crucifixion and resurrection."

"Boy, news like that would certainly rock the world... It's no wonder the Crux Redemptoris have had Gaius on the case to shut you down."

"Exactly," I grumbled.

After two hours of sitting around worrying, I had nearly worked up the courage to take the next call from Gaius.

"Do you want me to take the call, love?" Jackson asked.

"Yes, I think it'd be better. I've got the yearning, but I fear I'm lacking the fortitude."

The phone rang right on time. Again, Chris put us through the ritual of waiting until she could start a trace. She nodded, and Jackson triggered the speaker and answered.

"Dr Bolt speaking."

"So, you're my point person?" the gravelly voice asked.

"Yes, get on with it, Gaius... Incidentally, is that your real name?" he said to provide more time wasting.

"In fact, it is a name given to me by my religious order. Have you prepared as per my instructions?"

"Is Cleo okay?" he looked at Chris with furrowed brow for her approval. She nodded back with a tight smile.

"She is fine. Now, here is what you will do. You will list everything that you have in relation to the book. I won't call it a gospel... It is an abomination. The lock of hair, test results, tape recordings of hypnosis sessions, and the transcripts, etc., etc.... Then you will send the list to an email address I will give you. During that time, you will collect every item on that list... I will instruct from there. In two hours' time, I will email you, so you will have a return address."

He terminated the call.

"He's smart. Using an email makes it impossible to trace. It would be bounced all over the net," Chris said as her phone rang. "They got a trace from a SkypeOut pre-purchased credit. Difficult to trace; it would take hours, and we don't have the time. They're on it, but with not much hope, I'm afraid."

"Look, we'll need to get back to the manor to put all this together. It's a fifty-minute drive, that'll only give us an hour," I told Chris.

She immediately pulled out her phone and dialled a number.

"Who are you calling?" I asked.

"HQ, I'm ordering a chopper for us. I'll have someone drive your van to the manor," she replied.

Her efficiency was most comforting.

"Judith, can you ring ahead to the manor and get them started on the list?" I said.

"Yes, Ahmed and Brigitte will know what to do," Judith said.

Just then, two detectives came in, saw Chris on the phone, and confronted me.

"Doctor Leigh, I presume? I'm Detective Inspector Carney, and this is Detective Sergeant O'Brien. We've been assigned to your case," Carney introduced.

"Good, I hope you will do a better job than what has been done to date," I snapped.

"You're not satisfied with the investigation, ma'am?" O'Brien snarled.

I didn't like the look of either of them. Carney had an air of arrogance, while his sidekick looked more like a robber than a cop.

"No, I'm not. Twice they have failed to trace the kidnapper's call," I replied.

Carney, a tall man with a long thin nose, beady eyes, and a seriously receding hairline, looked as poorly as perhaps his paycheque was, while O'Brien was stout with a moon face, indicating he consumed his paycheque in hamburgers and donuts. In looks, they vaguely reminded me of Dan Aykroyd and John Belushi in the Blues Brothers, but certainly not in personality.

"It's not as simple as it may seem to trace a phone call, Doctor. It's true that they haven't been able to..." Carney growled, attempting to subdue me.

I angrily cut him off. "What do you mean you can't trace his phone call? What rubbish! You and I both know what you can do... You can turn his cellphone off and on remotely, you can follow his GPS phone's signal..."

"I'm afraid you've been watching too much television, Doctor," Carney said behind a scornful smirk.

"Don't you fucking patronise me, DI Carney. Why are you not using what's available to you to catch this kidnapper? Is it that you don't want to catch him?" I seethed.

"Seriously, madam, why on earth would we want to do that?" O'Brien barked.

I ignored him and focused my rage on Carney.

"Are you a religious man, DI Carney?"

"I don't see what that has to do with the case, Doctor," Carney said, offended.

"Everything, DI Carney... everything! Do you realise we have been persecuted by this militant religious zealot for the last forty years?" I thundered.

"You can't say that, I—" he stammered.

"You fucking listen to me real good, this bastard has murdered two people and got away with it... When I was twenty-five, he rammed my car with his and crushed my pelvis so I could never have children, then ten years later he stabbed me in the leg... See!" I irreverently lifted my dress to my knee and showed them the ugly scar on my calf. "Look at it, both of you... he did that and got away with it... And then four weeks ago, he stabbed Agent Chris Kelly over there in the stomach. He has continued to threaten us even with your intervention. Interpol has a dossier on him six inches thick... you can't catch him... they can't catch him, and then you have the audacity to question my reasoning! I asked if you are a religious man, now answer me, please."

"Look, Doctor, you might talk to the police like that in the colonies, but not—" O'Brien began.

"Shut up, O'Brien. I wasn't talking to you, Carney!" I shrieked.

"Yes," Carney answered, irritated. "I'm a devout Catholic."

"Then I want you off the case!" I roared.

With her call finished, Chris came running over to step between us before there was bloodshed.

"What's the matter, Bonnie?" she barked in a panic.

"I don't want this pair on our case," I folded my arms defiantly.

Jackson wandered over.

"I don't think we've got any choice, love," he said.

I was at my wit's end... frustration had taken an awful toll on me, I knew. But nevertheless, I didn't want anyone I couldn't trust in charge of Cleo's welfare. I broke down and sobbed on Jackson's shoulder.

"Hush now, love. It's all getting a bit much for you, isn't it?" he lovingly whispered, holding me close.

"Jackson, take Bonnie and the others outside to the helipad. It will be here very soon. I'll join you there in a moment," Chris said warmly.

We left her talking with Carney and O'Brien.

CHAPTER
XLVI

The chopper landed on the lawn of the Manor, leaving us an hour and a half to prepare everything for the deadline. The team had managed to get a lot done in our absence. I was still upset from my encounter with Carney and O'Brien when we gathered in the library, so Jackson suggested having a drink to calm our nerves. Dylan, Jane, Brigitte, and Ahmed went to help Mike in the study, while Jackson, Judith, Chris, and I had a drink and discussed our next move. The chopper pilot, Henry, went to the kitchen for a cup of tea before heading back to Luton airport. I noticed Wayne lagging behind but then he seemed to make a decision to speak up and approached me.

"Excuse me, Bonnie, but I just want to offer to do anything I can to help find Cleo... I... I," he said, tears welling in his eyes.

I took his hand, his genuine care for Cleo soothing my hostility.

"Thank you, Wayne."

"I was wondering?" he hesitated, reluctant to speak up.

"Go on, Wayne," I urged him.

"Well, the others said the cops haven't been able to locate Gaius even though he's called several times."

"That's right, it makes me angry that in this day and age with all the best technology at their disposal they can't even trace a bloody phone call," I growled.

"When I was packing Cleo's few personal effects, I found her watch. She'd taken it off during the scanning because it was raining."

"Her father gave her that watch, I'm surprised she took it off."

"Well, you know how Sharlene used psychometry on the gospel hair, could she use it on Cleo's watch to locate her?"

I froze with realisation. He was absolutely spot-on. Sharlene had worked with the police before to locate a missing person and succeeded. I jumped up.

"Guys, listen up!" They all immediately focused their attention on me. "Wayne has come up with a brilliant idea. He has Cleo's watch and suggested we get Sharlene to use it to locate Cleo."

"Psychometry, well thought out, Wayne," Judith said.

"Didn't she locate a young girl for the police in the States?" Jackson said.

"Yes, I just hope she hasn't left for France," I admitted.

"Phone her, Bonnie. I can have Henry take us to her in the chopper. If she's still in town, she'll only need to hop a cab to the London Heliport. I'll arrange clearance for her," Chris said with efficiency.

I dialled Sharlene's number. She and her boyfriend were at the Mayfair Hotel, about to leave for the airport. I didn't even have to ask. After explaining the situation to her, without hesitation, she offered to help. I told her about Cleo's watch, and she asked for items of clothing as well. Wayne rushed upstairs to get some clothes.

Within minutes, Chris and I were in the air en route to the London heliport.

"What's the ETA, Henry?" Chris yelled above the engine noise.

"Six minutes, Agent Kelly."

"Excellent," she checked her watch. "We've still got seventy minutes."

Our hearts were pounding. It was cutting it close to the next call from Gaius.

"Don't worry, if this works, it'll give us an advantage," Chris said.

I looked out of the window at the greater London area below us. It was vast, made me feel small, and made me wish for this whole thing to end well.

As we touched down on the helipad, I could see Sharlene waiting by a stretch limousine near the exit. Chris had Henry wait while I rushed over to the limo. I hugged Sharlene, and she introduced me to Maurice, a stunning young man—so typically French. We got into the limo.

Sharlene immediately sat back in the rear seat and began the process of meditation. When she felt she was in the right state, she opened the palm of her right hand, and I placed Cleo's watch in it.

Twenty minutes later, we were back in the air, headed for the manor.

On our way across the lawn to the manor, Chris stopped to answer her phone. It was DI Carney returning her call. She turned her phone on speaker for me to hear.

"We've had an American friend of the Bolt's, a psychic, use psychometry to locate Cleo," Chris informed him.

"I'm not interested in that mumbo jumbo, Kelly, nor do I like meddling Yanks after publicity. Next thing, it'll be all over the papers. You've gone ahead on this without any consultation—"

"I'm going to interrupt you there, DI Carney, because you're wasting our time. I don't need your bloody permission to act in a case that I've been handling long before you became involved. Do I make myself clear?"

"You have no jurisdiction in a kidnapping, Agent Kelly," he snapped back.

I was furious. I just wanted to tell him to piss off so we could get on with it.

"I don't think I have anything more to say to you, DI Carney," Kelly said aggressively.

"I warn you, Agent Kelly, there will be no more interference from you in this case."

"I'm losing your signal... oops," she winked at me. "Gone... What an arse!"

We raced inside the manor to the library, where Jackson, Wayne, Judith, and Mike were pacing the floor. As we entered, so did Chris.

"How did it go, love?" Jackson asked excitedly.

I spoke up for everyone to hear. "She was in a dark room, a cellar perhaps. She is gagged, and there's running water like a brook outside. And every now and then, a low rumbling sound. Sharlene had an overall feeling of religious significance," I explained. "That's about all. Let's brainstorm."

"A church!" Judith said.

"Good, yes?" I invited more ideas.

"An old disused church with a stream nearby," Mike suggested.

"I just Googled abandoned churches in Hertfordshire, and there's only one: Saint Gregory's," Wayne said, looking at his Galaxy notebook.

"Where is it from here?" I asked.

"Borehamwood," Wayne replied.

"That isn't far from Watford, where the police lost him. About forty-five minutes on the M1 from here," Mike added.

"There's a brook near the church," Wayne exclaimed.

"Running water," I reiterated.

"I'm pretty sure Saint Gregory is a Benedictine saint, so that would add up as well," Mike mentioned.

"I just Googled Saint Gregory, and you're right, Mike. He is a Benedictine saint," Wayne confirmed.

Chris and I exchanged a unified expression of interest. It was worth a try. Then, my phone rang. All sound in the room fell silent, leaving only the intimidating ring of the phone. I swore to myself to change the ringtone once this was all over—I didn't want to be reminded of Gaius whenever my phone rang. Chris had immediately dialled a special police number to trace the call. I waited for her signal. It was going down to the wire. One more ring, and my voicemail would pick up. With my heart in my mouth, I stared wide-eyed at Chris. She signalled. I clicked the speaker and answered.

"Hello."

"Ah, a new point person. Got your nerve back, Dr Bolt? I will give you instructions. You follow them without question. Put one foot wrong, and I will inflict an injury on the girl. Is that clear?"

"Yes."

Chris had instructed me to stay calm and listen hard for background sounds—anything that might provide a clue to the location.

"Pack everything you have in three easily transportable boxes. List the contents on the outside of each box. Load it all in a van. I will ring in two hours and give you a location to drop the van off. You will be the driver. If you leave anything out, I will injure Cleo with a fatal wound. I already have a list of everything compiled by her to check off against. No police. If I see any, Cleo will suffer."

"Thought you were going to email—" The phone went dead. I looked up at Chris. She shook her head. No trace.

A few minutes later, Judith, Mike, Jackson, and I were in the study with Chris, planning the next move.

"DI Carney refuses to act on Sharlene's insight," Chris said.

"We can't afford to waste time worrying about the police. We need to act on our own," I argued.

"How come Gaius changed from emailing the instructions to calling again?" Jackson wondered.

"It seems he's in a hurry. He might be worried that the net is closing on him," Chris said. "Anyhow, Carney was monitoring the call. He'll call any minute with how they'll want to play it. You can be sure that will translate to little involvement from us," Chris growled angrily.

"Fat chance. Not with me driving!" I snapped.

"Leave Carney and company to me. You follow up on Sharlene's foresight. It's our best chance," Jackson said sternly.

"Yes, there's no time to debate it, Bonnie," Judith added.

"You're not suggesting they go after him alone, are you?" Mike questioned.

"It will have to be. Are you up for it, Chris?" I asked.

"Yes."

"Are you armed?" Jackson asked.

"Yes. We'll take Wayne as our driver," Chris said.

"No, he said I have to drive. I'll take the van, and you follow in a car, Chris," I said.

"What if Borehamwood isn't the right place?" Mike suggested.

"It won't matter. If we fail to find him there and he calls with the drop-off location, Bonnie just needs to tell him she's coming from somewhere near Borehamwood, Ruislip, or something to buy us enough time," Chris explained.

"Okay, no time to lose. I'll get the others started on loading the van," Jackson said, hopping out the door.

As predicted, Chris's phone rang. It was DI Carney with the outcome of their ransom call discussions. I could tell by Chris's expression and tone of voice that their response wasn't to her satisfaction. She told them she'd call back.

"They insist on taking over the ransom exchange, claiming that if they don't, we'd be putting Cleo's life at risk. I said that wasn't an option," Chris relayed.

"Going by their performance to date, I'd say they'd be the ones putting her life at risk," I snarled.

"We're going to have to make a decision right now on how to play this," Chris proposed.

"I think it's up to Bonnie," Judith said.

"I agree," Mike said, sitting back in his chair and folding his arms. "Why not take advantage of the cops?"

"That's smart thinking, Mike. Why don't I tell Carney we've packed the van and it will be in a holding pattern in Borehamwood, waiting for the next call from Gaius? I'll tell him I will be concealed in the van and armed," Chris said.

"Are they likely to accept that, considering they're trying to cut you out?" Mike asked.

"I don't think they have much choice. They know they can't put up a chopper or a roadblock—"

"And we know he won't hesitate to maim or kill Cleo if he gets the slightest whiff of the police," I interjected.

"I will have to kill him... he's not going to exchange Cleo for the van. He'll keep her for insurance against the contents. I'd say he'll want Bonnie to deliver the van to an airport—he'll have a plane ready to go just like before—that's why he wants everything packed in three easily transportable boxes. As soon as he has them, he'll load them and Cleo into the plane and take off," Chris said with conviction.

"Are you sure of that, Chris?" I asked, genuinely curious.

"As sure as I can be, Bonnie," she smiled.

"So, we won't need two cars if you're going to ambush the bastard," I said bluntly.

"I owe him one," Chris said bitterly. "Come on, let's get rolling."

She phoned Carney back and laid down the law. He wasn't impressed, but as we knew, there was little he could do about it. She agreed for them to put a tap on her cell phone to track her, and Carney promised to keep a five-mile radius no-go-zone for the police around Borehamwood. He had word from his superiors to let us handle it. After all, I was risking my life by being the driver.

CHAPTER
XLVII

Standing in front of the manor, basking in the afterglow of the day, I noticed a worried expression in Jackson's eyes. It made me question my own actions. I gently brushed a strand of grey hair away from his eye and kissed him softly on the lips. Then, we held each other at arm's length, locking eyes.

"It all comes down to this, doesn't it?" I whispered, intended only for his ears.

"Yes, love. The last forty years come down to this. Are you—" Jackson began, but I interrupted him.

"Hush, love. It's not the time to question it. We both know what needs to be done."

Just then, Chris's phone rang.

"You're right, but it doesn't make it any easier. I should be the one going instead of you," he said.

"You'd look terrible in a dress, love. You know that," I giggled.

"I don't know, I quite fancy that little black Chanel number of yours," he joked, and then he embraced me.

Chris approached us. "I just heard from Interpol HQ. The Vatican has officially denied any involvement with Crux Redemptoris in this matter. They claim they have not authorised the use of an aircraft and have no knowledge of the referenced gospel," she explained.

"Do you believe that?" I asked emphatically.

"I think we have to," Chris admitted.

"The Black Pope," Jackson interjected.

"What do you mean?" Chris asked.

"I'll explain it later, but within that powerful order, there are two factions. I believe Interpol heard from the white faction, whereas the faction responsible for this kidnapping is the black one," he explained.

Chris nodded and headed to the van. I turned and hugged Mike, then Judith, Ahmed, and Brigitte. Wayne walked over, tears welling up in his eyes.

"I wish I could—" he pleaded.

I took his hand. "Just stay positive, darling. You've gotten us this far. Chris and I are going to bring Cleo home. Okay?"

He nodded, emotionally moved.

I climbed into the driver's seat and called out, "Are you ready, Chrissy?"

"Bring it on!" she exclaimed emphatically from her hiding spot in the back, and we drove off into the sunset.

Having the Sat Nav simplified finding our destination. I usually avoided being the driver in a foreign country, but in this case, I had no choice. As we approached the turnoff to Saint Gregory's, I heard Chris checking her weapon.

"It's twenty minutes until he calls, and we're only a couple of minutes away from the church," I said.

"Park a block away from it."

"I'm getting cold feet, Chris. God, I hope they're here," I admitted, my voice trembling.

It was dark, and the streets leading to the church were poorly lit. The church itself was an 18th-century structure, far from the modern centre of Borehamwood. As instructed, I found a parking spot on Shakespeare Drive, a block away from the church. It was eerily quiet, with no signs of life—no cars, no people. Chris was rummaging in the back, and then the side door slid open. She came around to my window and tapped on it. I rolled it down.

"You stay right there. I'll quickly scout the area and be back before the phone call. Are you okay?" she asked.

"Don't ask," I replied nervously.

I watched her disappear into the darkness of the night. After a few minutes, I heard a train passing by at the end of the street, the sound of its rumbling confirming Sharlene's description. I glanced at my phone on the passenger seat, expecting it to ring any minute. Checking the clock, I realised only ten minutes had passed, though it felt like an hour. Suddenly, I jumped when a face appeared at my window—it was Chris. She climbed into the back.

"How did it go?" I asked, my heart pounding like a drum.

"There's a brook behind the church, and there's a black car parked at the rectory. I'll quickly text a check on the number plate now."

"The train line is at the end of the street," I added.

"Yes, I heard the train. Everything seems to match so far. If the car belongs to the church, we might have a problem," she said, texting. A reply came within seconds.

"We're in luck. The car is from Watford; it's probably stolen," she reported.

My phone rang.

"Here we go!" I said with trepidation, answering it on speaker. "Hello."

"Do you have the van packed?" he growled.

"Yes."

"Describe it."

"Three transportable boxes, as you requested, all labelled with contents."

"Where are you located now?"

Chris showed me her hand, on which she had written a name.

"Ruislip."

"Ruislip? Why there?" he asked.

Chris showed me her other hand, and I read the message written on it.

"There were some items stored here that we—"

"Be at the corner of Dagger Lane and Hogg Lane in Elstree exactly one hour from now. Park your vehicle there and stay inside it. Repeat those instructions."

"Corner of Dagger and Hogg Lane, Elstree, in one hour, park, and stay in the car. What about Cleo?"

He abruptly ended the call.

A phone rang, and Chris answered. "Yes, we're in position. I understand. No, can't you temporarily halt flight movements for the next two hours? Ridiculous. I'll inform you when to move in." Irritated, she hung up.

From her demeanour during the call, it was clear she was receiving little cooperation from the police.

"That was Carney... Hogg Lane leads to London Elstree Aerodrome. I asked him to stop departures for the next two hours, but apparently, he can't."

"He's utterly useless. They had better keep their distance then," I warned.

"I think I need to go in there. There's no way he's going to let Cleo live."

"What if we've got the wrong place?" I asked.

"It's not... believe me. I'm going in. I'll hit speed dial, and your phone will ring when I've identified him. That way, if he tries to escape in the car, you can tail him."

"What about leaving you here?" I protested.

"Yes."

There was no use arguing with her; she was determined. She got out of the van and disappeared into the darkness before I could take a breath. This wait was shaping up to be longer and more agonising. I sat in the darkness, wondering what she expected me to do if he tried to flee. Then, my phone rang once. She had sighted him. Now the nerves truly set in. It was crunch time. Two gunshots shattered the silence, and I nearly jumped out of my skin. I saw lights at the end of the street—headlights. Was he trying to escape? Instinct took over—I started the van. My phone lit up with a text message. It said, "Stop him."

I spotted the black car approaching. I revved the engine, and as it reached me, I yanked the steering wheel, jammed my foot on the accelerator, and prepared for impact. The black sedan collided with me with a deafening crash. Glass shattered, and the van rolled over onto its side, tossing me around like a ragdoll. After it settled down, and I realised I was still intact, I quickly thought and pushed open the door, crawling out. There was a hissing sound, and steam rose from the mangled wreck that was once his car's front end. Then, I saw him. He had been thrown through the windshield and lay on the road. Despite his bleeding wounds, he continued to move. I didn't know what to do—then I heard footsteps. I looked in their direction and saw Chris emerging from the darkness, running toward me with her gun aimed at Gaius. She frantically waved her hand, signalling for me to take cover. I swiftly ducked behind the van. She slowed down as she reached the tangled vehicles but kept her gun trained on him.

"Where's Cleo?" I cried out.

She glanced at me and froze. The pistol slipped from her grasp, and her knees buckled.

I gasped at the expression on her face and then suddenly realised what had happened. Gaius had thrown a knife that had pierced her chest. With my heart pounding, I watched her collapse on the road, twenty feet away from me. I peered around the corner of the van at Gaius—he stood there with an evil smirk on his blood-drenched face. His eyes suddenly locked onto mine.

"Now look at what you've done, Doctor Bolt," he growled smugly, blood dripping from his chin.

I suddenly caught a strong whiff of gasoline coming from the wreckage. Just as he started moving toward me, his car exploded in a fiery blaze. The explosion knocked him down. The van shuddered, rocked by the force of the blast, and I was thrown onto the ground. The intense heat from the blazing car forced me to shield my face with my hand. Through the flames, I could see poor Chris still sprawled on the road, still conscious, with the hilt of the knife sticking out of her chest.

There was movement. I looked up and shuddered—Gaius had survived the blast and was struggling to his feet. His clothes were smouldering, his face scorched, burned, and bloody. He staggered toward me, his hands clawed like a character from a zombie film. Fear paralysed me, but I knew I had to move. Pulling myself backward along the ground, I glanced at Chris. She had assessed the situation— her pistol lay on the ground a few feet from her. Gaius was closing in on me. Chris summoned all her remaining strength, fighting through the pain, and kicked at the pistol. Her foot connected, and it slid across the pavement within my reach. Summoning every ounce of courage I had, I dived for it, scraping my elbows and knees on the asphalt. I grabbed the gun, and as Gaius towered over me, I raised it and pulled the trigger, again and again until all four bullets were spent, and the gun just clicked. He froze, wide-eyed, blood gushing from his mouth, and collapsed at my feet. I stopped pulling the trigger; he was dead. I dropped the gun and crawled away from the fire toward Chris. The fire grew more intense, and I could sense that the van was about to explode. I reached Chris, about to pass out, when I felt someone's arms slipping under mine, dragging me away from the flames. A massive explosion shook me, and through the haze of smoke and confusion, I saw Carney.

The next thing I knew, I was in the back of an ambulance, breathing through an oxygen mask. I could vaguely see Chris on the opposite bunk. Then, I drifted off.

When I woke up, I found myself in a hospital bed, both my arms bandaged. In a daze, I watched a series of images flash by, familiar faces peering at me—Jackson, Judith, Sharlene, Cleo. I wondered if I was dreaming. Suddenly, the chaos ceased, and the sounds returned to normal. After blinking a few times to clear my eyes, I recognised Jackson asleep in a chair at the foot of my bed.

"Jackson?" I mumbled through cracked and parched lips.

He woke up startled, rushed to my bedside, and took my hand. "There you are, love," he said with a warm, loving smile. "How are you feeling?"

"Like a pork chop, but in one piece, I hope. How about Cleo and Chris?" I asked, gripping Jackson's hand tightly.

He looked up as Cleo entered the room. I reached up and took her hand, tears welling up in my eyes.

"There's more of Boudicca in you than you had reckoned, Aunty Bo," she said lovingly.

"What's with this 'Aunty Bo' stuff?" I chuckled, wincing slightly. "Are you alright, darling?" I asked, gripping Jackson's hand as if I would never let go.

"Yes, thanks to DI Carney and the bomb squad... Gaius had me hogtied in the rectory cellar and rigged with a bomb. It was set to go off two hours after he left."

"Long enough for him to check everything and then fly out with it," I deduced.

"That was the plan, but it was never going to happen," Jackson said. "Carney managed to shut down the Elstree airport by parking DS O'Brien's car with a strobing blue light right in the middle of the main runway. Gaius wasn't going anywhere."

"What about Chrissy?"

"She's still in the emergency room... the blade punctured her left lung, narrowly missing her heart," Cleo explained.

"Poor thing, if it hadn't been for her, I'd be dead," I said, my eyes welling up again.

"Me too," Cleo said gratefully.

Mike and Judith came into the room and hugged me.

"Sharlene is outside with the others. Oh, love, I'm so glad you're alright," Judith said, her eyes filled with tears.

"We lost everything in the fire," I said dejectedly.

"No, we didn't. I made copies of everything, and we kept some of the hair. The only thing gone for good is Gaius," Mike quipped.

"That's no great loss," Judith added.

Wayne entered the room and put his arm around Cleo. It was clear they meant a lot to each other.

"This might cheer you up a bit, Bonnie," Wayne said happily. "Dylan is convinced he has found Boudicca."

An hour later, I was discharged from the hospital, and we returned to the manor, where Detectives Carney and O'Brien met me. I provided a statement that seemed to satisfy them since witness statements from Shakespeare Drive residents corroborated my story.

Sharlene couldn't resist giving DI Carney an earful as he and O'Brien left the manor. I made it clear to both of them that if it hadn't been for Sharlene's foresight, Cleo would be dead. Reluctantly, Carney agreed, and to his credit, he apologised for his narrow-mindedness. After the police left, we settled in to relax.

The phone rang—it was the hospital, delivering relieving news. Chris was out of danger; she was going to be alright.

CHAPTER XLVIII

After a well-deserved rest, we all gathered at the breakfast table the next morning. Dylan was eager to report his findings and stood up to share them.

"After covering three-quarters of the Stanmore Common grid prepared by Dr Ahmed, we have located three hot spots, two of which definitely warrant digging."

"How deep are they, Dylan?" Judith inquired.

"The two promising ones are just under six metres, and the lesser one is three metres."

"What is the ground level, Ahmed?" Judith asked.

"Ground zero is approximately three metres, Judith."

"So, the lesser one is not in the ideal location, being on flat ground, but the other two at six metres certainly are. Okay, Brigitte, after breakfast, we'll start the process of obtaining a permit to excavate," Judith said.

"Yes, Judith," Brigitte replied.

There was a sense of optimism among us about Dylan's findings. Despite both Cleo and I looking worse for wear—me more than her—we all felt uplifted.

I had suffered third-degree burns on my arms, cuts, and lacerations on my face from windshield fragments. My knees and elbows were deeply grazed from crawling on the bitumen, leaving me walking like a zombie. But what bothered me the most, being the vain person I am, was my singed eyebrows and hair. I looked like an extra from a disaster movie, like 'The Towering Inferno' or 'Earthquake.'

Jackson took the floor. 'This morning, I spoke with Interpol HQ... Chris's injury is career-ending, I'm afraid. On the positive side, she's recovering and will be well compensated for the rest of her life."

We all responded with a round of applause. We deeply respected Chris for the sacrifice she had made for us.

"We are indebted to her, especially me. I wouldn't be here now if it weren't for her bravery," I said frankly, my eyes welling up with tears.

"She turned her back on the cops and believed in me, and that took a tremendous amount of courage," Sharlene said spiritedly.

Jane stood up. "Um, I went for a run this morning and picked up the local newspaper." She showed us the front page, which featured a photograph of the burnt-out wrecked vehicles with the headline: "Man Dies and Woman Badly Injured in Terrible Car Accident in Borehamwood."

"Never let the truth get in the way of a good story," I grumbled dismissively.

Later that day, under gloomy skies that sprinkled us with rain, we bid farewell to Sharlene and Maurice. As we hugged, I couldn't help but wonder when I would see her again. Always a source of amazement, she gave me a cheeky grin with a sparkle in her eyes and said, as if she knew exactly what I was thinking, "Soon, love."

Jackson and I stood solemnly together in the drizzle, watching the red taillights of their minicab fade into the mist that had drifted in from the woods.

"There's always something mystical about the way Sharlene arrives and leaves, isn't there?" I said, tears welling up.

"You know, I was thinking the exact same thing."

Holding hands like young lovers, we wandered back inside the manor. Just inside the front door, Jackson stopped and drew me close, kissing me gently on the lips.

"Have I told you lately that I love you?" he softly sang in my ear, sounding just like Van Morrison.

"Have I told you there is no one above you?" I sang in reply, matching his soft tone. "I love being loved by you," I admitted.

With the threat of Gaius behind us, things were winding down. After bidding farewell to Ahmed and Brigitte, who left for Cambridge to secure the permit for the Stanmore dig, and Wayne driving Dylan, Jane, and Cleo to Costco in Milton Keynes for fresh food supplies, us 'oldies' gathered in the library to discuss the future.

"I think it's time to go home," I admitted with a deep sigh. "I feel emotionally drained, and I believe we need to continue our studies independently for a while. What are your thoughts, Judith?"

"My only concern is the dig," she affirmed. "But I completely understand your desire to go home after all you've been through here love."

"Do we need to be here for the dig?" I asked.

"It might be best left to the younger ones," Jackson suggested.

"You're probably right, Jackson. I, for one, would prefer to focus on unravelling the gospel," Mike agreed.

"Yes, you're absolutely right. We can leave more to Ahmed, Brigitte, and Cleo. Cleo will stay, won't she?" Judith inquired.

I looked at Jackson with a questioning expression.

"Yes, I suppose so. Is that alright?" I requested.

Judith reached out and affectionately touched my knee. "Goes without saying, my dear... Besides, by the looks of it, she has struck up quite a friendship with Wayne," she said with a cheeky grin.

"But I don't think they should impose on you any longer, Judith," Jackson said.

"I've already thought about that," Mike explained. "Cleo and Jane can stay at the manor, and Dylan and Wayne can stay at the gatehouse. That way, they'll be nearby, and the house will be peaceful. But as a team, they'll be close enough for us to keep an eye on them. On the other hand, Ahmed and Brigitte are considering renting a house together in Bushey Heath, quite near Stanmore Common."

"Together?" I repeated.

"Yes, it seems that after all this time, they've become a couple," Mike smiled.

"I don't know how he knows all these things," Judith muttered. "But it sounds fine to me."

"That's excellent news! Those two are so perfect for each other. We've always said that, haven't we, love?" I said to Jackson.

"Yes, I'm amazed it took this long," he chuckled.

"Oh, I think it might have been going on as a well-kept secret for quite a while," Mike sniggered.

"Now, let's talk about the work," Judith announced, sporting her academic face.

"Okay, look, I'll be honest here. Given the circumstances, I believe that only the people in this room and Cleo should be aware that we have a copy of most of the gospel and the lock of hair. For the rest of the world, it all went up in smoke in the car wreck," Mike proposed.

"I agree. In fact, I think we should publicise the fact that it all went up in smoke to completely throw off Crux Redemptoris once and for all, without mentioning the gospel but saying enough for them to understand," Jackson added.

"You mean using it as a cover story, but without revealing the gospel, just enough for them to grasp the situation?" Judith asked.

"Exactly. Otherwise, they'll simply replace Gaius with another merciless person like they did with Edward, and it will start all over again," Mike concluded.

"So, the gospel and the hair, along with the story, will revert to being a First Light secret," I said.

"Classified until we feel the time is right," Judith agreed.

"Then, one of us will need to come up with the best method of exposing the secret. In the meantime, we can focus on Boudicca while confidentially studying all the information we've gathered on Joseph and the hair," Mike added.

"Sounds sensible," I agreed.

"We had already compiled everything we have for Gaius, so before you go, I will make a duplicate so there's one complete copy for you and one for us," Mike said.

"And we'll continue to discuss matters concerning the gospel via the First Light website using our established code," Judith submitted.

"Precisely," Mike agreed. "I'll even build a new firewall security system."

"Do you honestly believe Crux Redemptoris will buy it?" I asked.

"I don't think we have much choice really. It will be a matter of a convincing cover story and how well it's distributed," Judith said. "Easy-peasy," she added with a sly grin.

"I'm sure we can safely leave that up to you guys," Jackson said confidently.

The sun sparkled like diamond facets on the lake at the end of the street, and the sound of a Kookaburra warmed my heart. I was glad to be back in the sanctity of our home at Tuross Head, nestled in the rustic isolation of the South Coast of New South Wales. Sitting on the balcony with the warm morning sun on my face, my mind at ease with the world—I closed my eyes and thought, I have been a time traveller—I have seen the world at a time in history that was not meant to be seen by the likes of me. I hold the truth of the world's most influential organised religion in my hands. I have witnessed that truth stolen from the people by a bigoted greedy extremist religious order intent on maintaining the mythos of their doctrine at any cost. I have been a member of a dedicated group of seekers of the truth prepared to risk their lives for the greater good of humanity. I made this journey hand in hand with my partner, my lover, and my best friend, and together we built friendships with like-minded people who we look upon as our extended family. This journey, however, is far from complete—it won't end until the truth is finally revealed. For some uncanny reason, we were made gatekeepers of that truth—if you are a believer in spirituality and destiny, then perhaps all that has taken place in my bizarre tale makes perfect sense to you. As for Cleo and myself, until we can determine a genetic link to Boudicca, it all falls into the misty realm of the supernatural. Why were we able to connect with Queen Boudicca? Was the gospel buried in 61 AD for us to find in the 21st Century? Why? Which secret does the gospel contain that needs to be exposed in the 21st Century?

"Coffee, my love?" Jackson said, breaking my reverie and handing me a cup. "You looked deep in thought."

"Oh, it's just so lovely to be home, Darl," I said.

He sat in the chair beside me.

"Ah yes, Australia—the lucky country. I've missed all that it has to offer. But it is difficult to make sense of it all, isn't it?" he smiled knowingly.

"Can't hide anything from Mr Perceptive, can I?"

"Difficult for someone who knows you so well."

"Too true, my love... and yes, it is tough to make sense of it all. But when I do, I want it to be scientific fact rather than an episode from the Twilight Zone like it is at the moment," I admitted.

"Well, maybe we're getting closer to scientific evidence," he said with a cheeky grin and then paused to build suspense.

"Stop it," I growled playfully. "What is it? Something has happened?"

A gleam appeared in his lovely eyes. "I just received an email from Mike... they've found something."

"But they've only been digging a week... what is it?"

He slowly unfurled a sheet of paper and then handed it to me. It was a photograph of Cleo and Dylan grinning at what they were holding in their hands: a large wedge-shaped slice of rotted timber.

"What on Earth is that?" I asked, squinting to see the detail.

"Well, that photo was taken three days ago, and since then, Judith has had the wood dated to between 20 AD and 80 AD," he grinned. "Right on the money, there's a close-up. Do you want to see it?"

"Stop teasing me, you. Of course, I do!"

He unfurled a second sheet of A4 paper and handed it over.

"They think there's a carving on it... see?"

"Yes, there is, and I recognise it. Two figures, a raven and a hare." My hand was shaking the paper. "It's hers, there were three hares and a raven," I muttered excitedly, my eyes welling up with tears.

"That's what Mike thought you'd say," he smiled. "Cleo remembered it as well."

My heart was pounding like a drum—we'd struck pay dirt—thoughts flashed through my mind, but the dominant one was how lucky we were.

"It's her grave," I cried and immediately hugged Jackson. I let go, jumped up, and screamed at the lake so loud it echoed into infinity, "We found it!"

An elderly neighbour trimming his front hedge looked sharply up at me screaming from the balcony and gave me thumbs up.

I looked back at my husband.

"Boudicca's shield—that's definitely Boudicca's shield!" I could tell by the look in his eyes that Jackson knew as well as I that a new day had just dawned for this incredible adventure.

The End

BIBLIOGRAPHY

Blake W. 1997. The Illuminated Books of William Blake: Jerusalem-The Emanation of the Giant Albion V.I. Princeton University Press. USA. e-Book.

Church A. & Brodribb W. (translators) 2003. "Tacitus: The Annals & The Histories. Agricola Book." The Modern Library Classics.

Delaney J. 2015. "The Roman Conquests of Britain'. University of Central Florida, Orlando, Florida.

Gedge, P, 1978. The Eagle and the Raven. Penguin Books. London.

Graves R. 1976. The White Goddess: Grammar of Poetic Myth. Faber & Faber. UK

Greer G. 1970. The Female Eunuch, MacGibbon and Kee, London, England, 1970.

Hunter C & Eimar, B. 2012. "The Art of Hypnotic Regression Therapy', Crown House Publishing. London.

Magarey S. 2014. "The Encyclopedia of Women and Leadership in Twentieth-Century Australia." The Australian Women's Archives Project.

Kappas J. 1978. "Professional Hypnotism Manual." Goodreads.

Roud S. 2010. "London Lore and the Traditions of the Worlds Most Vibrant City," Arrow Books. London.

Yeates L. 1996. "A set of competency and proficiency standards for Australian professional clinical hypnotherapists: A descriptive guide to the Australian Hypnotherapists' Association accreditation system. The Australian Hypnotherapists' Association.

INTERNET RESEARCH

Ancient Order of Druids. Viewed: July, 2022.
<http://thanetdruids.co.uk/>

Andrasta/Andraste. The Celtic Goddess of Victory. Viewed July 2022.
<https://celticnative.com/andraste-celtic-goddess-of-victory/Australia>

Druidic Order of the Golden Dawn. Viewed: May, 2022.
<http://www.druidical-gd.org/>

Barcelona: Monserrat Monastery: Viewed: May 2022.
<http://www.barcelona.de/en/barcelona-excursions-monastery-montserrat.html>

Wikipedia – Boudican Revolt - Battle of Wattling Street. Viewed: April, 2017.
<https://en.wikipedia.org/wiki/Battle_of_Watling_Street>

Paulden Jenkins. Burrowbridge Mump. Ancient Landscape around Glastonbury. Viewed: July, 2017.
<http://www.palden.co.uk/leymap/burrowbridge-mump.html>

Paulden Jenkins. Butleigh. Ancient Landscape around Glastonbury. Viewed: April, 2017.
<http://www.palden.co.uk/leymap/butleigh.html>

Wikipedia. Boudica. Viewed: December 2016.
<http://en.wikipedia.org/wiki/Boudica>

Skye-net. Boudicca. Queen of the Iceni. Viewed : March 12, 2017.
<http://skyelander.orgfree.com/b1.html>

Wikipedia. Britain in the Iron Age. Viewed: December, 2016.
<https://en.m.wikipedia.org/wiki/British_Iron_Age>

Wikipedia. Cadbury Castle. Viewed: December 2016.
<https://en.wikipedia.org/wiki/Cadbury_Castle,_Somerset>

Wikipedia. Celtic Languages. Viewed: December 2016.
<http://en.wikipedia.org/wiki/Celtic_languages>

Wikipedia. Crataegus. Viewed: December 2016.
<https://en.wikipedia.org/wiki/Crataegus>

Wikipedia. Cunobeline & Joseph of Arimathea. Viewed: December 2016.
<https://en.wikipedia.org/wiki/Cunobeline>

Workman, B.K, Druids in Britain, ca. 54 BC. Viewed: July, 2010.
<http://www.eyewitnesstohistory.com/druids.htm>

Wikipedia. Dobunni. Viewed: December 2016.
<https://en.m.wikipedia.org/wiki/Dobunni>

Ford. M. 2001. Church of the Great God. Joseph of Arimathea. Viewed: July 2010.
<http://www.cgg.org/index.cfm/fuseaction/Library.sr/CT/artb/k/24/Joseph-of-Arimathea.htm>

Wikipedia. Goidelic Languages. Viewed: December 2016.
<http://en.wikipedia.org/wiki/Goidelic_languages>

Wikipedia. Gaius Suetonius Paulinus. Viewed: December 2016.
<http://en.wikipedia.org/wiki/Gaius_Suetonius_Paulinus>

Glastonbury Grove. Glastonbury History. Viewed: June 2010.
<http://www.glastonberrygrove.net/reference/history/glstnbry/history.html>

Megaliths, Menhires and Stone Circles of Somerset. Hillforts, Somerset. June 2010,
<http://www.somersetinfocus.co.uk/history/ancientsites.php?r=w>

Wikipedia. Hill forts of Somerset. Viewed: January, 2015.
<https://en.wikipedia.org/wiki/List_of_hill_forts_and_ancient_settlements_in_Somerset>

George F. Jowett. Historic & Akashic info on the Grail Family in Great Britain. Joseph of Arimathea in Britain. Trustee of the Gospel. Viewed: November, 2016.

<http://www.spiritmythos.org/TM/AP/grailfamily.html>

Vatican Confirmation. Joseph of Arimathea in Britain. Viewed: January, 2015.
<http://jahtruth.net/joarim.htm>

Murdock D/Acharya S. Jesus the Druid: Was Christ in Britain? Viewed: January, 2015.
<http://www.truthbeknown.com/christ-great-britain.html>

Reilly B. Bran The sleeping Guardian. Viewed: March, 2020.
<http://www.druidry.org/library/sacred-sites/bran-sleeping-guardian>

Wikipedia. Roman units. Viewed: May, 2020.
<https://en.wikipedia.org/wiki/List_of_Roman_army_unit_types>

Wikipedia. Roman Britain. Viewed: April, 2023.
<http://en.wikipedia.org/wiki/Roman_Britain>

The Old Way. Viewed: 17th July, 2023.
<http://www.angelfire.com/de2/newconcepts/wicca/moons2.html>

WikiCompany. The Vatican and the Jesuits. Viewed: August, 2023.
<http://www.bibliotecapleyades.net/vatican/esp_vatican37.htm>

Tintagel. Tintagel and Glastonbury. Viewed: March, 2021.
<http://www.angelfire.com/ak3/dailyword/travelfive.html>

Eye of the Psychic. Glastonbury: England's oldest sacred landscape? Viewed: August, 2023.
https://www.eyeofthepsychic.com/glastonbury/
Wikipedia. Unknown years of Jesus. Viewed: July, 2022.
https://en.m.wikipedia.org/wiki/Unknown_years_of_Jesus

MAP

Twelve Hides of Glastonbury (Whitstone and Wells Forum)